F.

LARGE PRINT

Central Support Unit
Catherine Street Dumfries DG1 1JB
tel: 01387 253820 fax: 01387 260294
e-mail: libs&i@dumgal.gov.uk

Dumfries and Galloway
LIBRARIES
Information and Archives

UK

CUSTOMER
SERVICE
EXCELLENCE
The Government Standard

24 HOUR LOAN RENEWAL ON OUR WEBSITE - WWW.DUMGAL.GOV.UK/LIA

ABOUT LAST NIGHT

ABOUT LAST NIGHT

Adele Parks

WINDSOR
PARAGON

First published 2011
by Headline Review
This Large Print edition published 2011
by AudioGO Ltd
by arrangement with
Headline Publishing Group

Hardcover ISBN: 978 1 445 85852 4
Softcover   ISBN: 978 1 445 85853 1

British Library Cataloguing in Publication Data available

Printed and bound in Great Britain by
MPG Books Group Limited

This novel is dedicated to police and medical staff everywhere.

30 Years Ago

Stephanie Amstell is the type of child that does not create any sort of impression—not even a bad one. She goes through her days unnoticed, she has mousy hair, mousy ways and mousy grades. No one appears to be aware of Stephanie, she is ignored and in response to being ignored she seems to shrink. The more she shrinks, the harder she is to spot. It is a vicious circle. She's just like Mrs Pepperpot, in the large hardback book that Mrs Iceton reads to the Year Threes as they sit on the itchy school carpet, waiting for the school bell to signal home time. Just like Mrs Pepperpot except not grey haired and not cheerful. Just small. That's the same.

Stephanie is happy and chatty enough at home, where she's reasonably indulged by her devoted and loving (although somewhat insular and blinkered) parents but she positively shrivels up on the short walk to school. Stephanie lies awake at night and seriously considers the possibility that the other children aren't just ignoring her but that they can't *actually* see her. Maybe they need a telescope (her parents *do* both wear glasses). Is it possible that she is truly shrinking, fading, disappearing like a leaf in autumn? Will she go brown and crinkled and then break apart altogether? Stephanie is terrified that she might totally vanish before she even gets to Westfield Comprehensive. This is not a completely wild thing for her young mind to surmise because she's spent the first three years of school frequently repeating her name to all those who ask, but no matter how often she tries to reinforce the fact that she's called

3

Stephanie, her name always seems to be forgotten in an instant. *Stephanie Amstell*, for goodness gracious goshness, it is an unusual name! By rights it should be the type of name that people remark upon and hold on to. But it seems that Stephanie's averageness somehow erases the splendid name and teachers often slip up and call her Sarah or Susan or Bethany. Teachers, librarians, dinner ladies, other kids. Everyone.

Everyone except Pip, that is.

Philippa Foxton splashes down at Stephanie's little Surrey state school when Stephanie is eight and three-quarter years old. Stephanie learns that the new girl comes from a place called Upnorth. Stephanie assumes Upnorth is an exotic, far-off foreign country where people speak a different language and are somewhat wild. She wonders whether Philippa Foxton has a passport, whether she is used to different stamps or coins. Stephanie thinks that Philippa's accent, while obviously *odd*, is not unpleasant. The tone is soft and gentle and her speech is so rapid it sounds as though she is constantly singing a very pretty and soothing lullaby. Philippa Foxton's voice is quite different from anything Stephanie has come across before. Everyone in Stephanie's world uses clipped, careful speech which, while rarely unkind, always seems to be the verbal equivalent to a firm handshake, the sort you have to give to the Brown Owl at Brownies if you get a badge. When Philippa speaks, it is like being wrapped in a huge hug.

The assumption that Philippa hails from somewhere wild is founded on the fact that not only does Philippa Foxton send shock waves throughout the hopscotch-loving community because she rejects the green gingham dress (which is most girls' much preferred part of the school uniform) but she also refuses to wear the grey skirt alternative. Instead she invokes her right to wear *shorts* in those first few bright days of the September term, just like the boys do, and she says she intends to wear trousers when it rains. Her clarity on the matter causes gasps; whether they are of admiration or horror is uncertain. Stephanie's daddy had already told her about *genetic predispositions*. He was explaining why Mummy got cross with him when he went to the betting shop 'more times than was good for him'. Stephanie can't believe that a little girl, not even nine years old, would be quite so *sure* without some sort of genetic or cultural predisposition.

Pip laughs loudly and often. She laughs in the classroom, the playground, the gym hall and even the library. Her laugh is careless and, while Stephanie doesn't know the word at the time, she later will identify Pip's laugh as irreverent. Pip never waits to be approached or introduced to strangers, instead *she* makes herself known to everyone.

'I'm Philippa Foxton, but most people like to call me Pip, it's much easier, so you can call me that!' she says. Lots and lots of times.

She assumes (rightly as it turns out) that everyone will want to know her. Straightaway she joins the trampoline and gymnastics club and excels at both as she is thin and tall like a maypole. She is a demon with the skipping rope and is able to juggle with three bouncy balls, which quickly and firmly makes her the undisputed queen of the playground. Then in November Pip is picked to play Mary in the Nativity production, *even though* she's only been at the school less than three months and the part is usually awarded to a Year Six girl. The strange thing is, none of the other little girls mind, everyone agrees she'll be perfect in the part. Pip's parents host teas and sleepovers, even when it isn't her birthday. They let the guests eat pizza in front of the TV and drink hot chocolate in Pip's bedroom. Pip's dad plays the guitar and her mum wears dozens of fluorescent lime and pink bracelets all the way up her arm. It takes no time at all before it is agreed and accepted that the newest girl at school is the coolest girl at school. Everyone wants to be her best friend.

Stephanie has watched all of this from a wary distance. She has never had the ambition or self-confidence to place herself in Pip's way, although like everyone else she is fascinated by the tall, slim, poised creature. Then Pip introduces herself to Stephanie—just as she has introduced herself to the swim instructor, the caretaker and all the other boys and girls, older and younger, throughout the school. Stephanie's life will never be the same again. With some effort, Stephanie Amstell manages to mumble her name.

Pip gasps with unfeigned awe. 'I have *never, ever* heard such a beautiful name in all my life.'

Stephanie is overwhelmed by the compliment and doesn't know what to do with her hands. Her knees (which are both dressed with Elastoplasts) tremble. She also thinks her name is gorgeous and has always wondered why other people fail to notice its gorgeousness or draw attention to the fact. Stephanie is uncertain how to reply to such longed-for flattery, but finds she has no need to, as Pip carries on.

'Stephanie and Philippa. Stephanie and Philippa. StephanieandPhilippa.' She rolls their names around her tongue, pulling them together, joining them. Entangling them in a way that hints they will never be separated again. 'We sound like we go together, don't you think?' she asks happily. 'We sound noble.' Stephanie thinks it's a strange word to pick but she likes it. She loves it in fact. The way she loves everything about Pip. 'We both have bazooka names! I'm sure it's a sign that we're always going to be friends.'

'Are you?' Stephanie asks, shy but thrilled.

'Definitely,' Pip replies with a confidence that seems broad enough to buoy up both small girls. 'I'm usually known as Pip. Would you like to be shortened to Steph? We can keep our noble names for important times. Steph and Pip sound like the sort of girls who have lots of fun and secrets and a club,' Pip continues with enthusiasm and certainty. 'Stephanie and Philippa sound like the sort of ladies who wear lovely clothes and live in big houses and have husbands who love them very much,' she adds firmly. 'We'll save those names for later.'

Stephanie is flattered that this intoxicating child has singled her out and is immediately enthralled with the idea of both lifestyles that Pip has conjured up. A childhood full of fun, and secrets and a club sounds wonderful and a grown-up life with lovely clothes, a big house and a loving husband sounds perfect.

Stephanie is enchanted by the fact that whenever Pip pairs their names together, she

7

always says Steph's name first—no matter whether she uses the full name or the derivative. It makes Steph feel valued. Pip is the world's best at making Steph feel esteemed, needed and prized.

So it takes just a split second and it's decided. Steph and Pip love one another with an instinctual, instant intensity that only little girls can muster. Theirs will be the sort of love that thickens and solidifies over the years, a love that will become unremarkable and expected rather than intoxicating and enthralling, but it will be all the more real and cherished for that metamorphosis.

And so it is decided, Steph and Pip are best friends.

Monday 22 March Last Year

CHAPTER ONE

'Hi, Steph, sorry to ring so early,' said Pip, in a garbled, slightly frantic voice that she'd used more or less constantly for the last two years. She'd used this tone so often, in fact, that no one, other than perhaps Steph, could remember the cheerful, careless, sometimes sexy voice that Pip had used before her husband had skipped the country without leaving a forwarding address.

'That's OK, we're all up,' assured Stephanie kindly.

'I thought you would be. You're a morning person.'

'Hmm,' mumbled Stephanie, neither confirming nor denying. This presumption, like many of the presumptions her friend Pip made, was not especially accurate but it was in no way offensive, it was flattering. Stephanie liked to think that other people considered her to be a natural morning person. Generally speaking, morning people were positive, opportunistic, breezy sorts. Think Holly Willoughby, Lorraine Kelly and Phillip Schofield. They also all had glossy hair and perfect make-up, even Phil. That was just the sort of club Stephanie liked to belong to. Stephanie had no interest in being one of those women who had a demanding social life, or stayed up late watching reality TV or even stayed up to attend all-night vigils to highlight the predicament of some worthy prisoner of conscience who had been unlucky enough to be born into some harsh, far-off regime. Those types of women were invariably slovenly in the morning and had an obvious dependency on caffeine, their children often went to school with the wrong PE kit. The thought made Steph shudder.

Yet, secretly, Stephanie was afraid that she was rather gloomier and, well, *normal* than the archetypal morning person. Yes, she had glossy, rich chestnut-coloured hair but it came with a cost (both financial and in terms of the time she devoted to eliminating all signs of her dowdy, natural colour, which was mid-brown, interrupted with the odd grey stray), and it was a cost she sometimes found herself resenting. As she occasionally resented the on/off dieting that she'd practised for the last five years. She was an uncomfortable size twelve, her body relentlessly fought to be a relaxed size fourteen. Secretly Stephanie worshipped elasticised waistbands but her garments with this unfashionable feature were hidden at the back of her wardrobe and only allowed out when she was alone. She sometimes thought it would be just such a treat to go to the school gates without having to apply full make-up. Plus, privately, there wasn't a day that passed when she didn't inwardly curse the damned alarm clock that dragged her into consciousness. Not that she'd *ever* admit as much, even to Pip. Stephanie liked to cultivate the idea that she was a Mary Poppins sort of character, free from unreasonable gripes and excessive moaning. Besides, it was pointless to grumble about something like spending hours in the hairdressers, let alone early mornings. Early mornings were an unavoidable fact of life. It was much better to brace oneself, plaster on a smile and efficiently start serving out the cornflakes.

'I didn't want to have to call you again but I'm

stuck,' Pip admitted, somewhat pathetically.

'How can I help?'

Steph wondered if she sounded a bit like one of those automated voices that asked you to 'press one if you are paying by direct debit' (code for 'we enjoy taking your money'), 'press two to hear opening hours' ('we're closed'), 'press three if your call is to do with tracking an order' ('which we've lost'), 'press four if you'd like to renew your subscription' ('to the service or product you've never utilised'), 'press five if you want to speak to an assistant, or please hold' (until you lose the will to live). Did she sound irritatingly calm and, while very polite, a tad insincere? Steph hoped not. She *was* sincere in her wish to help her friend, it was just a little bit difficult to sound so when this was the fourth panicky early-morning call she'd received in just three weeks. Luckily, Pip was far too immersed in her own concern to identify the nuance of exasperation in her best friend's voice. She ploughed on.

'I have a meeting in London and I need to be there by nine thirty. I'll be late if I don't get to the station within the next fifteen minutes but it's too early to take Chloe to school. I can't very well leave her outside the gate for an hour.'

'No, of course not. Absolutely not.'

Stephanie briefly wondered how long Pip had known about this meeting, it couldn't be a surprise to her. Her daughter was eight years old, so the issue of sorting childcare wasn't a newie either. She must have known yesterday that she would need some help and yet she hadn't mentioned it when they'd come to Steph's for Sunday lunch. Chloe could have stayed over last night or at least

13

they could have arranged a pick-up time. Sometimes it seemed as though Pip was incapable of thinking more than five minutes ahead. Why couldn't she be more organised? But then Steph realised saying as much (while truthful) would seem churlish. Steph was struck with a thought. Chloe was eight! The very same age as she and Pip had been when they met. A generation ago and yet Steph remembered it with such vividness, as though it was yesterday, so she found it easy to breezily respond in the way that was expected. 'Drop her off here. I'll take her to school. I insist.'

'Really?'

'No problem.'

'Thank you, thank you, thank you,' gushed Pip. She sounded at once relieved and surprised to be helped out of a hole, which Stephanie thought was daft because Pip must know by now that Steph always helped her out of any holes she found herself in. In the past couple of years, Steph had helped Pip choose a flat to rent, move into the flat and decorate it. She'd helped her apply for school places and part-time jobs. Steph sometimes helped Pip with shopping, gardening or even washing if required, so taking Chloe to school wasn't a big deal.

Not that their friendship was all one way, Steph reminded herself, Pip brought a lot to the party too. In fact, Steph often thought that Pip actually brought *the* party. Pip was chaotic, yes—but she was also chatty and charismatic. Pip might often be frantic but she was always funny. She was also gentle, loyal and trustworthy. Even now. Even since Dylan had left. She was not as consistently positive, true. Maybe her humour was tinged with a harshness that could occasionally explode into something approaching bitterness, but no one could blame her. Pip was wounded. Not fatally but critically.

Dylan Harris. The name still caused Steph to shudder so it wasn't unreasonable that when his name assaulted Pip's ears (or, more frequently, when it fell from her lips) she was prone to throwing a total fit—judders and tears and all. Steph hated to think of the destruction that man had caused. Bailing out on his relationship with Pip and Chloe, when Chloe was only six years old, was crime enough—that was the crime everyone understood and referred to—but there were times when Steph thought that was the best thing he'd ever done. The years he stayed with them, when he no longer gave a damn, were the really vile ones. Steph had come to call the last three years of her friend's marriage the angry years, at least she did so in her head. The angry years were filled with loud rows, embarrassing public displays of resentment and—ultimately—lazy, unconvincing lies about his infidelities. Those were the years that had ripped away Pip's confidence in herself and in her world. Those were the years that had thrown her into disarray. She'd always been such a buoyant, capable woman before then but for a long period of time, whenever Steph brought her friend to mind, she thought of a drowning kitten that had just managed to push its head out of the sack that she'd been thrown into but had no chance of escape. A kitten, helpless, hopeless and so damned surprised by the betrayal.

Pip had been devastated by Dylan's desertion (as she liked to call it). Desertion had a nineteenth-century ring to it, a hint of tragedy and drama that rather appealed to her. Saying, 'when Dylan left me' simply didn't cover it in the same way and she never used the neutral form, 'when we split'. Besides, to be accurate he didn't walk out on them, he threw them out. He changed the locks when Pip and Chloe were out seeing off Pip's parents' plane; Mr and Mrs Foxton were emigrating to New Zealand that very day, Dylan's timing being nothing short of sadistic. Pip came home from Heathrow to a note pinned to the door; it had the address of the lock-up where he'd stored all their stuff. Then before she could yell 'lawyer' he'd sold his apartment and left the country too. Unquestionably, Pip was a wronged woman.

Her paleness and thinness testified as much. True, Pip had always had a tendency towards both physical traits. She was a poor cook and rarely got excited about food the way Steph did, plus she preferred holidays where she energetically marched across dark northern moors rather than lounging around the pool in Europe, so she had never had much opportunity to pick up a tan. But following the split, Pip plummeted alarmingly from the description 'slim' to 'skinny' or 'scrawny' and her pale skin was less likely to be described as porcelain and more likely to be noticed as ashen or pallid. Stephanie had watched her friend's *joie de vivre* slip away with the inches and any hint of colour. She thought it was a tragedy. Pip was a natural beauty. She was five foot eight and had long tapering limbs. She had naturally blond, wavy hair and, as she'd always resisted the temptation to either straighten or colour it, it fell in a thick, healthy, undulating mass around her shoulders.

16

She had wide, slightly slanting green eyes that shone out above her sharp cheekbones. Following her split from Dylan, it was impossible to ignore the fact that she bore a remarkable resemblance to a wronged pre-Raphaelite model, drowning in disappointment and regret. Divorce was sometimes thought of as a very modern disease, an epidemic of the twenty-first century, and yet a broken heart was the oldest ailment known to mankind. Well, certainly to womankind.

'Don't worry about it,' Steph assured Pip.

'I didn't know who else to call.'

'Always call me, Pip.'

'I just knew you'd be organised and you'd manage.'

Stephanie glanced around her kitchen; her eyes darted from one micro-scene of domestic carnage to the next. Yes, normally she was organised. If anyone caught her at, say, eleven in the morning or two thirty in the afternoon, even 9 p.m., she definitely would be able to proudly wear the badge 'organised'. But the times in-between, the times when her family spilt out into her domestic perfection, were rather more chaotic.

Her family were all awake and up, waging war on her calm and pretty environment. Her three boys lolled around the kitchen in various states of undress and distress. Harry, her eleven year old, was increasingly unpredictable as he was battling with a premature onset of hormones. His voice was unreliable and as such caused him great embarrassment. One moment he sounded like the child she thought him to be, the next he'd say something in a deep and gravelly tone which would cause Steph to look around the kitchen in order to find the intruder. It was disconcerting for everyone. Alfie, her eight year old, was noisily stating his case for watching TV, specifically the episode of *Phineas and Ferb* on the Disney channel that he'd recorded the night before. Julian (her thirty-nine year old—husband, rather than child) was rather more keen on watching Sky news and the pair of them were robustly quibbling over the remote. Freddie, her five year old,was sitting under the table feeding Coco Pops to his guinea pig.

'No trouble!' Stephanie assured her friend.

Although Chloe and Alfie were the same age they did not go to the same school. Alfie and Freddie went to Mansfield, a boys-only prep school, Harry attended St Joseph's, the local fee-paying grammar school (a place hard-won and pricey) and Chloe went to the local state school, Woodsend Primary School. The school Stephanie and Pip had attended. Stephanie made a quick calculation in her head. Providing Pip dropped off Chloe in the next ten minutes as she'd promised (possible but by no means certain as Pip wasn't the best timekeeper, even when she had a train to catch) and all the children could be herded into the Audi by five to eight then she could still deliver them each at the relevant schools before bells rang.

'Does Chloe need a packed lunch?' asked Stephanie.

'Steph, that would be wonderful! She does and I was just about to start making one but if you could do it that would save me a few minutes. You're an angel. What would I do without you?' asked Pip, just as she'd regularly asked over the last thirty years.

'You'll never have to find out,' replied Stephanie, just as she'd replied over the past thirty years. Then she rang off. Steph bent down and swooped up Freddie, firmly and fondly she plopped him back into his chair and instructed, 'Eat your cereal at the table, Freddie, not under it and Coco Pops are not a good thing to feed to the guinea pig.'

'But are Coco Pops good for me?' Freddie turned his curious, open face towards his mother and waited for her reassurance.

'Yes,' she replied without thinking about the question, as she was too busy dashing around the kitchen picking up homework books, Pokémon cards and stray pens and then redistributing them in the appropriate rucksacks and pencil cases.

'Other than the sugar content,' muttered Julian drily.

Stephanie made the decision to ignore her husband's comment because if she gave it any thought she might consider it to be an undermining contradiction (at best) or an underhand criticism (at worst). Coco Pops was not always Steph's cereal of choice for her boys' breakfasts and she usually insisted that the children eat Bran Flakes or Weetabix but Freddie had not wanted to go to school today because he had a new teacher, a strict and demanding middle-aged woman who terrified Steph let alone her five year old. The last, beloved teacher had just moved out of the area and now taught at a different faraway school and so this morning Freddie had needed a bit of extra persuasion to eat any breakfast at all. Steph didn't think there was any point in bothering Julian with this level of

19

domestic detail. Besides, Julian was not a morning person and unlike his wife he had no designs on appearing to pass himself off as one. He was especially grumpy this morning; it was understandable, it was Monday and, hand on heart, no one liked Monday mornings.

Stephanie remembered a time, over a decade ago now, when she used to have to reluctantly say goodbye to the weekend—which had been full of cinema visits, energetic walks in the countryside and long, boozy pub lunches—and face the morning commute on trains and tubes, it was always a trial. Besides which, Julian hadn't even benefited from the rejuvenating powers of a family weekend. He'd had to work most of the time. He'd spent a lot of Saturday afternoon holed up in the room she liked to call her library and he called his den, answering emails and taking calls about some deal or other, he'd had his Sunday roast interrupted by a work call and then last night, just as Steph was beginning the process of ushering the children off to bed and anticipating a night in front of the TV (catching up on some drama or even the guilty pleasure of a repeat of a *Friends* episode), Julian's boss had rung him again and Julian had spent another hour on the phone. On a Sunday evening! It wasn't reasonable. He looked incredibly stressed and agitated after he'd taken the calls. Steph wasn't sure what deal Julian was currently brokering but it must be big and important if the extra hours needed were any sort of indication. The man would be worked into an early grave. Stephanie sometimes wished that Julian would tell his boss where to stick his job and his inconsiderate demands on their family time

20

but, then, she never had that thought when they were holidaying in the Maldives or when she was hosting a coffee morning in their—five bedroom, three bathroom, three reception room—house.

Stephanie handed Alfie his school tie and as she did so she surreptitiously sniffed the top of Harry's head to check he didn't smell of anything other than shampoo or conditioner. Harry was beginning to suffer with greasy hair and Stephanie dreaded the moment when angry hormonal spots would start to blister his smooth skin, skin that she still thought of as baby skin. With a sigh she turned her attention to preparing a packed lunch for Chloe. She'd make ham sandwiches, with tomato but no spread which was Chloe's preference. She had a small pot of organic yoghurt (apricot), a packet of raisins and cranberries, an apple and a carton of Innocent smoothie. Stephanie prided herself on her healthy eating habits. Or rather, her dictatorial skills that meant her children and the children she knew ate healthily, although she wasn't above sneaking a king-size Mars Bar for herself.

Julian pushed his empty muesli bowl about twenty centimetres away from him (this was a habit of his that mildly frustrated Steph, she wished that, just once, he'd pick up the bowl and put it in the dishwasher, instead of leaving it for her to clear). But she was glad she hadn't grumbled when Julian stood up from the table and commented in a jokey, good-natured tone, 'You like that woman more than you like me.'

How could she grumble at her husband for not clearing his breakfast bowl when she was prepared to go to lengths for her friend? He never complained about her continual invitations which meant Pip shared their lives. Pip and Chloe came round at least once a fortnight for Sunday lunch, they stopped by several times a week, they spent Christmas, Mother's Day, birthdays and bank holidays together and last summer Pip and Chloe had even joined Steph, Julian and the boys on their family holiday in the south of France. When she gave it any thought, Steph realised that Julian had the patience of a saint, really he did. You didn't often come across a husband who was prepared to share his wife's time quite so generously. Not just her time but his money too, if she was going to be vulgar about it. The fact was, there was no way Pip could have managed to pay for a holiday since her divorce but Julian rented a large four-bedroom gîte—when they could have got away with three or even two bedrooms—then he'd practically insisted that Pip and Chloe come along to 'fill the rooms that would just stand empty'. Stephanie smiled to herself, he was so generous. Yes, she'd married a good one. What a joy. What a relief. She often told herself how lucky she was.

'Go on, admit it, if you were in a life or death situation and you had to choose between Pip or me, you'd pick her,' he teased as he walked away from the table. He was looking around for his BlackBerry; he didn't like it being out of reach or sight.

Steph heard the smile in his voice and continued the joke.

'Without hesitation, darling,' she laughed. 'As much as I love you, you simply don't offer the right sort of advice when it comes to which shoes go with which outfit and you know absolutely nothing about removing stubborn stains from school shirts.'

22

'Which is of course all you women ever talk about,' added Julian.

They both knew this wasn't the case but were quite enjoying the silly, flippant banter. It was fun and a tiny bit flirtatious, which was an achievement on a Monday morning for any couple, it bordered on an absolute miracle for a couple who had been together nearly twenty years. Sometimes Steph thought that they both behaved as though they had an audience and a role to play in front of that audience, as though they were self-conscious participants on a reality TV show. No doubt their habit stemmed from the fact that they had been parents for eleven years and invariably there was at least one pair of sharp eyes and ears following and interpreting their every move and conversation.

'That, and men,' confirmed Steph. She kissed her husband on the lips.

It was a brief, habitual sort of kiss. What it lacked in erotic passion it compensated for with genuine warmth. Sometimes, it seemed to Steph that Julian didn't really notice her kisses anymore. Was she unreasonable to expect him to after all these years?

From time to time it occurred to Steph that Julian didn't seem to notice most of the domestic stuff that surrounded him. He didn't know that Harry had not been picked for the grammar school football team (despite five consecutive years of playing for the A team for his prep school). He'd been offered a place as a sub in Cs but had haughtily refused the position. Harry had come home last Tuesday in a terrible mood and systematically stripped his room of all the Chelsea paraphernalia that he'd been carefully collecting for years. He'd melodramatically piled the annuals, posters, badges and caps into a cardboard box and dumped it next to the wheelie bin in the garden, insisting that as his 'career was now so *obviously* over, there was no point in keeping this rubbish *stuff*'. Steph had simultaneously fought laughter and tears. Naturally, it broke her heart that her son was disappointed and felt rejected but on the other hand, his indignant tantrum had been quite entertaining. She'd long ago learnt to roll with the metaphysical punches that a child flung out when disappointed. She'd secretly retrieved the cardboard box while he was playing a game on his Wii. Her plan was to reintroduce the memorabilia once the first sting of disappointment had abated or when he was installed on the A team.

Julian had missed that domestic drama because he was in Geneva at the time. In fact he missed most domestic dramas because of the time he spent in Geneva or Paris or Frankfurt or at the office in London. Julian was unaware that Alfie was especially argumentative this morning because he was irritated that on Saturday his mother had won a long-fought battle and had all his hair chopped short. Although only eight, Alfie had an acute sense of the impression he made on other people. Normally he wowed them. He'd inherited his father's looks. The combination of his huge blue eyes, framed with long and thick lashes, and his curly surfer-length hair meant that he was perfectly suited to play Zac Efron as a child if the need ever arose. He was a star at his weekend Stagecoach class, in fact he managed to create quite a stir just walking along the high street. Stephanie found she was ever so slightly uncomfortable with the fact that her eight year old was so aware that he was already immeasurably cool; shouldn't he still be simply concerned with climbing trees or riding his bike at a dangerous speed, rather than whether Crocs or Converse trainers looked best with his khaki cut-offs? Not that she'd insisted he had his hair chopped just to temper his vanity, the headmaster had sent out a note on Friday afternoon, reminding parents that pupils' hair ought not to hang over ears or reach the shirt collar. While the note was ostensibly addressed to all parents, Stephanie was convinced that Mr Granger had Alfie in mind and so she had duly marched him off to the hairdressers.

Julian hadn't commented on the new crockery that Stephanie had bought (it was white with a silver rim around the edge and they used to have a brown set with a dense cream floral design). He would see these things, though, when he looked at the Visa statement at the end of the month. He might notice that trims for Harry and Freddie, Alfie's chop and Stephanie's highlights had totalled over £400 in the fancy London hair salon that she liked to go to. He would then certainly question whether Stephanie needed to spend £900 on a new dinner service. He'd comment that the old one was adequate, he might even ask was there any difference at all. Stephanie would then promptly point out that the brown set had a transient appeal while the white crockery was a classic. Then, most likely, he'd mumble as though he was affronted that she spent his money so freely. That was how these things normally played out. The truth was she knew he liked the fact that he earned so much and she spent so much, it was a way of showing the world that he was an effective hunter-gatherer.

The kiss he'd never notice because that wasn't on a bank statement.

CHAPTER TWO

Pip frantically ran to the platform, she took large strides, the soles of her shoes slammed painfully on to the tiled floor but she couldn't think about that now as she had less than a minute to spare before the train departed. Pip only just managed to leap on to the train and collapse into the first available seat before the automatic doors swished shut behind her and the train started its speedy journey into London Waterloo.

The moment she caught her breath she realised that the seat she'd chosen was a mistake. Not only was she sitting next to a large, greying man who had inconsiderately taken up far more than half the seat, leaving her to perch precariously practically in the aisle (a target for anyone lugging bags from the door to their seat and back again) but he was wearing headphones. The distinctive, heartfelt tunes of Tina Turner were blaring out at a volume which meant that no other passenger could reasonably expect to hear his or her own thoughts. Pip had nothing against Tina Turner but the question, 'What's Love Got To Do With It?' belted out in that slightly desperate, overtly mournful pitch, so early in the morning, wasn't one she felt able to tackle. Besides which, she soon realised that she was also very close to the train loos.

Somewhat predictably, whoever had last used the convenience had failed to bother to press the button that would close the door after use, that or the automated lock was broken. The door gaped open, treating Pip to a front-seat view of the actual pan. Why was there always something swishing about on the floor of public loos? Pip wanted to think that the liquid she spotted rolling around the floor was water, shaken from hands of people in a desperate hurry to leave the cubicle, but she couldn't help but fear it was more likely to be a leak from the toilet or simply a matter of poor aim, a thought that was solidified as there was a faint smell of urine drifting into the carriage. Regrettably, Pip had an incredibly keen sense of smell. She was like a bloodhound, Steph would always say. On more than one occasion Steph had invited Pip around to her home to help sniff out something not quite savoury (a cheese sandwich carefully hidden in a jigsaw box or a stray trainer carelessly lost at the bottom of the music cupboard). There were a couple of things worth commenting upon there. One, Steph had a music cupboard, an actual and entire designated cupboard (not much smaller than Chloe's bedroom) where Steph stored the boys' instruments (two violins, a cello, a classical guitar, a flute and three recorders) and secondly, Pip loved Steph enough to sniff around her potentially toxic cupboards, if it helped. No greater love hath a friend.

Pip wished that it was one of her other senses that was as acute. It would be useful to hear more than she did. She wasn't certain whether it was a sign of age or some sort of allergy but last night, as she'd kissed Chloe at bedtime and they'd both recited their usual, 'Night night, don't let the bed bugs bite' (a bit of nonsense from Pip's own childhood), Pip could have sworn that Chloe said, 'Night night, don't let the red Uggs bite.' Pip admitting as much had made Chloe laugh raucously, in a way that Pip treasured, but even so! Pip couldn't help fearing that it was distinctly, and regrettably, middle-aged that her hearing was becoming unreliable. She already wore glasses (well, lenses), she'd done so since she was a teenager. Her sense of taste wasn't up to much. She had little interest in food and would often forget to eat at all until her stomach rudely rumbled. If she could take a pill that would provide all the necessary proteins and nutrients to keep her alive, then she would do so. Her lack of interest in food meant that she was a hopeless cook, guilty of resorting to ready-made meals more times than she liked to think about, let alone admit to. Her taste buds had very low expectations and yet she still managed to disappoint them.

This left her with the sense of touch.

Ohhh.

The word *touch* stirred such an uncomfortable mix of emotions for Pip nowadays that she barely dared consider the word. It set off a spiral of associated thoughts that were bittersweet. Touching, stroking, caressing, feeling, holding.

Having.

She supposed touch had been the other sense that she used to heavily rely upon, the sense she had most enjoyed. Put simply, Pip liked to touch and be touched. She was definitely what was known as a tactile person, however unfashionable such a thing had become in this age of cool reserve. Pip was known for her big, hearty hugs (that were surprisingly robust and reassuringly comforting for a woman so willowy), she used to have a habit of gently laying her hand on a person's arm when she wanted to tell them something important or when they were telling *her* something important, she liked to ruffle kids' hair, sprinkle loud raspberries on babies' chubby thighs and kiss the cheeks of friends and family, not just the air in the vicinity of their cheeks. But Pip no longer did any of the above as much as she used to, as much as she'd like to.

It wasn't just the fact that she and the majority of her friends had children of school age now (there were no longer as many babies in her life), it was also the fact that being a tactile person needed a certain amount of self-confidence. A self-confidence that Pip used to be famed for but had now bled away. You had to believe that someone might want to be on the receiving end of one of your hugs before you could effectively bestow it and, frankly, Pip wasn't sure. After all, Dylan hadn't wanted to be on the receiving end of her hugs, or any other intimacy she could offer. He'd preferred the company of *that slut*. Pip knew that referring to Dylan's mistress as *that slut* was infantile and clichéd but still she couldn't help herself. In fact, it had taken her two years to be so refined, in the early days she'd called the woman things that would make a sailor blush. It was some sort of vent for her pitiful, impotent fury. Slut was one of the kindest things she'd called her rival. Not that the woman he fled to God-knows-where with

29

was Pip's only rival, not if you categorise rivals as women Dylan slept with. There had been a trail of women who fitted that description. Pip tended to focus on the one he left the country with, although, considering Dylan's attention span, it was very likely that *that slut* had been replaced by another slut by now. Pip couldn't decide whether she hoped so or not. She didn't want Dylan to find his happily-ever-after with *that slut* but then being the ex ex held no cachet. It didn't bear thinking about.

The truth was, besides all the friendly hugging, and hair ruffling and baby kissing, the intimacy Pip missed most was sex. Pip thought she was probably quite good at sex. Besides the fact that she had been told as much by old boyfriends (admittedly a long, long time ago), she enjoyed it enormously and, in her experience, the things a person enjoys tend to be the things that person excels at. Pip hadn't had any sex for nearly three years. She hadn't had good sex (the caring, caress-packed variety) for longer still. She missed the thought, the anticipation, the act and the afterglow of having sex with her husband, the man she thought was her life partner.

Of course she knew she no longer had a husband.

She'd been on her own for two and a half years now. Two and a half years and yet every time she thought about the fact that she was no longer Dylan's wife she felt a whole new wave of anguish, regret and deep, deep sorrow wash over her. When would that fade? People kept reassuring her that time healed and they urged her to 'get back out there' but it was easier said than done. Pip knew it was wrong, pointless and illogical, Pip knew that

Dylan had cheated on her, bullied her and deserted her, she knew he was unreliable with regard to his responsibilities to Chloe and yet she still missed him.

She missed the way he liked to throw lavish dinner parties on a Saturday night for their friends, she loved the sense of fun and indulgence such festivities inevitably created. She missed his sense of humour which was intelligent and demanding (although occasionally could be a tiny bit sharp, some might say cruel), she missed his ambitious and stylish plans for their home and their garden (a home and garden that now belonged to someone else), she missed him sneakily grabbing her arse whenever she walked past him or stood close to his side, even if they were out in public. She missed the smell of his aftershave, mingled with the smell of his leather jacket. She missed sex. Pip ran her cool fingers up and down her own forearm, not a substitute for the matter on her mind but a comfort.

Pip stared out of the window and watched as stations began to whizz in and out of sight. They were all similar to look at (grey, grubby, boasting nothing more exciting than faded posters advertising West End shows or the latest bestselling novel). The stations could not distract her. She glanced around the carriage. Other than the large man she'd sat next to, and a scattering of serious-looking commuters, the carriage was populated with a cluster of anxious, middle-aged women. They were a group, this much was signalled by the fact that they were all wearing a uniform of loud, long-sleeved shirts in a floral print and bright chunky necklaces, the sort of necklace

31

that is often given to a mum on Mother's Day by a child who watches makeover programmes. The floral shirts were currently fashionable and indeed they worked well on women of a certain age. The bright colours implied they'd made an effort, and the generous length covered the bulges that belied the fact that the effort hadn't been enough.

These women endlessly checked that their bags were secure, that they had their tickets with them and that they knew which tube line they'd need once they arrived at Waterloo. It was obvious that they were unused to travel and intimidated by the idea of a trip into the country's capital. They were probably planning on visiting a gallery (one of the free ones, nothing too modern) and then wandering around Harrods' food hall for a few hours. Chances were that they'd only been persuaded to make the journey because their bossy teenage children had muttered that they needed to 'get a life', or maybe they were keen for something new to talk about with their husbands at the tea table. If they still had husbands.

Pip knew these women without having to be introduced to them, as they were a prevalent breed. She at once pitied them and feared them and she wondered whether she was one of them. True, she was ten or even twenty years younger than them, but while she might not have been cut from the same cloth, she thought there was a real chance that she'd since been sewn into the same pattern. She was surrounded by women who were permanently well-intentioned and therefore plagued with endless worry as to whether they were doing the right thing. The combination was unintentionally (but irrevocably) irritating. The worry was etched in their foreheads and engraved in their weary eyes, which had seen the best and worst of life. Their bosoms were low and slack but, still, their intentions were worn loud and clear, on the sleeve where hearts used to be kept, until they were broken.

Pip wondered whether she ought to move seats. Of course she should. She could so easily stand up and wander along the train until she found a seat that she did not have to share with a loud and large chap or a view of the lav but Pip was reluctant to do so. She did not want to draw attention to herself. She did not want to admit that she'd picked the wrong seat in the first place. This was, of course, ridiculous and she knew it. As though anyone would notice if she changed seats. As though anyone *cared* what she did. Pip briefly chided herself, then stood up and shuffled along the aisle into the next carriage where she sat down on one of those seats designed for three, facing another seat designed for three.

'You couldn't stand the smell either, eh?' asked the man sitting opposite her.

Pip looked up, startled that anyone should decide to strike up a conversation on a London commuter train. She swiftly concluded that the man must be an out-of-towner, otherwise he would be aware of the unwritten (but clearly understood) code which dictated that strangers never spoke to one another on public transport, not unless the matter up for discussion was one of life and death, and even then seasoned commuters knew to proceed with caution. Could this man be drunk so early in the day? It was the only excuse.

Pip didn't know whether she ought to answer or

not but found there wasn't any need to because the man didn't wait for her response, he ploughed on regardless.

'I don't know why people can't at least close the door after them. It's so inconsiderate, let alone unhygienic. Would they pee on the floor in their bathroom at home and then leave the door wide open so that everyone could see the evidence?' He shook his head in disgusted disbelief.

'Erm, no. I suppose not,' muttered Pip.

She briefly considered whether the man was likely to be a school teacher. School teachers often felt the impulse, and the right, to express their opinions, plus that thing he'd said about whether people would pee on their own bathroom floors was just the sort of thing a teacher would say. She clearly remembered her own teachers asking, 'Would you put your feet on the table at home, Philippa Foxton?' 'Would you swing on your chair at home, Philippa Foxton?' Pip wondered whether she could move seats again. The last thing she wanted was to have to make small talk with a stranger for the entire thirty-five-minute journey, especially the sort of small talk that she imagined teachers preferred, talk about league tables and degeneration of the standard of the current exam system. Pip froze whenever she thought about league tables (or MMR vaccinations, or the effect of pylons on a child's health). She relied heavily on Steph for guidance on all that sort of thing.

Pip was much better at the fun parts of parenting. She loved playing with Chloe and never got bored of dressing up dolls, making dens, sculpting play dough, threading beads. Not that she was simply the 'fun parent', for one thing this would assume Dylan was the disciplinarian parent and he wasn't. He was the absent parent, which meant she was the everything-she-could-be parent. Besides being a great playmate, Pip was very competent about ensuring regular bedtimes, regular exercise and, despite her lazy habits when it came to preparing her own food, she tried to offer her daughter a balanced diet. She policed teeth brushing, hair brushing, tidying of the bedroom and completion of homework. She also answered the difficult questions—'Where do we come from?' and 'Where has Daddy gone?' Both had been handled with the sort of sensitivity that reassured Chloe that her world was safe and fine even when Pip sometimes doubted that this was the case. Pip and her daughter laughed together, stropped together and played together. They worked well together. Pip was supremely competent at everything to do with being a parent in their home but was less able when any sort of official bodies came into their private arena. It was another instance of her lack of confidence. She found it difficult to be discerning or definitive when faced with the sea of sometimes contradictory advice that washed up at every mother's feet.

When Chloe was first born, Pip was fully able to join in on the aspects of the post-natal club she thought worthwhile and yet she felt happy to reject the overly fussy, paranoid parts. She thought pumping her breast milk to measure the fluid ounces before she fed them to her baby was a ridiculous suggestion and would not do it, no matter how many of the other new mums told her that it was essential to know how much milk Chloe had digested. She was also certain it was unnecessary to play the sounds of frolicking dolphins to your baby to aid sleep or to develop cognitive reasoning. But now she was never quite so sure about anything and frequently asked advice on matters to do with parenting. How should she best treat Chloe's verruca? Should she insist Chloe continue her piano lessons, even though she professed to hate them and seemed to have no ear? Would it be a good idea to watch Disney movies in French? Pip's breathing speeded up as these thoughts whizzed around her head. Being a parent was such a huge responsibility. She'd been at it for eight years now, and while there were aspects that she'd obviously become comfortable with, each day seemed to present a cluster of new challenges. How would she manage to protect her daughter until she reached adulthood? Not that the job ended there, not if her own mother's fretting was anything to go by. The problem was Pip so often felt out of her depth and, more specifically, alone.

She glanced at the man travelling opposite her. He had slightly tanned, lucent skin with a sprinkling of dark freckles on his cheekbones. He probably was a teacher, she decided. He probably did know about learning French by ear. He certainly looked a bit like a teacher. He was wearing chinos, rather than jeans, but a casual jacket rather than a suit. Pip thought his outfit definitely ruled out lawyer, city trader or bank manager. Besides, his hair was quite long and still held a colour (dark brown); all the lawyers and bankers she knew were balding or grey or both. He was tall and thin, although his broad shoulders

36

ensured that he was lean, not lanky. He clearly had not shaved that morning but rather than making him look scruffy, the slight shadow made him look earnest and industrious. He'd picked up a newspaper and was holding it open but he was still looking at Pip as though keen to continue chatting. Maybe it would be OK to ask this stranger, who was opinionated about the train loos, whether he thought there was any merit in watching Disney DVDs in French.

'Are you a teacher?' she blurted, almost demanded.

The man looked surprised and faintly amused. 'No, are you?' he replied politely.

'No,' replied Pip. It was at this point she saw the flaw in her conversation-opener: it was unusual to the point of making her appear slightly crazy.

She hurriedly reached for her handbag and searched for her novel. She carried a large bag full of things that she carted around 'just in case'. Carrying an umbrella, Elastoplasts, Savlon cream, hand sanitiser, her address book, a sewing kit, tissues, a tin holding an assortment of paper clips, elastic bands and biros, the London *A–Z*, nail clippers and a small bottle of lavender essence was an attempt to make her feel more secure. She weighed herself down with this stuff in a futile effort to ward off disasters; in fact, all it did was give her a bad back. Once Pip located her novel, she started to read it, holding it high to her face in an effort to block out the curious gaze of the loo man, who was not a teacher.

God, she was pathetic. Pip swore and muttered to herself. She was so incompetent! She was apparently incapable of simply mixing in the real world! Why had she made that assumption about a complete stranger on the strength of one throwaway comment? And how could she think that opening gambit might be suitable? Even if he was a teacher, why would he be interested in talking to her about her child's education? Her problem was she had an overactive imagination, her mother must have thrown manure at her head when she was a kid. It was clear she didn't get out enough, and no wonder considering the embarrassment she caused herself when she actually was out and about. What did she know about this stranger? Other than he had really attractive eyes (light brown with flecks of green). Thoughtful eyes, ones that seemed considerate and trustworthy. Oh. My. God. There she went again. Making assumptions. It was pathetic. She knew nothing about this man (except that he wasn't a teacher). Just because his eyes were attractive (damned attractive, exceptionally so) it didn't mean that he was considerate or trustworthy. In fact the opposite was more likely to be the case, if her experience was anything to go by.

That had always been another one of her problems, she was too ready to think the best of someone. Too ready to fall for a handsome face. His was a handsome face, very strong jawline and an interesting little scar just above his right eye. She wondered where that had come from. Perhaps he'd sustained an injury while carrying out some heroic act, like wresting an old lady's bag back from some thug or jumping into a river to save a drowning puppy. Stop it! Pip tried to rein in her thoughts. Seriously, she pitied poor Chloe for being lumbered with her as a mum. She was like a kid herself, she was hopeless! She didn't understand why her friends still talked to her. She understood why Dylan had left her.

No, actually she didn't understand that. Not fully, not ever.

After a few minutes of determined reading of her barrier book, Pip felt the man's gaze fall from her as he seemed to settle into reading his newspaper. Good. Phew. That was a relief. Now she could concentrate on what she'd planned to concentrate on during this journey, she could prepare herself for this meeting.

She might never have an opportunity like this one again. This could be huge, she simply must not blow it. She wanted to reach into her bag and fish out her designs but didn't want to move in case that was interpreted by the not-a-teacher-man as an invitation to talk. Besides, she knew the designs like the back of her hand. All she had to do was think through her pitch. Remain focused. Be eloquent. Appear considered. Keep a cool head. And turn her life around.

Oh crap.

CHAPTER THREE

Kirsten pouted into the mirror. Held the pose, admired the gorgeous young woman pouting back at her, winked, grinned and then blew her a kiss. Yes, she was stunning. It was official. Even in the hideous, ugly, old-fashioned mirror she looked a.maz.ing.

No wonder they couldn't resist her, thought Kirsten, giggling with glee. Somehow, somewhere on a subconscious level, she continually acknowledged her spectacular youth and beauty, although if quizzed she might have said she was giggling at the thought of drinking champagne tonight and staying in a decent bed, rather than the dismal, lumpy, skinny apology for a bed that she had to sleep in in this lousy flat share.

She glanced around her bedroom. It really was quite pathetically miserable. The furniture was from the ark. Her mother had chuckled when she saw it and commented, 'I used to have this exact suite! Your nan bought it for me from MFI.'

Suite! Suite? When Kirsten talked about a suite she meant a suite of rooms, like they'd once had when they went on holiday to Los Angeles or the suite of rooms she'd once got Jules to upgrade to at Highview. Mummy meant three-piece suites (which were so *over*, everyone knew an eclectic mix of chairs and a daybed were the thing nowadays) or she meant this bloody repulsive, veneered dressing table, matching headboard and chest of drawers that crowded Kirsten whenever she had to stay in this dingy room.

Mummy liked to reminisce about the old days. Nothing she liked more than to remind them all of what they had come from. She was always going on about stuff like buying furniture from MFI, or being excited at finding a clementine stuffed in an old pair of tights at Christmas time, or the strikes that she'd endured throughout the seventies which had led to mountains of rubbish piling up in the streets and meant people had to share baths or something. Kirsten didn't quite get why the binmen going on strike meant that her mother and such needed to use candles, or why people stockpiled loo roll. But then, she didn't really listen that carefully when Mummy took a trip down memory lane—frankly it was all a bit of a bore. Kirsten didn't see the point; talking about how you were once poor and had crap stuff was deathly. Kirsten liked all the lovely, expensive things her daddy had lavished on her since she was a tiny girl; at least *he* realised that the only point to being filthy rich was for you to enjoy it. What could be more fabulous than splashing your cash around and wallowing in it? If her mother had her way, they'd still be in the poky flat that her parents had rented when they first married, the claustrophobically small place that her mother still referred to as 'cosy'.

Kirsten *definitely* preferred her father's way of doing things. He'd buried his appalling accent and now sounded a little like Prince Charles, he was a member of the right clubs and friends with the right people. Admittedly, her mother's accent wasn't terrible, it was friendly, but still not something Kirsten aspired to. Kirsten had been careful to round her vowels, careful to call her mum and dad Mummy and Daddy, and careful to finesse a languid drawl so that she had fitted right in at her lovely little chi-chi girls-only independent school, Queen Charlotte's School for Girls.

Kirsten had just turned twenty-two, which seemed really *adult* to her although Mummy often said she didn't seem to have the sense she was born with. Mummy was always going on about the fact that in her day girls were much more independent and savvy but Kirsten thought her mother was wrong about this too. After all, she'd started having Brazilian waxes when she was seventeen and now she'd had the entire area lasered except for a tiny thin runway line. She was never in the embarrassing position of having to turn down an invitation to go swimming or to a jacuzzi because the odd stray hair might spoil her day, whereas her mother (with all her common sense and supposed savvy!) had to rely heavily on sarongs whenever they were on holiday. But then, maybe this wasn't a terrible thing, if you considered her mother's age— forty-six! Wearing a sarong was probably the most dignified option if she was going to insist on going on a beach at all.

Kirsten worked in the city, as a personal assistant to a group of hedge fund managers. She did her job well enough not to get fired, although probably not well enough to ensure she would be promoted to PA of a CEO or even a CFO. Not that Kirsten was planning on hanging around that long; the PAs to the CEOs were *really* old, like thirty-four, or thirty-five. Kirsten planned to be married before she was twenty-five and then she wouldn't need to work ever again. Kirsten could never understand why her mother had tried to 'keep her hand in' with the family business once they could afford a proper PA to do all the boring filing and stuff, why would Mummy want to bother? Kirsten's father didn't like it *at all*. He argued that *his* wife didn't need to work, that it was a man's job to provide for his family; he said she showed him up by coming into the office, and in the end she'd *finally* listened to him and stayed away. Although her mother still occasionally grumbled that she missed the buzz of office life. Buzz! Ha, that was a joke. Her parents' office was on a sleepy industrial estate, there was no buzz! All there was in the office was parched spider plants and a wall calendar, with undecipherable critical deadlines. Daddy didn't spend any money on interior decorating because none of his clients ever saw it. If he wanted to shake on a deal he took his clients to his members-only club in London.

At least there was some sort of atmosphere in Kirsten's office. Kirsten knew it made sense to work in the city, if she had to work at all (which apparently she did now!). The city was where all the money was. The money men. Potential husbands. Kirsten had been a bit surprised that there were women hedge fund managers too. She didn't have a problem with that, if some girls wanted to charge around getting stressed about stuff, that was their lookout but she'd never fancied the idea. It looked like a lot of effort and effort wasn't her thing. She supposed they must like their jobs because they all got to wear beautiful suits (designers such as Joseph and Calvin Klein), they got to carry Gucci bags and they always wore absolutely stunning shoes with killer heels! But it wasn't for her. She'd once tried to read those huge newspapers but what did it mean, 'BASF set to buy Cognis for more than €3bn'? What was an equity? Or a capital market or bond buying, come to that? And was it really necessary to use quite so many initials in these newspaper reports? 'ECB seeks tougher eurozone rules'? 'Iran bars IAEA inspectors'? She would have had a better chance at understanding something if the journalists had bothered to write out the words in full.

Maybe, maybe not.

She'd only managed a very average C grade for her GCSE in maths. She'd hated her maths teacher at school. She was such a bore, her catchphrase was, 'Sit up, Kirsten, and do try to be serious.' Why would she want to be serious? Serious people tended to wear hideous clothes and often had frown lines on their forehead. Her headmistress had been very stroppy with anyone who got Cs as Cs brought down the school average. As if Kirsten cared about the crappy school average. That was their problem. They should have taught her better. Daddy had paid them enough over the years. It wasn't as though she was a total *idiot* with numbers, she always knew how much she had in the bank (or rather how much she didn't have in the bank, right now she was £408 overdrawn and she had £742 on her credit cards). This was modest compared to some of her friends, or compared to Mummy, come to that. She often put over a thousand on the credit card in a single transaction and Daddy just paid it off at the end of the month. No biggie. He was loaded. He used to do exactly the same for Kirsten and could again if he wanted to.

Problem was he didn't want to. Not any more.

After twenty-two years of complete and utter indulgence the cashmere rug had now been pulled from under Kirsten's feet. It wasn't fair!

The oldies had both got a thing about her becoming more independent. Daddy had grumbled that he wasn't going to work like a Chinaman to feed her drug habit. It was ridiculous, of course, to say such things. Kirsten had pointed out that his comment was racist *and* inaccurate. *He* liked

44

working, he'd done nothing else for as long as she could remember! Besides, no one could call the odd spliff a drug habit. The real issue was neither of them had forgiven her for throwing a party at their place when they went on the cruise for their silver wedding anniversary. They said it was 'the straw that broke the donkey's back'. Kirsten was at a loss as to exactly which other straws had previously stacked up to lead to this catastrophe. Surely, the various suspensions from school, the bumps in the cars and even her going on an impromptu holiday to the south of France with that gang of hippies she met at Glastonbury were all discrete incidents that had been forgiven and forgotten. They'd really overreacted to her holiday, calling the police and yabbering on about abduction or elopement—as if! It was just a bit of fun. It was unfair to bring up all that ancient history as examples of her supposed irresponsibility.

And a cruise! What a cliché. They'd written the script by being so ridiculously, predictably middle class. Since they were such a cliché, she felt duty bound to act within stereotype too and have a party that would inevitably be crashed and get out of hand, especially as she'd posted an open invite to it on Facebook. Retrospectively, that had guaranteed *interesting* guests, she supposed. But knowing everyone at your party was so boring!

It wasn't just her to blame either. Darryl had brought about a dozen friends home from uni and they'd been the ones that drank Daddy's cellar dry. Not that anyone ever got cross with goody-two-shoes Darryl; her baby brother who'd got a place at Oxford to read Politics couldn't put a foot wrong.

You'd think he was already prime minister the way they idolised him and hung on his every word. Admittedly, it was her friends that were most likely responsible for peeing in the aquarium, but who knew it would alter the pH balance of the water so drastically and all the fish would die?

But, after the party, Daddy had turned purple (it was finding vomit in his Burberry shoes that really finished him off) and he started demanding she got a job, move to London, share a flat with someone. Who? The same losers that had peed in his precious fish tank? That didn't seem right. He said it was time for her to stand on her own two feet. He'd made some weak joke about her two feet no longer being clad in Kurt Geiger, now that he wasn't paying. Ha bloody ha.

Frankly, Kirsten had thought her father's reaction was quite hurtful. She'd always assumed he liked having her around. She was his little girl. Maybe not as bright as Darryl but significantly cuter to look at. That's what he was always saying, what a pretty little thing she was.

Daddy liked to tell everyone that *he* got her the job in the city but that wasn't true. She had a degree from Thames Valley University, didn't she? OK it was a third class but still it was in Events Management and Hospitality which had come in really handy when she was helping to organise the office Christmas party. Everyone talked about how cool it was to serve the canapés from mirrors and that had been her idea. She did have a flair for that sort of thing; when she was married and had a gorgeous house, she'd throw the *best* parties. She'd be the hostess with the mostest! She'd invite her parents and Daddy would be really proud of her

46

then, when he saw her glittering in the middle of all her exciting friends. It really was annoying that, even though she had her degree and everything, Daddy still took the credit for her getting a job in the city. He said she got it because of the strings he'd pulled with the men he'd dined with for years.

He might be on to something there, thought Kirsten, grinning slyly. It was certainly about something being pulled! The old men that her father played golf with and had lunch with and sat across boardroom tables with had taken an interest in her. An exceptional interest. Not because of her degree in Events Management and Hospitality, admittedly, and not because they did business with Daddy. She knew the most likely reason for their interest was that she had silky, long, blond hair and silky, long, bronzed legs. The guy at the interview barely looked at her CV, he couldn't tear his eyes away from her double Ds. He didn't care about her A level results or coursework average, the only statistics he was thinking about was 34, 22, 34. It was gross if you thought about it. The HR guy was probably Daddy's age!

She could tell the woman doing the interview was grossed out too. She kept sighing deeply and rolling her eyes. Kirsten felt a bit sorry for her. It was clear she took her job really seriously, she'd prepared a whole list of questions for Kirsten and Kirsten wouldn't have minded answering them but she never got the chance. The old bloke kept saying, 'Oh, I'm sure Kirsten has plenty on her CV which she can be proud of. I bet you're a girl who likes a bit of extra-curricular, aren't you?' The woman had muttered something about inappropriate behaviour and lawsuits but he'd just laughed. Kirsten thought it was a good thing the woman interviewer took her job so seriously though because, to be honest, she was so plain it was probably the best thing she could do.

Daddy was right in a way, working had broadened her horizons and made her grow up. Not that she'd learnt that much about standing on her own two feet though, what she'd learnt was that it was much better to lie flat on her back.

The thing was, it was expensive living and working in the city. Take Friday, for instance. Her cab drive into work had cost thirty quid. She'd had a hangover and just couldn't face public transport. The thought of all those people who smelt of farts and garlic and didn't take baths pushing up unnecessarily close to her was so disgusting. Even the sweet-smelling girls, who douched and doused themselves in perfume, were annoying because sometimes one of them was prettier or better dressed than she was and that could put her in a really bad mood all day. In fact, she might get a cab in today too. She just loved looking at all the beautiful things in the shop windows as she drove past.

And there were so many beautiful things! There were Alexander Wang handbags to die for, Agent Provocateur lingerie that left her hot and flustered, Burberry coats that were eternal classics, Stella McCartney dresses to flatter, Miu Miu shoes that she'd trample over her granny to get hold of. It was just too exciting to be constantly surrounded by utterly fabulous things all the time! Kirsten wanted it all. She *needed* it all. And her salary of twenty-one thousand, three hundred pounds a year didn't go anywhere, not after paying for rent, food and taxis. Kirsten couldn't understand how some of the girls she knew from Queen Charlotte's managed on what they did. Gemma Kirk was working as a journalist and earned sixteen thousand. That seemed weird, why would she agree to that? She'd always been a brainiac. And Ellenor Carter-Jones wasn't even earning yet because she was at med school and that took years and years to finish! Duh, what was she thinking? By the time she completed training, her ovaries would have practically dried up. Then there was Rebecca Ellis, who was on about eleven thousand, working for a charity! Madness! And to think all the teachers at Queen Charlotte's School used to go on about how those particular girls would go far.

So, yes, Kirsten knew that some girls managed on less, just not girls like her.

It wasn't as if she took hard cash off any of her boyfriends, she wasn't a prostitute. But if they wanted to buy her gifts, why would she stop them? And if they didn't really understand her hints as to exactly which gifts she'd like bought, then was it unreasonable to ask them for a store card instead? She'd been working in the city for eight months now and she hadn't had to buy much more than cereal and Tampax for most of that time. Men loved dressing her up almost as much as they loved undressing her. It was a territorial thing, maybe. She saw most of her boyfriends just once a week, which fitted in with their families' lives and her social life. They liked to imagine her wearing their gifts on the days when they didn't get together. They bought her coats to keep her warm, underwear to get them hot and just about everything else in-between. What did her brother call it when he saw the Tiffany bracelet that Brian gave her? Darryl had asked her where it was from and when she told him to mind his own business he'd guessed its origin. He was pretty cool though. He didn't threaten to tell Mummy and Daddy. He'd said she should look at it as an economical redressing, men are paid more than women, most times, for doing the *exact* same job and that's not fair, is it? She was just getting a bit of that back. It was her due. She was quite the feminist, really, if you looked at it like that.

Kirsten liked her brother's way of looking at the matter. So she didn't point out that she never had sex with men who did the same job as she did (as though she'd look at a PA!). Plus, the other reason she wasn't a prostitute was that she liked all her boyfriends, at least she liked them well enough, more or less. She had three at the moment, it was four until last month but she'd had to ditch Alan Edwardson because he was getting a bit too involved, he kept talking about wanting to leave his wife for her. Why would he think she wanted that? Madness!

Alan had been the first lover she'd taken in the city and truthfully he was a low-grade starter. It wouldn't be unfair to compare him with a very average prawn cocktail, smothered in cheap mayonnaise, and now she'd moved on to much finer delicacies. For a start Alan was the least senior out of the men she'd screwed, he was also the least good-looking and the most boring. As such he'd been so flattered by her attentions that he'd practically begged her to let him buy her stuff. Ugly men were always the easiest to seduce. Duh, no-brainer. But while she didn't mind him buying her stuff, she had to eventually admit that she didn't particularly want a balding husband with glasses. His wife might be consoled with the house in Chiswick and then the cottage in the south of France but Kirsten wanted the whole package. Money, yes, there was no shame in that. But besides the cash, when she got married she wanted to net a handsome husband, someone a bit more like Jules. He was easily the most handsome out of the four. Easily.

Frankly, sometimes, she was a bit embarrassed to be spotted out with her other boyfriends. She made sure that they took her to the sort of restaurants that her friends could never afford in a month of Sundays, so she was generally pretty safe. But she had been spotted twice. Mortifying! There had been one occasion when she was with Brian and she was trying on dresses in Harvey Nics when she bumped into a girl from college who was out shopping with her mum. Kirsten just pretended Brian was her father. The second time was much worse in a way. She hadn't been spotted in a shop or a restaurant but she'd been in the lift with Mark Deally. Mark Deally headed up the EMEIA division and was a big deal, he had a big gut too (small willy!). Kirsten was adjusting his tie when suddenly the lift doors sprang open and who should walk in but Jake Mason.

Jake Mason was this really hot guy, who she'd had quite a thing about throughout uni, not that she'd ever let him know. He was totally gorgeous, dead funny and clever and, you know, smiley. Yeah, smiley. He'd got a job in the city, same firm as Kirsten, as coincidence would have it. A couple of months back, when they first started working

51

together, he'd asked her to have a sandwich with him but she'd had to say no because she'd already arranged to meet Brian Ford in a nearby hotel for a lunchtime quickie (and she didn't mean drink). Jake had said, 'Some other time then,' and while she'd nodded he hadn't ever asked again. The other PAs were always going on about Jake. They said that he was on a fast-track management scheme or something and would be heading up EMEIA himself in a few years. Kirsten hoped so, for one thing then she could ask him exactly what EMEIA stood for, but besides that she privately thought he was the sort of person who deserved success. He reminded her a bit of Jules. Not an arrogant arse, like so many of them. Anyway, he got into the lift and gave her this odd look. Not that he'd seen her give Mark Deally so much as a peck on the cheek, she was just adjusting his tie, but the look Jake gave her was as though he knew she'd just been giving head in the washrooms.

He looked as though he'd just stepped in something nasty.

CHAPTER FOUR

'Well, how did it go?' Steph demanded with excitement.

'Brilliantly!' yelled Pip, not able to hide her own excitement but also exposing the surprise she felt too. 'They placed an order! They didn't even go away and mull it over, which is what I'd hoped for *at best*! But no, they bit my hand off!'

'I knew it!' shrieked Steph, who always seemed

to have more confidence in Pip's skills and creativity than Pip did herself.

For years Pip had enjoyed spending hours poking around old bric-a-brac and vintage shops and buying up all sorts of interesting fabrics and laces, simply because she'd always loved materials. She adored the softness of velvet, the fun of felt, the simplicity of cotton and the luxuriousness of silk. Pip got excited about a piece of gingham or hessian in exactly the way artists became excited about their paint pallet or musicians loved their instruments. When she lived with Dylan she'd stored the lovely fabrics in the spare room, occasionally wearing a vintage cocktail dress or trimming a baby blanket with a piece of lace but not really doing anything particularly structured with her treasure. Then, one day, she found an especially bonny, wide 1950s skirt which she bought for a few quid. Because she'd loved the print above and beyond any that she'd ever discovered before, she carefully unpicked the skirt and used the material to make a peg bag and some sweet bags as gifts for Chloe's guests to take home from her third birthday party. Everyone had loved the bags, they were unilaterally agreed to be adorable keepsakes. Six of the mothers at the party had asked where Pip bought them and had been suitably impressed when she admitted to making them herself. Pip had so enjoyed the process of creating something new out of something once loved but now forgotten that she sorted through her entire collection of pretty vintage materials, stashed in the spare room, in order to do the same thing again.

She soon found that the 1950s skirts were so

generous that she could transform one garment into two or more little knick-knacks, so alongside the party bags and peg bags, over time Pip started to design and make bunting, rosettes, badges, aprons, tray cloths, reusable shopping bags and suchlike. In her more confident moments, Pip thought that all her products were incredibly pretty and feminine and totally unique but sometimes she worried that she was simply peddling exactly the same artsy-fartsy stuff as the next bored mum who happened to be in possession of a sewing machine. In these moments of wavering confidence it was always Steph who would insist that her pieces were charming and dead on trend. Steph was adamant that Pip's unique and attractive items had enormous commercial potential. She said that the accessories promised serenity and old-fashioned values that everyone would want to buy into.

'They subliminally suggest childhoods full of fluffy ducklings, skipping ropes and games of hopscotch rather than Pokémon cards, violent video games and text speak that corrupts grammar lessons,' Steph had argued firmly.

Pip wanted to believe Steph but she knew Steph was biased and also, she sometimes wondered whether privileged Steph lived in the real world and therefore whether her view was relevant. She wasn't criticising Steph when she allowed this thought to drift around her head; it was just that Steph didn't have to live in the real world, so why would she choose to?

'Does anyone want that, nowadays?' Pip had asked gloomily.

'Absolutely every mother in the country would want to buy that!' Steph had said fixedly. 'The fact

54

the fabric is recycled appeals to the eco-warrior mums and the fact that all the pieces are handmade and many are one-offs appeals to those who continually strive to find some sort of individuality while staying well within the boundaries of doing exactly what everyone expects of them.'

'Suppose.'

Just this morning Steph had asserted, 'If there was any justice in this universe, the people at Selfridges will fall over themselves to sign you up to a massive deal. I'm sure of it!'

Pip very much doubted there was any justice anywhere so hadn't been especially comforted but she couldn't bring herself to say as much to Steph who liked to believe there was.

'I've literally just left the meeting. I'm still in the store. It's actually pretty difficult finding a door out of this place, isn't it? I had to call you straightaway.'

'So tell me *exactly* what happened,' Steph now said excitedly.

'Aren't you busy?' Pip could hear the distinct buzz of light, not especially sensational, gossip and chatter in the background.

'I'm hosting a coffee morning for the mothers of the boys in Freddie's class,' explained Steph. 'Hang on one moment.' Pip heard Steph hurriedly say, 'Will you excuse me. I have to take this, it's important. Do help yourselves to tea or coffee. The scones have just come out of the oven.'

Pip imagined her friend dashing out of the kitchen, away from the gaggle of well-groomed, eternally polite ladies that Steph baked scones for. She would hide away in the room that she referred to as the library (although in reality it was just a room with two small bookshelves, a desk and a rather smart gilt antiqued armchair that the sales assistant had described as a library chair). The books were stacked in size order and the heavy hardbacks suggested a serious-minded interest in Victorian architecture and other equally worthy matters. Pip knew that Steph was always fastidious about removing all her romantic novels from the newspaper rack, kitchen units or the coffee table whenever she expected guests. Even though she derived so much pleasure from those sorts of books, it was an awkward, secret pleasure and not one she wanted to advertise. Both Steph and Pip were aware that at thirty-eight (nearly thirty-nine, nearly forty!) Steph shouldn't really give a damn what anyone thought of her reading matter, but she did and Pip understood that, possibly better than most. Stephanie also cared if people thought she'd selected the correct heel height for a function, or whether she'd cooked the appropriate number of courses depending on the formality of the entertainment she was offering. Sometimes, she even worried what the neighbours thought about the length of the grass in her front garden. It was a strange comfort to Pip that despite the hundreds of things, large and small, that Steph cared about and worried over, Pip knew she was top of the charts—second only to Steph's children. To be frank, Pip was glad that *someone* worried about her so intensely, even if that someone was her best and oldest friend rather than a caring and sexy boyfriend.

Steph wanted every last detail of the meeting, she wanted to chew it over and fully digest it, just as much as Pip wanted to deliver it.

'Are you sitting comfortably?' teased Pip.

'Yes.'

'Then I shall begin.' This was their old joke from the days when they watched *Jackanory* together, glasses of milk and custard creams grasped tightly in their small hands. Steph instantly forgot that there were fourteen mothers in the kitchen who expected to be intravenously dripped Fair Trade Colombian bean coffee.

'Well, they adored the fabric-covered photo albums and the fabric-covered photo frames. They even complimented me on the bunting. I didn't know what they'd make of that. Everyone offers bunting nowadays.'

'But your bunting is personalised,' pointed out Steph. Besides the usual triangles, Pip strung up the letters of the kid's name. 'No mother could resist advertising her own darling.'

'They even talked about devoting a window section to my stuff. A nostalgic tea party set-up. With the bunting and tablecloths, party bags and aprons.'

'Oh, my gosh!' squealed Steph. 'How bloody fantastic.'

Steph didn't often swear, it was clear that the excitement, the relief, the *achievement* had overwhelmed her. This was not just Pip's achievement but Steph's too. After all, it had been Steph's idea to turn Pip's sewing skills into some sort of a career, or if that was too grand a word then certainly an income. An income independent of Dylan. It was Steph who repeatedly insisted that Pip had an extraordinary talent and needed to be expressing herself. It had been Steph who had encouraged and cajoled Pip into expanding beyond making the odd apron or tray mat as a birthday gift for a pal and instead to concentrate on producing a range of samples of all her work and collating a professional portfolio, in order to find someone who could retail the stock in a robust way. It had been Steph who insisted that Pip write to Harrods, Harvey Nics and Selfridges to ask for a meeting with the buyer. Pip would have been happy with selling her goodies at the school craft show.

Pip had once been considered a luminary and everyone expected she'd have a glittering career (herself included). She hadn't shone at school at anything other than art and biology but her work was so outstanding that, after a year's foundation course, she won a place at the prestigious St Martin's School of Art to study textiles. She'd never have had the basic GCSE requirement for entry if it hadn't been for Steph. Steph had always done Pip's maths and English homework when required, in return Pip had dissected Steph's rat during lab work (while Steph sipped water and looked in the opposite direction, not wanting to faint like Stephen McCarthy had) and Pip had also got Steph an undeserved A in art.

After graduation Pip was lucky enough to secure an enviable apprenticeship in a celebrated Parisian haute couture fashion house. Pip was adored by her employees, as she was a captivating mix of diligent and inspired. Her role ought to have been limited to coffee-making and silently observing but swiftly became one where she was allowed to unofficially brief designers on trends in fabrics, colours and shapes. Her flair and competence meant that within half the time anyone could reasonably expect, Pip was visualising ideas and making hand sketches that the powers in the fashion house respected enough to work up into complete designs. Within just two years her designs were dripping off the world's most stunning models as they flounced down the catwalks in Milan, Paris and New York.

Pip was noticed by the right people, she was invited to the right nightclubs, restaurants and parties. She wore the right things (to be accurate, whatever she wore became the right thing). She knew the right designers, artists, photographers and musicians. She was more than an It girl, she was the right girl.

It all seemed such a long time ago now.

Pip's downfall was her creative heart. She had a clear belief in her own talents, that was never up for question, but she also believed that the only way for her to be truly happy was for her to be in love. She respected career women who worked relentlessly to claw their way to the top of whichever field they excelled in and she gasped in awe at women who smashed through glass ceilings but she couldn't help but notice that those women seemed to have bloody knuckles. Their success came with a price, a price she wasn't prepared to pay. Actually, Pip believed male success also came with a price. She only had to look so far as her best friend's husband to see what sacrifices were demanded to excel in a career, irrespective of gender. Julian rarely managed to attend his children's birthday parties, he didn't know what colour his own bedroom wall was painted and when his mother had been treated for cancer in a wonderfully plush (some might say swanky) hospital (which he'd paid for) he'd only managed to visit her four times in the last four months of her life. Pip had visited more than Julian had (although nowhere near as often as Steph). Julian didn't like being in the hospital, not just because he baulked at the sight of his mother wasting away and angrily felt his impotency to affect her end, but also because he couldn't switch on his BlackBerry. His office didn't like not being able to reach him.

Was he finding the cure for the cancer that was killing his mother? No, he was buying and selling shares. Successfully, Pip realised that. But that was her point. Glittering careers seemed to cost such a lot. Too much.

Put simply, Pip was a romantic. Deadly so. She was certain that she wouldn't be able to enjoy a loft apartment, a corporate silver card or even an expensive bottle of champagne if she didn't have someone to enjoy them with. She would have loved to enjoy those things *and* pursue a lover but if forced to choose one over the other, Pip Foxton would always plump for passion before promotion.

For example, when Pip met Philippe (a French musician) at an arty fashion party and he'd invited her to live with him on his barge, *Le Bleu* (he made the offer the night they met, before the clock had struck midnight), she barely paused to pack her toothbrush but embraced the romantic opportunity with her two skinny arms. Their names matched, it was meant to be! He had dark brown eyes that seemed to stare directly into her innermost thoughts, thoughts that glittered and glistened in his presence! She had not for a moment considered the fact that a nomadic life sailing up and down the Seine might affect her commute to work.

But soon it transpired that while it was undoubtedly utterly romantic to moor right next to the Eiffel Tower one night and then at Port d'Arsenal near Notre Dame the next, it did play havoc with her sense of direction. Each morning Pip woke up, not quite certain which metro line she was near to, which meant she rarely arrived at the fashion house in time for dark coffee and croissants. One night Philippe quietly trudged *Le Bleu* along the Seine, sailing right through Corbeil to Melun. Of course, when Pip woke up she could appreciate that the market town was beautiful, *très jolie*! And that the Château de Vaux le Vicomte was very likely worthy of a visit and yes, how fascinating that Philippe knew that it was built from 1658 to 1661 for the superintendent of finances of Louis XIV, but how was she going to get to work? Philippe persuaded her that she didn't have to. Better to lie in his arms (or to be accurate sit on his penis, he preferred her on top although Pip found that position rather uncomfortable). *Le Bleu* was cramped and Pip was forever banging her head against the wooden ceiling. The bathroom facilities were basic and it was easy to burn oneself when preparing even the simplest of meals. All in all, the barge did not turn out to be as idyllic or romantic as Pip had imagined. Nor did Philippe, come to that. Or, to be strictly accurate, he continued to be incredibly romantic and attractive and continued to bore holes in hearts with his dark brown eyes; only they were other women's hearts, not Pip's.

So, Pip ran back to Paris where her first tragic love affair (and, more importantly, her sudden

61

departure from the fashion house) was forgiven. The French understood a love affair and generally believed that a little drama was good for an artiste.

But then Pip met Jacob. Jacob was a Californian fashion photographer, very 'up and coming', studying in France. Pip was certain that their careers were more complementary and refused to notice all the signs that indicated the place Jacob most liked to come up was different women. Jacob wanted Pip to open her legs and her contact book but keep her heart firmly closed. After two years he still insisted that theirs was just a casual thing. Pip not being a casual sort of girl had to walk away while she still had the power to move.

She walked right away, on to an aeroplane and back across the Channel. The memories of Philippe and Jacob had stained Paris for ever for her and she could not live there. The *grand fromage* of the French fashion industry could not understand why she had made the exact same mistake twice. To be gripped in a passionate fever once is poor luck, twice—then, it's a sickness. The bigwigs in the UK believed that her one true love ought to have been her art; workaholics and martyrs to their careers, they believed she lacked commitment. Pip had been pretty sure that when she returned to London her haute couture experience would guarantee that she'd be snapped up by a UK ready-to-wear designer or, at least, have the opportunity to work developing affordable high-street fashion. But, sadly, Pip struggled to find a job of comparable prestige to the one she'd so carelessly chucked away. Her former employers were irritated by her casual attitude towards the opportunity they had bestowed upon her and didn't hesitate to say as much when potential ones called for references. Other would-be employers stifled Pip's chances without even going so far as to request references by insisting she was overqualified and that she'd soon be bored working in the studios they ran.

'Let me be the judge of that,' Pip had insisted but to no avail, her spectacular CV was slipped back across the desk and an interviewer waved goodbye to a fabulous opportunity.

After months combing the papers, trailing around agencies and hauling her portfolio to fashion houses in order to find the dream job, Pip settled. She settled for a job as a fashion buyer in a previously prestigious but slightly tired department store on Bond Street. She was made to feel truly grateful for her position as swim- and cruise-wear buyer. No one worried whether she was overqualified. They just told her that she wasn't allowed to go to the toilet without advising a more senior member of staff on the shop floor, that the jacket potatoes in the staff canteen were good value because they were subsidised and that a free weekly check-up with the store's chiropodist was a perk that she'd need to take advantage of because standing on her feet all day took its toll.

Pip's heart mended rather faster than her career prospects and pretty soon she was dating different men. Only they were really all the same man. They might not have been called either Philippe or Jacob, they might have been called Tom, Dick or Harry, but they were the same shallow, selfish womanisers, who underestimated and undermined. They were the sort of men that some women have the good fortune to avoid throughout their lives, the sort of men that other women attach themselves to like filings cling to a magnet. Somewhere, out there, in the immense, complex universe there was an unwritten rule book, full of secrets, sayings and sliding scales that some people instinctively understood and others learnt through experience but Pip simply couldn't get her head around. The fact was, the sharper the chiselled cheekbones, the harder the heart.

Pip still believed that a successful career was enhanced if it was shared with the one you love and she still believed that a blazing career demanded sacrifices she wasn't prepared to make. The difference was she no longer thought the perfect companion in her life had to be tall, dark and handsome. Rather she was small, blonde and cute. Pip's one true love was Chloe. Any career she now carved out would have to be one that would allow her to be around for Chloe's school holidays and, ideally, one that afforded them the opportunity to do more than potter in their (tiny) back garden for the duration of those holidays.

'I have to start straightaway, they want—'

'Sorry, Pip, can you hang on a moment,' said Steph apologetically.

Pip listened as some woman asked Stephanie whether she had any organic raw sugar because the woman in question was, apparently, slightly intolerant of refined sugar. Pip heard Steph reply that there was refined and raw (both organic) sugar in the bowls which she'd find just next to the cream jug. Yes, the white jug with the yellow rim was cream, and yes, the white jug with the red rim was skimmed milk and yes, the white jug with the blue rim was full fat milk. If Steph was feeling any frustration that this woman had hunted her down in the library, she did not show it. Pip thought that the woman was a moron and should use a bit of common sense, instead of expecting Steph to run around after her. Just because Steph was brilliant at looking after people and had a knack of anticipating needs before the needy even recognised them for themselves didn't mean that her goodwill should be abused. Although Pip had enough self-awareness to realise that she probably only felt this strongly about this particular issue, at this particular moment, because she needed Steph to share her success and was always a tinsy bit resentful of Steph's other friendships.

Stephanie returned to the conversation. 'Sorry about that. Look, I'm being a bit rude to my guests, much as I'd love to spend all morning on the phone with you, I better go.'

'I get it. You've invited people into your home, the very least you can do is avoid causing the allergy lady an angry rash.' Pip didn't actually believe that the woman had an intolerance, she was probably just dieting, but Pip knew that Steph would feel an extreme responsibility and wouldn't be able to concentrate on the conversation properly anyway. 'I'm going to find the food hall and do a quick treat shop,' she added, feigning nonchalance.

'I'll come to yours, this evening. You can give me a blow-by-blow account then,' suggested Steph.

'No, not tonight, you can't.'

'Why not?'

'I have to run up a sample skirted apron in a heavy stripe by tomorrow. I promised the Selfridges buyer.' True, Pip was showing grit and focus but, less nobly, she was making Steph wait because she was fighting a flash of irritation that Steph was not available when she wanted her. Pip wasn't proud of her co-dependency and she made a mental promise to herself that she'd work on it, just not at this moment in time.

'Oh. Wow. OK.' If Steph noted the rebuke, she elegantly chose to ignore it. 'Well, tomorrow then. I'll need to get a babysitter because Julian is away but I should be able to manage to do that.'

'Perfect. I'll give you an entire debrief then.'

'I'll bring champagne. I'm so proud of you!'

CHAPTER FIVE

All of Steph's guests left by eleven thirty. She waved goodbye to the last of them as her cleaner, Mrs Evans, arrived. A number of the mothers had lunch appointments and needed to refresh make-up or change clothes, others had to meet their personal trainers or some 'divine lady' they had 'found' who was making curtains for their second reception room. Pip always joked that she wondered where all the 'divine' ladies who made curtains, highlighted hair and catered for parties were hiding until the mothers of the pupils at Mansfield School for Boys 'found' them. Stephanie tended to ignore this line of sarcasm as she knew that Pip was just the sort of talent that would be 'found' by these women and once she was, she'd be considerably less resentful of their exuberance when opening their fat chequebooks.

Steph had had all her curtains made by a divine

lady just three years ago and she fully expected them to last for quite a few years yet. She (reluctantly) saw her personal trainer on a Tuesday and Thursday, straight after school drop-off (Julian had bought her the twice weekly sessions for Christmas, although she'd have preferred the duck-egg blue Le Creuset pan set which she'd long since had her eye on), and she didn't have any lunch appointments, the charity committee that she sat on tended to lunch on a Friday. She had nowhere she needed to be.

Out of the corner of her eye Stephanie noticed Mrs Evans cast a despairing and disproportionally disgruntled glance around the kitchen. She clearly thought the debris from the coffee morning was excessive and muttered that she would start in the bedrooms, as though the task of cleaning the kitchen was simply too overwhelming and horrifying. Steph immediately felt guilty and at once carefully stacked all fifteen cups, saucers and side plates in the dishwasher, then she popped the remaining scones in a Tupperware box (three left, which was lucky, they'd be a perfect after-school snack for each of the children) then she swooped around the kitchen with a brush and dishcloth to eradicate any stray crumbs that had the nerve to loiter, she didn't want to upset Mrs Evans. Steph was very lucky to have a cleaner (even if the said cleaner was a bit of a slacker). Stephanie was very aware of her privileges. Her luck. She thanked God for it. Literally. Unlike many of her friends, she actually gave a lot of thought to religion and she regularly attended church. In fact she always felt rather relieved to be on her knees, counting her many blessings and repeatedly verbalising her gratitude to whoever orchestrated the world so that she managed to be up here, on the top of the pile. She wasn't exactly sure how she'd been so lucky. Did she deserve it? She hoped so, but frankly, deserving good fortune seemed to have little to do with the matter. Incredibly kind people, earnest, funny, hard-working, gentle people found their lives suddenly blighted with tragedy just as often as the vicious, the miserable, the deceivers and the crooks of this world. It all seemed such a lottery to her, which was a terrifying thought. If you didn't know what you were doing right to ensure such a fortunate set-up, then how could you possibly avoid it all going wrong?

It was a capricious world. Steph constantly navigated the choppy waters by working hard and abiding by the rules.

She'd studied hard at school and gained decent grades, enough to allow her to read Economics at Birmingham University. It was often said that, unlike Pip, Stephanie had been lucky in love, she'd never had her heart broken. Whether that was luck or careful management was a matter of opinion. It's true to say that Steph had not been the sort of girl that felt a need to run to Paris or run away from it either. She didn't have any of that artistic bent (which often led to that type of wild and extravagant behaviour). Steph thought that the lack of an artistic bent was a matter of luck. She believed that some people had it and that was their misfortune because an artistic bent could not be managed or tamed, it would always break free and wreak havoc. Stephanie liked being so supremely sensible however unfashionable that made her. Much rather that than be in Pip's position. Pip was somewhat like an emotional grasshopper, either flying high in the sky, leaping from one love to the next, or being carelessly crushed underfoot.

Stephanie had met Julian Blake at university; he was also studying Economics, proving they had so much in common from the start. She'd watched him from a distance for many weeks before she actually spoke to him. This was not just timidity (although that was part of it), she used those weeks to observe him, to weigh him up. He was not the most gorgeous man in the lecture hall (that honour fell to a boy called Eddie Black—and yep, Pip did sleep with him when she once came to visit Steph and no, he did not call) but Julian was certainly attractive. He was over six feet tall, he had a huge smile and big blue eyes that flashed with intelligence and amusement by turn and dark blond curls that she wanted to glide her fingers through. He had a few pimples around his hairline and upper lip that tended to bleed when he shaved but they all had pimples at that time. Steph knew that he'd grow out of them and she suspected that he'd be the sort of boy that suited his looks best when he was a man (she'd been right about that, he definitely had a solid handsomeness to him now, sometimes when she looked at him her breath caught in her chest). Steph had noticed that Julian had hobbies (he liked rugby and football then, and golf and cycling now). Her mother had advised her to marry a man with hobbies because hobbies kept a man out of trouble. Not that she was thinking of marrying Julian. Well, at least not straightaway. She wasn't the sort of girl who expected, or intended, to fall 'madly in love', as the phrase went. She thought that was pure folly which would

69

lead to inevitable heartache. No, Stephanie took a long view.

Steph became Julian's friend first. She manoeuvred things so that they kept bumping into one another at the library, on the sidelines of the rugby pitch, in the student union bar. Nods of recognition became smiles and then they naturally drifted into comfortable conversation. To this day, twenty years on, Steph still hasn't confessed to Julian how carefully she studied his timetable and extra-curricular activities so that she could always be in the right place at the right time. She sometimes wondered whether she should tell him. Would he be flattered? Would he be impressed by her cunning? Maybe they could laugh about it now. Maybe, but she didn't want to spoil the illusion that he'd nurtured. He seemed to quite like the idea that they'd somehow just stumbled into one another's arms.

For a year she had enjoyed that status of best friend and she'd never once hinted or suggested that they should be anything else. At close quarters, without any romantic notions that might entangle and confuse, Steph had been able to clearly judge exactly what sort of man Julian was.

She'd found out that they shared the same family values (marriage was for life), that they wanted the same number of kids (three), and that they wanted those children to be privately educated (even though neither of them had had that experience). She learnt about his ambitions to go into the city and work as a hedge fund manager (at least she now understood how the kids' education would be paid for; even if, back then, she didn't understand exactly what a hedge fund manager did, she knew enough to understand that it meant a huge pay packet). And she discovered that he also wanted to see a bit of the world.

'Not backpacking, God forbid.' He'd spat out the word in disgust. 'No way. I like using loo roll to wipe my arse, not my hand, and I like beds where the only beasts sharing with me are the girls I've invited along.'

'So, five stars all the way for you, is it?' she'd asked laughingly.

'Yup,' he'd replied simply and firmly. 'I'll work hard, earn a fantastic salary and my family and I will be very well looked after. Always.'

Stephanie had found his confidence overwhelmingly attractive and reassuring. She still did. And the man was as good as his word, they never went without anything. She'd discovered that he wanted to move to London after graduation, to live in Fulham for eight or nine years and then move out to the country, with his wife and firstborn. The rest of the kids would follow later.

This was exactly the plan they followed. After a year of being friends there was a drunken kiss at a house party that led to a change of status. Both Stephanie and Julian were ready for the shift. Steph had begun to feel secretly jealous of various, temporary girlfriends Julian dated. As he tended to date pretty but vacuous types, she felt that the women he held beneath him, when he was between the sheets, were in fact beneath him. Happily, Julian reached a similar conclusion at the same time. He seemed to increasingly appreciate Stephanie's sagacious manner more than the salacious manners of his other girlfriends. When he was with Steph he notably relaxed, probably because he felt appreciated and respected. He often mused that they made a great team; that they were bigger than the sum of their parts, and she knew that he liked it that she got his jokes (which were few and far between, both the jokes and the people who got them). Admittedly, she suspected that the very first time he kissed her was because she was in the room when he wanted to kiss someone. Not an especially noble reason for starting up a romance but a fairly typical one for most nineteen-year-old boys. He'd probably expected the kiss to be comfortable, pleasant; he'd no doubt been surprised when he felt fireworks rocket through his body, causing his fingers and lips to quiver. Later he told her that from the moment he kissed her, he thought that perhaps he'd found the woman he should spend the rest of his life with. From then on Stephanie was sure that Julian kissed her not because she happened to be in the room when he wanted to kiss someone, but because she was the woman he wanted to kiss.

Oh yes, Stephanie Blake was a lucky woman.

She had a husband she loved, who loved her back, three healthy children she adored more than she could express (more than she could ever have imagined), a beautiful home with all the trappings anyone could hope for and today her best friend in all the world had had some good news too. Steph punched the air. Not a gesture she was ever likely to do in public but something that felt right at that moment. Pip's good news was the icing on the cake. It was about time Pip had something to celebrate. Steph felt relieved, satisfied. She let out a deep breath. She hadn't been aware that she was breathing in, holding it all in, but she had been.

Now, she could relax. See, good things did come to those who deserved it. What a relief; she'd always clung to that belief.

The telephone rang shrilly through the house. Steph's first thought was that it would be Pip ringing back, unable to wait until tomorrow evening to impart more details about the meeting after all. Before Steph got to it, Mrs Evans, who was now doing some light dusting in the hall (very light, Steph noticed, she didn't actually pick up the ornaments but dusted around them) reached the phone. A moment later, Mrs Evans crossly banged the handset back into the cradle.

'Sales pitch? New windows? New kitchen?' said Stephanie.

'No. One of those nuisance calls again.' Mrs Evans looked at her employer with a mix of irritation and sympathy. 'I thought they'd stopped.'

'I thought they had too,' replied Steph.

'You should get on to the police about them,' said Mrs Evans darkly. She did enjoy a drama and since she'd recently resolved a five-month tussle with her insurance company (over a ruined carpet, the result of a burst pipe or a bowl of deliberately spilt mucky washing-up water, depending on what you believed), now she was keen to find something new to get her teeth into.

Stephanie was by nature the extreme opposite and preferred a life with as few confrontations as possible. 'I really don't think that's necessary. It's not like the caller actually says anything, do they? They're not offensive or threatening.'

'No, that's true,' admitted Mrs Evans reluctantly. 'They don't say nothing at all. I pick up the phone and say "Blake residence", all polite and

73

everything, and then they put the phone down.'

'Probably just a wrong number,' assured Steph breezily.

'Then why don't they say so? It's darn right rude. Besides, it's happened too often for it to be that.'

'Maybe there's a fault on our line. I'll call BT. Don't worry about it, Mrs Evans. Look, I'm going to pop to the supermarket now. I need to pick up some champagne. My friend has had a bit of good news and we'll be celebrating tomorrow evening. I was wondering, do you think you could babysit for a few hours tomorrow? As you know, Julian often stays in town on a Tuesday because he has telephone conferences with the offices in the States. If he gets home at all it will be after midnight.'

'Oh, yes, no problem. You know I love looking after your kiddies. Such nice manners on them boys,' replied Mrs Evans. 'If only all kids minded their Ps and Qs the way your bunch do, the world would be a nicer place.'

Stephanie happily accepted the compliment without recalling how argumentative and grumpy her boys had been at breakfast. Stephanie found that a little self-deception, now and then, went a long way when mothering.

CHAPTER SIX

Pip's journey home was entirely different from her journey into London. She decided that rather than take a tube, which meant entering the bowels of

London and risking fatal injury in a stampede for a seat, she'd walk back to Waterloo.

Pip breezed along Oxford Street, dodging shoppers with large bags full of early season bargains and turned right on to Regent Street. The name alone made her straighten her back and hold her head up a fraction higher, it offered such promise, the street was swollen with grand history and achievement. Usually, Pip slunk along Regent Street, enviously staring at the glamorous windows which framed garments with out-of-reach price tags, but today she thought the pretty window displays, incorporating Easter bunnies and frolicking lambs, seemed fun and frivolous. She did not find them intimidating. She actually twirled around, arms spread wide, when she reached Trafalgar Square. Every step she took was a celebration in its own right. She crossed the Hungerford Bridge to Waterloo and actually smiled at passing strangers, forgetting her own rule that dictated by doing so she might appear insane. She beamed unselfconsciously and was pleasantly surprised that most people smiled back at her—who knew? Her steps were vivid. Her hair lifted in the breeze. She turned her head to The Gherkin, St Paul's and the OXO tower and felt she was part of it all.

Part of the history. Part of the future.

Finally life was falling into place. Easily, naturally, like a routine by impressive synchronised swimmers. She belonged. She was a success. Nothing was the same as it had been this morning. For a start she was carrying two rather large, sleek, yellow cardboard bags. Selfridges bags. Hurrah! Somehow the quality card and jaunty colour said it all—the person carrying these bags is having a fantastic life.

Everything had changed in a matter of forty-five minutes. In forty-five minutes Pip had become the sort of person who could buy an expensive jar of whole kalamata olives (in a marinade of fresh oregano, garlic, peppercorns and extra virgin olive oil), when usually she bought basic green ones, by the quarter, over the counter in the supermarket and then only as a treat. She had been transformed into the sort of person who bought organic hand-cut crisps (cracked sea salt and refined balsamic vinegar), rather than Walkers. She was the sort of person who could buy a chocolate fountain. No one had a real need for a chocolate fountain, Pip realised that. But she and Chloe had once seen such a thing in action, at Pip's uncle's sixtieth birthday party, and Chloe had been mesmerised. She thought the fountain was magical, that the chocolate was unlimited which was surely the stuff of girls' dreams everywhere. Pip wanted to make Chloe's dreams come true. If she could, she'd buy her a pony, give her the ability to recall her eight-times table at will and conjure up a prince for her to marry; as it was, she was limited to buying the chocolate fountain. Still, it was a start. A glorious, indulgent, wrapped-in-a-yellow-cardboard-bag start! Not that she'd actually earned any hard cash in those forty-five minutes but the promise of it was enough to buoy her up.

She stepped on to the train with a full three minutes to spare. She felt secure and organised. She paused and looked for a free seat facing the direction of travel, away from a skanky loo. She settled into a seat and placed her shopping bags on

76

the one next to her so as to discourage anyone sitting close by, she wanted to have a few moments to privately luxuriate in the glorious thought of her success.

Pip stared out of the window as the train sped, unstopping, through small stations. She noticed that at each station there was a tiny drama playing out. At the first, there was a mother frantically trying to persuade her reluctant, plank-like toddler to submit to sitting in the buggy. Pip knew from experience that the toddler was unlikely to do so, preferring instead to carelessly charge around the platform, causing the mother's heart to leap into her mouth time and time again. At the next station Pip briefly glimpsed embracing lovers. The girl was holding the lapels of the boy's jacket, he was holding the belt loops of her jeans, they pulled one another close. They melted into each other, unaware that a train had just whizzed by and unconcerned that they were being watched. At another station a middle-aged couple silently shared a sandwich, rather than an embrace, but Pip saw that there was something quite marvellous about the sandwich sharing, it had a special intimacy. Pip spotted business people with laptops, waiting for their trains. They stood shoulder to shoulder with grandparents visiting their offsprings' offspring and at a cautious distance from moody and bleak teenagers, hidden under heavy hoods.

Pip wanted to lean out of the window and yell to the teenagers that it was all OK. She wanted to reassure them that they did not need to feel so bleak or look so glum. Life was stretched out in front of them, just like a long rail track, it was all theirs for the taking, but she couldn't. The windows of modern trains were not designed for such romantic gestures. They were designed to open just an inch or so, to allow ventilation but minimise the amount of rubbish that could be thrown on to the tracks (or maybe minimise the amount of bodies thrown on to the tracks. Something that Pip thought was *more* likely to happen because people were unable to shout encouragement to one another when the urge took them).

Pip was in such a fabulous mood that everywhere she looked she saw potential and possibilities. She wondered if the group of middle-aged ladies, with bright blouses, that she'd travelled with this morning was having fun in London. She hoped so. Now, she imagined that perhaps they'd have lunch in a smart restaurant and then buy expensive cosmetics.

'Hello, again.'

Pip looked up and saw that the man who wasn't a teacher was sitting diagonally opposite her. She was stunned. What were the chances? Minuscule. Less than that. And yet here he was, on her train. It took Pip just a fraction of a moment to decide that this second coincidental meeting must *mean* something. Something beyond the fact that he too must have had a meeting in London, which just happened to last as long as hers had and therefore he was going home at about the same time too.

'I'm not stalking you,' exclaimed Pip. The instant she said as much, she regretted it. She would have been better advised to simply smile and say hello back.

'No, I realise that. You sat down first. I saw you

and moved seat. I came to sit near you on the off chance we could strike up a conversation,' he said, with a wide and cheerful grin which exposed slightly crooked teeth.

Pip was somehow reassured by his frank confession *and* the small imperfection. Crooked teeth were standard issue for a kid growing up in Britain in the 1980s, nowadays dentists worried about overbites and whitening as though all their patients were destined to have careers as TV presenters but it wasn't always the case. He looked about her age, maybe a bit younger, it was hard to tell with men, people her age only had perfect teeth if they'd bought them as an adult and that level of spare time and spare money was alien to Pip. Somewhere deep inside she felt something urgent that made her sure that she didn't want this man to be alien. Besides, if it wasn't for his slightly dodgy teeth, this man might be ridiculously attractive and then she would do something stupid like lose her ability to speak.

'Oh,' she replied.

'So, you might think I'm stalking you. Except that you moved seats first on the journey in. That makes it one all. Not so much stalking as mutual appreciation.'

'Oh.'

He spoke quickly and confidently. He had a Scottish accent, a soft lilt that made her feel instantly at ease with him. She was incredibly flattered by his attention.

He was probably a serial killer.

'Robbie Donaldson.'

Robbie stretched across the aisle to hold out his hand for Pip to shake. A polite serial killer, she noted.

Pip looked around the train. It was full of teenagers who had spent the day in London shopping, although they'd probably tell their parents they'd been researching in galleries and libraries for their GCSEs. She thought it was probably safe enough to have a conversation with this man, in public, in broad daylight.

'Pip,' she said, taking his hand and shaking it. She decided not to offer up her second name, just to be on the safe side.

'So you've had a pretty good day at Selfridges,' he asserted, in his charming, attractive tone.

Was he a mind-reader? wondered Pip. How could he possibly know about the contract? Then she realised he was looking at her huge yellow bags, stuffed with goodies, and he simply meant she'd had a good day shopping. For reasons that she didn't have time to fully analyse Pip realised that she wanted to draw a distinction between her and all the other shoppers on the train, she wanted to impress him.

'Actually these are congratulatory treats.'

'Who are you congratulating?'

'Myself.'

Robbie Donaldson cocked an eyebrow which invited her to go on and Pip didn't need to be asked twice. Delighted with her own success, she told him all about her fruitful meeting.

'So you're going to be one of those women that I read about in the *Guardian*. Women who become cottage industry millionaires,' he commented, with a broad grin, clearly impressed.

'Maybe,' she laughed, enjoying the unfamiliar feeling of being impressive.

80

For the first time in a long time good fortune seemed possible. Probable, even. Why the heck couldn't she become a millionaire? Well, at least a success. Maybe a stonking success. He was right, you *did* read about it all the time. It happened. Why might it not happen to her? She beamed at Robbie and he grinned back at her. The strangest thing happened. It was probably the successful meeting that was making her feel so free and frivolous but Pip couldn't deny it. His smile detonated a fizzy bomb of sensations throughout her body. A fizzy bomb that, if she scurried around her deepest memories, she vaguely recognised. Yes, yes it was. Lust. Oh. My. God. She checked, mentally taking her own temperature and pulse. It was true. A definite, intoxicating mix of curiosity, delight and magnetism sloshed and swished around her stomach and head, with the rapidity and determination of a babbling stream rushing over a stone. There was nothing serial killer about him, she was pretty sure of it. Everything about him was glowing and positive and gentle.

'So, we've established you're not a teacher then?' she commented.

She'd been talking about herself for twenty minutes, it was only polite to ask a bit about him and besides, she wanted to know *all* about him. In fact, she had an urge to start compiling a dossier because while it had been only twenty minutes, Pip was beginning to think that Robbie Donaldson might be someone she'd like to get to know a little better. A lot better? Pip was surprised to feel any sort of interest or attraction. True, before Dylan she'd been in the habit of falling utterly in love, or at least in lust, within the first three minutes of setting eyes on a bloke. But since Dylan she hadn't met anyone she felt the slightest bit curious about, despite well-intentioned friends occasionally arranging dinner parties that often had a spare man, who just happened to be seated next to Pip. While Pip understood that these meddlesome friends were trying to be helpful, her repeated response to a situation like that was to stay in the kitchen for as long as possible. She sometimes washed up (even when the hosts had a dishwasher), just to avoid the embarrassing and cloying set-ups. And yet, here she was having a conversation with Robbie Donaldson that while not actually flirty was certainly encouraging.

'I'm a nurse,' said Robbie.

Pip put a lot of effort into resisting quipping that she thought he'd have a terrific bedside manner. 'What sort of nurse?'

'I'm a fertility nurse.'

Pip gasped despite herself. She didn't know what to say to this man who looked at vaginas for a living. She silently berated herself. What a shallow thing to think! She pushed the thought out of her mind but was distressed to find it was replaced with the question, 'What sort of man becomes a fertility nurse?' She shook her head a fraction, in order to clear it. That was a petty, small-minded thought too. Pip was not in the habit of being small-minded. She knew full well that gender should have nothing to do with career choice. Hadn't she always been in favour of equal rights? Hadn't she often staunchly defended a woman's right to become an astronaut, or a footballer or a forklift truck driver (if the desire struck) with the more sexist men she'd come across in her past (usually in Steph's front room, Steph knew a lot of conservative people)? Pip had worked in fashion, a traditionally feminine industry where men thrived. Gay men mostly, she admitted reluctantly. She stole a look at Robbie. Was he gay? Oh please, God, don't let him be gay, she silently muttered.

'It always throws people,' said Robbie, flashing an understanding smile that seemed to communicate that he'd read her mind and that he'd forgiven her prejudice. 'It does take a bit of getting used to. But I love my work.'

Pip wanted to ask what bit did he love exactly, but before she could, Robbie commented, 'The hours are long and sometimes unpredictable though. Shift work is an assassin to a social life.'

'Oh.'

'But I am free tonight. I don't know if you have any plans?'

It had been so long since Pip had been asked on a date that, for a moment, she didn't compute that she was being asked on one. Once she had registered as much she was completely at a loss as to how to respond. Should she instantly snap up his offer? Should she be demure and say she had plans? After all, she did have plans. She was supposed to be knocking up a skirted apron for the Selfridges buyer. Pip was extremely tempted to ignore her responsibilities and scamper off into the sunset with this man, as she had always done in the past. She fought her instinctual response and thought of Chloe. She would need a babysitter for her if she went out tonight and she could hardly ask Steph to do the honours, as she'd refused Steph's offer to celebrate on the grounds she had to work.

'We could catch a movie,' added Robbie. She still didn't respond, so Robbie began to adjust his offer. 'Or grab a bowl of pasta. Whatever you fancy doing.'

He didn't know whether he was being too full on and therefore off-putting. Should he downgrade to a less demanding offer, like a drink? Or wasn't he being impressive enough? Did this woman expect champagne cocktails in a trendy London watering hole and then theatre and an after-show dinner, at least three courses? He had no idea. He was out of practice when it came to asking women out.

'I'll need to get a babysitter,' said Pip finally.

'You have children?'

'One child. A daughter, Chloe. She's eight.' Pip waited to see if the lovely fertility nurse liked offspring in theory but recoiled from them in reality, the way some of her prospective dates had in the past.

'Beautiful name,' he commented. Pip scanned his face but couldn't see any outward signs of panic. 'So going out tonight is a bit unrealistic. I imagine you'll need more notice to find a sitter.'

Pip hardly dared breathe. Was he back-pedalling? She hoped not and feared so. Naturally, the moment there was the slightest hint that he might be at all reluctant or recanting, she found she wanted him with a certainty and ferocity. It wasn't her fault so much as her habit.

She realised she had nothing to worry about when he added, 'How about Friday? Do you think that might work? That will give you time to find a sitter. If I give you my mobile and my home number then you can call me to confirm.'

'OK,' she mumbled.

Damn, damn, damn. If she took his number, it was up to her to make a call to him. She hated that idea. She already knew that either she'd lose her nerve and never call, or even if she had the intention of calling, she might lose his number and not be able to do so! At the very least, assuming she managed to keep hold of the number (and her nerve), she would then be faced with that awful dilemma of wondering *when* exactly she ought to call. Was it right to call as soon as she had a sitter confirmed or should she wait a little longer? She'd probably phone Steph to ask her to sit as soon as she got off the train, but she couldn't call Robbie *today* to confirm for a *Friday* date, could she? That would appear far too eager. Too desperate. She'd have to leave it at least twenty-four hours, maybe forty-eight. What were the rules nowadays? Pip didn't know. She'd always got it wrong. Even before Dylan. She blamed the plethora of self-help guides and rule books that she'd read on the subject. They were confidence-sapping, confusing, contradictory and yet compulsive.

It all started when someone or other wrote an entire book of dating rules, detailing exactly when a woman should call, how long the call should last and what she should say if she got voicemail. Pip had devoured that book and played by the suggested rules for some months (although admittedly without finding true love). Then someone else had come along and written another book which said the first rule book had got it all wrong. The second author claimed there were no rules and that you had to treat each case on an individual basis and exactly like a business deal. Then there was the third book that argued, no matter what, a girl must *never* approach a romantic situation like a business deal but she must follow her heart instead.

Pip had read all the books, *The Definitive Rules for Dating, More Rules for Dating, The Little Book of Dating Rules, The Big Book of Dating Rules, The Ten Essential Dating Rules, The Lifetime of Rules, The Text Rules for Dating.* What had she been reading when she met Dylan? she wondered. The truth was, while she knew all the rules and had sometimes followed them, sometimes broken them, it didn't seem to make any difference. The only real winners when it came to dating guidebooks were the authors, who no doubt laughed all the way to the bank. Pip felt fretful and anguished. Why couldn't she just take his number and enjoy the moment? Why was she paralysed with indecision?

Then, like the sun coming out from behind a huge storm cloud, Robbie said, 'You better give me your numbers, too. I hate it when one person or the other has the responsibility to call and there's all that horrible agonising about who promised to call who and when. It's such a waste of energy. Should we just agree to make sure we speak by Wednesday? It doesn't matter when before Wednesday and it doesn't matter who calls who. OK?'

Pip nodded, relieved. She was more than happy to be swept along by his frank and uncomplicated approach to making arrangements, although she was pretty sure that someone somewhere in one of her many books must have written a dating rule that advised women not to be led but to assert their independence as early as possible.

'Shall we go to the movies?' Pip nodded. 'What sort of movies do you like?'

'Nothing too violent or arty or miserable,' she said quickly. 'Ones with happy endings.' Pip wondered whether such a confession could be considered an assertive, independent act.

CHAPTER SEVEN

Stephanie walked down the aisle of the supermarket, slowly pushing a shallow trolley with, typically, a funny wheel that meant the trolley veered off towards the right. This meant she had to push harder with her right hand and as a consequence she had a slight pain in her shoulder. She'd had a funny twinge on that side for a few weeks now, she should probably book herself an appointment for a back and shoulder massage. Julian was always encouraging her to do that sort of thing but Steph was a bit funny about being that—well—that *naked* in front of a stranger. OK, she knew that they didn't actually see *anything*, and she knew that absolutely everyone had massages nowadays—the Queen probably did. Massages weren't sexual, necessarily. Silly to think they were. But. Even so. She might just settle for a deep bath and a generous slosh from her bottle of Radox.

Her intention had been to just dash into the supermarket and pick up the champagne, she'd done a big shop on Thursday, but on the drive over here she'd remembered they were out of garlic paste, kitchen roll and leather cleaner. She'd forgotten to buy these few items the last two times she'd visited the store because generally on her weekly shop she rushed around, grabbing replacement produce for the things they'd consumed in an efficient, mechanical way. Unfortunately, her haste and the repetitive nature of shopping meant that she had a tendency to forget anything slightly out of the ordinary. But she wasn't in a rush today so this was a great opportunity to buy all those outstanding bits and bobs that made a home run smoothly, there was only so long a woman could manage without garlic paste.

Besides, she really didn't want to go home right now. She didn't much like being in the house when Mrs Evans was cleaning (however inefficiently) because on some level it made her feel strangely useless and displaced. Stephanie still wasn't convinced that they needed a cleaner or that she deserved one, her mother had never had one and her house was always spotless. Steph could comfortably manage the housework now the children were all at school, in fact her problem sometimes seemed to be *filling* the hours. But when she'd suggested as much to Julian, he'd said she was nuts. Why would she want to put on rubber gloves and put her hands down the loo when they could pay someone else to do that and all the other grubby jobs—like emptying bins, scouring the oven and washing kitchen tiles? Steph had not said that Mrs Evans was rather hopeless at any of these elbow-grease jobs, she realised that wasn't the point, instead she replied that she might get some sense of satisfaction from scrubbing their home. But then he'd pointed out that Mrs Evans had been cleaning for them for almost ten years and she depended on the income, he said it was a contribution to the economy (as was employing a gardener, people to repaint the rendering and buying organic meat off the local farmer). Stephanie had then felt rather guilty and silly that she'd failed to think about her responsibility to Mrs Evans. Julian was so considerate, he saw the wider picture. Stephanie sometimes worried that she was becoming increasingly myopic as the years went by. When they'd graduated (she'd gained a first-class degree, Julian had a respectable 2:1) she would have looked at the employment of a cleaner in terms of economic value too, she was sure she would have. Although, frankly, the issue would never have arisen because when they graduated they'd both earned a pittance and could hardly afford cleaning products for their little rented flat in Fulham, let alone a cleaner.

Anyway, today, it wasn't the issue of feeling displaced in her own house that made Steph reluctant to go home, the thing was she could not face the inevitable chatter about the nuisance calls. Mrs Evans would more than likely go on and on and on about it all afternoon. Stephanie could do without it.

So instead she had decided that she'd saunter up and down the aisles, at a snail's pace, carefully considering the produce on offer and see if she did indeed need a chemical to stop the build-up of hard water ravaging the innards of her washing machine or ready-to-roll pastry (she tended to make her own but having a packet in the cupboard—just in case she was ever horribly short of time—seemed wise).

It took her forty-five minutes to reach the

alcohol section but no time at all for her to snatch up the most expensive bottle of champagne, tomorrow was a Bolly occasion, not an own-label occasion. Steph was fully expecting to gain a certain amount of vicarious pleasure from the resurrection of Pip's career, it was only right that she launched the ship with the very best champers on offer. It would probably surprise and confound Pip to know that, in some small way, Steph envied her. Of course, it was a genuine shame that Pip was struggling financially and even with a contract from Selfridges Pip's income was likely to be a relatively modest one. She probably would still not be able to afford the things that were scattered at Steph's feet, yet Steph still faintly remembered the thrill, the sense of achievement, the sense of satisfaction that she used to get when she bought something *she'd* saved up for. It was wonderful to own something that you'd earned. Julian was fond (a little too fond) of saying, 'There's no need for you to work, Steph.' Steph knew there was no *need* but being needed was rather lovely. Of course she understood that her role as mother to three boys was work enough and it was fulfilling (and exhausting, thrilling and strenuous) but Steph thought it might be nice, on occasion, to buy Julian a present that she had actually paid for.

Not that Steph's career had ever been as glittering and fascinating as Pip's. She'd worked as a civil servant, an administrator in the health sector. She'd been rigorous, focused and disciplined, yes, she'd been rather good at it, although admittedly on some days it had been simply dull. Steph, her parents and Julian all agreed that the civil service was the perfect place for a bright woman to be employed, specifically one who was thinking of starting a family in her mid-twenties. The maternity leave was especially generous, she could have up to a year off. Not that it was relevant in the end. Despite her intentions, she never did return to work after Harry was born. How could she justify continuing? Her salary wouldn't cover the childcare costs, even if she'd wanted to leave her boys with someone else (which she didn't). Besides, few careers could withstand three maternity breaks. One or two an employer might not notice (some assume a woman is yo-yo dieting as she balloons up, disappears and then reappears some months later—in fact, she is precariously balancing her home and work life) but a third pregnancy seemed to tip the scales.

Steph carefully loaded the shopping into the boot of her new Audi. It was a roomy boot attached to a roomy car. Julian had surprised her with it, just the week before last. He brought it home without them having had any discussion about buying a new car, a late birthday present, he'd called it. Her birthday had been last month and he'd bought her a simply lovely dress and a pair of gold stud earrings then. A new car was so unnecessary.

'Quit grumbling and hop in,' Pip had insisted excitedly. She'd been at theirs when Julian handed over the keys. 'I'm desperate to go for a spin, even if you're an unappreciative, miserable bag.'

Steph was not a miserable bag and she really did appreciate the gift. It was just that the car was extremely long and Steph sweated buckets whenever she had to park it. Although she had to admit the roomy boot was so useful when she had three sports kits, three instruments and three school bags to lug from A to B to C to D and back again. Steph got into the car and took a deep breath, it was just a case of getting used to the size, she told herself.

Steph's thoughts were interrupted by the sound of a phone. She reached for hers which was nestled in her handbag but it wasn't ringing. She looked around, confused. Could the sound be coming from outside? No, it seemed to be closer than that. She followed the noise. Ah ha. That's where it was coming from. There was a mobile lost beneath the back seat. Steph stretched to retrieve it, her fingers made contact just as the ringing stopped. The phone then beeped to say there was a new voicemail message. Steph was perplexed, she didn't recognise the phone. It wasn't Julian's or Harry's and the younger children weren't allowed a phone yet. Steph pressed 121 to listen to the message, no doubt it would be some frantic mother of a friend of Harry's, regretting that she'd spent so much on her son's first mobile and swearing that from now on she would only buy standard issue.

But the voice was not that of a stressed mum but a rather formal, slightly loquacious male voice. Stephanie had heard the same tone a hundred times before from overly keen shopkeepers, car salesmen and waiters. The tone was used by anyone who worked on commission or depended on tips; Steph understood the effusive manner but didn't enjoy it.

'This is the concierge at Highview Hotel, Mr Blake. I've just been checking our reservations for tomorrow evening, sir, and I've noticed that while your regular room is reserved, there's no order for your usual champagne or fresh cut flowers. Nor is there a booking for dinner. I'm concerned this might be *our* oversight, so I have taken the liberty of reserving you your regular table at nine p.m., sir, and I've arranged for you to enjoy an upgrade to our suite tomorrow. I'll personally make sure that there are flowers in the suite and champagne on ice for six p.m. as usual. This week, we'd like to offer those with our compliments, Mr Blake, sir. Just in case there has been any oversight on our part.'

What could this mean?

It could mean only one thing.

This was the most horrible moment of Steph's life so far, although she couldn't computerise and categorise it as such as it was happening. All she thought was Highview Hotel? Highview Hotel? Stephanie felt her body go slack. It slipped away from her and she looked at the ground, fully expecting her liquid being to be in a mushy pool on the floor. Flowers? Champagne? She had no bones, no guts and no heart. They'd all vanished in that single moment. Spontaneous combustion. Disappeared. Left her. She was resourceless. She was a void.

Except her head, she could still feel her head. It seemed to be expanding and contracting and she could hear a wailing sound, like a siren but she didn't know where that was coming from, she could not make sense of it. Had someone called the emergency services? They should have. This was an emergency. Regular table? This was a horrific, unspeakable disaster. She felt her head swell and push angrily against the car interior. The cushy leather seats no longer appeared plush and comfortable but instead, momentarily, she imagined she was inside a padded cell. She was insane. But then, in the next microscopic instant, her head began to shrink, to implode. She felt it heavy in her hands. Her hands were wet. Why was that? Where was the wailing siren coming from? She wanted it to stop. Suddenly Stephanie realised that it was her making the siren sound. She was howling. The wet on her hands was an undignified mess of tears and snot. Instantly Steph clasped her mouth closed and swallowed the agony. She scrambled to press the button to lower the car window. She needed fresh air, she was suffocating. She stuck her head outside and took panicked gulps. The howling had created an instant and intense pain inside her head. The betrayal had created a yet more ferocious pain in her heart.

She'd heard other women, in similar circumstances (because, yes, there were always women in these circumstances), say that at first they didn't understand or accept what was going on when they discovered their husband's infidelity. It wasn't that way with Stephanie, Stephanie understood immediately. She wished the knowledge—the bleak, cruel awareness—had seeped into her consciousness slowly. Even a moment longer in blissful ignorance would have been wonderful. But she knew. She categorically knew. Affair. Adultery. Treachery. Ruin. She knew. Such ugliness.

She knew what it was. She just didn't understand how it could be so. Not her Julian. Julian Blake was an upstanding member of the community. He'd started a Neighbourhood Watch scheme on their quiet private road. He paid all his bills by direct debit—on time and in full—he donated to charities, he worked so hard to give his family a good life, he was an adoring father, a loving husband. A filthy adulterer. These descriptions didn't sit together. They didn't make sense.

Stephanie blew her nose. Right, that was a bit better, she couldn't think properly with goodness knows what running down her face. She picked up the phone again and forced herself to relisten to the message from the concierge at Highview Hotel. There was no mistake. The man had said Mr Blake twice.

Stephanie knew the Highview Hotel. Everyone in Surrey did. It was a beautiful country hotel with a luxurious spa and a Michelin star restaurant. It was the sort of hotel young girls imagined they'd host their wedding receptions in, it was the hotel that Stephanie and Julian had celebrated their last wedding anniversary in. It was the sort of place people took their lovers if they wanted to impress them, Steph knew this for a fact.

Stephanie used her own phone to call the Highview. With extraordinary self-possession, she pretended to be Mr Blake's new personal assistant. She said she was standing in for Rosie O'Grady, his usual PA, as Rosie was off sick. 'I might be around for a few weeks,' she lied. Steph did not care about telling the lie. She was not alone in telling lies, it seemed. She pleaded ignorance about the usual arrangement and asked for details about the booking. The kind receptionist understood what it was like to get a bollocking from a boss and so helpfully ran through all the details so that the temp PA would have all the minutiae on file for future reference. Good PAs were supposed to know as much about their bosses as their wives did—well, more in this case, clearly.

'Yes, Mr Julian Blake stays with us every Tuesday and has done so for three months now.' The receptionist didn't add that sometimes Mr Blake left the room during the course of the evening but his friend always stayed the entire night, she felt doing so was unnecessary and unseemly, the PA would understand. 'He and his companion often take advantage of our spa facilities by booking a massage for early evening.'

A massage! 'What time does Mr Blake arrive?' interrupted Steph. She didn't have to disguise her voice, it was unnaturally high anyway. Her breath was caught, trapped.

'Between six and seven. Occasionally a bit earlier. He likes flowers and champagne in the room. They used to order room service but recently he's been making a dinner booking for nine.'

Knives sliced Steph's flesh. The deepest thrust was not the thought of the chilled champagne bubbling down his throat, perhaps being passed from his mouth to this other woman's during a passionate kiss, it was not the thought of the fragrance of fresh flowers drifting through their room or even the thought of Julian indulging in a sensual, aromatherapy massage before he touched this other woman's body. The most malicious and merciless words that the receptionist had inadvertently delivered was the fact that he arrived at the hotel at 6 p.m. The hotel was only a few miles away from their home. To arrive there by six, Julian would have had to leave work in London at 5 p.m. on the dot, at the latest. Stephanie realised that silent fat tears were rolling down her cheeks again. She saw them splatter on to her Mark Jacob handbag, the leather would be marked. She didn't care. There should be stains. There should be outward signs. How could these things happen and the world go on unchanged?

In all the years they had been married, Julian had never made it home in time to help with homework, teatime or bathtime. Never. Oh OK, maybe once or twice, her birthday or one of the kids' birthdays possibly, but very, *very* rarely. And she had never, ever allowed herself to grumble that she could do with another pair of hands during those fraught and chaotic few hours. Not once. Her restraint was superhuman. Oh, she'd wanted to, often enough. And of course she'd moaned to Pip and even some of the other mothers at the school gate who identified with her position. Every parent who had battled with a fractious kid who didn't want to eat broccoli or practise their piano scales understood how hard those relentless, unpredictable evenings could be. But Steph had always believed that moaning to Julian about her evening responsibilities would be unfair. She'd believed that he was in the office working like a dog, for their family. She'd nurtured the idea that he'd actually like to rush home and complete these tasks that she sometimes considered mundane, if only he could. She'd told herself that he'd have considered it an honour to do so and so she'd never grumbled.

The bastard.

Stephanie thanked the receptionist for her help and assured her that all the details for Mr Blake's bookings were now on file and that she wouldn't have to inquire again. She resisted doing anything obvious like cancelling the dinner reservation or asking for Blue Nun instead of champagne, she knew if she did so, she'd alert the receptionist that something was wrong and she could not risk doing that. Obviously Julian was a valued client of theirs and the hotel staff might feel a responsibility to inform him of his new PA's inefficiencies or idiosyncrasies. No, Steph had to think clearly before she did anything at all. This was too dire for a hot-headed response.

Stephanie's fingers felt like lead weights and were having difficulty cooperating with the instructions her brain was sending, her head was pounding and her back and legs still felt like liquid. She wanted to get out of the car and stretch but wasn't sure if she'd be able to stay upright. She knew what she had to do next but the thought was about as appealing as picking through the wardrobe of a recently deceased relative. She had to check the phone for text messages, incoming and outgoing. She screwed her eyes closed and then forced them open, she had to focus.

She opened the text inbox and discovered forty-two messages from one number, there were no messages from any other number. The number didn't have a name attached to it, clearly only one person could reach Julian this way. The phone had been bought for the purpose of deception. It was a filthy adultery phone.

The messages read as she'd expected them to. No one reinvented the wheel when they had an affair, no matter how special they thought they were. Some were banal texts that just read, 'Will be leaving work early and waiting for you! x' or, 'On

98

my way! x.' Julian's mistress, it appeared, was fond of the exclamation mark and she always signed her texts with a kiss. Other texts were horribly explicit and left nothing to the imagination. The texts hurt Stephanie deep in the pit of her stomach and, deeper still, in the pit of her soul. The tone was confident, jaunty and upbeat. Stephanie tried to concentrate on reading the messages and not allow herself to start imagining the woman behind the jaunty, upbeat messages. Was she blonde? Steph thought she probably was. This was irrational and unfounded but history shows that blondes tend to be blamed by brunettes for all the world's ills. Or maybe she had lashings of magnificent red hair, porcelain skin and sparkling green eyes. Julian had a thing for redheads. He could always be persuaded to go to see a romcom if Amy Adams or Isla Fisher were starring (he'd been devastated when Nicole Kidman had become a blonde). Stephanie thought the woman must be stupid. Of course she must be, because it was stupid to be so jaunty and upbeat when you were sleeping with another woman's husband, screwing someone's father, ripping apart a family. You'd have to be stupid not to know how wrong that was. How vile. Stupid or callous. A callous, vicious hellcat. That was possible. Probable.

Stephanie scrolled back to the first message. It was sent on 15 February, the day after Valentine's Day. Had this woman bought Julian the phone as a gift? Was it a gift to himself so he could carry on this clandestine affair? He certainly wouldn't want to risk sending this sort of message from his BlackBerry, as it often lay around their home within easy reach of their curious boys. Steph

99

thought back to Valentine's Day. She and Julian had exchanged cards and a perfunctory peck on the cheek as usual. A vicious shaft of pain and humiliation spilt through Steph's body. She'd always been so smug that they still acknowledged Valentine's Day at all, so many of their friends in ancient marriages didn't bother. OK, long gone were the days when Steph would cut his toast into heart shapes or buy scanty panties, but then nor was Julian likely to come home with a huge bunch of flowers or book a table at a restaurant. This Valentine's Day Steph's most treasured gift had been the finger painting Freddie made at school. He'd used his thumbprint to make hearts in silver glitter paint, the picture was pinned to their fridge with a magnet that read, 'If You Believe It You'll Achieve It'. Steph had bought the magnet for Harry when he was taking his Common Entrance exams. He hadn't been very impressed with her motivational gift, he would have preferred a video game.

Steph couldn't even remember if she and Julian had spent the evening of Valentine's night together. Perhaps he'd been with this other woman.

The receptionist at Highview Hotel had said that Julian had been visiting there for three months. It was late March. Did she mean January or December? Christmas? The thought was another vicious kick. Steph already felt as though she was lying, bloody, bruised and defeated, in the gutter, yet the blows kept coming, relentless and agonising. When had the affair started? At some gaudy, excessive Christmas party? Was this woman a colleague who had taken advantage of the fact that everyone behaved ridiculously at office parties? Had he had sex with this . . . this . . . Steph was stumped. She searched around every crevice in her mind but she didn't have words that were vile enough to describe the woman, or fair enough, because she knew it wasn't just the woman's fault. Julian had betrayed her. Her pathetic prudery, even at a time like this, *especially* at a time like this, made her feel weak and ashamed. Of course there were words for people like Julian and his whore. See, there was one. Why couldn't she stand up for herself more? She'd been such a mug. The archetypal mug.

The thought of Julian touching this woman, whoever she was, kissing her, caressing her, entering her, caused Steph's heart to race dangerously, she could barely breathe. She laid her head against the cold glass window. 'Oh dear God help me,' she whispered. Julian might have done those things and then still sat in their sitting room on Christmas morning, watching the boys' innocent and delighted faces as they opened their gifts. He'd still put himself in charge of the afternoon games and he'd still set fire to the Christmas pudding, as though everything was normal. How was that possible?

Maybe it started after that? In the dull, dark January afternoons? Had the constant rain and gloom sent Julian out on a search for something sparkling and shallow? Some callous, vicious hellcat.

Reading the texts would give her more information. Reading the texts would rip her heart out.

Many, many of the messages were sexy,

uninhibited, candid messages. This woman liked to text about licking, sucking, fucking. She wrote those words down! Stephanie was shocked. Her shock made her feel like a ridiculous prude, a simpleton. She never said the f word to Julian. They didn't fuck, they made love. Or at times, if she was honest with herself, they simply had sex because he wanted it and she just wanted it over with. Love-making required energy and occasionally she didn't have the right amount of energy or she wasn't in the right sort of mood, or whatever. Anyway, the truth was sometimes it was just sex.

Stephanie read every single one of the forty-two texts. Texts her husband valued so much that he hadn't deleted them, although he must have known keeping them was a risk. Or was it? Did he think she was so stupid, so gullible, so naive that she'd never suspect him of having an affair?

Well, he'd be right. She did trust him. *Had* trusted him. It had never, ever entered her head that Julian would have an affair. His work demanded foreign travel. True, since they'd moved to Riverford he had stayed overnight in town if he'd had to work very late or if he'd attended a business dinner that had dragged on. The last train home ran at midnight and the bank had a corporate flat that all the senior employees were entitled to use so it made sense. Or it had seemed to. She hadn't been suspicious, just pleased that he was getting a decent night's sleep. She hadn't thought it odd when those spasmodic nights in town became more frequent or that they nearly always occurred on a Tuesday. Although clearly, Julian wasn't using the corporate flat (if such a

102

thing existed!), he was staying in a five-star hotel. How was he paying for it? Steph had never noticed any irregularities in their bank account. Surely he wasn't passing this off as a work expense and paying on his corporate card? Did he have a separate bank account? How deep was this deception?

Fathoms deep.

Bottomless.

Of course it happened, she knew that. Infidelity was depressingly commonplace, but Julian? *No.* He was better than that. They were better than that.

Yet the proof was incontrovertible.

Of course the worst was to come. She checked the sent box and discovered sixty-seven texts sent. Her stomach lurched. Did she have the strength to read them? Did she have the strength not to? Wouldn't it be better to try and ram the lid on this particular Pandora's box? Now, before any more havoc could be let loose. But it was impossible. She had to read them. She had to know.

CHAPTER EIGHT

'Kirsten, can you come to this meeting and take notes, please,' said Brian. He was standing at the doorway to the boardroom. He used his firm, deep, professional voice to fire the command across the office. Kirsten understood. You never knew who might be listening.

Kirsten rather liked Brian being masterful, it reminded her of the reason she was with him in the first place. In bed he liked baby talk! Who'd have guessed that? There was nothing about his serious, dark pinstripe suit or conservative blue striped tie that hinted at such a thing. But it was true, he liked her to talk with a lisp and he'd once asked her to dress up as a schoolgirl. She found that a bit odd, to be honest. She didn't mind dressing up as a nurse, or a French maid or even wearing the usual slutty stuff, because that was all very adult, but a schoolgirl outfit was borderline weird. She'd said no. Admittedly it wasn't a flat and absolutely non-negotiable no (like the one she'd issued when Mark Deally wanted anal sex), this no was more a 'maybe one day' sort of no. She'd said that if Brian did something really, really lovely for her, she might want to thank him by dressing up in a naughty Saint Trinian's outfit. But it had to be something really, *really* lovely. Not just a new bag or a pair of earrings, she was thinking about something like a mini break, maybe Paris or Venice.

It would be nice to have something fun to do at the weekends because the thing with the way her social life was panning out was that she was often at a loose end at the weekend. She didn't really like the dives her mates went to, not anymore. They were really tatty in comparison to what she'd got used to during the week and there was no point going shopping with her friends because there was no one to pay for anything. Her mates were pretty jealous of her clothes, she reckoned, because she'd noticed they didn't call as much as they used to. But being on her own every weekend was a bit zeds-ville. What was the point of having three boyfriends if not one of them was available to so much as take her telephone calls on a wet Sunday afternoon, let alone take her to the movies? Thinking about her lonely, boring weekends made Kirsten reply in a tone that was significantly less pleasant or enticing than usual.

'It's not my job to take notes in a meeting,' she replied grumpily. 'I've a bunch of emails to answer and, besides, who will answer the phones?'

Kirsten noticed one or two of the other group PAs bristle. Most of them knew why Kirsten got away with being a bit cheeky with Brian and they didn't like it. More jealousy, Kirsten reckoned, not her problem. One or two of them were really pretty and probably didn't have to work as hard as they did, but some people chose to do everything the hard way—that was their lookout.

'Divert your phone through to Rosie and get in here,' said Brian firmly.

Kirsten sighed and made a big show of laboriously gathering up her bag and laptop. Brian sounded a little bit irritated with her, in fact he sounded horrifyingly like Daddy when he was ticking her off about borrowing the car without asking. But what could Brian be cross with her about? Nothing. He was probably appearing gruff just to try to throw everyone off their scent.

Kirsten briefly wondered if there really was a meeting in the boardroom or whether, when she got in there, the place would be deserted and Brian would throw her across the table and shag her senseless. As a rule, Brian wasn't one for risks and thrills of that nature but you never knew for certain, her mother was always saying that still waters ran deep. Yes, it was the quiet ones you had to watch.

As she walked towards the boardroom she decided that if he wanted to fool around they could, as long as he was careful with her hair. She'd managed to squeeze in a quick visit to an Aveda hair salon at lunchtime and she'd treated herself to an expensive up-do, she didn't want it tumbling down. Plus, she was going to have to make it clear that it was an either/or situation. If they had sex now in the boardroom, she wasn't going to bother this evening, he could take her out for a yummy meal instead. She really wanted to try the Whitechapel Gallery. Some of the other girls in the office had gone there last Friday, they hadn't invited Kirsten, not that she cared. They knew by now that she'd never dream of going to such an expensive place without a date to pick up the cheque at the end. Or, she and Brian could go to Orso in Covent Garden, she'd long since fancied trying there, or maybe The Avenue in St James—there were lots of lovely restaurants to choose from. Generally speaking, her boyfriends took her to hotel restaurants. She wasn't complaining because the hotel restaurants were some of the very best, she adored Rhodes W1 Brasserie at the Cumberland Hotel and Windows at the Park Lane Hilton, but their motivation for picking these restaurants was transparent. It was fair to say they never let her linger over coffee.

Kirsten entered the boardroom and since she was now anticipating a seduction scene she was surprised that there were five guys and one woman sitting around the table, she was expected to take notes after all. She was unsure whether or not she was pleased about this. On the one hand, her hair was safe, on the other she'd have to do some real

106

work. She sat at the end of the table, pulled out her laptop and greedily eyed the tray of sandwiches. They were totally untouched and because of the hair appointment she hadn't had the chance to eat. Would it be bad form to help herself?

The managers started to talk. And talk. And talk. Tedious, tedious, tedious. It was a stiflingly hot room, the air conditioning didn't seem to be doing anything other than humming which added to the sluggish atmosphere. Kirsten thought her eyes might actually close and she'd nod off to sleep if she had to listen to much more of this. She didn't have a clue or *any* interest in what they were on about so it was tricky taking down the meeting's minutes. As best she could she half-heartedly typed every word she picked up. She'd get Brian to have a look at it this evening, he'd help her to pull her messy notes into some semblance of coherence. Probably, he had a slant that he wanted to impose on the minutes anyway. That was what usually happened in business meetings, wasn't it? Someone always had some fixed agenda, she'd seen that on loads of TV dramas. Brian had most likely called her in here because she could help him with achieving his particular agenda, whatever that might be.

Kirsten rather liked the idea of her helping Brian with his business dealings. She drifted off for a moment, thinking of a scenario where they shared an office (she was wearing a really cool grey suit from Calvin Klein, and Jimmy Choo shoes, plus an extremely wide belt that emphasised her tiny cinched waist. Would she carry a bag? If so it would be a relaxed slouchy number, maybe a Marc Jacobs). In her daydream she walked with real purpose and he asked her to countersign something. Other than her clearly imagining her outfit, the details of the fantasy were a bit blurred so she wasn't sure what she might be asked to countersign or why she'd be working alongside Brian in his office in the first place. Kirsten emerged from her musings when she heard Brian say, 'I think that about wraps it up.'

'Yes, agreed. Let's get the minutes out this afternoon,' added one of the other grey guys who looked a bit like Brian. They dressed alike—expensively but what was the point of them wearing a tailored, made-to-measure suit if they were cut from the same fabric? Kirsten wondered how much a made-to-measure suit cost. She made a mental note to ask Brian later.

There was a chorus of agreement. 'Absolutely, high priority. This afternoon.'

The woman added, 'Extremely sensitive, can't afford to fuck this up.' Then she strode towards the door.

Kirsten had noticed that busy people rarely spoke in full sentences, it was as though they didn't even have the time to say, 'Extremely sensitive, *we* can't afford to fuck this up,' or, 'Extremely sensitive, *you* can't afford to fuck this up,' or even, 'Extremely sensitive, Kirsten can't afford to fuck this up.'

Which was it?

Kirsten looked down at her laptop and reread some of her notes. The sentences merged into one another—well, they weren't even sentences really, more an assortment of words loosely grouped together. The most unifying thing about them being the fact that they were all on her laptop and she must have typed them!

A wider range of investment and trading activities. Risks inherent in their investments. Shares, debt and commodities. Notably short selling and derivatives. Limited range of professional. Regulations governing short selling, derivatives, leverage, fee structures and the liquidity of interests in the fund. The fund's open-ended structure. Run into many billions of dollars. Dominate certain specialty markets.

It didn't make sense. She recognised one or two names as well. She'd heard Jules mentioned and Mark but she didn't understand the context. Crap, had that man said that she had to distribute these minutes this afternoon? Crap.

'Kirsten, can you stay back a moment?' said Brian.

Oh, thank God. Kirsten let out a big sigh of relief. He would help her write the minutes—that had been his plan after all. Once the others had left the boardroom, Brian went to the door, glanced outside into the office and then firmly closed the door so that they were alone in the room. Bloody hell, he *was* after sex, thought Kirsten. Would they have time if she had to get these minutes sorted this afternoon?

Brian turned to Kirsten and she saw at once that he wasn't thinking about sex, he looked vexed and harassed.

'OK, did you get all that? Are you clear?' he barked.

'Erm, well, not entirely,' admitted Kirsten. 'I couldn't type quite as fast as they talked.'

'Don't you know shorthand?' he asked, as he dug around his jacket pocket and then pulled out a

109

cotton handkerchief.

'No,' replied Kirsten. She was offended. Did they even teach that nowadays? She didn't know. She hadn't gone to bloody secretarial school! She had a degree! Besides, no one had mentioned anything about shorthand at the interview.

'Well, how fast can you type?' asked Brian, as he blotted his forehead with his cotton handkerchief. He was very sweaty. Did he have a gland problem? Kirsten wondered. She'd never noticed him sweat before but now he looked like someone had turned a tap on. It was totally gross. Grey hair she could forgive, slightly balding, slightly paunchy or wearing glasses she'd come to expect. She'd accept two out of four. But profuse sweating was a deal-breaker. A girl had to have standards. Kirsten very much doubted that she and Brian would have sex tonight, or ever again, come to that. She couldn't do it with a sweaty guy. No, she really couldn't, she was certain of that. But she needed a gentle way of letting him down. She didn't want to piss him off, he was one of her direct bosses after all.

'Let's see what you've got,' said Brian wearily.

For a moment Kirsten thought he was asking to see a glimpse of her stockings or something but then he reached for her laptop and she understood.

'Fucking hell. You idiot!' he yelled the moment he read a paragraph of her notes.

'Excuse me!' Kirsten replied indignantly.

'You fucking idiot,' he added, for clarity. 'Is this all you took down? In over an hour? You haven't got any of the salient points. In fact you haven't got any points at all, this is total crap.'

Kirsten didn't understand why Brian was getting

so worked up. He was at the meeting, he knew what had been said, even if she didn't. He could just tell her and she'd write it down now. Or better yet he could just write it himself and she could get back to her desk, she fancied doing a little online shopping.

'Don't shout at me. I've never taken down notes before,' she pleaded. She mustered the pout that she'd been practising in the mirror this morning, she knew it made her look adorable, she was sure to win him over.

'No, it's not notes you're known for taking down, is it?' muttered Brian nastily.

'What do you mean by that?' She wasn't thick. They always made the mistake of thinking she was so thick that she didn't even know when she was being insulted. But she wasn't thick.

'This was a fucking important meeting, Kirsten. Why can't you just do your job?'

Kirsten thought Brian was the thick one. He, more than most, was aware of her skill set; if the meeting was so damned important he should have asked Rosie to take notes. She glared at him. He glowered back. Suddenly she noticed something very cold and hard in his eyes that she'd never noticed before. She'd always thought of him as such a teddy bear but now he looked like a hungry Rottweiler, straining at his leash. All at once, Kirsten felt quite vulnerable. A scary thought flashed into her mind—she was out of her depth.

The last time she'd felt this vulnerable was a few weeks back, when she'd let Mark tie her, spreadeagled, to a four-poster bed. She hadn't really been too comfortable with doing that. Mark was always going on about the fact that what he

111

liked about her was that she was so adventurous and daring, and it was nice to be appreciated, so in the end she'd agreed to him tying her up. She'd asked him to use bows rather than knots though, so she could get away if she wanted to. He'd laughed and said that was defeating the purpose. He'd pulled very hard on the straps, she'd tried to joke that he must have been a good Boy Scout and earned loads of badges as a kid with knot-tying skills like his. He'd said that there was nothing Boy Scout about him. This was true. Sometimes, she did just wish that they could have straightforward sex with kissing and hugging and stuff. Even with Brian it always had to be an athletic sprint through the entire Kama Sutra. He said that he could get that boring stuff at home, which was fair enough, she supposed. She wasn't the woman who had to visit the in-laws or even discuss whether the insulation in the loft was sufficient, she was the woman who had to do it doggy style and talk dirty.

Mark hadn't hurt her. She wasn't saying that. It was quite exciting really, in a scary sort of way. All the way through she'd had to keep reminding herself that she'd agreed to do it, he hadn't forced her. It was exactly like going on a loop-the-loop— terrifying but thrilling. She'd stood in the queue, got on the fairground attraction, and belted herself in for the ride. Once she'd given in to it, she got into it and she had to give in to it because when she struggled, the straps tightened and hurt her ankles and wrists more.

Kirsten felt similarly vulnerable and trapped now, but there was none of the excitement.

'Look, shouting at me isn't going to fix things,' Kirsten pointed out to Brian. 'Can't you help me

112

write the minutes?'

'I'm not a fucking secretary,' he yelled. Then, muttering under his breath, he added, 'I should fire you over this.'

Kirsten heard him. The shock of the threat reverberated through her body. How could he be talking of sacking her? It was Monday, *his* night. They were supposed to be going to a lovely restaurant. They would drink wine that cost thirty quid a bottle, he'd probably have bought her that gorgeous top from Karen Millen that she'd been hinting at and they'd have sex in the sort of hotel that puts chocolates on your pillow. There should be no talk of her being fired, she was protected from that sort of thing. She was fast track, in her own way. She needed to remind him.

Icily, Kirsten commented, 'You might not *be* a fucking secretary but you are fucking a secretary so if you try to fire me I'll go straight to HR and tell them what we've been up to.'

'Kirsten, you're the office bike, no one will give a toss what you say,' replied Brian coldly. He did not seem at all affected by her threat, he swatted it away as though she was a filthy, annoying fly and turned back to her laptop. 'Go back to the phones. Send Rosie in here at once. She'll be able to sort your mess out. I should have asked her to do the job in the first place.'

Kirsten felt whipped. He'd said she was incompetent at her job; she wasn't incompetent, she was adequate. That's the grade she'd been awarded in her six-month appraisal. He'd called her the office bike. She wasn't! OK, so maybe she had a few boyfriends in the office but that didn't make her a bike. Kirsten hunted around her head for something hurtful to throw at Brian.

Nothing.

A total blank.

She never thought of really good insults until ages after she needed one.

'Yes, maybe you should have asked Rosie. I don't need this sort of hassle,' spat Kirsten as she flounced out of the boardroom. But even to her own ears, she sounded pathetic and childish.

Wounded, rather than wounding.

CHAPTER NINE

After a rather damp and chill start to the day, the sun had battered the solid layer of grey clouds until they'd lost the will, fallen apart and disintegrated into picturesque, white, bite-size clouds that looked like blobs of cotton stuck on the blue, just the way children drew them on pictures. Now the sun had taken rightful possession of the sky, the streets appeared litter-free, the leaves on trees were as vitally green as it was possible to be and the women who drove their four-by-fours were managing to park and smile rather than stare one another down as they raced for the spaces closest to the school gate. Pip thought the clement weather was an acknowledgement of her glorious luck, or better yet, a sign of more good things to come. She mentally hugged herself.

Pip had always loved spring. It was her favourite season, it was more than pleasant in its own right but also full of promise and expectancy about what would come next. A season full of hope and second chances, something Pip firmly believed in (some might say clung to). To her shame, she had barely noticed spring for the last two years. She was so deep in the doldrums of despair that the tight buds bravely pushing their way through the still nippy mornings had not caused her to smile. She hadn't bothered to chop up apples for the birds that had babies in their nests, as she'd done practically every year of her life since she was seven, even though she knew that garden birds depended on this sort of consideration during spring. She hadn't even found the energy to take Chloe to the working farm along the road, where kids were encouraged to ride ponies and feed goats. Since before Chloe could have any understanding of what was going on, Pip and Steph had taken the children to the farm to see baby chicks hatch and lambs birth. OK, the process was all a bit bloodier than Pip had envisaged and it led to more questions from Chloe than she was ready to handle.

'What's that thing hanging out of—'

'Should we go and get a teacake and perhaps a glass of orange juice?' Pip had interrupted.

Yes, bloodier, but even so Pip enjoyed the event. Birth was a marvellous thing to witness. She'd enjoyed feeling part of new beginnings. In farms, fertility hung in the air, was lodged under her fingernails and sailed on the wind, lifting her hair and causing her heart to quicken. She liked being close to the land, savouring the smell of mud and grass and animals. Living in a town it was easy to feel removed from the seasons, the passing of time became marked with nothing more sensational than turning over the calendar that hung on the wall. So visiting the farm in springtime had become a tradition, a ritual. But after Dylan left the country, all normal practice was abandoned.

Robbie Donaldson's face loomed into Pip's consciousness. She playfully batted it away. Best not to get too excited, she told herself, although she wasn't listening—not really. She thought of his grin, it was heartfelt and sincere but it was more than that, it was cheeky, almost mucky. Pip trembled with a rare and virtually forgotten sense of anticipation.

'You're very cheerful today,' commented Angie, mum of Toby, a precocious, freckled kid in Chloe's class.

'I am,' agreed Pip. Angie smiled but didn't ask any questions. The mums at the gate were generally fairly nosy but they were also invariably totally distracted. Angie started to discuss the chances of Toby emerging from school with his waterproof jacket.

'We couldn't find it this morning. He said it was on his peg but they say that, don't they, when they don't want to say they've lost it. I do hope he's got it because it's meant to pour down again tonight and he's lost the hood off his other coat and we've got to get to the swimming baths by four and then on to his music tutor by six. Plus, I have to get Evie to trampoline club, not to mention homework. Note to self, don't buy a detachable hood. I think he left his other coat in Bude. We were there at the weekend, to surf. Did I mention that my mother-in-law has a place there and she likes us to use it whenever we can?'

Angie had mentioned the cottage in Bude, Cornwall, to Pip several times, actually. When she first did so Pip had thought the information might precede an invite but it hadn't. Soon, Pip gathered that Angie simply liked to drop into conversation the existence of the Bude cottage in order to inflame a little envy amongst the mums clustered at the school gate. She mentioned her children's packed extra-curricular agendas for the same reason. The galling thing was her technique worked, Pip was usually a little envious. She thought it must be wonderful to take your daughter *and* son (the salt and pepper set) every other weekend to paddle in the rock pools that frame the sandy Cornwall beaches, to let your Labrador pound along the vast expanses, dashing in and out of the foam, to have a husband clambering on the romantic, craggy rocks in search of whelks to amuse the children. Of course she was envious of any woman who had the whole shebang. She and Chloe often seemed fractured when compared to such sketches of domestic bliss. Plus, Pip didn't have the cash to enrol Chloe in endless after-school activities, the way so many of the parents did. But today Angie's words slipped like butter off Teflon. Today, Pip had her contract with Selfridges to shore her up and her date with Robbie, the fertility nurse, to look forward to. Soon she would be bringing in regular extra cash and, if the mood struck her, Chloe could join a trampoline club, ballet club, pony club, ninja arts club or a Morris dancing class for that matter.

And who knew, maybe Robbie the fertility nurse had a mother who also had a cottage in Cornwall and it was that woman's greatest dream to throw open the doors of said cottage to a single mother Robbie had met on the train. Pip let the thought

117

skitter through her head. Immediately her new and fragile confidence faltered.

Get real. There were higher odds of Chloe wanting to join a Morris dancing class.

The sun splattered down on to the school tarmac and Pip listened to the song of kids chattering excitedly as they exploded through the school door like bubbles from a fizzy drink after the can has been shaken. Then, in that instant, Pip spotted Chloe standing by the school doors. She was standing on tiptoes and craning her neck trying to spot her mum in amongst the hordes of mothers and other carers. Even to the most affectionate eye, Chloe looked distinctly gangly and scruffy. Her silky hair had worked its way out of the plaits that Pip had conscientiously knitted together that morning. Pip noticed that Chloe wasn't wearing a pullover, even though she set off with one— missing in action then, she assumed. The little girl's socks had run down her legs and taken refuge by her ankles. She was struggling with a PE kitbag that was about twice her size. Pip grinned and started to wave both her hands above her head in order to flag her daughter. Chloe beamed, a gap-toothed smile, when she spotted Pip waving so heartily. To Pip, Chloe was the most beautiful thing in the world and she wouldn't swap being her mum and everything that came with it (including an unreliable bastard of an ex being the dad) for a lifetime at a Thai spa, let alone a weekend in Cornwall.

Pip suddenly but quite firmly had an overwhelming sense that all was well with the world. Everything was one hundred per cent perfect.

CHAPTER TEN

Stephanie could not focus. She'd checked her watch ten or more times in just fifteen minutes but still couldn't quite plot the evening. Normally, she was so organised but then nothing was normal. Her world was irredeemably, irreversibly changed. There was then, a time when she'd been happy, content and able. And there was now, when everything was ruined. Everything was soiled.

She'd managed to collect the boys (three different pick-up times, two different schools). She'd remembered that Harry had a tennis lesson after school and that Alfie needed to bring home his cello to practise for the concert this Thursday. Doing just this much required such effort. Her feet, her arms and her stomach felt like clay. She dragged her reluctant body from place to place but they drove home in silence as Steph simply could not muster the energy to talk to them about their days as she usually did. Even if she had found a way to subdue the nasty, filthy fears and accusations that were flinging themselves around her head in order to feign an interest in what they had for lunch or who they'd played with at breaktime, her efforts would most likely have gone unrewarded. The boys were all sulking because she'd forgotten to bring their afternoon snacks. Normally, she arrived at the school gate furnished with ham sandwiches and apples, but the needs of their constantly rumbling bellies had washed from her mind.

Kiss.

Lick.

Cock.

Fuck.

The alien words of the texts kept leaping into her mind like gunshots.

Now, she had to oversee their homework. Harry had some serious-looking geography worksheets and half a dozen maths problems to complete, so she told him to log on to Google. He scampered off, not needing to be asked twice, delighted that his mother hadn't insisted that his first reference point had to be the dusty encyclopedia that she normally favoured. He sensed her distraction and wondered if she'd notice if he logged on to Warhammer instead.

Alfie's assignment was writing a letter of complaint. He told his mother that he was going to write to his hairdresser and tell her that he didn't like his latest cut.

'Don't you think it might be more appropriate if you wrote to a toy manufacturer and said you'd received a toy for your birthday that had a piece broken?' she asked with a sigh.

'But I didn't,' said Alfie. 'That's not true.'

'No. But this letter-writing is an exercise in imagination and Mrs Young might be more interested in a letter to a toy manufacturer.'

'But I don't like my haircut, not at all,' said Alfie firmly.

Sod it, thought Steph. She was taken aback by the curse erupting in her head but really—sod it. What did it matter if Alfie wrote about his haircut or a broken toy? What did it matter if the children impressed their teachers? If they got good grades, went to university, met nice women, married them, had children? What did any of it matter? It might all disappear anyway. It might all be faulty, no matter how much effort she put in.

Steph started to sway. She felt dangerously adrift. Lost. She needed to sit down. She realised she was probably still in shock.

Freddie needed to practise his reading.

Her body had switched to some sort of automatic emergency programme but she felt like a robot with a broken control panel. All day she'd managed to lumber on, following a pre-set pattern, yet sparks were flying through her system—nasty, sharp jolts that burnt her and were undoubtedly flagging alarming short circuits and, possibly, an impending explosion. Somehow or other Steph stumbled through teatime, bathtime and bedtime. She only broke down crying once but explained it away by saying that she'd burnt her hand on the oven. She *had* burnt her hand on the oven, she also dropped a bowl of peas and she'd allowed the children to watch TV for far longer than the usual weekday quota but she couldn't bring herself to regard these things as disasters. They were simply consequences of the one enormous, overwhelming disaster.

When Julian walked through the door, Steph gasped dramatically. She was annoyed with herself for doing so, that wasn't her plan. Her plan was to behave exactly as normal, no hysterics, no fuss or commotion. She was not going to yell accusations or feverishly demand a divorce, God forbid. She wanted to try to regain some sort of control or at the very least offer up the semblance of it. She needed time to think clearly. Carefully. To work out what she could do for the best.

121

She had gasped because he was the same. Illogically, she'd expected some outward change. A manifestation of the horror that she'd discovered. Of course, that was nonsense. This Jekyll and Hyde did not physically morph to conveniently flag his diabolical, altered status.

Or had he? Julian had worn glasses for reading, driving and watching TV for as long as she'd known him and it had never bothered him beyond a mild irritation when he couldn't find a pair in the morning. But some months back, he'd suddenly started talking about having laser surgery, and when Steph had discouraged it, he'd settled on lenses. For the first time Steph questioned the motivation behind his sudden vanity. Did he only wear lenses on Tuesdays or more regularly than that? When exactly had he started to care about wearing glasses? Was it about the same time as he started mucking about with the Atkins diet?

Steph hated the Atkins diet, she liked carbs. There was nothing better than chunky slices of warm, homemade, wholemeal bread, slathered in butter, or a steaming bowl of *al dente* pasta with a fresh tomato sauce. She thought the Atkins diet was ludicrous and inconvenient, it did not promote healthy eating habits and therefore defied good sense as a lifestyle choice. Steph valued good sense above just about anything. Yet, she had still prepared the meals he requested. She had been quite surprised when Julian had embraced the diet with such enthusiasm. He'd said Rosie, his PA, had lost half a stone on it and she swore by it. He insisted he needed to move seven or eight pounds that had started to cling to him over the past couple of years. He seemed to suddenly know everything there was to know about metabolic advantage. Had Rosie really introduced him to the diet? Or was his mistress a skinny, carb-loathing bitch? Steph didn't know. She didn't know anything.

Julian walked through to the kitchen, put his laptop and the *Evening Standard* on top of the breakfast bar and his regular mobile in his trouser pocket. As he did so he briefly scanned the kitchen. Steph wondered whether he was looking for his other mobile. The one she'd secreted in her bedside drawer, hidden beneath her nighties and tights. Had he been searching for it all day? Fretting about it? Was he inconsolable because he couldn't send dirty, flirty, filthy texts to his mistress today? Had he had to stick to *The Times* Sudoku for his entertainment this lunchtime?

'The kids are in bed, are they?' he asked, as he always did.

'Yes. I'm sure they're still awake. They'd appreciate it if you popped your head round the door,' Steph answered automatically.

Why was it her responsibility to remind him to go upstairs and say good night to his children? she asked herself. Surely, after eleven years of being a father, he knew what was expected of him. She thought of the text messages and had her answer.

No, Julian didn't know what was expected of him as a father.

Julian nodded and dragged a smile to his face. Steph thought it was a painstakingly designed smile that had something of the martyr about it. He wanted Steph to know that after a hard day at the office he was absolutely fried, but still willing to 'be dad' before he helped himself to a well deserved G&T. Normally, this smile cut through any exhaustion Steph might be feeling, routinely she dashed to the cupboard and poured him a drink, checked on the dish that would be simmering in the oven, sometimes she even pulled him into a sympathetic hug. This evening she said, 'I haven't had time to read with Freddie, will you do it? He needs to read at least eight pages.' Then she poured herself a glass of wine and pressed the start button on the microwave. 'This takes five and a half minutes and a minute standing time, so don't dawdle.'

'A microwave dinner?' Julian couldn't hide his surprise or disappointment. The lines around his mouth sharpened. He'd only eaten a sandwich for lunch. He was starving and those plastic dinners never left him feeling full, the way a home-cooked dinner did.

'I found it lurking in the fridge, thought it needed eating up,' said Steph. 'I've already eaten, with the children.'

Steph was lying. She hadn't been able to swallow a morsel.

This morning she'd planned to cook roasted haddock on chickpea and chorizo sauté for their supper. She'd even started to prepare the dish this afternoon, before she collected the children, as that was her habitual time to do any prep that might be required for the evening meals. She had considered that it was rather strange that she was cooking their dinner, under the circumstances, but she didn't know what else to do. She had to do *something*.

While she'd chopped the large red onion and the coriander leaves into fine parts, she had

124

suddenly been filled with such an overwhelming, unstoppable fury that she'd flung the chopping board, the knife, the onion and coriander against the kitchen wall. She hurled it with all her might. A deliberate act of violence. The board fell with a satisfying clatter. So satisfying in fact, that next she'd thrown the bowl of chickpeas (already decanted, drained and rinsed). It was a heavy wooden board and it had taken a huge chunk out of the wall. The ingredients had scattered everywhere, settling like confetti under cabinets, under the breakfast bar, near the fridge. Steph could see a piece of red onion right now, next to the dishwasher. She hadn't cleaned up very well.

The violence had been such a release. To see the wall stained and chipped felt wonderful, exhilarating. She wanted to smash something else. Their glassware perhaps? Or the new crockery? Both. She wanted to continue to hurl, smash, shatter and sever until everything they owned was ground into tiny parts, too small to offer any satisfaction when breaking them further. She wanted to pick up the chopping knife and plunge it into the cushions in the sitting room and gouge out their innards. She'd like to see feathers from the pillows on their bed flutter around their bedroom. She wanted to rip and shred their bed sheets. Steph's heartbeat had trebled; adrenalin caroused through her bloodstream like a stag party hurtling through city streets on the lookout for trouble. Who knew what damage she could have wreaked if Mrs Evans hadn't come tearing down the stairs and stopped her.

Not enough damage. She knew that. Whatever she smashed, ripped or flung, she couldn't cause as much harm as he had. She couldn't even the score. Least, not like that.

'What's the matter?' Mrs Evans had yelled as she ran into the kitchen with a speed Steph had never witnessed before, in all the ten years Mrs Evans had been cleaning for the Blakes.

'Nothing,' lied Steph. 'I dropped the chopping board.'

If Mrs Evans wondered how Steph had dropped the chopping board up the opposite wall and the bowl of chickpeas too, she was discreet enough not to ask for any more details. All she said was, 'Evening primrose capsules are very good for PMT, you know.'

'Thank you, Mrs Evans. I shall go out and get some. Just as soon as I've cleared up here,' replied Steph carefully.

'I think that wall might need a spot of paint,' Mrs Evans muttered and then she'd shuffled off back to the ironing.

Stephanie didn't go and buy evening primrose capsules or paint but instead she went out and bought Julian a microwave roast chicken dinner. She simply could not chop, dice, stir and sauté food for him. Not when he'd sent another woman a text saying he wanted to take her bent over, in front of a mirror. She couldn't cook for that man.

Julian was now seated at their fine dining-room table, wolfing down the tasteless supper. Part of him wanted to grumble about its inadequacy but a bigger part of him knew that doing so was impossible as they were not living in the 1950s.

'Are you happy?' His wife blurted the question just as his teeth had closed down on a particularly hard piece of chicken gristle. With his tongue he

126

worked the unyielding piece of meat to the side of his mouth, so that he could retrieve it as politely as possible and leave it on the side of his plate.

'Funny thing to ask,' he replied.

Steph noticed that wasn't an answer. 'Do you like your job? Our home? Do you like living in Riverford?' She spat out the questions like a round from a machine gun.

'Yes, of course,' replied Julian without looking up from his plate. 'Why wouldn't I?'

Why indeed? It was Julian who had wanted to leave London and come to Riverford, a prosperous and pleasant county town in Surrey with good schools and large gardens. Steph sighed at the hopelessly inadequate questions she'd posed and the predictably defective response Julian had offered. They would never get to the heart of the matter like this. They weren't the questions that needed to be asked but how could she say, 'Do you like me?' How could a woman ask her man of nearly twenty years such a humiliating, reducing question?

Steph sat still for a moment or two, concentrating on the sound of Julian's knife and fork scraping on his plate, the sound of his wine glass clinking against his front teeth and him gulping and swallowing. She couldn't ask the question she wanted to ask.

How could you do this to me?

Steph wondered what she ought to do next. What to do in the next five minutes? What to do with her remaining fifty years. Her mind was a blank. Trauma had temporarily erased everything. Stupidly, she couldn't remember how she usually spent her evenings with her husband. How did they behave with one another before she had this vile knowledge swirling around her head and threatening to spill all over their dining-room table, all over their lives?

She normally had some little bit of news or an anecdote to tell him. Often it was about the kids, their daily triumphs and disasters. Sometimes she had a snippet of info about his father, she called Julian's father every couple of days to ask how his golf game or his vegetable plot were faring. Or she'd tell Julian about the places they had been invited. This year they'd seen a trickle of invites to fortieth birthday parties, next year she anticipated there would be an avalanche. Stephanie had already started thinking about Julian's birthday party, even though it was a while off. She envisaged a jazz band and fancy dress—the house full of molls and gangsters, as Julian had an interest in that period of history. She'd thought a Sunday afternoon party might work well so that people could bring along their children. There was nothing so lovely as to watch your offspring and the offspring of your friends play together.

Now, those plans seemed pathetic.

Stephanie and Julian always accepted the invites to parties, weekend, dinner or lunch dates, they had a full social life. Thinking about it now, Steph had to admit that Julian was rarely what you'd describe as enthusiastic about these invites. He went along, of course. He chatted, ate the food and drank the wine that was served, but he didn't seem to look forward to these socials the way she did. He often said he'd be just as happy staying in. Stephanie had thought that it was a huge compliment that Julian found everything he needed with his family, that he was content within the walls of his castle. Now she reasoned that no doubt the walls of the castle were enough for him because when he was out alone he spent his time ravaging and pillaging, which provided more than enough entertainment to privately reminisce on while they watched the evening news. But, even before she'd known about his ravaging another woman, she'd patiently explained that while he got plenty of social interaction at work, she was mostly confined to brief snatches of conversation thrown out and sponged up at pick-up and drop-off. She needed to go somewhere at least once a week where she could enjoy a glass of wine and expect a sentence to be finished.

A dinner or lunch invite necessitated a reciprocal one, it was simply a matter of manners. Stephanie didn't mind, in fact she loved entertaining. She approached hosting with a keen sense of order. She would spend hours flicking through recipe books deciding what to serve (she kept a note of who had eaten what and been invited with whom, so as to avoid ever serving the same guest the same dish twice). She spent hours in the local butchers, fishmongers, deli and bakery, carefully selecting the best ingredients she could track down. She regularly served three courses, cheese and then coffee and chocolates. She lit candles and arranged flowers in the hall, dining room and downstairs loo. Julian opened the wine.

The realisation that Julian's contribution was minimal sent a shiver scratching across Steph's body. On so many occasions she'd told herself that Julian was happy enough to go with the flow, and that he had no problem at all with their endless stream of house guests but now she had to wonder. What was he thinking about when he carved the pistachio nut crust rack of lamb or set a match to the Bombe Alaska? Her? *That* woman? While Steph was in the kitchen carefully inching the pudding out of its case, did he nip to the library to send a text to his mistress detailing how he wanted to inch down her pants with his teeth? Did he find their friends tedious? Did he think Steph's form of entertaining was a painful symptom of their settled existence?

Julian had not always been quite so indifferent to entertaining their friends. Before dinner parties (before kids) they used to throw wild parties which people anticipated for weeks in advance and talked about for months afterwards. At those parties Steph would weave amongst the guests, handing out canapés, topping up glasses, laughing at their jokes, and Julian would flay around on the rug that was making do as a dance floor. He loved dancing. He wasn't trained and was unlikely to ever find himself compared to Justin Timberlake but what he lost in expertise he made up for with enthusiasm.

Julian used to say that dancing was unadulterated fun, a pure extravagance. Not something to be self-conscious about, not something to even think about. For him it was all about instinct. He liked to throw his limbs and shake his head. He was often careless of the actual tune or rhythm but still he was admirable and mesmerising because his dancing exuded pure, unadulterated joy. He used to like to gyrate and whirl so madly, he'd often have a head rush. He used to dance until he had a sweaty body, hair

130

sticking to the back of his neck, sometimes he'd even whip off his T-shirt, bravely showing his squish-pack. The copious amount of alcohol they served at their parties definitely helped.

Steph was a fair dancer too, although her style was totally opposite to Julian's. She did not have the confidence to rely on her instincts and so she used to take classes to painstakingly learn steps and routines. She had always been guarded and considered. She danced because Julian asked her to, not because she enjoyed it. She'd been rather relieved when clubbing and loud parties became a thing of their past. Steph hadn't had to dance since—oh, when was it? she wondered. Her cousin Jenny's wedding reception, which was almost four years ago.

Looking at Julian now, Steph couldn't see the young man who used to dance until he was clammy. Did he miss it?

Oh God, did he go dancing with this other woman? The carb-loathing bitch was probably an awe-inspiringly cool dancer. She probably parted crowds with her sexy moves. They probably looked like Fred Astaire and Ginger Rogers. And everyone knew—it was universally agreed—that good dancers were always phenomenal in the sack. Steph was too numb to know what hurt her most, the thought of her husband shagging another woman (a fact she'd allowed to slosh around her head for some hours now) or this latest thought, the thought of her husband dancing with another woman. Falling in love with another woman.

Possibly the worst of it was the thought that she had not as yet dared examine.

She'd had chances too.

And she'd let them go.

Stephanie was aware that their evening meal was unusually quiet, so quiet she could hear the clock on the wall tick and her heart beat. It seemed some sort of cruel irony that her heart seemed so determined to pound on, drawing attention to the minutes slipping away. Hadn't she wasted enough time? Her heart and her head knew the answer to that question at a deep and terrifyingly profound level. Yes, she'd wasted enough time. Too much time. But what could she do about it? What were her choices? Was divorce a choice? She'd always said she'd rather Julian died than divorce her. She'd seen what a divorce could do to a woman, to a family. She thought of Pip and Chloe. The pain was gargantuan. It put her in mind of going to one of those space exhibitions that Harry was so fond of, one that tried to offer perspective about the size of planet earth in relation to the sun and then the size of the sun in relation to the galaxy. It was impossible to comprehend.

Julian didn't seem to notice the silence. The onus of conversation was never on him and it was disturbing and distressing to discover that her endless past efforts to chat, to be interesting, had probably been futile, he appeared to be happy enough to eat in silence. Julian exuded a sense of self-possession. He did not sift through his post, flick through gift catalogues or read newspapers at the dinner table, the way Stephanie was inclined to do, especially if she was eating alone. She liked to keep busy. She found it helpful. It stopped her thinking.

About him. About chances. Julian wasn't the only one with secrets.

132

Steph shot Julian another resentful glare. No doubt he was thinking about *her*. That's why he could dwell in an all-consuming silence. He'd allowed himself to think of his other woman. More than think—obviously. What a luxury. What an indulgence.

What a bastard.

Stephanie wondered whether she ought to tell him about Pip's triumph with Selfridges. She decided she would, if he asked. She could not be so ungenerous as to keep the information to herself, not if he showed any genuine interest in the outcome of the meeting. But as Steph stared at his head—dark blond hair that was brushed with grey now (rather fortunately giving the effect of expensive highlights), thinning at the temples, exposing a delicate scalp that had a small mole to the left of the crown—she doubted he *would* think to inquire.

Julian's blond scalp had long since been a worry to her. He was careless about wearing a hat on holiday and would sit for long periods of time beneath the blazing sun while she fussed that he'd scorch his head. She lived in dread of him, or the children, suffering from sun damage, or clogged arteries, or being involved in a ski accident. Julian called her Little Mrs Worrypants and his teasing encouraged the children to take up the nickname. It had long since occurred to Steph that their playful mocking was a little patronising. Julian and Harry (perhaps even Alfie) thought she was ludicrous to worry so much about applying suncream, eating antioxidants or avoiding double black diamond ski runs, and perhaps they were right. The most insidious threat had snuck up on

133

her without her realising and she'd been powerless to prevent it.

Could she have made a mistake? Steph clutched at burning straws. She thought back to the texts. Most of them were splattered on to her memory like a farmer brands his sheep, a red slash. There was no mistake. In one he'd said he was *dying* to see her, counting the seconds. In another he'd said he couldn't get through the day without her. He'd boasted that he'd had to go into the gents and 'sort himself out' because he was so horny thinking about her. Whoever she was.

The texts were gross. Ugly. Nasty.

Yet passionate. Yes, Stephanie had to admit that. They were passionate. She recognised that much, understood that much.

But there was no place for passion between a man and a woman who weren't married to one another if they were married to other people. It was wrong. It broke all the rules.

Stephanie looked at her husband. He had something green stuck between his two front teeth. She wouldn't tell him. It seemed that there was no place for passion between a man and a woman who were married to one another.

'I have one of my headaches coming on. I think I need an early night.' Her voice was not much above a whisper.

'Oh, OK.' Finally Julian lifted his head and met his wife's eyes as her admitting to discomfort was unusual. 'You look terrible.'

'Thanks. I'll sleep in the guest room so you don't disturb me when you come to bed.' She couldn't stand the idea of sleeping next to him. How had he slept next to her for all these months?

'Yes, OK. Sounds like a plan.'

Did it? Steph didn't think it was much of a plan. She had to come up with something more. She could hardly convince herself that serving her cruelly deceiving husband a microwave dinner was punishment enough for his infidelity.

Tuesday

CHAPTER ELEVEN

Pip woke up to the sound of birds chattering. They were not real ones, the sing-song came from an electronic recording on her alarm clock, but still, she embraced the illusion. She felt like a character in an animated Disney movie, one of the old ones—*Cinderella* or *Snow White*, someone like that. For a moment she relaxed and let the recorded bird chatter float around her bedroom, as she wondered exactly which character she most related to.

Cinderella, a pauper who is suddenly elevated beyond her wildest dreams? Yes, yes, possibly. By placing an order, the buyer at Selfridges had behaved as a fairy godmother with a magic wand. Or Snow White? Who was originally destined to great things, but then was cheated out of her birthright and had to endure years of suffering in the wilderness but was ultimately restored, reinstated and rewarded.

That one, Pip decided. She was Snow White.

She stretched her coltishly long limbs up and down the bed and began to hum. Sunlight slipped through the gap in the curtains and blossomed across her duvet. So, this is what being happy felt like. A song in her head, lightness in her body, all feelings of depression and oppression banished. Pip beamed and ran the words Selfridges, Robbie Donaldson, Selfridges, Robbie Donaldson through her head, pinned to the tune of 'Some Day My Prince Will Come'. Her bedroom door creaked open and Chloe scampered in. She expertly leapt over the piles of discarded clothes, open magazines and books, belts and bangles which Pip had abandoned on the floor (creating the impression that there were a series of drunken women passed out in Pip's bedroom) and jumped into bed in order to bestow and receive morning cuddles.

This was Pip's favourite part of the day, the part of the day when they had ten minutes when they had to answer to nothing and no one. A time when she could convince herself that clocks had stopped, a time when homework, chores, bills, even conversations did not have to have a meaning and the only thing that mattered was whether Chloe's feet were warm or cold against her shins and whether her daughter's kisses fell fluidly or had to be extracted. Both females felt like fireside cats, contentedly curled in one another's warmth.

Normally, Pip only relinquished these tender and amiable moments after she'd twice pushed the snooze button on her alarm, often Chloe grew impatient and broke free of Pip's hot, tight embraces and scampered into the kitchen to make a start on breakfast which forced Pip to drag herself, with great reluctance, out of bed and into her dressing gown.

But today Pip was alert and playful rather than anguished or pensive.

'Knock, knock,' said Pip.

Chloe instantly caught on and asked, 'Who's there?'

'Alfred.'

'Alfred who?'

'Alfred the needle if you sew.' Pip delivered the punchline knowing that the joke was lame but would be appreciated anyway.

140

'That's terrible!' groaned Chloe.

'Of course! OK, OK, how about this. Knock, knock.'

'Who's there?'

'Harold.'

'Harold who?'

'I'm thirty-eight. Harold are you?'

'That's quite good,' admitted Chloe with some seriousness. 'Have you any more?'

More. More. Pip scrabbled around her head for some more jokes. 'Knock, knock.'

'Who's there?'

'Winnie Thup.'

'Winnie Thup who?'

'And Tigger too!'

While Chloe was groaning and laughing, Pip threw back the duvet and announced, 'How about I make us pancakes for breakfast?'

'Really?' Chloe paused, it was clear that she was wondering how to tactfully respond. After some moments, she carefully replied, 'We could have two bowls of Crunchy Nut Cornflakes instead of one. That would be a treat.'

Pip understood her daughter's response and felt a flush of guilt surge through her body. Chloe was enjoying her mum's unusually buoyant mood but experience had shown her that any interaction between her mother and cooking utensils, however brief, would almost certainly bring an abrupt halt to the festive mood. It was likely, almost inevitable, that the pancakes would stick to the pan, or Pip would drop an egg on the floor, or she'd lose track of the time and they'd arrive late at the school gate. Chloe probably didn't want to admit that she doubted her mother's ability to make pancakes *and*

141

remain cheerful as that would certainly ruin the atmosphere within an instant.

Pip felt ashamed that no doubt Chloe was thinking of all the occasions when she'd insisted on making birthday cakes but burnt them because she was tired or distracted, or maybe Chloe was thinking about the times when Pip insisted they had to go on a picnic and had dragged them both up the Surrey Downs, lugging an enormous, delicious and nutritionally balanced picnic, only still to be found lacking because she'd forgotten the rug or drinks or something else imperative. These failures would leave Pip fighting tears while her young daughter insisted that, 'It doesn't matter. We're having a good time, aren't we? Mummy isn't a stupid, not at all.'

Yes, Pip was often guilty of trying too hard and being bitterly and obviously disappointed when her attempts at providing the perfect childhood ended in anything less than perfection. She put herself under too much pressure and Chloe, not yet nine, had already recognised as much and tried to protect her mother from her own failings. It wasn't as it should be. Things often hadn't been as they should be for them, thought Pip. But now they were as they should be or, at least, they might be. There was a shot, a chance, an opportunity at least and Pip wasn't going to blow it.

'Good plan!' she agreed and she resisted commenting that the risk of her mucking up pouring cereal was significantly less than her mucking up preparing pancakes. If she'd done so then Chloe would have been forced into uttering reassurances.

Over the Crunchy Nut Cornflakes Pip

optimistically promised that her sunny outlook was going to last *for ever*, and that they would *always* be happy.

'Doubt it,' commented Chloe in a matter-of-fact fashion.

'Why do you say that?' asked Pip aghast.

'Well, *for ever* is a really, really, really long time,' pointed out Chloe. Pip watched as the end of her daughter's hair trailed into the bowl of cereal, Chloe followed her mother's gaze and then tucked the milk-soaked strands behind her ear. 'I sometimes promise my best friends that I'll love them for ever and I've told my worst enemies that I'll hate them for ever but I always forget and either fall out or make up before for ever has anywhere near happened.'

Pip smiled at her amazing daughter; she knew this was true. Sometimes it was the same person at the other end of Chloe's pledge and all the promising might take place in one day but be forgotten by the time Chloe settled down to tea and CBBC. For ever was a long time. How come her eight year old was wiser than she was? wondered Pip.

'And no one is always happy, Mummy. I don't think that's possible,' added Chloe with a calm acceptance that Pip envied.

The promise of eternal happiness and optimism was just the sort of thing that Pip said, which only Pip believed, and therefore only Pip was ever disappointed when the promise proved impossible to keep.

Even so, Chloe was no doubt delighted that Pip's relaxed and jaunty disposition lasted at least until she was dropped off at the school gate and looked set to last all day. Her upbeat mood meant that Pip made an effort not to fall into bleak self-criticism when they reached the school gate and realised that they'd forgotten Chloe's swimming kit. Chloe looked relieved that she didn't have to listen to her mum calling herself stupid as usual. Pip suddenly understood that no doubt it was annoying and embarrassing enough that Chloe had to regularly wear one of the costumes from the lost and found box (baggy and worn thin so that people could see the colour of her flesh on the shoulder strap, a pity when Chloe had a lovely lilac bathing costume, with a deep scoop back and a red cherry print) but the situation was clearly made worse if Chloe had to listen to her mother go on and on and on about how hopeless she was and Chloe had to say over and over and over again how it didn't matter. Pip knew that despite Chloe's assurances, sometimes it did matter. Today Pip was determined that she would not allow the role-reversal where her child had to prop her up.

'I'll have time to go home for it and then bring it back. I'll leave the bag on your peg. We don't even have to tell Miss Fletcher,' she said simply.

After Pip had briskly walked to Chloe's school for the second time that morning and had stealthily delivered the forgotten swimming kit to the correct peg, she still felt the rare but robust sense of wellbeing and satisfaction. It was a windy day and the fat, pearlescent clouds raced across the pale blue as she dashed through the busy streets; her jacket flew open and fluttered around her in an energetic way. She felt full to the brim with possibility and excitement.

The door of her flat slammed behind her and

the flap on the letter box rattled noisily. Often, returning home to her flat conjured up a vague sense of dissatisfaction. Sometimes, no matter how much she tried to, it was hard to think of the tiny rooms as cosy and the fraying wallpaper as shabby chic. Sometimes, she couldn't help but long for the space and light that were abundant at Dylan's live/work 'space' (as he'd liked to call his apartment in Clerkenwell). Sometimes she did miss London. She never said as much to anyone, certainly not Steph. It would seem ungrateful; after all, Steph had been so wonderful, so resilient and so practical when she searched for a flat for Pip.

When Dylan had given her no alternative, she had only one place to go—Steph's. Pip hated to think of that time. That bleak and desolate time of her life when her heart ached, her dreams snapped and her future vanished. Pip and Chloe stayed with Steph, Julian and the boys for a couple of months and then, when it became obvious that they would need somewhere permanent to live, it seemed logical to pick somewhere close to Steph and her family, Pip's main support. Of course, Steph had been absolutely right, the schools were lovely around here and the cost of living so much more manageable compared to London. As Pip was without a regular income, this was an overwhelming factor. The high street was exceptionally pretty and always bustling; still, she occasionally longed for London and all its giddy promise. It made sense to move out here to Riverford. But why was it that the sensible option was always the most likely to be the dull option?

Pip's flat was modest, two small bedrooms, a sitting room, bathroom and kitchen. Five rooms in total. Steph had fifteen rooms, if you included the downstairs loo. Sixteen if you counted the conservatory separate from the dining room. Three times as many. Was that fair? Pip often wondered but tried not to obsess whether it was or wasn't. It was a ridiculous thing to care about. It was silly to compare; just because they'd grown up in the same area and had gone to the same school, there was no reason to expect that they'd end up living in similar sized homes. Or have similar sized families.

Or have a husband each.

Life didn't work like that. Pip never found herself wondering how much space the Queen had at Buckingham Palace, although she must have masses, so why compare herself to Steph?

Pip was pleased that today the kitchen did not strike her as grubby and neglected, instead she saw a thriving hub of activity. The kitchen was the largest of the five rooms in Pip's flat. It was big enough to fit a substantial dining-room table into the centre. Pip had found the dining-room table in a house clearance warehouse years ago, when she poked around such places through curiosity rather than necessity. It sat six comfortably and eight if needs be. Pip had bought the table and had it delivered to Dylan's where she'd lovingly stripped back the varnish and then daringly stained the table a deep plum colour. She and Dylan and their friends had often sat around the table, laughing, eating, and drinking. Chloe's highchair had been drawn up to the table and there she'd made handprint pictures, rolled pastry in a cloud of flour, modelled play dough and painstakingly started to drag a pencil across a page in order to form letters.

Pip had been relieved to find the table in the lock-up when she and Chloe were evicted from Dylan's. Her only stipulation when she was looking for somewhere for them to live was that she could fit the table into one of the rooms. She cared about this more than she cared about whether there was a washing machine or how far she'd have to walk to the train station. Stephanie had talked to so many letting agents. She'd explained that even if the room were large enough, if it was on the fourth floor and the table couldn't fit through a window or up the stairs, then the flat simply wasn't suitable—no matter how reasonable the rent was. Pip thought she might have exasperated Steph on occasion during the flat hunt but if she had, Steph had never given into petty irritation and actually said so.

The table was now ensconced in the kitchen. It dominated to the point of impracticality but Pip did not care. A long time ago she'd harboured visions of her family growing up around this table, one baby popping up after another, until all the seats were occupied. She'd thought that they would eat, struggle, squabble, chatter and laugh around the table, as they played with Lego and refused their peas. Things hadn't turned out that way, there was just Chloe and her—a little amputee family—but still, she could at least hold on to the precious memories that had already been created around it and they could make more. True, there wouldn't be any squabbling siblings but there would still be Lego models and rejected vegetables.

Pip's sewing machine was pushed to the far end

of the much-loved table. It was near the window so that she could benefit from any natural light and almost hidden in amongst the reels of cotton and fabric offcuts that gathered on the table. Pip loved sitting down in front of her sewing machine, sewing lulled her, the way aromatherapy or certain pieces of classical music relaxed other people.

She took pleasure in selecting the most suitable colour thread, sometimes a match, sometimes a contrast. She saw nuances in scarlet, crimson, cherry and ruby, where other people might only see red. She enjoyed the preparation of carefully threading her machine, readying it for action, for *creation*.

She liked the checks and balances that placed her in control of her craft and she was meticulously careful in adjusting the needle position, stitch length and width before she finally held the thread with her left hand and turned the hand wheel with her right. She loved placing her foot on the peddle and creating a whirl or hum depending on the force she exerted. The ritual always brought her joy and today it brought her a long-lacking sense of purpose too. The things she was about to create were wanted in a London store.

Pip was so engrossed in her craft that she almost failed to notice the phone ringing. She stood up, hunted around for her mobile and eventually found it between a box of tea bags and a carton of orange juice.

'Hello, Pippa. It's Robbie here.'

Pip practically dropped the phone. He'd rung! So soon! She glanced at the kitchen clock, only twenty hours after they'd last spoken.

'Hi,' she mumbled.

'I just wondered whether you'd had a chance to fix up a sitter yet?' he said matter-of-factly, as though this was a normal thing to wonder, perfectly average, whereas Pip was certain that his wondering about such a thing was a miracle, a sensation. His tone ought to reflect that.

'Erm, no, well, yes. Maybe.'

'Which is it?' Robbie asked, he sounded amused rather than fazed by her uncertainty.

'I'm waiting for confirmation,' added Pip with more clarity. She was aware that her knees were shaking. They were actually wobbling as though she was in a cartoon. Quickly, she flopped into one of the kitchen chairs.

She'd called Steph the moment she got off the train yesterday, before she'd even passed through the ticket barrier, but Steph hadn't picked up. Pip had called twice since and had finally been forced to leave a message asking Steph to call back. She didn't want to give too much away on the voicemail, so she hadn't said that she needed a sitter because she'd been asked on a date. That sort of news was reserved for direct conversation only! Pip was looking forward to seeing Steph's jubilant reaction.

'I had a look at what's on at the movies. There's a crime slash action thriller, a costume drama, some romcom starring Anna Friel, or how do you feel about vampires?'

Robbie started to read out the blurbs attached to each film. Pip was aware of the vampire craze that had started a couple of years ago but hadn't seen any of the movies or read the books and she hadn't heard of any of the other films, she didn't so much as recognise the actors' names. She'd stopped taking notice of that sort of stuff quite some time ago. When exactly? Chloe was eight now. Before she'd been born Pip had loved going to the cinema, it wasn't Dylan's thing.

'Kristen Stewart is so very un-Hollywood, don't you think? Which makes her success all the more striking.'

'Kristen Stewart? I don't think I know her,' Pip replied honestly.

'You must know her. Dark hair, frail-looking. Born for the part.'

'Not ringing any bells,' admitted Pip.

'She was in *Panic Room* with Jodie Foster. As a child actor,' added Robbie, which suggested he had some idea that Pip hadn't mooched out of her house since Noah was taking woodwork classes.

'No.' Of course she knew who Jodie Foster was although the last thing she saw her in was *Bugsy Malone*, at Christmas, on TV. Jodie Foster was a child actor in that.

Pip would usually have been very embarrassed at this point in a conversation. Often when she chatted to mums at the school gate she pretended that she was aware of the latest TV drama or news issue or heart-throb that was grabbing the headlines, she didn't let on that all her cultural references started with CBBC and finished with the Disney channel. She might as well have worn a hat saying, 'out of touch', or worse, 'opted out'. Not so much a huge D for dunce, the way disobedient kids used to have to wear in schools of long ago, but more likely a great big L for 'Loser' or more accurately 'Lost'. But, with Robbie, Pip felt that it would be OK to say, 'I haven't been to the movies for an absolute age. My ex didn't like

150

the cinema. He hated the sound of people eating, so the popcorn crunching really got to him.'

Robbie started to laugh.

Pip was initially a little taken aback. 'What?'

'He hated the sound of people crunching popcorn?' Robbie asked, not bothering to hide his amused disbelief. 'And for this reason you've never seen *Avatar* or *Lord of the Rings* or *Slumdog Millionaire* or even *Mamma Mia*?'

'I did see *Mamma Mia*. My friend, Steph, bought me the DVD.' Pip felt comfortable with him. Relaxed, frank. 'And slurping drinks.' She giggled as she thought about it now. 'He really couldn't bear slurping drinks. He wasn't that keen on any bodily function actually. Sort of squeamish. A bit of a prissy prig, Steph says.'

Pip wondered, not for the first time, whether Dylan used to wash his hands after he'd had sex with his mistresses the way he always did with her. It was something only Stephanie knew. Dylan had womanised, criticised, lied and disappeared but the thing that had been the cruellest, the hardest to understand, the most humiliating was that after sex he always washed his hands and brushed his teeth. If there was time and he wasn't too tired, he'd shower too. As though she was dirty. Pip longed to curl her body around his or have him hold her tightly but the moment he came he slipped from her and washed her away. Every time. Over a period of years, he'd washed her away until all they had went down the plughole.

As though reading her mind, Robbie let out a low whistle of disbelief and murmured, 'The man must have been insane. How could he have been married to you and remained prissy? You're the sort of woman that makes men grateful they have primeval urges.'

'What do you mean, like howling and thumping your chest?' Pip was pretty sure this wasn't what Robbie meant but she wanted to make him spell it out. It had been a long time since she'd been certain she'd made a man feel hot and bothered in the right way. Infuriating traffic wardens didn't count.

'I mean something more animal than that.' His voice cracked a bit under the weight of the confession.

Pip was suddenly aware of his humanity, his manliness and boyishness all mixed together. It seemed as though he was a little nervous; that he was wondering, was his hint a bit much, too early? Pip started to smile to herself, the smile grew to a huge beam that was so wide her face was in danger of splitting. All at once, Pip no longer felt relaxed and comfortable with Robbie, suddenly she felt wildly, delightfully excited. He liked her. Like *liked* her. In a lusty, healthy, thrilling way.

'I fancy the romcom,' she said.

'Great.'

So this is it, she thought, this is what it's like to rejoin the human race.

It's good to be back.

CHAPTER TWELVE

Mrs Evans always rang the doorbell when she came to babysit the Blake children. She did have her own key, which she used to let herself in on

Mondays and Thursdays when she came to do the cleaning, but she never let herself in in the evenings. She thought it was overstepping some or other invisible boundary, so she always rang the bell to announce her arrival. When Steph answered the door, Mrs Evans thought she must have made a mistake, she'd obviously come on the wrong evening. Far from her usual immaculately turned-out self, Mrs Blake looked—well—frankly, terrible. She was wearing the same skirt and top as she'd had on yesterday. Had she slept in it? It was creased enough to make you think so. She wasn't wearing even a lick of mascara and she hadn't pulled a comb through her hair, that much was certain. In summary, Mrs Evans thought Mrs Blake looked a right bloody mess.

Stephanie held the door wide open and mustered something approaching a smile. It didn't reach her eyes. It was a fragile, unconvincing sort of smile, quite like the type Mrs Evans dredged up for her daughter-in-law whenever she visited, polite but not heartfelt.

'Come in, Mrs Evans. The boys are watching TV.'

'Am I early?'

'No.'

Stephanie watched as Mrs Evans' gaze fell on her grubby top and, like some sort of homing missile, lock on to the tomato ketchup stain. Steph sighed. She should have changed. She supposed she would have to now, not that Pip would notice the stain or, even if she did, she would not care about it one way or the other, but Mrs Evans clearly expected more from her employer. Did she have the energy to change her clothes? Steph

153

didn't know. The very idea was overwhelming. She'd have to make a selection, lift her arms and perhaps even fasten buttons. These simple tasks seemed insurmountable.

Unsurprisingly, Steph had not slept last night. She had heard Julian retreat to the library at about nine thirty. She'd dashed out of bed and stood on the landing, straining to hear whether or not he made a telephone call. He hadn't, not on this occasion, but Steph could recall many, many times when he'd excused himself from dinner parties, family lunches and evening TV viewing with the excuse that he had to make or take a work call. She'd always felt sorry for him for having to work so hard and so proud of him, as she believed he must have a round-the-clock influence and be very important in the office. Now she felt ridiculous. He hadn't been brokering deals, making an impact on the nation's gross domestic product or even reordering stationery, more likely he was whispering with his mistress or perhaps calling Highview to check that the champagne was on ice. Bastard.

At ten minutes to midnight Stephanie had heard Julian go to bed. She'd listened to the buzz of his electric toothbrush as he cleaned his teeth, she'd heard him gargle and pee. She knew his routine so well that she could count the moments it would take between him switching off the bathroom light, walking to the bed, checking that the alarm was set for the next morning and then, finally, switching off his bedside table lamp. She had counted the seconds and listened as his feet fell in a predictable beat. She knew that he would throw one pillow on to the floor and knead the other into the shape he

154

preferred. He'd turn on to his right side. He'd fall asleep almost the instant his head hit the pillow, as though he was a man with a clear conscience. As this certainly wasn't the case, she wondered whether he had a conscience at all. He would snore, very gently. She knew his routines so well but she didn't know him at all, apparently.

Even though it was after midnight and even though Stephanie had never felt so weary in her life, sleep had eluded her. She'd lain alone in the spare bed listening to the sounds of the house and wondering what she'd done wrong. All she'd ever wanted was to do the right thing. So where had she gone wrong and was there anything, anything at all, she could do to fix this? If only she'd had some warning, some clue that their marriage was a farce, but she hadn't had any clue at all.

Something shivered and shifted inside Steph's stomach. Was she being honest with herself? A huge feeling of self-doubt, an acknowledgement that she was self-deceiving, sloshed through her system. No, she was not being absolutely honest with herself.

The truth was that for months now she'd been putting all her effort and energy into *appearing* perfectly happy but of course she knew that wasn't the same thing. Every day, she'd *told* herself she was perfectly happy. She was so *lucky*. She had everything every woman wanted, didn't she? Or at least, she'd thought she had (although retrospectively she could see that no wife wanted a faithless bastard of a husband). But before she knew about Julian's affair—before yesterday— she'd thought she was so lucky and lucky was right next door to happy, wasn't it? Because if you

155

weren't perfectly happy when you were so lucky, then you were simply ungrateful and Steph never wanted to be ungrateful.

So she had reasoned.

Over and over again.

But last night Steph had forced herself to think harder about the matter. She'd considered the phrase 'perfectly happy'. Was anyone really perfectly happy? Did perfect happiness exist? Reluctantly she admitted that no, she thought not. Rallying, she told herself that she had, at least, been perfectly content. She chose not to think about the times when she'd felt a little bored and frustrated. She told herself it was a marvellous thing to always be the wind beneath everyone else's wings (although truthfully she hated that expression since it had been immortalised in a song). But she was content to support, someone had to, everyone couldn't be the lead role. Content. Yes. That was good, wasn't it? Good enough? She'd thought so.

Again, she paused.

Truthfully, she hadn't been content for quite a while now. She'd *tried* to be, she'd *wanted* to be, she'd told herself that she was. But she was *not*.

Not since the tenth of May last year.

Yes, she could name the exact date when her contentment had flown out of the window. Only, she hadn't accepted it to be the case. She hadn't wanted it to be the case. For the hundredth time Stephanie lay awake, stared at the ceiling and catalogued the 'if onlys' that might have preserved her contentment, if only one of them had been an actuality.

Quite obviously there were the 'if onlys' that

every betrayed wife clung to. If only she could turn the clock back twenty-four hours. If only she hadn't found the phone or listened to the message or read the texts. If only she didn't *know*.

Steph had listened to the occasional car sweep along the road outside, sometimes she'd caught snippets of tunes from late-night radio as the drivers often had their windows down, hoping the combination of fresh air and loud music would keep them alert at the wheel. She'd listened to the trees in the garden sway and shudder in the robust spring wind and she'd heard an owl hoot its objection to being blown about. Only once the house fell utterly silent, and Stephanie had been absolutely certain that her sons and Julian were fast asleep, did she give in to her pain which was somewhere deep and dark, it had been buried like a dead body under six foot of dirty ground. But now it was legitimate, now she was entitled to bay, howl and wail like an animal, like a beast—wild, rough and unfettered. She felt nothing like a civilised human being. It had taken every iota of self-discipline for her to push her face into the pillow so that her fierce anger, her ugly and loud sobs, wouldn't wake her boys.

Somehow she'd got up this morning and taken the boys to school but then she'd returned home to bed and spent the rest of the day hidden under the duvet in the spare room, sobbing some more. It was as though now she'd started, she really couldn't stop. She cried until her wailing gave her a headache and then on past that, until she was so dehydrated her tears ceased but her body still shook and she was left with a throbbing head and a hoarse voice. She thought it was a miracle that she

157

had a voice at all considering the strain she'd placed on it with baying and then she wondered, what was the point of her voice anyway? What was the use of it? She could say the only thing that mattered. The only thing she thought.

Her life was a sham.

Because there were other 'if onlys'. Deeper, perhaps even bleaker ones. The other 'if onlys' were connected to missed opportunities, wasted months and her self-sacrifice that she had regarded as her self-discipline and now she wasn't so sure. The 'if onlys' that were connected to her secret.

Subhash Sharma.

Since last May, Steph had often lain awake thinking about the 'if onlys' that might have preserved her contentment. If only she had chosen a different coffee shop that particular morning. Or, if he had. If only she hadn't been in such a hurry and they hadn't actually collided. If only he hadn't cared that he'd spilt his cappuccino over the dry-cleaning she was carrying, if he'd just flung an insincere sorry her way and continued dashing out of the café. But he had cared. He'd immediately reached for his wallet and pulled out a crisp £50 note, insisting that he must pay for her coat and Julian's suit to be cleaned all over again. She remembered being slightly surprised by the £50 note, she hadn't seen many before, people rarely carried them. His ready and sincere apology and the unstinting nature of his offer had impressed her, although she couldn't possibly have taken the money, it was far too much. If only she had, then maybe he wouldn't have insisted that he had to buy her coffee and a slice of cake by way of making amends. If only she had accepted the newspaper

158

he offered her, then maybe he wouldn't have stayed with her as she ate and drank his apology. But she hadn't accepted it.

'Would you like a look at the newspaper?' He'd held out his copy of the *Guardian*, it was tightly folded into a manageable rectangle. She stared at his dark brown hands and noticed how clean and neat his nails were, it looked as if he was balancing creamy pearls on the tips of his fingers. Stephanie had shaken her head.

'Oh, no. I never read newspapers. They're so full of terrible news. There's never anything jolly in them at all. I liked it in the old days, do you remember? There used to be articles about the construction of marvellous buildings and no one ever felt the need to point out how over-budget the project might be or how much longer than originally planned the construction had taken. And after the main news on the television they'd have a slot about talking dogs or featuring the Queen Mum opening a car factory. Not that anyone opens car factories nowadays. It's all closures. That's why I don't read newspapers or watch the news. The Queen Mother is dead, of course, and everything is closing.'

Stephanie stopped talking. Finally. What had possessed her to blether on for so long to a complete stranger? She'd blushed because she knew she sounded idiotic. More idiotic, it ought to be noted, than she was in fact. Because Stephanie was a woman who had considered and careful views about many interesting issues (youths carrying knives, teachers' pay, tax bands, and support of single parents), but this man was dashingly handsome and she always found she was rather hopeless around men who were too good-looking. His eyes, big brown lakes of wisdom, were show-stopping.

If only he'd had a squint or a nervous tic.

These had been her bedtime thoughts for months. She'd thought that the problem was that she'd met Subhash Sharma. Now she thought, if only he was my lover. If he were, I would not feel so obliterated, so humiliated. If only.

Focus, focus! Stephanie dragged herself back to the here and now. She rummaged in her wardrobe and pulled out a black roll-neck jumper that might appease Mrs Evans. She'd bought this jumper hoping that it would somehow transform her into Audrey Hepburn as she had looked in the old movie *Funny Face*, sophisticated, modish, elegant and chic. An impossible desire. For a start Steph had size 36C boobs (which were more flab than breast) and, well, a normal face and a normal everything else for that matter. No woman could ever be Audrey Hepburn, the angels broke the mould after she'd been born. Steph knew this but it never stopped her (and just about every other woman on the planet) trying to be a little more Audrey-esque at some moment or other.

Steph stared at the roll-neck with resentment. In that moment it seemed to represent another broken promise, another unrealised dream. She was not and never would be Audrey Hepburn. Steph felt tears threaten again. It wouldn't do, it was exhausting. With a long sigh, Steph dug about in the depths of her consciousness and mental resources for her more practical self—she needed that Steph to re-emerge. The jumper would keep her warm and since yesterday she'd felt miserably chilled, the heat had been well and truly snuffed out of her. She pulled it on and dashed down the stairs. She had to get to Pip's. She'd wanted to call Pip all day but with a Herculean strength she'd held off. She knew that Pip had to whip up some more samples for Selfridges and if she'd knocked on Pip's door this morning the samples would never have been completed. Pip was easily distracted by a drama on TV, this would wipe her out. But now Steph could go to Pip with a clear conscience, by now Pip would have completed the work she needed to get done. She had to get to Pip. It would stop her doing something stupid. It was her best chance at remaining sane.

CHAPTER THIRTEEN

Stephanie handed over the bottle of champagne to Pip but she couldn't manage a smile. It was a miracle that she'd remembered the gift at all and she wouldn't have, except Mrs Evans had run out of their house and almost thrown herself under the car in an effort to flag down Steph, just as she'd been pulling away.

'You can't turn up to your friend's for a celebration without the bubbles,' Mrs Evans had admonished.

Stephanie took the bottle and mumbled her thanks and something about losing her head if it wasn't screwed on. This wasn't true, Stephanie was generally the most organised of women but it didn't matter—people rarely expected to hear the truth, they just expected to hear something or other. Steph then automatically reiterated the carefully negotiated bedtimes to Mrs Evans (although she knew Mrs Evans would ignore her instructions, as she was far more interested in having the children's company and favour than she was in worrying about how tired they might be in the morning) and then Steph had pulled out of her driveway and driven across town to Pip's home.

The large detached houses in lush grounds, adorned with pretty flowers and the occasional swimming pool, began to shrink and huddle and all signs of green had disappeared by the time Steph pulled up outside Pip's 1970s flat. There was no driveway. Usually Stephanie was concerned about parking in the street, nervous that kids, rich on resentment but poor on resources, would be unable to resist scraping a key along the door panel. Frankly, today she didn't give a toss.

Pip was far too high on her own success to notice Steph's bleak mood. She squealed in delight at the Bolly.

'Is it chilled?'

Steph didn't answer. She didn't know. She couldn't remember if she'd put the bottle in the fridge or not. Pip patted the bottle and was surprised to find that it wasn't chilled, it was unlike Stephanie not to pay attention to that sort of detail. A little disappointed, Pip internally debated whether they should drink the champers now, at room temperature, or whether she should bang it in the freezer for ten minutes. That might do it. But could she wait? She wanted to celebrate *now*. It had been an age since she'd felt this happy. No, she couldn't wait, she decided to dig out some ice cubes and sling them into the glasses. OK, some might say that it was a waste of Bolly to serve it warm with ice but Pip didn't care. She opened the bottle to a discreet pop and started to chatter.

'Are you happy to stay in the kitchen? Then we can chat freely. Chloe is watching *Wizards of Waverly Place* in the sitting room and you know the rule, no talking when Selena Gomez is in the house. Although do nip in and give her a kiss, she's been so excited that you were coming round, even though she saw you yesterday and the day before that!'

Stephanie was Chloe's godmother and generally she was a conscientious and loving one. She adored Chloe like a fourth child, the daughter she didn't have. She knew that Chloe's favourite colour was lilac, that she had a small birth mark on the base of her back, she knew that Hama beads were out and braiding was in (this week, although a new hobby would dominate next), she knew the name of Chloe's schoolteacher (Miss Fletcher) and that the word sponge made her giggle. But this evening Steph dreaded the thought of making small talk to Chloe about hair accessories, and who was this Selena Gomez? A new kid at school? Had Chloe made a new friend? Steph did not care.

Not noticing Steph's pallid colour or unusual reticence, Pip carried on chatting excitedly. 'Thank you so much for taking Chloe to school yesterday. Imagine if you couldn't have managed it and I'd missed the train! I really am going to have to get more organised. If this takes off, the way the people at Selfridges think it might, I won't be able to be so slapdash. I can't always depend on you being my failsafe back up.'

'No, you can't,' muttered Steph gloomily.

Pip was taken aback. She'd made the comment thoughtlessly. If asked to consider her situation Pip would have admitted that she didn't mean what she'd just said and in fact she *did* believe that she could always depend on Stephanie being her failsafe back-up. She had been for thirty years, after all. Steph's response was unexpected and unwelcome. Pip continued to pour crisps into a bowl, the ones from Selfridges food hall, the ones Steph always served; her favourite. Perhaps Steph was having one of her migraines. She was always a bit of a grumpy bugger when she had a migraine, but she was too much of a martyr to simply go to bed in a darkened room, she liked to soldier on (and to make everyone suffer). Pip decided to ignore her friend's grouchy mood. She was too happy to be brought down and, besides, she didn't for a moment believe Steph. Of course she could depend on Steph, she'd said as much just yesterday and on countless other occasions before then. Steph practically encouraged her dependency, she enjoyed being needed.

Pip placed the crisps on the table but didn't take a seat because Steph was still standing and wearing her coat. Usually, she flung her coat to one side the moment she was in the house and she pulled up a chair without asking or waiting to be asked. Why the formality?

'I am so excited! I don't know where to begin! I think my luck is changing, *finally*. OK, are you ready for this? Besides the order from Selfridges, and I'm going to tell you all about that in detail soon . . . but that's not all. Guess what?' Steph didn't guess. Not really needing to be encouraged, Pip continued, 'I've met a man! A lovely man. A nurse. A fertility nurse actually.' Pip rolled the words and her eyes around the room. 'That's taking a bit of getting used to, if I'm honest, but he's so nice! He's asked me on a date. This Friday. *A Friday date.*'

Pip paused. The importance of a Friday date could not be underestimated; it showed a commitment and intent that a Tuesday or Wednesday date lacked. Of course, it might just be that Robbie's shifts at the hospital only accommodated a Friday date, but still! There must be a dozen things a man like Robbie could do on a Friday. He could meet his friends for a drink or he could visit his sister and her family, he'd talked about them quite a lot today, on the phone. It was obvious that he was really close to them which was a good thing because, while Pip knew the danger of projecting, she did think it was a good sign if a man had a decent relationship with his family, it showed an ability to commit. Or, and this was the scary one, he could choose to see another woman on a Friday night. But no, he'd chosen to invite her on a date.

'We've been on the phone to one another most of today. I haven't done a stitch of work. Literally!'

'You haven't finished the sample?' Steph could not disguise her distress. She hadn't called Pip because she'd thought Pip needed to be busy but Pip hadn't been getting down to it, at least not to work! Steph glared at her friend.

Pip smiled. 'Don't worry. I called them. I said I'd finish it by tomorrow.'

'Do you ever learn?' snapped Steph.

Pip didn't register her friend's anger or anxiety. 'So can you have Chloe? Is it too much? If you're

165

busy I can arrange for her to have a sleepover at a friend's. Not that I'm suggesting I'll sleep with him that first night,' Pip shrugged and then admitted, 'although I probably will, I always used to. I'm pretty certain sex is still fashionable.'

Still Steph didn't say a word about the fertility nurse. She stood like a statue, polluting Pip's cheerful kitchen with her horror and misery.

'Didn't you hear me? I have a date! My love life has been like the Gobi desert for years and I'm telling you I've been asked on a date, why aren't you whooping?' asked Pip, giggling.

'Because Julian is having an affair,' Steph replied.

CHAPTER FOURTEEN

'What?' The silence between them was sudden and sturdy. Pip could hear her own heart, Steph's laboured breathing and the jolly chatter from the Disney channel that was drifting through from the living room, but had she correctly heard what Steph had just said? No, she had misheard. She must have.

'An affair. Julian is having an affair,' Steph repeated for clarity.

'There must be some mistake.'

'No mistake.'

'But, but he can't be. Not Julian. He's . . . he's nice. He's . . . he's Julian,' Pip stuttered.

If Stephanie could get her heart to behave in the way that it always had—with feeling—she might have felt sorry for Pip. Pip looked stunned,

166

shattered, almost as confused as Steph herself felt. But Steph couldn't feel a thing. She was numb.

'What makes you think so?' asked Pip, whose first instinct was not to believe the charge, not for a moment. There had to be some sort of mix-up or misguided gossip, there had to be an explanation. Pip's experience of unfaithful men was extensive and that's what made her so sure that Julian wasn't having an affair. He wasn't the type to do anything so destructive, so thoughtless and selfish.

So pathetic.

Secretly, over the years, Pip had occasionally thought that Julian was the sort of man she ought to have married. He used to be dashing (although nowadays he was more likely to be described as dignified). He earned a fortune. It was impossible not to be just the tiniest bit envious of Steph's walk-in wardrobe and her en-suite bathroom. Of course, he was not the sort of man Pip could have ever married because he was not the sort of man she ever dated. Julian was sensible (in her less generous moments, if she'd had a glass too many, she might admit she thought he was bordering on the dull side). More positively she'd openly declare that he was ambitious, considerate and that he had an impressive game plan (something none of the men she'd ever dated could be accused of). A game plan he followed to the letter, in order to better his life and the lives of his loved ones. A mistress couldn't be part of a game plan, could she? In the final summation, Julian was respectable.

Pip had never dated respectable men, men who could play golf or had attended schools where the teams were called 'houses' and the terms were called Michaelmas, Lent and Trinity. She'd tended to date working-class boys who had made good. She always said she admired their tenacity, which was true, but the pertinent fact was that she was also wildly attracted to their dangerous, unpredictable, unconventional side. But she'd blundered with Dylan, she'd swum in waters too deep. He wasn't a working-class guy made good, proud of his roots and empathetic to the struggles of others because of it. He was a shallow, pretentious wanker.

Wow, it felt good saying that. It had taken a while. Years. The truth was, Dylan wasn't even called Dylan, even his name was a fake. He was born and baptised common or garden, good old-fashioned Ian. He'd changed his name by deed poll. He said it was to add a certain distinction, a certain class, which he clearly felt he lacked. Well, it would take more than erasing the details on the birth certificate to lend that man class. He was a horrid snob around other state school-educated people. He was cringingly lick-ass towards people he thought could help him in any way. Sometimes, in her bleaker moments, Pip wondered whether Dylan was ever attracted to her or whether he just wanted access to Julian and all of Julian's colleagues. She'd thought that his willingness to mix with her best friend and her best friend's family was a tribute to how much Dylan cared about her, but was it? Julian was a very powerful man and a generous one. He had opened up his contact book to Dylan. He'd arranged for him to be interviewed at the bank. He'd helped Dylan find a rung on the ladder. Dylan had first got a position in the bank's marketing department but soon left and went to work for the competition. He hopped around from job to job, as he did from bed to bed. Last she knew he was a fully-fledged consultant.

God, what was she doing thinking about Dylan at a time like this? This was Steph's crisis, not hers. She should be thinking about Julian, not Dylan. She had to pull herself together, she had to focus.

Pip grabbed the pile of magazines that were on the kitchen chair and tossed them carelessly on the table, where no doubt they would lie for several more weeks in amongst the rest of her clutter, library books, spools of thread, scraps of material, forgotten homework and the ketchup bottle. Carefully, she lowered her friend into the seat and then quickly pulled up another wooden chair which she slumped into. Pip handed Steph the glass of champagne. Neither of them thought to toast. Pip swallowed two large gulps and then guided Steph's glass to her lips, just the way she guided Calpol into Chloe's mouth when she had a fever.

'I found a phone in my car. There are texts to and from him.' Steph fished the nasty phone out of her bag and passed it to Pip. Pip took the offending item and started to read the messages. After a few moments of reading she turned so pale she was transparent, Steph thought she could see the picture hung on the wall behind her.

'Why do you think this phone is his? It might be someone else's.'

'Someone who has been in my car?' asked Steph sceptically.

'Julian might have given a colleague a lift. His colleague might be having an affair. This phone belongs to a friend of Julian's. It has to.'

Pip was desperate to reason away the evidence.

169

She wanted to believe in Julian's fidelity. She'd met countless faithless men in her time and it would be reasonable to expect that she'd be the first to condemn but throughout all her disappointments Pip had looked at Julian and seen some sort of beacon. He stood firm and tall like a lighthouse, guiding her to safer waters. Julian was proof that faithful, decent men were out there, somewhere. She just had to keep looking for one and stop crashing against the rocks. Julian had been so good to her during her splits from Philippe, Jacob, Tim and Andrew etc., and most importantly, throughout the aftermath of her split from Dylan. He might not have said much on these occasions but he'd listened and that had been a comfort at the time, the countless times. But what if Julian was a nasty bastard just like all the others? What then? What could she believe in?

'There's no chance of a mistake. There was a message from a hotel. I rang back. Mr Julian Blake has been staying there, every Tuesday night, for nearly three months,' said Steph flatly and firmly.

'Oh.' The bulb in the lighthouse flickered and then went out. There was no hope. Pip knew enough about Steph's family life to know that Julian was usually away from home on Tuesdays.

Somehow Steph had held the microscopic hope that Pip would be able to explain away this atrocity and defy the mountain of evidence against her husband. But Steph saw by the sad slouch that Pip thought the case was open and closed. Pip, the eternal romantic, the woman who once believed a boyfriend when he said the frilly, size eight panties in his laptop case were his—that he'd worn them at a fancy dress party—rather than think he might be

170

cheating, did not believe Julian was innocent.

Steph thought she might die. Just stop. Cease to be right now. It would be easier than carrying on, facing this. Instead, she chose a more conventional root, she began to sob again. Stephanie was not a crier by nature, except during her three pregnancies when her hormones turned her to mush and she was known to cry at adverts for cat litter if the kitten was cute enough. She lived her life on an even keel, rarely allowing indignation to bubble into rage, the way so many people did. It surprised everyone when she turned out to be a screamer during labour and now, she seemed to have tapped into somewhere in-between, something instinctual and primeval and terrible exploded from her. She howled. Between her howls she gulped out the impotent words that countless betrayed women had spilled before her. She called him an idiot, a cruel and two-timing, double-dealing, faithless bastard. She howled that she hated him. And that she loved him.

She had no idea which it was.

Chloe, who sadly was quite used to hysteria, stood up and moved to close the door between the kitchen and the living room so that her TV viewing would not be interrupted. She stopped in her tracks when she realised it was her Aunty Stephanie crying and not her mum. She stood in the doorway looking and feeling frail.

'It's OK, sweetheart,' said Pip. 'Aunty Stephanie has just banged her funny bone. You know how that hurts.'

'Yes, there's nothing funny about it at all,' said Chloe, immediately relieved and only too happy to accept her mother's spurious explanation.

171

'Give me a kiss and then hop off to bed, I'll be through in a moment to tuck you in and turn out the light.'

Chloe was a noticeably obedient child, especially in this instance—a kitchen with a weeping adult held no allure.

As soon as her daughter was out of earshot, Pip asked, 'Have you spoken to him?'

'I confirmed that he's planning on being away tonight. He said he was going to be late, probably stay in the company flat, in town. Of course, he said he'd try to make the last train home but it's all crap.'

'Are you going to confront him?'

'I don't know,' gasped Steph through her tears. She didn't know anything. Not anymore. Everything she'd known, everything she'd clung to and stood by—a happy home, a strong marriage, a devoted husband—was a fraud.

Pip understood that a confrontation would inevitably have consequences. Was Stephanie ready to face those consequences? What if a confrontation led to a request for a divorce, rather than him pleading for forgiveness? It often did. What a lot Steph would have to give up if they divorced. Not just the money and the security but the simplicity. No one knew better than Pip how complex everything became after a divorce. Because Dylan had gone AWOL, she at least did not have to worry about who saw who at Christmas but that was a tightrope that had to be limped along for many. Birthdays were no longer a simple celebration, more a minefield of sore memories and potential flare-ups. Then there was the responsibility to the estranged grandparents and

172

the restrictions on where it was viable and practical to live. So many complications.

On top of that there were other people's reactions to contend with. People didn't mean to be cruel but following a marriage breakdown, tactless and tasteless questions fell like confetti. Was he seeing someone else? Was he in debt? Had you been arguing for long? Did you see it coming? Yes, yes, yes and no had been Pip's honest replies but her sincerity hadn't quietened or quelled anyone. Pip realised that the reason for these questions was that people were trying to pinpoint *exactly* why her relationship had broken down, often in an effort to comfort themselves that their marriages were quite different and therefore not in danger. But the clumsy questioning led to the careless destruction of the gossamer-thin recollections and convictions as to what she thought the relationship had been. It was a little like watching a brutal, trainee cop stomp all over a crime scene, his huge boots bringing more havoc and reducing the chances of ever getting to the bottom of things.

It still hurt Pip to remember that, following her break-up from Dylan, a number of her friends and family told her that they'd never liked him anyway and they'd always been at a loss as to what she saw in him in the first place. Pip knew that they were trying to offer consolation but in fact their comments just made her feel silly and mistrustful. Why hadn't they said something at the time, if they felt so strongly? Were they the sort of friends who simply told her what they thought she wanted to hear and, if so, how could she trust what they had to say now? Others said he'd made passes at them at her house parties and some admitted he owed them money. Her tremulous memories were slashed, her beliefs detonated.

Some friends stopped calling altogether. It seemed that many couples were reluctant to mix with single mums. Pip couldn't decide if her old pals were envious or terrified of her unexpected freedom. Did they think divorce was contagious? Did they think she was going to lunge over the table and make a pass at their dull and plump husbands now that she was single? Did they think that she was a failure because she couldn't hold her marriage together? And therefore, simply, that she was no longer 'their sort'. It wasn't clear. All Pip did know was that the invites to dinner and lunch parties dried up. If it hadn't been for Steph, how would she have made it through those endless Sundays?

None of these thoughts helped. Pip sighed for Steph. And for herself. No wonder Steph had always said that she'd prefer Julian to drop dead than face a divorce. She was a woman who depended on approval.

'Such a waste, such a waste, so much time,' wept Steph. She had wrapped her arms around her body and was rocking backwards and forwards, a little like an old crazy in a horror movie. The analogy was disturbing. Pip felt as unnerved and fearful as Chloe. This behaviour was so unlike Steph. Unprecedented. That said, the situation was unprecedented. How could she judge what would be an acceptable amount of grief and fury?

Pip knew Chloe would not settle unless she went to give her a kiss, and tucked Mrs Scamper (her stuffed toy mouse) into bed. She didn't want to leave her friend in this terrible state, not even for a moment, and for the first time Pip understood how it must have been for Steph on those countless occasions when she had sent out an emotional SOS and Steph had had to answer the signal. That was probably why Steph had always suggested she come over to her home; once you have kids it's tricky to administer on tap TLC to your devastated best friend. Bouts of sympathy, however sincerely felt, had to come between overseeing homework, music practice, teeth-brushing and mealtimes.

'Will you be OK while I tuck in Chloe?'

'You don't have to hide the sharp knives if that's what you are thinking,' muttered Steph darkly.

It hadn't been what Pip was thinking, not exactly, and the scale of the macabre comment distressed her. Fuck. This was big. What should she say? What could she do? Pip felt helpless and under-qualified.

'I'll just be a couple of minutes, OK?' she said tenderly. Pip put her arms around Steph and tried to pull her into a huge hug but Steph would not, or could not, yield to her touch. She remained flint-like, rigid and isolated. Pip wondered what, if anything, she could do to comfort her friend. 'Here, drink your champagne,' she mumbled, holding out the glass.

Steph nodded obediently, although she thought that the frivolous drink had never been less appealing.

CHAPTER FIFTEEN

Stephanie's eyes stung as she'd cried such a lot today. Over and over again, heavy, ugly sobs had erupted, sometimes they'd faded into silent leaking and then re-erupted into raw anguish once again. It wouldn't do, she thought to herself. She'd had to wear sunglasses at the school gate and she'd told the boys that her allergies had kicked in early this year. Of course they'd believed her. Not for a moment did they imagine their mummy was upset. Their mummy didn't do upset. A lifetime of impeccable behaviour had strengthened her alibi. But still it wouldn't do. Steph slid her stinging eyes around Pip's small kitchen. The flat was very modest and the shortage of space was accentuated because the place was always strewn with life's stuff: magazines, books, Chloe's hair ribbons and brushes, comics, notes from school, party invitations, crayons, stray Lego, dice and toys, cartons of milk, boxes of tea bags, and the piles of washing that needed to be ironed but probably never would be (chances were that Pip and Chloe would pull on the crumpled clothes when they had nothing left in their wardrobes to wear).

The cat's litter tray needed emptying, it smelt and looked terrible. Normally Steph would oblige but this evening she couldn't summon the energy. Steph had never before really noticed how tight on space Pip's home was, of course she knew it was modest but today she felt distinctly claustrophobic. Usually, she only saw Chloe's delightful pictures pinned to the cupboard doors, today she noticed that the hinges were broken on two of the cupboards and that the cheap veneer cover was battered and peeling in the corners. The floor felt sticky due to countless spills that Pip hadn't bothered to mop up, and instead of admiring Pip's devil-may-care attitude to housework, the mess and chaos irritated her. People should take more care, she thought.

Stephanie looked around the kitchen and was swamped with a deep, murky feeling of despair. She could practically touch the sensation, it was so solid and real. She was sure she would be able to taste it. Tentatively, she poked out her tongue. Yes, the air tasted bitter and regretful. Why was she sitting here? Was she hoping that Pip could dig up some answers or offer up some consolation? Better yet that she could wave a magic wand and make the whole filthy mess go away? What would she give for the opportunity to rewrite her history? Anything. She would give anything, with the exception of her children. But the cold fact was, Pip couldn't do any of those things. She could not give her an opportunity to do things differently, to change the outcome and avoid the catastrophe. She probably wouldn't even be able to find the right words of consolation.

But maybe someone could.

Subhash.

An image of his warm, welcoming face filled Steph's head. For months now she'd told herself that Subhash was not real. Or, more accurately, what she felt for him was not real. She was a very sensible woman and thought the chances were that he was simply a diversion, a fantasy, nothing more than the result of her being a housewife of a certain age, stuck in a certain routine, with nothing other than certainties ahead of her (she'd been wrong about that as it happened, nothing ahead of her was certain). Now, she considered the possibility that what she'd felt all these months was real. Now, she could talk to him. Now, she could go to him. Julian had taken away everything. Everything but that. Unknowingly, but quite definitely, he'd given her that licence.

So far they'd shared four lunches, a couple of walks, seven phone calls, an afternoon visit to the theatre and he'd given her two gifts (a small box of pistachio and almond barfis and a book). She couldn't kid herself that this compared to fifteen years of marriage and three sons. But it was all she had to grasp at right now.

She had shared the pistachio and almond barfis with him as they watched the matinee performance. It was a good play, an Ayckbourn, but Steph hadn't been able to concentrate properly. She'd been aware of Subhash's elbow on the armrest next to hers and she'd found the proximity to said elbow ridiculously distracting. Besides, she'd been horribly aware of the inevitable sexual references in the play and the recurring theme of adultery. It had been excruciating. She hoped Subhash hadn't read too much into her choice of play and that he didn't think she was somehow condoning the shenanigans on stage. She hadn't actually given the choice of play much thought at all. They'd simply ended up watching an Ayckbourn (with inevitable sexual references and the theme of adultery!) because Subhash had asked her what she liked to do with her spare time and she'd been a bit stuck.

Truthfully, her free time was sucked up into the vortex of childcare. There was her book group, of course, she met those women once every six weeks and they always had a lovely chat, sometimes even about the book they'd read, but she'd wanted to sound a little more interesting, a little more dynamic. She had been to the local theatre a few times. Usually when one of the more proactive mums from school organised an evening out, she always enjoyed those trips immensely. She had only once been to Riverford's theatre with Julian. He'd been bored and during the interval he'd sent emails to work from his BlackBerry. When there was no champagne to be bought at the bar he'd rolled his eyes and pronounced the place provincial. Steph had defended the play, pointing out it was going to run in the West End the following month. He muttered that he'd have preferred to wait and to pay more rather than be cheek by jowl with the blue-rinse brigade. In London, vibrant young leftwing students made up some of the audience and Julian liked that. In Riverford the theatre was full of women on HRT with hairs on their chins. He did at least agree to join the entire family every Boxing Day for the pantomime (although she had heard him mutter to Harry that panto wasn't theatre, theatre demanded Hollywood celebrities or at least RADA-trained actors, not C list soap stars in purple wigs). Still, it was the nearest Steph had to a hobby, so when Subhash had asked her what she liked to do in her free time, she'd replied that she liked to go to the theatre.

Of course, he'd been as enthusiastic and interested as he always was about anything to do with her life. He'd said he'd like to visit the theatre that brought her so much pleasure. That was perhaps overstating the case, but she couldn't very well admit that, so she'd booked tickets for a matinee.

The book he had given her was a slim edition of poems by Tagore. She kept it in her bedside drawer, secreted away underneath another novel and her notebook. The notebook was where she jotted her night-time thoughts. 1) Book dentist appointment for boys. 2) Collect dry-cleaning. 3) Buy Harry new shin pads. That sort of thing.

Subhash had written an inscription in the front of the poetry book, his writing was florid and fluid, the words danced across the page. 'To Stephanie, who I honour.' He had not signed his name, people in their position didn't write their names on gifts. She knew why he'd chosen to write honour, it was just a question of semantics. Honour was very close to love. Its bedfellow, if you like. Just think about the traditional wedding vows, love, honour and obey. Subhash spoke about things like honour, respect and fidelity. He said he understood why she could not be his while she was married and while he was. He did not push as other men might. Not for sex, at least. But he pushed for her. He talked about their souls needing one another. It was very flattering. He made it sound simple. And now, now maybe it was. She was finally free to go to him, without any guilt. Wasn't she? Or at least it was justifiable. Understandable.

Stephanie gasped as she realised that in amongst all the pain and heartbreak and the disbelief and shock, there was a tiny, almost imperceptible, sliver of relief.

CHAPTER SIXTEEN

Chloe was not lying in bed as Pip had expected but sitting by the side of it, sorting through her button badges. She could spend hours subdividing her collection into categories of size, colour or subject. This evening she was grouping them by subject. She'd laid them out before her, like jewels, various small piles of colourful badges. Badges with slogans, fairy badges, animal badges, badges featuring hearts, *High School Musical* and *Hannah Montana* badges (really, the last two piles were sub-classes, as she only had two Hannah badges and just two didn't justify an entire class) and finally miscellaneous badges (a couple of charity freebies and some from old birthday cards). Pip often sat with Chloe pawing through the badges, discussing their origin or the graphics, pinning them on a cushion or simply enjoying the jingly sound they made as they were dropped into a shoe box, but tonight Pip didn't have the time.

'Have you cleaned your teeth?'

'No.' Chloe jumped up. Her skinny legs poked out of her pyjamas which were too short. Pip made a mental note that she should cut them off at the thigh and add a lace trim and then they'd see Chloe through for a few more months. Chloe's spindly legs caused a lump of profound affection to catch in Pip's chest, something between pleasure and awe and tender concern. Her daughter was so indescribably beautiful to her. Pip ached with the thought that, one day, Chloe might sit in a friend's kitchen sobbing because of her faithless husband.

Panic and rage flooded through Pip's body. She wanted to build an enormous wall around her daughter in an effort to protect her. From what? From life? That wasn't possible, that wasn't right and what was happening in Pip's kitchen right now was life. As sad as that was to acknowledge.

Pip listened to her daughter's difficult-to-understand light chatter which was spluttered out as she brushed her teeth, causing her to spray small flecks of toothpaste around the room. Pip effectively masked her mounting impatience as she waited until Chloe had put away her badges, found Mrs Scamper and rearranged her other soft toys.

Then Pip said, 'Come on, sweetie. In bed, lights out.'

'Will you read me a story?'

'Not tonight, my love.'

Chloe pouted and attempted to look crestfallen but her mother knew her well enough to be able to distinguish between genuine disappointment and tactics to delay bedtime and was therefore unmoved. Pip leaned in to kiss her daughter's soft cheek. As she did so she took a deep breath and inhaled the beautiful and unique smell of her skin, fresh from being dunked in bubble bath and her hair that smelt of strawberry shampoo.

'Can I read to myself?'

Pip was torn, she hated curbing her child's enthusiasm for books but this request was undoubtedly nothing more than an attempt to mastermind a later curfew.

'OK. Ten minutes and then lights off. I'm going to trust you to time yourself and turn out your own light. Agreed?' Pip really wanted to get back to Steph. Poor Steph. This was a nightmare.

'Yes.'

Chloe scrambled out of bed again and took a Jurassic age to choose a book to read. Pip waited to tuck her in for a second time and gave her yet another kiss before rushing back to the kitchen.

'OK, I'm all yours,' said Pip.

But the kitchen was empty, never more so. Steph had gone. Pip knew instantly that Steph must have dashed off for some sort of ill-advised confrontation.

'Crap,' cursed Pip. 'Crap, crap, crap. You should have waited, Steph. You should have waited.'

CHAPTER SEVENTEEN

Kirsten had made an extra special effort today, well, she always did for Jules. Frankly, if she'd had a straightforward choice in the matter, she would never have bothered with Mark, or Brian or Alan in the first place. She would have concentrated all her efforts on Jules from day one. But she didn't have a straightforward choice; she had to keep her options open. She wasn't as naive as to think getting a married man to leave his family was a simple thing to achieve, it took a lot of work and immaculate planning and even then things could still go very wrong; no matter what Mummy thought about her lack of common sense, Kirsten understood that much. People were always underestimating her, writing her off as silly and lazy and immature. But they were wrong and one day she'd show them. Maybe today.

Kirsten was feeling a little more buoyant than

yesterday because it had occurred to her that she could probably have been a hedge fund manager, if she'd wanted to be. It wasn't such a tricky a job, after all. Last night, she found herself sitting in her grungy flat, all *alone*. One of her flatmates was a health freak and spent most of the evening running around Victoria Park and her other flatmate had gone to the movies and, while she had been invited, Kirsten had turned the offer down, explaining she had more glam plans but as Brian suddenly turned into such an arse, she found out she didn't have any plans—glam or otherwise. Brian spent yesterday afternoon storming around the building, in a massive OTT temper tantrum, and Kirsten had been unnerved by it, to be honest. She'd decided she needed to be a bit more informed about what exactly she was supposed to be doing in the bank. It wasn't that she suddenly wanted to be one of those boringly serious career types but she just felt it might be important to understand her job description and (going the extra mile) the job description of her bosses, what with all this silly talk of Brian having her sacked! So, Kirsten had used the alone time to look up a definition of fund managers on Wikipedia. OK, she hadn't understood all the technical stuff but she had understood enough to get that what Brian, Jules and the others did was invest and trade other people's money. What was so special about that? That's what she did! She took her boyfriends' money and invested it in classic handbags or traded it for a few drinks at a happening nightclub. No biggy. Brian didn't need to be so bloody up himself!

At least this morning Brian was no longer

threatening to sack her, but then, he was not speaking to her at all. She didn't feel quite so secure in her position as when he'd been munching on her muff and therefore eating out of her hand. There hadn't been any cheeky emails or texts from him at all today. Or any of the others, come to that.

Sod Brian, thought Kirsten indignantly. The situation was a bit frustrating but not the end of the world. True, up until yesterday she had thought that Brian was her most likely candidate as an actual husband. He was always going on about how he only stayed with his wife for the kids, which was promising. Jules never said that and Mark didn't have a wife, just a string of women whom he treated in more or less the same way as he treated her. Kirsten was disappointed that Brian had, so suddenly and definitively, turned. She had enough sense to know this wasn't some insignificant lover's tiff, it was over. All because of some stupid note-taking in some stupid meeting! She'd been in the meeting—it had been deathly boring. She couldn't think that there was anything so vital to report that she and Brian should have to fall out over it.

She was just like a hedge fund manger, she'd spread her risk. There were plenty more fish in the sea, loads of ways to skin a cat, many bites at the cherry, etc., etc. She still had Mark and Jules, they were both younger than Brian anyway.

Kirsten had considered both men and drawn up a list of pros and cons.

Mark was single (pro) but resolutely so (con). Mark bought her great stuff (pro) but he literally made her beg for it (con). He was a bully (con). He behaved as though he thought she was stupid (con). He frightened her (con).

Jules was married (con) but he was sleeping with her so his marriage couldn't be so solid (pro). He'd bought her a fantastically cool phone and paid the bill every month (pro). He always took her to that lovely country hotel on Tuesday nights and she loved getting a spa treatment there (pro). He held the door open when she walked through it (pro) and stood up when she came into the room (pro). If he thought she was thick he'd never actually said so (pro).

It was clear to Kirsten that Jules was her best bet.

Her scare with Brian had been a wake-up call. She'd decided that she needed to focus. There was a fine line between keeping her options open by spreading her risk and losing out entirely by spreading herself too thinly. She was nearly twenty-three, well, in a few months' time. She needed to get a move on. If she wanted to be married by the time she was twenty-five she had to concentrate her efforts. A divorce took a couple of years, didn't it? Or could you get quickies now, did they take a couple of months? They seemed to take just a blink of the eye on *Desperate Housewives*, but maybe that was just America. Either way, before she could marry Jules she had to get him to fall completely in love with her, offer to leave his wife, actually leave his wife (she was bright enough to know that these two things weren't necessarily immediately consecutive), propose to her, get divorced and plan a wedding.

She had better get cracking.

The one thing that she absolutely didn't want to be was an old mum. You saw some mums pushing strollers along the high street and, honestly, they looked like grannies! She definitely did not want to be one of those. She wanted to be like the mums who 'introduced' their offspring in *Hello!* shoots, all glam and slim and colour-coordinated. Besides, it was always a good idea for second wives to get on with baby-making pretty sharpish; if their husbands had had children with their first wife, it completed the takeover. In fact, it was usually wisest for a second wife to have at least one more baby than the first wife had, because in that way she cemented things. Kirsten had seen that much when loads of her friends' dads had left them and run off to start a new family. Jules had three boys! She'd need to have four and at least one of them had to be a girl! There was no time to lose at all!

So, step one, getting him to fall madly in love with her. How close was she to achieving that? she wondered. He often said he couldn't stop thinking about her. He usually stayed all night with her at the hotel (although not always). He'd once said he'd like her to see the Himalayan Mountains, because he thought they were the most beautiful mountains in the world, and he made it sound like he'd want to be the one to show them to her. He said he loved things about her (like her arse and her toned thighs). His pupils would enlarge during sex so that he could barely focus and he said she was the only woman he'd ever had a simultaneous orgasm with (although, in fact, she'd faked it and so he still hadn't had that pleasure, but he thought he had and that counted for something). Was that love?

No, Kirsten admitted to herself, it was not. But it could become so.

Kirsten thought that if ever she became really

famous, and then was asked to go on *Celebrity Mastermind*, her specialist subject would be men. She was pretty sure she knew what made them tick. It actually wasn't that tricky, there were three main drivers—youth, sex, flattery. There were nuances, of course. Some men were tit men and others arse but, in the final analysis, that was all about sex. Some men liked blondes, others redheads or dark but they all liked young heads. Some men wanted to be flattered about the size of their brain, or their bank account, or their dick but it was always the same compliment—it's big, big, big!

After surfing the net last night, Kirsten had nipped into the local beauty salon to have a full body exfoliation and to freshen up her pedicure. She'd slammed both treatments on to her credit card but she didn't care, it wasn't debt, it was an investment. She'd decided against having a spray-on tan because Jules didn't like the smell, he once said it reminded him of the smell of digestive biscuits which had been dunked in tea. He never specified but Kirsten got the feeling that his wife liked digestive biscuits.

Then Kirsten had returned to her dingy flat and locked herself in the bathroom. She'd had a deep, perfumed bath and then carefully moisturised every inch of her bronzed, toned (young!) body. She'd taken her time, refusing to be rushed or hassled, even though her flatmate had hammered on the bathroom door, insisting that Kirsten get out of the bath as she'd wanted a shower after her eight-mile run and then, when Kirsten had eventually left the bathroom and locked herself into her bedroom, her idiot flatmate had hammered on that door and gone mad, yelling that there wasn't enough hot water left for her shower. Bloody hell! That was just the sort of aggro Kirsten couldn't wait to leave behind. Slowly, carefully Kirsten had massaged the body moisturiser into her elbows, her knees, her bum, her stomach and her thighs. When Jules put his hands on her she wanted him to think that he was diving into a bowl of cream. She wanted him to long to touch, stroke and caress her. She wanted him to feel loss every time he had to take his hands off her thighs.

She'd performed the same ritual this morning and then spent an age selecting her underwear. In the end she plumped for the Agent Provocateur basque, thong and stockings ensemble, which Mark had bought her a few weeks back. It was red and obvious but Kirsten didn't want to be subtle. Once, a few months back, Kirsten had got hold of Jules's BlackBerry and flicked through the gallery, where she'd discovered loads of pictures of his wife and kids. His wife was as expected—probably once pretty, now decidedly dowdy. Nearly all the photos showed the kids beaming at the camera while his wife's face was often almost edged out of the frame. Yet, even from half an eye or just part of her chin and mouth, you could see that invariably she looked harassed or worried. She did have decent highlights though, Kirsten would give her that. Kirsten knew from the shots that Jules's wife was not the sort of woman who wore slutty, red underwear and despite millions of years of evolution, the fact was, men were turned on by slutty red underwear.

Jules had bought her the phone just after he'd caught her going through his gallery and he'd bought himself one too, that was last February. He

189

said he wanted to keep things separate, obviously he wanted to avoid the risk of his wife ever finding her number in his BlackBerry or on a bill. He'd snapped that he didn't like her looking at photos of his wife and kids. She'd joked that maybe she should go and stare at his house and then he might buy her one of those too, since he wanted to keep everything distinct. But he hadn't got the joke. He'd looked really uncomfortable and said she didn't know where he lived. He was wrong about that though, of course she knew where he lived. He lived in Riverford, a pretty enough place but she'd make him move back to London when they got it together. She was far too young to be squirrelled away in the country. She knew more about him than he told her. She knew how much his bonus was last year, she knew his date of birth, which university he went to, where he banked, she even knew his exam results. It was really easy to get that sort of information out of HR, she'd just had to say that she was filling out a form for him and needed a few personal details. PAs got access to all sorts of stuff. See, people shouldn't underestimate her.

Kirsten had tried on six outfits this morning, before settling on a tight purple shirt and slate-grey skirt. She applied her make-up with infinite care and she booked another appointment at Aveda for lunchtime today. She hadn't been prepared to sleep sitting up last night, so the up-do hadn't lasted, and now she couldn't do anything with her hair, it was kinking in all the wrong places. Kirsten often thought that it was a nightmare having naturally wavy hair; seriously, it was a living hell. It was just like a disability, really. Even when waves were in, it was still rubbish having wavy hair because it didn't wave in the right way. Better to have straight hair that could be teased into the appropriate style. At lunchtime she'd have a shaggy, surfer chick blow-dry, nothing too finished or prissy, that wouldn't do at all. Kirsten wanted Jules to look at her and think sex, or—specifically—young sex. Wild sex. Irresistible sex. Sex was her thing. And of course Kirsten knew that sex wasn't the same thing as love but, happily, not many men were that brilliant at spotting the difference.

Kirsten had sent Jules a couple of really mucky texts today. *Really* filthy, even by their standards. He liked her to tell him exactly what she was imagining he'd do to her and what she'd do to him once they got to Highview. Her experience had been that she could never be too explicit. But he hadn't texted back, which was bothering her. Yesterday she thought perhaps he might be working from home and so she'd taken the risk of calling him there, something she usually only ever did at a weekend or in the evening if she'd had a few; she always hung up if anyone else answered, some old woman answered yesterday. She tried to tell herself that she was being paranoid and that Brian's silly behaviour was stopping her from thinking straight, but she couldn't help but feel a bit nervous. What if Jules went off her too? That would be too much for her to stand. She sent him another cheeky text, waited ten minutes and then sent him an email, ostensibly confirming that they'd meet at the same place and same time but also teasing and seducing him. It bounced back. It turns out that while you might not be able to be too explicit for your lover, you could be too explicit for the internal email profanity filter.

Kirsten and Jules always met at a wine bar, Jeroboam, it was just five minutes away from the office. From there they'd go to the station and then catch a train to Riverford, pick up his car and then drive to Highview. Or sometimes, if he was out of the country, she'd get a train and a taxi on her own and he would drive in from Heathrow, his unsuspecting wife assuming he was abroad for one night more than was actually the case. Today, Kirsten had a surprise for him, she'd borrowed Daddy's Alpha for the week and she was planning on driving them to the hotel, so that he could chillax.

On Sunday, she'd spent the afternoon talking to her boyfriends on the phone but it had been a bit unsatisfactory. Brian was busy in the office and hadn't been in the least bit interested in her plan to meet up and do a bit of shopping, Mark hadn't picked up her call and Jules had been distracted, he'd said it wasn't a good time to chat—maybe later. By Sunday evening, boredom had driven her back to her parental home for a visit. It wasn't an entirely wasted evening, at least she'd been able to drop off her washing and cadge some groceries and she'd used their landline to call Jules back again. She'd stayed at theirs until late and then her mother had insisted that she borrow the Alpha to drive home, rather than take public transport (just as Kirsten had hoped she would). Her father didn't need the car as he could drive his Jaguar, it was her mother who would be most inconvenienced and yet Daddy had grumbled and said he wasn't going to pay any parking fines *this time*. This ridiculous 'time to stand on your own two feet' mantra was really beginning to grate! She'd told him that Mr Kormos, the man from the kebab shop below her flat, would give her some permit passes to allow her to park for the week and then she'd return the car next weekend. Mr Kormos adored her and would do anything she asked, for nothing more than a big beam. He was a real treasure. Kirsten knew it was a bonus to have men in your life that would do things for you and not expect sex. They had to be much, much older and/or poorer so that it was very, *very* clear that you were way out of their league and they didn't stand a chance of anything more than an affectionate peck on the cheek. That said, it never ceased to surprise Kirsten how many old, ugly or poor men still thought they'd have a crack at her. Men were so often unreasonably and unjustifiably confident about their own powers of attraction.

It had been a nightmare driving the car into work today. People were so impatient and far too ready to honk their horns! The constant honk, honk, honk didn't do anything to steady anyone's nerves and she'd had to pay a fortune at the NCP to park the bloody thing. She'd hoped that she'd get a parking space at the office, she imagined it was just a case of being very nice to the security guard but he'd insisted that the spots were for director use only and she didn't have the nerve to ask Mark if she could borrow his spot. But it was all going to be worth it, she wanted to make Jules feel extra special tonight. She hoped the traffic wouldn't be too mad on the journey over to Highview, otherwise she was unlikely to aid Jules's relaxation, and after the journey into work this morning she had needed a shot of whisky in her espresso.

Kirsten liked meeting at Jeroboam. Admittedly it was a bit quiet at this time in the evening but it was uber-smart, all white leather tub chairs and booths, with glass ceilings and floors. They had a huge cocktail list and the bar snacks were so utterly trendy it was impossible to know what you were eating. When Kirsten first started working in the city, she'd had a number of wild nights in Jeroboam as this was the place of choice for everyone to congregate after work. It was where they'd go to let their hair and knickers down, the sort of place where excess and vulgarity were practically *de rigueur*. City boys tried to out-spend one another, as though that proved their success, while the city women tried to out-pout one another in order to effectively hide their success. Management and newbies rubbed shoulders, quaffed champagne and then rubbed other less neutral parts of the body. It was in this bar that Kirsten first caught the attention of Jules et al. But once she started her affairs she noticed that her boyfriends were less likely to bring her here. It was the perfect place for a flirtation but too busy to hope for any level of discretion. Jules would allow one quick drink and then they would be on their way before things became hectic in there.

When she and Jules met at Jeroboam, she always arrived first as she was happy to run away from her desk the moment she could. Obviously, they couldn't leave the office together, they had to put a respectable five minutes between their escapes. He was a married man, it wouldn't be a brilliant career move for him to flaunt their relationship and, in fact, she also preferred a bit of carefulness. She'd always allowed all the men in her life think they were the *only* men in her life. From time to time she'd had to forcefully deny rumours to the contrary when they inevitably reared their ugly heads, that's why she'd been so taken aback when Brian had called her the office bike yesterday. He couldn't know about the others, could he? Not for definite. That would be a disaster because if he knew about the others, then the others probably knew about him, and *that* wouldn't be good. It was daft really that she had to make each one of her boyfriends feel special and exclusive. Mark openly multi-dated and Brian and Jules both had wives, it was totally double standards! But Kirsten got it that women had to deal with double standards—it was just a fact.

Kirsten was comforted and calmed when she saw Jules stride into the bar. She let out a deep sigh of relief. She hadn't realised that she'd been holding her breath in anticipation or that she was stressed and concerned until she actually laid eyes on him and that cloud lifted. Now, as the fear had passed, she could admit that she'd feared he might have got a sniff of the office gossip and would therefore stand her up. She bounced off the bar stool and rushed towards him, flinging her arms around his neck and landing a huge smacker on his cheek. Normally she didn't behave so girlishly, with Jules she played the vamp, but the relief was affecting her concentration. Usually, she sashayed up to him, or waited until he came to her. Sometimes she wouldn't say a word to him until he'd bought her a chilled glass of champagne and she'd taken her first sip. Then, only then, she might lean close to him and whisper in a breathy urgent way, 'Fuck me.' Today she was ebullient and joyful although Julian wasn't. He unclasped her hands from around his neck.

'Not in here, Kirsten, we might be spotted.'

'Sorry, Jules,' giggled Kirsten. She pouted as she'd practised in front of the mirror yesterday. 'But you *are* irresistible.'

He was vain enough to believe her and so rewarded her with a brief smile, before sobering and adding, 'Kirsten, I've asked you before. Please call me Julian. It is my name, after all.'

'No. I won't,' she replied playfully. 'I like us having special names for one another. You're supposed to call me Kirstie and you're my Jules.'

Kirsten placed her hands on her hips, becoming a subconscious pastiche of the nagging wife when all she'd hoped to do was draw attention to her tiny waist and slim hips.

'Jules is all mine. Julian belongs to your colleagues, your family and the friends I haven't met yet.' She thought it was brave to add 'yet' but didn't dare go so far as to say that the name belonged to his wife. They both knew as much. 'When you're Jules you can leave all your stresses and demands behind. Jules deserves a bit of fun.' She flashed him a grin that left neither of them in any doubt as to exactly what form that fun might take.

CHAPTER EIGHTEEN

It was a slow, broad and sexy smile. It spread across her entire face and seemed to radiate out of her eyes too and, beyond that, into the air surrounding her. It struck Julian as a delightfully carefree smile. It was entirely about the moment and her absolute unfettered pleasure in that moment. There was no hint of distraction, disappointment or even familiarity, which were the main ingredients of his wife's prosaic and automatic smiles. Kirsten's smiles were dangerous. It reminded him of how she was in bed. There, she was adventurous, uninhibited, boundless, released. She had a youthful, vital effervescence and it was contagious. During sex she always remained in the moment, she bubbled, she gurgled and she simmered. He knew that she had no expectations of him, no plans for him, there was nothing she wanted from him, which was immensely attractive and refreshing. It was going to be difficult to say what he needed to. He should have been stronger on the phone on Sunday night. What made him think this would be easier face to face? Especially considering hers was such a remarkably pretty and young face.

The problem was he and Steph hadn't had that sort of sex for years and years, the adventurous, uninhibited, boundless, released kind. Steph always had one ear on the door expecting to hear a child cry out and one hand on her dressing gown, aware that if that child did call out for her she must modestly cover up and then dash across the landing to tend to their needs. But what about his needs? He had needs. How long was it since Steph had made him feel like he was her priority? Too damn long.

Oh yes, Steph loved him, he knew that, and he loved her too. Of course. But their love was

197

familiar, accepted, expected, freely granted and taken as such. Such a ready surrendering of love shouldn't mean that it meant less but somehow it did. In life it was always the rare things that were valued, not the stuff that was liberally scattered about. Think truffles, diamonds or oil. Kirsten made him feel unique, particular, valued. *He* was Kirsten's priority. He was sure of that.

Well, almost sure.

The thing was it had become harder to ignore the vulgar talk in the washroom and the after-hours gossip in the bar, there were whispers she was making a handful of men feel just as unique. Jules had tried telling himself that he didn't believe the rumours. Yes, of course she probably stroked a few of the old guys' egos, that was only sensible in her position, but he couldn't suspect her of anything more. Admittedly, she had a light and flirty way about her that fanned the flames of scandal but he couldn't believe that she was screwing them all, like Brian Ford had been saying recently. Ford had said Kirsten was good to go if you picked up the restaurant bill and dangled a few baubles in her direction. Could that be true?

At first Julian was incredibly affronted by the suggestion. Not only on her behalf but mostly because if such a thing were true, or even being seen to be true, it didn't reflect well on him, did it? He looked like a dick. A prize dick, who had just fallen for a pretty face (an exceptionally pretty face, no one would argue with that, but a dick all the same). A man of his calibre, with a respectable family and important job, didn't risk everything for some daft tart. So, he'd told himself that no, the rumours could not be true. Kirsten wasn't playing him, he was sure of it. Almost sure. She wasn't a good enough actress to make them *all* feel that they were her priority. She was still young and a bit naive. Her face was an open book. Julian could imagine what had happened. Chances were, Ford had tried his luck and she'd knocked him back, that's why he was making up these facile rumours. Men weren't above petty and destructive character assassination, although it was a good trick of theirs to insist that bitching and undermining were exclusively female domains.

Still, he didn't like the rumours.

Julian sighed to himself.

It was true he was nobody's dick. He was an intelligent man and therefore he was very well aware that the rumours might be true.

Women who dated men of a certain age and income to supplement their paltry wages did exist and they clustered in the city, like vultures around a rotting carcass. But was Kirsten like that? All his life, Julian had followed a game plan and he'd stuck rigidly to it. A mid-life crisis wasn't part of the game plan. Not that he was saying he was actually *having* a mid-life crisis. MLCs were so tacky, so pitiful, messy and stupid. What he had with Kirsten was different to that. It was. What they had was . . . It was . . .

Thinking about it, he didn't have a fucking clue what it was, frankly.

Not love, he was sure of that. He couldn't love a woman who didn't know any three-syllable words unless they were brand names of designer shops. What they had was a bit of fun. A lot of fun, actually. His treat. Steph took pleasure in buying tea sets and curtains and things and he took pleasure in Kirsten. He deserved a treat. He worked hard. Really, bloody hard. In the office, in the gym and at home.

Julian went to the gym regularly. He had to as his metabolism simply wasn't what it used to be. It was becoming increasingly difficult to stay lithe but it was impossible to say no to business lunches. Many of his big business deals happened over expensive bottles of Burgundy at the Ivy. You had to be in it to win it—fact. So, Julian felt it necessary to go to the gym four or five times a week, but he *hated* it. It wasn't just that he silently resented his body for letting him down—for ageing—and the gym was the place where he had to wage a time-consuming war on his own body fat. It wasn't just because the locker-room chat was aggressive and competitive (he could hold his own). It wasn't anything to do with the crappy coffee they served. No, he hated the gym machines. Specifically the running machine.

To Julian the running machine represented all that was wrong with his life. With everyone's life, come to that. He thought the concept of running, ideally outdoors in the fresh air, was a great concept. As a kid and young bloke he'd liked nothing more than to run until his muscles groaned and his chest heaved. Running felt so free. It was full of benefits (like discreetly checking out the hot lady joggers and watching seasons change). Running always seemed full of possibility. It was just a matter of placing one foot in front of another and he could go anywhere, be anything. The whole world was at his feet. He liked going for a run and coming home covered in mud and sweat, it always felt like an achievement.

But then some tosser took the concept of running and ruined it. They sanitised it by inventing the running machine. The ultimate going nowhere machine. Running machines smelt of rubber, not mud or grass. The view was always the same (the fat arse of the puffing bloke on the machine in front). There was no sense of possibility or freedom. Or escape. It ruined running.

Logically, Julian knew that it was well within his power to simply reject the running machine and all its sterility but he knew he would not because the running machine had undeniable, logical advantages. He could come to the gym and complete an entire body workout. It was not possible to lift weights or to row if your exercise of choice was pounding the streets. The very fact that he didn't get muddy on the running machine was now seen like an advantage, he didn't have to waste time cleaning his shoes after the run (and time was money for Julian nowadays, never more so). He could monitor his heartbeat, the calories he'd utilised, vary his gradient and accurately time his five-kilometre run. The running machine made sense. It spoke to his head but not his heart and Julian hated himself for becoming the sort of man who put convenience above the feeling of possibility. He resented every last step he took on the running machine and, as he sometimes visited the gym five times a week, that was a lot of steps to resent. Hell, he so did resent the going-nowhere machine. The machine that ruthlessly exposed his life for what it was.

A life of sensible choices and extended periods of monotony.

What was his life about, exactly? Besides the monotony and tyranny of the going-nowhere machine, what was there? Well, Julian spent relentless, stressful hours in the office, where his arse of a boss took all the praise, all the time. Then he came home to the kids. Yes, of course he loved his boys but they did have a tendency to be noisy and demanding and at times sulky, which was the last thing he needed after a twelve-hour day and a cramped commute. When he was a kid his mother ran to find his father's slippers the moment he walked through the door after work, yes, even in the eighties, and neither he nor his brother dared speak to his father until they were spoken to. Not that Julian was suggesting such draconian ways would work in the modern world but a *bit* of respect would be nice. Respect, rather than the constant demands and criticism that he was inevitably greeted with.

'Read to me, Daddy. No, not that one. I finished *that* one *ages* ago.'

'Have you brought me a treat, Daddy? To make up for being so *late*?'

'Why did you miss sports day, Daddy? *Every* other daddy was there.'

There was never any acknowledgement that he was late and tired because he'd spent all day in the office working like a dog to give them the stuff he never had. Private schooling, foreign holidays, video games, music lessons, new bikes, flash trainers. They were just kids, he supposed. Of course they couldn't understand everything. But when he'd drawn up his game plan, Julian had not factored in the truth that sometimes being a parent was simply a chore, an expense and a deadening responsibility.

And Steph. Sometimes he thought that Steph was just like the boys, really. She needed taking care of, she was expensive and she was always asking for something. Julian knew she was a 'good wife', if being a good wife meant running an expensive home with impeccable taste and efficiency. But when they'd married he'd defined a good wife as his best friend, a woman he could drink a bottle of wine with (while they put the world to rights) and laugh with (until they couldn't sit upright). Not that sitting upright was their thing in those days. They spent a lot more time being horizontal. Steph's best friend was Pip, not him. Of course, that made sense. He wasn't jealous of Pip or anything pathetic like that. Women needed their women friends. Men, not so much. He had lots of mates but not a soulmate. Steph was always describing Pip as a soulmate. It was just that the hours Steph spent talking Pip off the metaphorical ledge were intrusive and unremitting. Men didn't do that for each other, they were more likely to urge the other fella to jump just to see what he'd look like when he splattered. He and Steph never drank bottles of red wine together in the evenings anymore. They were both far too concerned with hangovers and body fat and teeth staining and other crap that just didn't matter when they were young. As for laughing until they couldn't sit up? He couldn't bring to mind the last occasion when they'd done that. Wallpaper samples, his father's heart medication and discussions about what to serve to the Joneses for supper on Saturday weren't laughing matters and that's all they talked about nowadays.

Julian's whole life was a thick soup of responsibility. Now that his mother had worked herself into an early grave, his father seemed to expect that he, Julian, should pick up the slack. It was bloody typical of his brother to sod off to Canada just when the oldies needed looking after. His father had been a bad-tempered bugger all his life, obstinate and critical, but Julian had got used to that. He knew where he stood with that. He understood it, it was manly, it was what a father was supposed to be. Now, he was this needy mess that Julian didn't get. He was always on the phone asking for something or other. Could Julian put up a shelf? Could Julian clear out the garage? Could Julian manage the sale of his house? More demands. Julian knew his father missed his mother. They all did. When she was diagnosed, no one had expected that to be it. Well, at least Julian hadn't. He'd thought they'd be able to fix it. To do something. But it had all happened so quickly. There hadn't been enough time. Not everything was said. Julian shoved the thought out of his head.

He didn't like thinking about his mother. It upset him. No good came from thinking about her death. There was only one lesson to be learnt about death. Life's short, make the most of it.

In fact, the first time Julian had hooked up with Kirsten was about a month after his mother's funeral. Some bloody psychologist might make something of that, he supposed, but Julian wasn't the sort to over-analyse.

It had been a tough day today. The staff in the office were recovering from the ramifications of the memo that Brian Ford had issued yesterday afternoon. Four members of the team had been made redundant, just like that. Asked to empty their desks and go within thirty minutes. Bloody hell. Poor performance was the only explanation required. Results were all. Culls were a hazard of this game and, over the last couple of years, they had become horribly familiar but, nonetheless, it was always upsetting. Julian was safe, at least in the short term. He had an impressive portfolio of clients and he'd ridden out the worst of the economic downturn with notable composure, meeting and breaking through targets as though they were paper streamers at a finish line.

At least, that was the impression he liked to give.

In truth, he was only safe because of the effort, the enormous effort, he persistently put into his work. Besides surpassing his targets, he was everyone's friend. He was friendly with the bods in HR, he let his boss take the credit for his most spectacular achievements and he generously provided alibis for his clients if their wives were asking questions about where they spent their evenings. He was sleek. He was good but he wasn't indispensable. No one was. The minute you thought you were was the minute your arse was kicked out the door. It didn't do to get complacent. What was it that Harry was always saying to him? You had to keep your head in the game. That was it.

Julian wasn't sure if, recently, he had been keeping his head in the game. He had a busy life— a stressful job, three children, a wife, a commitment to his personal trainer, a social life and now he had Kirsten too. Kirsten was supposed to be his treat. His antidote for all that responsibility and all those demands but he now feared that Kirsten might be the straw that would break the proverbial camel's back. Yes, she was fun. It was undoubtedly fun to lick champagne out of a young woman's navel, especially if the young woman in question had a stomach that was harder than an ironing board. When Steph had still been in possession of a hard stomach (many moons ago) they hadn't been able to afford champagne or room service in country hotels. Kirsten was his indulgence. She was fun. But maybe he'd be better buying himself an Aston Martin instead. It would be safer. Because, frankly, it wasn't fun when your horny mistress rang on a Sunday and told you she had her finger up herself and asked you to talk dirty over the roast potatoes. He couldn't allow that sort of risk. His boys had been within earshot. Rather than make him feel hot, she'd put him right off his lunch. There was a time and a place for everything and he couldn't afford for things to become blurred.

There was no question that when it came down to the wire, of course he'd choose Steph over Kirsten. Stephanie was his wife. They were a team. They were Mr and Mrs Blake. End of. The thing was, he had hoped he'd never have to choose one over the other but that somehow he'd just manage to run the two women in tandem. He wasn't so sure now. The blurring made him uncomfortable. It was one step away from being revealed. He and Steph had history together and three boys together, he fully intended them to have a long and happy future together. That would be scuppered if Kirsten turned out to be a dangerous, money-digging bitch rather than a lovely, good-time girl.

Money-digging bitches tended to cause trouble. It might start with a phone call over the roast and the next thing she'd be turning up on his doorstep telling Stephanie she was pregnant with his triplets or something equally hideous. The thought alone made his balls shrink. If the gossip was true he had to disentangle himself and quickly. As a trader he was very aware of the fact that while he'd had a good run of it, there was always an optimum time to make an exit. He'd had fun but all good things must come to an end.

He knew for certain that he never, ever wanted Steph to find out about Kirsten. She wouldn't understand that it was just about sex. She'd be hurt. Hurt beyond words. He never wanted to hurt Steph, she was too valuable to him.

So, this lunchtime Julian had decided that he needed to do some culling of his own. Things were getting complicated. Sometimes it was hard to keep track of his lies. Occasionally, he'd forget whether he'd told Steph he'd be out of the country or just working late and staying in the firm's flat. He'd had so much on his mind lately that his day-to-day organisation was suffering. In the past month he'd lost a rather decent sports jacket, a set of house keys and now his mobile phone had gone missing. It was only a matter of time before he mucked up at work. One slip and it was over.

Those were the words he was going to use. Three little words. 'Sorry, we're over.' Or was that technically four? Julian didn't know for certain, grammar wasn't his specialty, numbers were more his thing. But looking at Kirsten right now, he did know something for certain—those words were not the ones she wanted to hear. What was she waiting for? What was she hoping for? This was a bit of fun for her too, wasn't it? He'd always thought so, but from the way she was gazing at him now, full of lusty adoration, he'd put money on the fact that she probably wanted to hear him say three other little words. 'I love you.'

That ball and chain.

That exquisite promise.

What to do? What to do? That couldn't be what she was expecting, could it? He couldn't have got her all wrong, could he? Julian rubbed his temples. This was just the sort of complication he could do without. Truthfully, he had no idea. He didn't know much about Kirsten at all, they didn't do much *talking*. Which was she? Hard-faced whore, good-time girl or a naive young woman who had fallen in love with him?

'Look, Kirsten, I think there's something we need to talk about,' said Julian.

Kirsten, sensing some hesitation and distance in Julian's demeanour this evening, gently chewed on her bottom lip and she slowly, deliberately batted her eyelashes. 'Talking is so boring,' she said, stretching the word 'boring' so far that it lasted a week.

'No but really, I think we should. The thing is, while what we have is a lot of fun—'

'Oh yes, so much fun,' giggled Kirsten. She was practically dancing on the spot. Julian wasn't sure how to calm her. He glanced nervously around the bar. Time was ticking. Someone they knew might walk in here at any moment. He had better get to the point as quickly as possible. He pulled her to one of the booths and then stood the cocktail menus up in a line so as to hide them from anyone

208

glancing their way.

'The thing is I think it might be time that we called it—'

'Don't look now, you'll never guess who has just walked in,' interrupted Kirsten.

'Who?' asked Julian, trying not to show his panic.

'That woman who heads up the HR team. Can't remember her name. Something creepy-crawlie. Terrible suits, huge backside.'

'Lyn Fly?'

'That's it.'

'Oh shit.'

Kirsten giggled. 'What will she think if she sees the two of us together?'

Julian scowled at Kirsten. Was she being deliberately thick? It was obvious what anyone would think if they saw the two of them together, in a bar, after hours, they were so clearly here to discuss quantum physics. Some colleagues might be inclined to turn a blind eye, most would feel the need to spread a bit of gossip and the head of HR would have him out on his ear before he could say P45.

'We can't be seen together,' he snapped. 'You better go home. I'll nip to the gents and leave ten minutes after you.'

'I don't want to go home!' Kirsten said in a loud and indignant voice. Julian was pretty sure that the trendy, ambient background music had just screeched to a poignant silence and every eye in the bar was turned on them, just as though Clint Eastwood had walked into the saloon at noon to break up a gang of poker cheats.

'Shush,' he said urgently.

'I've brought Daddy's car. I was going to surprise you by driving you to Highview. Are you saying we're not going?' asked Kirsten crossly.

There was something steely and determined in the way she asked this that terrified Julian. He was pretty certain that if he didn't agree to go to Highview in Kirsten's daddy's car then she might scream and scream and scream until she was ill, or at least until she'd well and truly secured the attention of Lyn Fly. He couldn't risk it. He would go to Highview. Once there, he'd tell her that it was over between them. If she made a scene, at least they'd be in a private hotel room and no one would witness it. And surely she wouldn't make a scene, would she? She was a good-time girl. She'd know he was talking sense when he told her all good things had to come to an end. He'd let her have the room for the night, he'd even throw in a manicure or whatever she wanted at the spa if it made her happy. She loved that spa. It would be OK. The lid didn't have to blow on this.

'OK. Where are you parked?' he asked.

'Just round the corner, in the NCP.'

'I'll go and say hello to Lyn and while I'm talking to her and have her attention, you slip away. I'll see you at the NCP in ten. OK?'

'Maybe I should keep her talking and you slip out,' offered Kirsten.

'No, Kirsten, she'll notice me. She won't notice you,' pointed out Julian gruffly.

Kirsten thought Jules was wrong about that actually. She wasn't invisible. She was just the sort of girl that women with big asses always noticed. But whatever, she would follow his plan if it made him happy, as long as he paid for the car park she

210

didn't really care.

CHAPTER NINETEEN

'I never imagined you'd ever call.' He could not
disguise the mystification and the pleasure in his
voice although he wished he could as he knew both
emotions were unwieldy and that Stephanie might
find them slightly oppressive. He was so incredibly
happy to see her and, for the moment, that was
enough—that was everything, although he was no
fool, one glance at her confirmed that she did not
feel at all happy. Her face was ashen and her
eyes—normally wide and beautiful—were tiny slits
that just pushed through her red puffy lids. It was
obvious that she'd been crying hard. 'Are the boys
OK?' Although he'd never met the children he'd
seen plenty of photos of them and had a genuine
interest, not least because he knew those small
boys held their mother's heart. She nodded. So not
the boys. Then it had to be her husband.

'I never planned on calling,' she confessed.

'But you have.' Subhash treaded carefully. He
knew from past experiences that Stephanie would
only surrender as much as she wanted to. If he
hurried her, she might vanish. She was always
disappearing from his life. She would argue that
she wasn't ever really in his life and therefore,
technically, she couldn't disappear from it. He
didn't agree. She was very much part of his life.

He thought about her all the time. He ran
through the conversations they had had and he
imagined those he'd like to have. If he tasted

something new he wondered whether she might like it, when he was listening to Bach or Vivaldi he wondered whether she'd be moved by it. Subhash was a fan of classical music although he was rather self-conscious about admitting as much because people thought it meant more than it did. They thought it meant he might not enjoy watching *Little Britain* or that he was above grabbing the occasional burger from McDonald's if he was starving and in a hurry, both of which Subhash did. But since he'd met Stephanie, Subhash had started to see what people liked about pop songs. They spoke to him. They were all about him. Songs, poems and literature, the same! Alicia Keyes really knew a thing or two about love, as did those boys in that band Scouting For Girls. They knew about loss and women who wouldn't pick the guy who most deserved her. Not that it would be something he'd rush to admit to either but he'd got into the habit of staging what amounted to private mini karaoke sessions. First, he'd check the windows were shut (so as not to disturb the neighbours) and then he liked to play these songs at full blast. I'm not over you and I know that I should be. He'd sing along until he was practically hoarse, it was some sort of relief. And he'd bought himself a copy of Carol Ann Duffy's love poems. Now, she'd *nailed* it.

For all these reasons Subhash couldn't resist repeating, 'But you did call me.'

'It seems that way,' said Stephanie.

She probably didn't appreciate him making her spell it out but she must understand why he needed to. She'd refused him often enough. Pushed him away. Knocked him back. Again and again. She

212

used to react so angrily when he called her and she'd insisted that he leave her alone because she'd always firmly believed that was the right thing to do, but if it was so bloody right, why did it feel so awful? he'd asked. By way of an answer she'd repeat the facts. She was married. He was married. Yes, technically, he was. But Paadini spent nine months of the year in India with her family. She only came back to England from time to time for appearances' sake, to pretend to the world they had a marriage, when in fact they had a son, a history and a respectful partnership. He'd thought that was enough, he knew it was quite a lot more than many couples enjoyed. He'd imagined he'd be with his wife until his dying day. That was, until he'd met Stephanie.

It didn't make any sense on any level. He had never been unfaithful to Paadini in all their years together and, normally, he didn't even find western women particularly attractive. In comparison to Indian women, westerners could sometimes seem brash and clumsy, or even needy and irrational but Steph was none of those things. She was kind, warm and angelic. She was dignified and intelligent and, he'd long since suspected, she was more than a little bit undervalued by her own husband. Against his better judgement Subhash had pursued her. Gently, with little kindnesses. Softly, with thoughtful words. Stephanie had said he had no business being kind, no business calling her. Wanting her. That's what she'd said, many, many times. Oddly, while her morals certainly stood in the way of what he wanted, he couldn't help but admire her for them. Without them she wouldn't have been a woman he could love. So, logically, he had to respect her wishes and eventually he had stopped calling her. He'd hoped that she'd miss him then, he dreamt that she'd be desolate once he'd done as she'd demanded. Maybe she was. That would explain why they were here, back where it started.

He couldn't take his eyes off her. He drank her in. What was it that was making her so sad? How could he help? Always, that was his first thought. He wanted to protect her. He wanted to become invaluable to her. Indispensable. She wouldn't meet his eye. Instead she glanced around the steaming, bustling coffee shop. It was packed full of teenagers, the pleasant sort, who were too young and innocent to be in a pub. She watched as they flirted with one another—laughing and teasing—then eventually she was moved to comment.

'Life is so uncomplicated when you're their age.' She sounded weary. He wanted to lift her spirits but it was hard without knowing exactly what was wrong. He could guess, he wasn't an idiot. He knew what made women cry—their men. It was probable Julian was having an affair. The idiot. The blind idiot. How could he fail to value what he had, when what he had was so extraordinary? Subhash had never believed that the man worked the hours he claimed to. Subhash ran a very successful business and he knew what it was to work hard and he also knew that some men hung around their offices if their assistants were pretty and their wives no longer held an allure. It was extraordinarily commonplace. Still, Julian was a fool not to appreciate Stephanie, thought Subhash, he must be certifiable.

'I think that might be a nostalgic, rose-coloured-glasses opinion,' he said gently. 'Life is complicated for everyone.'

'Yes, maybe,' she sighed and he got the feeling he hadn't cheered her up. 'I'm not used to being in the coffee shop at this time of evening, normally I pop in just after drop-off or before pick-up.'

Subhash noticed that Stephanie structured her life in such a way that she used the terms 'after drop-off' and 'before pick-up' almost as an alternative to a.m. and p.m. She was a mother first and foremost. He realised this must be a great comfort to her children and a safeguard for her husband but it was a difficulty for him. He wanted the woman behind the mother. He was happy she was a mother, he saw a world where he would be a marvellous stepfather to her boys but he knew she could not see that world.

'Throughout the day the café is always full of harassed mothers with buggies and one or two retired old guys, who nurse coffee cups and read newspapers that they don't have to pay for,' she mumbled.

It was so like Stephanie to try to fill their silences. He appreciated her manners and her efforts but his habit was different. He allowed silences to sit between them, he liked them. Silences were the stage for the really interesting acts. Still, while she took in the scene of youthful, hormonal activity and avoided his gaze, he could stare at her with an overwhelming longing.

He was used to openly acknowledging the fact that he wanted her and he was used to her denying that the feeling was reciprocated but he didn't always believe her. Sometimes he thought that maybe she wanted it just as much. He had to have that hope or else it would be unbearable. Anyway, they'd constructed a fragile charade that allowed them both to appear to believe that what he was offering was friendship, what she was accepting was friendship; it had been that that allowed them to meet up on the few occasions they did, she could tell herself that it wasn't threatening. He supposed she'd eventually stopped believing in the charade, that's why she'd said they had to stop meeting. And now? Had the pretence—which sometimes suffocated her, terrified her—today, had it been the thought of him that had sustained her? Maybe. He took a punt.

'My God, I've missed you,' he muttered. 'You know how I feel about you. You know I—'

'Please, please don't say that. Those are not the words I want to hear from you. Not right now,' said Stephanie with surprising firmness. He had no way of knowing that she wanted to hear the rude words that had appeared on the texts. He would never imagine Stephanie had a need to hear words like licking, stroking, fucking. 'It's better if there are no words at all,' she added. 'I've heard the sweet words. Over the years they've been said. Love, forever, only you, until death do us part. Words mean nothing.'

Subhash understood this to mean that Julian's words meant nothing. Poor Stephanie. She'd thought Julian's words had meant something. She'd lived her life as though her vows had meant everything, even more than her happiness. Those words had had a dignity that sustained her and guided her. She must be devastated to see where that had landed her—disappointed, with puffy

216

eyelids. Subhash wondered whether Steph had decided that two wrongs might make a right in this case.

'It's Julian,' admitted Steph.

'Yes.' Subhash nodded to let her know he'd worked it out. He understood everything.

'He's having an affair.' Steph shot Subhash a resentful look which he considered unjust. 'Ironic, hey?' she muttered bitterly.

'A little. I'm sorry.'

'You've nothing to be sorry for,' she retorted sharply. 'We haven't had an affair!'

He couldn't keep up. Her emotions were firing in every direction, he could practically feel the sparks coming off her. She put him in mind of one of those swirling fireworks you pinned to a fence. What were they called? A Catherine wheel, that was it. Dangerous-looking things that seemed to constantly threaten to come unstuck as they whizzed round and round, spitting out fizzling white embers.

'Well, that must be some sort of comfort. At least you've always done the right thing,' he murmured.

'It's no comfort, actually,' she snapped. 'In fact, that's the worst of it.' Stephanie took a moment to stare directly at Subhash. 'It's been hard, so hard to . . .' She paused and grinned for the first time since she'd found Julian's phone. 'It's been hard to resist you,' she added finally. Subhash was gratified. 'Do you know, there've been so many times when no matter how busy I made myself, the days still felt empty or tedious.' Steph's right hand fluttered to her other wrist and she played with her watch strap. This was a terrible thing to admit to

217

him but she just couldn't sum up the necessary strength to silence herself anymore. 'There were so many days when I thought nothing would be nicer than spending time with you.' She allowed herself to smile at him again. Greedily, he sponged it up. He'd thought, or rather hoped, this was the case and it was such a joy to finally hear her confirm it. 'And only once or twice have I weakened and allowed myself the luxury of calling you. Only once or twice in all these months.'

He reached out to catch the hand that fiddled with her watch strap. As his fingers clasped around hers, his tips briefly brushed against her bare wrist. She shivered. He brought her hand to his lips and lightly kissed the tip of her middle finger. It was not normal behaviour for a couple their age, least not while they sat in the middle of a busy coffee shop.

'So now you think it's time to change tack?' he asked carefully.

'Yes.'

He understood. Now, she wanted action. Actions meant something. Actions could be depended on. It was what you did, not what you said, that counted. And it seemed that she knew what she wanted to do when she whispered, 'We need to find somewhere we can be alone.'

'Are you sure?' he asked. Concern and delight battled in his heart.

'Certain,' she said and so they stood up and headed for the door, he following her, although neither of them really believed her.

CHAPTER TWENTY

Kirsten thought that, in retrospect, driving to the hotel had been a mistake. She had wanted to treat Julian, to take care of him, but it had backfired. He'd been really patronising about her driving skills. He'd actually asked her if she'd passed her test yet, just because she stalled at the lights and that arse in the white van had nearly shunted them! It was the white van man's fault, he'd been driving too close and any decent boyfriend would have said as much, he would not have screamed out, 'Jesus, Kirsten, look out! You nearly took out the guy on the bike.' Everyone knew motorbikers were a nightmare! There were adverts telling drivers to look out for bikers, probably because they couldn't look out for themselves, it wasn't as if she was the first person in history to fail to spot one in her mirror. When Jules had snapped at her to, 'just cut out the chattering and concentrate on what you're doing or let me drive', he'd reminded her of her father! Twat.

Maybe she should have let him take over the driving but she hadn't and by the time they arrived at the hotel her nerves were in total shreds. She needed a drink. Julian did too by the look of him. He didn't even crack a smile when the receptionist told them that they'd been upgraded to a suite, free of charge! Before now, Kirsten had never really noticed what a miserable sod he could be. The moment they were in their room Kirsten opened the champagne and poured two glasses. She glugged hers back in seconds before Jules snapped, 'I didn't order champagne. That shouldn't be here. It's a mistake.' He glared at the bottle as though it had just said something racist.

'Why didn't you order champagne?' Kirsten demanded, quickly downing the second glass that she'd originally poured for him.

'It's overpriced here,' muttered Jules, showing himself up to be a tight bastard as well as a grumpy one. Kirsten was furious. Wasn't she worth it? She knew that when men started to question cost, they were questioning her value. For the second time in two days anger and disappointment threatened to overwhelm her. Why had Jules started to question her value? Fucking Brian Ford, was he gossiping? The problem was no man wanted something another man had passed over, it was a pride thing. What had Jules been going on about when he said they needed to talk? Men didn't do talking. Not unless the thing they wanted to say was goodbye. Oh shit.

Kirsten decided she had no alternative but to rally. If she turned up the heat then she was certain that she could pull Jules back under her spell. There was no need to panic. He was probably just being testy because the journey here had been so frantic and hair-raising. Kirsten took some deep breaths, then plastered on a smile and turned to face her lover.

'How about I run a deep, deep bubble bath for us both to share?' she suggested in a breathy, sexy voice that was usually extremely effective. She snaked her arms around his neck but Jules broke away from her and walked determinedly to the other side of the room. She noticed that he still had his laptop in his hand, was he planning on working tonight?

'I think I'd prefer a shower,' he replied.

'OK.' Kirsten started to unfasten her blouse. She managed to flash a bright, cheeky grin and a bright, cheeky cleavage at the same time. Jules put his hands on hers and stopped her.

'On my own,' he said firmly. 'I'm a bit sticky from the car journey.'

They both knew that normally he liked to be sticky with her but Kirsten decided not to push the point. She allowed him to shower alone while she turned her attention to the room. She drew the curtains on the evening rain and dimmed the lighting. She fished about in her bag until she unearthed the massage oil that she'd brought with her and she placed it on the bedside table, within convenient reach. She stripped down to her underwear and then carefully positioned herself on the bed. The pose she struck was a little artificial and uncomfortable. She wanted to pretend she was reading, so she lay on her stomach but it was hard to keep her arse raised at the exact angle so that when Jules emerged from the bathroom the first thing he'd notice would be her two peachy cheeks and a slight hint of lacy gusset. Then, as he was significantly longer than expected in the shower, her right thigh became numb. She got up and walked round the room but there was nothing new to look at and tedium started to run through her veins. She touched up her already perfect make-up, finished off the champers, reapplied her lip gloss *again* and then ordered a second bottle. She got the room service guy to take away the empty one so that Jules wouldn't know she'd knocked it back, at least not until it came to paying the bill.

Frustratingly, even after the effort she'd put into getting everything right, Jules appeared from the bathroom just as she was rooting through his jacket pockets.

'What are you doing?' He looked miffed.

'Erm, I was just looking for a label. I was wondering who'd made it. I was thinking of buying you a treat and wanted to know which designers you like,' she replied without pausing for breath. Obviously, this was a total lie but she was quick like that. She'd been scrabbling about for items undefined. She'd flicked through his wallet countless times so she knew which credit cards he had, she'd seen his picture of the boys and sometimes, if he was carrying loads of cash, she helped herself to a twenty (today there was only a single tenner, which was no use at all). She'd been poking about in his pockets hoping to find something—anything—*interesting*. She didn't know exactly what. A new photo, a notebook, a condom? His pockets were empty. Jules took the jacket from her and flung it over the back of a chair. Kirsten pouted, not like a sex siren but like a seven year old. She felt scolded and exposed and she didn't like it.

'I don't want you spending your money on me,' he said flatly.

No worries, not much danger of that, thought Kirsten sulkily. She couldn't remember when she last bought a present for someone else although she did like to buy herself little gifts from time to time, just to cheer herself up or reward herself if she'd done something really good, like stick to her diet for the entire day. Kirsten sighed. This evening was not panning out as she'd expected.

Yes, the room was just as lavish and trendy and big as it had ever been but something had changed. Kirsten couldn't enjoy her reflection from the heavy gilt mirrors or the feel of the silky, luxurious bed throws quite as much as she usually did. Suddenly the beautiful room, so solid and—well— *rich*, had an angsty, really negative vibe to it. The room and everything in it seemed a bit intimidating and unreal, including her relationship with Julian. Kirsten felt huge waves of panic swish around her body. Fuck it. Fuck it. She hated it when she wasn't in control of stuff. She liked to call the shots. She liked to be the one making people drop to their knees. This was all fucking wrong! Jules had a white towel wrapped around his waist and normally he strode around their room naked. On some level Kirsten understood that the white towel was like some sort of yellow warning card. She didn't like it.

'Come and lie down. You seem really tense, babe. How about I give you a really long massage? Hey?' Kirsten flashed her best smile.

'No, I'm fine. We need to—'

'I'll start with your shoulders, then work down to your back, your buttocks and then—'

'If you want. OK.' Kirsten couldn't help but notice that Jules's manner was akin to a man being led to a torture chamber, not one being offered a handjob. What was wrong with him? What was wrong with her?

He lay face down and she straddled him, careful not to put any of her weight on to him. Even though she only weighed eight stone one (seven stone nine, if anyone asked) and he probably weighed about thirteen stone, she didn't want to

223

squash him. She deliberately brushed her lacy panties against him, though. She massaged him for ages and ages, her thumbs had begun to hurt with the effort of working out the tense knots. She didn't get it, normally if she was straddled across him, in her scanties, she only had to be working the oil for five minutes—tops—before he flipped her over and they started shagging. After shagging they'd go for a treatment in the spa and/or dinner. If he didn't get on with it, there wouldn't be time for either one, let alone both. That wouldn't be fair. She wasn't operating a charity here! She expected something back for all her effort. Besides, she was starving. She hadn't had time to eat at lunch because of her hair appointment, fat lot of good that had been. Jules hadn't even noticed her new and wanton style.

What was that sound? Kirsten became still so she could listen properly. The combination of no food and quickly glugging the champagne meant she wasn't as sharp as usual. Was it the air conditioning or the wind blowing against the windows? No, it was Julian. That was more like it. Kirsten grinned as she registered his groans of pleasure. Now things could get moving at last. She clamped her thighs a fraction tighter and waited for him to respond. But he didn't respond. The groans continued at exactly the same pitch and rate, they were not deeper or longer. It took her a moment but then suddenly she understood. Julian was not moaning in ecstasy. Julian was snoring.

CHAPTER TWENTY-ONE

It had started to rain again. April showers, a little earlier than due. This shower was the most ferocious of the day and neither Steph nor Subhash was carrying an umbrella. As they ran from the café towards her car, spiky raindrops fell down his collar and caused her hair to frizz into an unflattering nest. She fingered the ends shyly. He didn't care. He hardly noticed that sort of thing. To him she was a presence, not a tangle of details. She allowed him to hold her hand as they dashed through the wet streets. They had once or twice held hands before, that much she had permitted, although never more than that. This time it seemed she really was going to allow more. Allow it all? Everything? Would she be his? He hardly dared believe it.

He was thinking about where to take her. Not his house. Paadini was in Mumbai, so theoretically the coast was clear but it wouldn't be right. He could not take Stephanie to be amongst his family photos, he couldn't take her between his matrimonial sheets. Not that he and his wife had had sex for nearly three years now. It wasn't that sort of marriage anymore. Subhash didn't really mind. There were many sexless marriages all over the world, he knew he wasn't alone in this and such things could work. It had worked, until he met Stephanie.

He scrabbled around his head for alternative places they could go to be together. An in-town hotel was far too risky. Someone who knew either

225

one of them might spot them coming or going. They would draw attention. Even nowadays, when such things shouldn't justify a second glance, they did, and a mixed-race couple was always noticed. He wouldn't want to take that gamble. If it was up to him, he would be comfortable taking out an advert in the local newspaper declaring how he felt about her but he knew she would not think this was the time to announce their love to the world. Or even if it was, being spotted sneaking into a B&B was not how the announcement should be made. He was sincere when he said he'd leave his wife for her. Men sometimes said such things to seduce a woman. Subhash said it because he wanted to spend the rest of his life with Steph. He'd been the happiest man in the world when she called this evening. And one of the most surprised.

Damn, he wished he'd had more notice, he'd have liked to have had time to consider the details and make everything perfect for her. That's what she deserved, perfection.

They could drive to Highview Hotel. It was beautiful there. A stately home set in elegant groomed grounds, not more than a few miles out of town. It was secluded and elegant, just the sort of place he thought she deserved, the sort of place he'd imagined making love to her. It was a nuisance that it was raining, in the rain it might take half an hour to wind through the country lanes and he didn't want to waste a moment. Part of him was worried that by the time they got there she might have changed her mind, again, like that time last summer when he'd tried to persuade her to meet him there for lunch. He'd planned on booking a room as well as a table because, yes, he'd hoped for afternoon delights, after all he was only human, but she only ate one course, wouldn't even stay for pudding. At first, he'd thought she didn't like the restaurant but it was only weeks later that she admitted that she'd celebrated her previous wedding anniversary at Highview. Of course she was going to be squeamish about his hints that they might take coffee in his room.

Would that anniversary dinner stand in the way now? Things were different now but still in flux. He knew she wasn't yet firmly committed to him. She belonged elsewhere but it appeared she was his for the moment. It was enough, he'd take it. He'd take whatever she offered him and cling on to it.

She was parked behind the town library in the doctor's car park. No one used that space at this time of the night. As soon as it was permissible to park on single yellow lines, people preferred to settle directly outside the off-licence or under a street lamp in the high street. The car park was dark and gloomy. There was a solid line of trees and bushes that were lush with fleshy leaves which acted as a curtain against the light. The tarmac— framed by nettle patches and a cracked path leading to and from the high street—was strewn with dented drink cans and litter.

They paused beside her car, hesitant in the pelting rain. He didn't know whether she wanted him to take control and drive them somewhere, or ought he to get in the passenger seat? Maybe she had worked out where they could go. Maybe she'd thought through the details and consequences of the offence that they were about to commit, the transgression that he could only regard as a celebration. He studied her. She was clearly nervous and agitated, he could tell by the way she continually played with the strap of her shoulder bag, but her mouth was set with a new determination that he hadn't come across before. Oh God, he wanted to kiss that mouth. He'd waited so long.

'Shall I drive?' he asked.

She glanced from left to right, recognising that the dusky evening was fading into a much more solid black now, soon they would disappear behind the night's shroud. 'No. I will.'

'Are you sure you're not too upset to drive?'

'I'm OK. Get in.'

He did as she asked him. It was good to be out of the rain and a moment's calm shrouded them. Subhash watched a raindrop slide down Stephanie's nose and splash on to her lap. From the clean smell it was clear that it was a new car, luxurious and roomy with grey leather seats and a shiny walnut finish on the doors and dashboard, a car for the plush and wealthy.

'Where shall we go?' she asked.

'Highview?' he suggested because he hadn't come up with anything better.

Stephanie flinched, then nodded her head—just once, a brittle movement—and then she started up the engine.

CHAPTER TWENTY-TWO

Asleep! Asleep! Kirsten couldn't fucking believe it. Her first instinct was to punch him in the back.

That would wake him up. The cheek of him. The fucking cheek of him. She'd never had a man fall asleep on her before. It was unbelievable.

Blow him! Well, not literally. Not now! Not a chance. What she meant was sod him, just because he wanted a nap didn't mean she had to miss out. She was incredibly hungry but she could go to the restaurant or order room service anytime, what she needed now was something to calm her down. Tequila? Maybe not. She didn't fancy drinking alone in the bar and, truthfully, experience had shown that tequilas didn't exactly calm her down, more likely she'd end up dancing on the tables. Then the answer came to her. She could go and have a full body aromatherapy massage and charge it to the room, she had earned it. She had to salvage something from this crap night.

Kirsten had thought her evening couldn't get much worse, which only went to show how little she knew because it did get worse when the snooty woman at the hotel spa's reception said that there were no available appointments.

'I recommend that in future you book in advance to avoid disappointment.'

The snooty spa bitch smiled as she said this but Kirsten wasn't fooled for a minute, she knew that all the women in the spa hated her. Over the past few months she'd noticed their jealousy. When she floated into the spa, on Jules's arm, she'd seen the nasty looks that passed between the therapists. She didn't give a toss. They were just jealous because her boyfriend was rich and distinguished and because while she was about the same age as most of them, *they* had to work for *her*.

'Would you like to book an appointment for

next Tuesday?' asked the snooty spa bitch. 'Tuesdays are your day, aren't they?'

There was something in the way the bitch had phrased the question that caused Kirsten to hesitate. It was as if she was saying Tuesdays were her day and on a Wednesday Jules brought someone else to the hotel and someone else again on a Thursday. That couldn't be right, could it? No, definitely not. She was the one who juggled different partners on every night of the week, not Jules. Jules only had his wife to worry about. Even so, the thought was unnerving. Besides, there was something else. Kirsten would have liked to have had the confidence to say yes and to have booked the works—facial, manicure, pedicure, massage and Hopi ear candles—but something niggled. She had a vague, hideous feeling that Jules was about to break up with her and that there might not be a next week, at least not for them. The thought was sickening. She'd put so much effort into him. What had gone wrong? Why did everything always go wrong for her?

'No, it's OK. I have a very busy work schedule. I'm not certain that I'll have time to be here next week,' replied Kirsten coolly. She wanted to save face. Saving face mattered. Really mattered.

But she wasn't sure she had when the snooty spa bitch bit down on her lip, as though she was trying to suppress a smile and commented, 'Whatever you say, *Mrs* Blake.' Kirsten had never said her name was Mrs Blake. Obviously, when Jules booked the room or paid for treatments and room service, he gave his name and the snooty spa bitch had no doubt noted this. She'd put two and two together and come up with four, she was just

230

pretending she had calculated to three. Kirsten looked at the woman behind the reception and knew that she knew Kirsten was not Mrs Blake. She probably also knew that there was a Mrs Blake, sitting at home with a gaggle of kids. She was trying to make a point. No doubt the bitch got a kick out of reminding Kirsten of Mrs Blake's existence. Probably she was trying to embarrass her. Well, shows what this silly cow knew, Kirsten didn't do embarrassed.

There had been that time she'd got so drunk at her mate's house party that she'd performed a pole dance on the pool table, using a cue as a prop. She couldn't remember the actual incident at all. The first she knew of it was when her brother had gone ape and shown her the video on YouTube, he'd been all narky and was mortified, saying she'd made a show of him. She pointed out that it had had over fourteen thousand hits in less than a week, which Kirsten knew was something to be proud of, not get arsey about. Imagine, fourteen *thousand* men admiring her performance.

'Jacking off to your performance, more like,' her brother had shouted angrily.

'Well, I hope you didn't,' she'd replied. That had shut him up.

After the disappointment about the massage, Kirsten confirmed their dinner reservation. She was pleased to be told they were booked for nine and less pleased when she discovered that it was already five past.

Fuck. This really was turning out to be a crap night.

CHAPTER TWENTY-THREE

When Subhash touched her hand she thought it was almost unbearable, not because she didn't want his touch but because she burned for it. Part of her, a part she had tried to ignore, had been thinking about this for months now. Thinking about Subhash had meant that she didn't sleep soundly, the deep and insistent curiosity about him had sometimes made it hard for her to ever finish an entire meal and it meant it was often difficult to follow the plot of the latest Sunday night costume drama—her mind could not stay focused but preferred to wander into her own fated romance. She'd frequently reminded herself that she hardly knew Subhash (how could a handful of lunches and telephone calls amount to knowing someone?). She hoped that reminding herself that their relationship was in its infancy and would never grow to maturity would make him less real and vital. She told herself that this tremendous excitement she felt was only her imagination playing tricks on her. The passion she felt did not really exist. She was simply flattered.

Her strategy hadn't worked. Her certainty that she would stop thinking of him was as solid as it was misguided. The inevitable result of haughtily demanding, 'So what do I know about him, after all?' was simply that she'd stay awake all night counting the things she did know.

1) He was forty-three. 2) His name meant softly spoken, which he was. His parents had invested in elocution lessons in order to ensure that his

English was perfect. There was no trace of an accent, but he still sounded somehow foreign. His perfect speech and grammar, which he'd learnt from a well-to-do old lady, seemed to draw attention to his foreignness, rather than away from it. As his teacher remembered and championed a gentler past, Subhash spoke in a way that that did not so much root him in another country, more in another time. 3) He ran his own, incredibly profitable but niche business, something to do with solar power (silicone wafers and supply chain management to Germany occasionally cropped up in his conversation). 4) He had just one nineteen-year-old son, who lived in LA. His son was studying at UCLA and he wanted to be a film director in Mumbai after he graduated. 5) Subhash was married.

This fact was always the hardest to call to mind. Sometimes she managed to go for weeks and weeks without thinking about his wife, sometimes she thought of her all night long.

6) It had been a traditionally arranged wedding and a successful, happy marriage until he met Stephanie. 7) He'd always been faithful in deed and thought until he met Stephanie. 8) He respected his wife and, in a way, loved her. 9) He was not in love with his wife.

Not in the heady, dizzy way that books and films and songs described. He claimed he'd never even believed in that sort of love, never understood it and certainly never hankered after it. That was, until he met Stephanie.

She'd been angry and confused when he said this. And a tiny bit thrilled. She'd told him that it was inappropriate and that they couldn't have lunch together again if he was going to say such things.

'I don't want there to be untruths between us,' he'd said simply.

'No, Subhash, you mustn't go there,' she'd insisted nervously.

He'd shrugged. 'We are there. Whether it is said or not. Say the word and I'll leave her.'

Stephanie had simply glared at him.

She had been absolutely certain that Subhash would eventually tire of her. She'd almost looked forward to the day when he'd move on and yet, equally, she'd dreaded it. They hadn't seen one another since November. There was something about the Christmas decorations that appeared in the shop windows that had tugged at her conscience. She'd known that she was not capable of dressing a tree, attending midnight Mass and cooking a turkey if Subhash weighed in on her conscience.

Julian had not been so squeamish. She knew that now.

So, last November, Stephanie had said to Subhash that if he really did love her, then he must leave her alone because he was destroying her peace of mind. He was destroying all that was good about her, all that he claimed to be attracted to— her morals, her values, her decency. They'd been sitting on a bench near the river, watching the ducks scramble about on the muddy slopes.

'All right,' he'd said, sighing his disappointment into the chilly air (she thought she could see it cloud their existence). 'I accept your logic and respect your decision. I will stop calling you. I'll wait for you to call me.'

'I won't call,' she'd said quietly, hoping to convince herself as much as him.

'I hope you do. I'll wait. And I'll want it and I won't stop wanting it. Remember that, Stephanie. I'll be waiting for you.'

He'd stopped calling her as she'd asked him to and as he'd promised he would. She'd got what she wanted, so why did she then feel so wretched? For months it had been intolerable to think of life without him and therefore she'd chosen not to think about life much at all. Instead she filled her days with doing (she joined the committee for the local historical society, served tea at school concerts and volunteered as a sales assistant at the cancer research charity shop in the high street). Through good old-fashioned self-discipline she'd taught herself not to expect to ever feel his fingers on her skin, not even to hope for it. If she wavered and thought of him, thought of calling him or encouraging him in any way, she would imagine something terrible—something like having the boys taken away from her, seeing her mother's face collapse with grief or causing her father-in-law to have a heart attack with shock. Steph conjured these horrendous fears whenever she reached for the phone, whenever she so much as thought of him. She was like a lab rat running against an electrified barrier and eventually she taught herself to associate him not with pleasure, but with the undoubted pain that a liaison with him would inevitably lead to.

Now she could think of him and not feel pain.

Couldn't she? Wasn't she entitled to that much now? Surely.

The hotel room was lovely. There was no doubt

235

about it, under other circumstances Steph might have got excited about the clever little touches, the teddy bear on the pillow and the complimentary fruit and port. Under other circumstances coming to a place like this might have been a real treat. But it was hard for her to notice the sumptuous bed throws and opulent cushions without thinking about what it was her husband had been doing in this hotel for months now, what he was likely doing even now; without thinking about what she had come to this hotel to do. The thought made the hairs on her arms stand up and prickle, like spiky blades of corn bristling in the wind.

She'd looked for Julian's car in the car park but couldn't see it. She wondered how he managed the logistics of this infidelity. She'd always believed that he drove to the station, left his car in the car park and then caught the train into London. Did that mean on Tuesdays he caught the train back to Riverford, picked up his car and then drove to Highview? He brought that woman to their home town? He practically passed their door! While she and the boys were having tea, he was—oh God, she couldn't think about it. She couldn't think about how deep this deception was. Infinite and indecent. A fresh wave of anger and a sense of injustice surged through her body. It bolstered her and attacked her at once.

'Would you like a drink?' asked Subhash. He had his back to her as his head was buried in the mini fridge. 'There are spirits—gin, whisky, vodka—and there's wine, both colours. Or a soft drink or I can order something from room service.'

'A cup of tea?' she said. She wasn't sure if she wanted a cup of tea but it was the drink she most

236

frequently requested and the response had simply rolled off her tongue.

'I was thinking of something a little more special. Champagne perhaps.'

Stephanie nodded. She didn't really feel like drinking champagne but it might help her get in the mood. What sort of mood did she want to be in, anyway? What sort of mood did you need to be in to become an adulteress? She wasn't sure. This was all so alien to her.

Subhash was trying so hard to please her and to impress her. He'd asked at reception if they could book the suite. Steph had known the answer even before the receptionist had explained that the suite was occupied by one of their regular guests. Steph imagined the manager kicking himself when he heard that the suite might have been taken by a paying guest rather than wasted on an apologetic gesture to Mr Blake, who was after all no more than a grubby adulterer. Then again, what was she? No different. Besides, it was unlikely that the Highview cared about their guests' morals. Maybe the Highview even went so far as to have a discount rate for grubby adulterers. What was Julian doing right this moment? she wondered. Was he in the jacuzzi or had they got straight down to it and was he taking her over the dressing table, one hand on her arse, another stretched round to cup her tit—just as that woman had described it on one of her texts today. Stephanie closed her eyes. It didn't keep the image out but it held her tears in.

Stephanie carefully lowered herself on to the edge of the bed. She wished she knew which room was Julian's 'regular room'. Was it possible it was this very room? This very bed? Steph felt gases

237

charge upwards from her stomach, push up her oesophagus and erupt into her mouth. If she'd eaten anything in the last day or so it would no doubt be a dark stain on the immaculate coir matting flooring by now.

Subhash called room service and asked for champagne and then he gently sat down next to her. Sitting side by side she could feel the heat of his body. Slowly, he turned to her and tentatively cradled her face in his two great big paws of hands. She mirrored his action. His hands then edged down so that his thumb rested on her chin and his palm and fingers reached around her neck. It was calming. Surprisingly so considering how churned and impossible she felt. His touch was healing. His gaze stopped her speaking or moving. She was rooted in his presence. She was completely unaware of the rain hammering down on the window or the sound of a catering trolley being pushed through the corridor just outside their room, she was even unaware of her wedding ring glistening on her left hand—everything other vanished. She could feel his bristling whiskers, peeping through his skin, tickling under her fingertips. Such an ordinary thing and yet she was struck by his manliness, his difference, and she gasped. He felt like a miracle. She felt chained and yet free. They were elsewhere. Other.

Suddenly aflame, she wanted to just get on with it. She wanted to lean into him and kiss him. Dare she? Ignited, he would kiss her back, she was sure that he would, even though she'd turned her head away from him on several occasions in the past. Not that she'd wanted to turn him away. She'd often wondered what his lips would be like to kiss.

Never had she allowed herself the indulgence of finding out. Would his kisses be charged and challenging or soft and gentle? What would it feel like to have his hands skim her body? Would he be sturdy and determined, firm and passionate? He'd been necessarily cautious, respectfully tentative for months and months; now she'd agreed to come to a hotel with him he would be unlikely to exercise any sort of self-control, no matter how much of a gentleman he was.

Kiss me. Kiss me, she silently urged. Make me yours. Wipe away all previous traces. Fix me. Even up the score.

And when he did finally kiss her, she would be a changed woman. She would not be pathetically passive. She was now unwilling to be overwhelmed and swallowed up, she'd meet the challenge of his kisses and she'd kiss as she'd never kissed before, with abandon and longing. All she had to do was initiate it. Just move a fraction closer. Tilt her head, just a smidgen.

Or she could simply reach for his trouser belt and scrabble to unfasten it. Get to business. Hadn't they waited long enough? Wasn't that what she was here for? She should tell him straight, clear up all doubt or hesitation. Let him know that she was finally ready for him. But she was unable to find the words that meant what she wanted to say. Instead she continued to silently will him to slide his hands up her roll-neck jumper and find her breast. She closed her eyes and imagined his fingers touching the edge of her bra, then slipping inside the cup to touch her nipple and perhaps gently circling or tugging on it. She felt the thrill of the thought of his caress throughout her body, in her heart and deep down, low, low in the parts she could never find a reasonable name for. Yes, truthfully, she had dreamt of his touch. She'd woken on more than one occasion, sweating and guilty from dreaming of his fingers inching across her, all of her—her breasts, her heart, her lips, her bits. And now, now her body hummed at the thought of his imminent attention. She could do it. She was entitled.

Tit for tat.

The expression struck her as hopelessly inconvenient and confusing and, more importantly, rather vulgar. What did it mean, exactly? Her tit for her husband's tatty behaviour? Maybe. The thought made her shudder.

But why shouldn't she do it? Subhash loved her. He'd said so. And she thought perhaps she loved him back. Or at least, she could, if she allowed herself to. Julian didn't love her. That was certain. He'd lied to her. He'd cheated on her and on their children. Was that love? He was at this very second kissing some other woman's— Steph couldn't say the word, not even to herself, but she saw the image in full technicolour, Julian with his head between this other woman's smooth, slim thighs.

If she had sex with Subhash now, here in this hotel, no one could blame her. It would be justified. Maybe a little grubby, but revenge was rarely anything other. It would take just one swift, deft movement. She could leap on to his lap, legs astride his body and she could grind into him. Part of her did want it.

But such a leap would be out of character and probably terrify him as much as it would surprise her. She wasn't a leaping, legs-astride sort of girl—

240

more was the pity.

'Are you sure this is what you want?' Subhash asked gently.

Stephanie put her hand over his, which was still cupping her face and she pressed him so close, it felt as though his hand might melt into her. She liked his question. He understood her hesitation. He always got to the root of the matter.

'It hurts,' she replied by way of explanation. She didn't need to explain exactly what hurt. All of it. Julian had caused such pain. Julian had changed. He'd changed everything. Everything, it seemed, other than Stephanie's ability to kiss a man who wasn't her husband. It wasn't fair.

Her throat was parched and constricted, by contrast her palms were moist and loose. She'd thought that they would pull at one another's clothes, scrabbling to find flesh. She'd imagined her skirt gathered up around her waist. Their lips merging into one another, kissing so hard she'd struggle to compute who was doing what to whom, who was saying what, promising what. Who was encouraging whom? As she'd manically driven from Pip's to meet Subhash, she'd been certain about what she needed and certain that this was it. Finally, the words that had passed between them, and the many more that she'd stifled and never dared allow escape from her head, suddenly seemed irrelevant. After all, it was what you did that counted, not what was said. She had always known as much. That was why she had never done this because she knew it would count. Now, they were left with nothing other than an exposed hunger. An unadorned and basic craving. She wanted him to be inside her. To sink into her. But it was harder than she'd imagined. Would it be totally different? Or just the same?

With her eyes closed she leant forward and finally kissed him, not wanting to see but needing to feel. He kissed her back, eyes wide, drinking up every flicker and flinch on her face. His hand slipped down her neck, resting when he cupped her breast. Gently, slowly he caressed her through her jumper. He was no virgin, in fact he and his wife had enjoyed a healthy, some might say adventurous, sex life when they were younger and yet this first base caress felt like one of the most erotic moments of his life. Was she enjoying him? She must be as it felt amazing. It felt important. It felt right.

Stephanie felt everything was wrong. Her world was binary, black and white, yes and no, good and bad, beginnings and endings. Other people had shades of grey and flashes of colour. Not her.

As, no doubt, Subhash was soaring—as the kiss filled him, sealed him, satiated him and encouraged him—she was devastated to acknowledge that the kiss failed to comfort her as entirely as she'd hoped. He could not block everything out. He simply accentuated a whole new stack of problems. Two wrongs simply made two wrongs. Damn it. She pulled away from him. Snapping their moment before it became something more solid.

She collapsed back on the bed, lying across it rather than along it, she stared at the ceiling. Subhash lay down next to her and feigned an interest in the ceiling too. After some minutes had sauntered past he reached out to her, resting his finger gently on the inside of her elbow.

242

'I need you, Stephanie,' he whispered. She liked the way he said her name. He pronounced it in such a way that it was heavy with sincerity, and tonight especially she craved sincerity. 'I want you to stay with me,' he added.

Stephanie sat up suddenly and searched around for her handbag. Once she located it she scrabbled inside it looking for a tissue and avoiding his eye. 'I know you do,' was the most honest thing she could reply. But how? How was that going to be possible? 'I can't have an affair,' she stated solemnly. 'I just can't do it. Everyone else seems to find it so easy but not me.'

She'd said this so many times that there was a strange comfort in the familiarity of the words. Of course, in the past they had meant a different thing. Was she now technically having an affair? she wondered. Over the months, when they'd met for the occasional lunch, a visit to the theatre and once or twice a walk along the barge route, she'd always been sure it wasn't an affair because she hadn't kissed him, she hadn't been physically intimate with him on any level. She'd ignored the fact that she'd spilled the minutiae of her mind to him and he'd hoovered up her chatter, her stories, memories, gossip and musings. She'd ignored the fact that there had been an emotional intimacy. Did a kiss ruin her argument? Was she now an adulteress? The thought made her stomach churn again.

'I mean, I can't go on doing what we . . .' Stephanie dropped her head into her hands, 'What we nearly just did. What we haven't done,' she added eventually.

'You can't go on *not* doing it?' he tried to clarify.

243

'Yes, that's it. I think.'

'No. Of course not. I don't want that either. I don't want you to go on *not* doing what we nearly did.'

Stephanie smiled despite herself. Even the semantics were difficult.

'We have to be together,' added Subhash with a gentle firmness that almost convinced Steph, almost comforted her. 'Properly together.'

'But how?' she demanded. Was it an option? Was it a hope? 'How?' Hysteria and desperation had begun to creep into her voice, probably because she knew the answer to her own question.

'You have to leave Julian,' he whispered.

'The children.' Stephanie shook her head in anguish.

'I'll look after you all.'

Steph wanted to believe him. She wanted someone to take control, to scoop her up and to take care of her. She wanted to feel safe and cherished as she had when her mother had tucked her into bed when she was a sleepy child. She'd like to be carried away. Somewhere far away. But it wasn't that simple. Stephanie could not, would not, divorce. That was not the life she'd envisaged for her children, for herself. But how could she stay with Julian after what he'd done?

'You have to divorce him,' said Subhash confidently. 'Because what else can you do now? It's not as though he's going to conveniently drop dead, is it?'

'Don't joke about such things, Subhash.'

'I am not joking,' he said seriously. 'I'm facing the facts.'

244

Wednesday

CHAPTER TWENTY-FOUR

Pip should probably hate herself. She really should. Probably. What kind of woman was she? What kind of friend? What kind of mother? With every question she demanded of herself, shame, embarrassment and a vague sense of self-loathing swelled up in her stomach, it pushed up through her body and then seemed to spurt out of her mouth and spill in the form of a scarlet blush across her cheeks and neck.

She was a terrible friend and an irresponsible mother and a slut. That's what she was. A slut.

Carefully, with tiny imperceptible movements, so as not to wake him, she inched her head around to look at him.

Oh, he was gorgeous!

Even so, it was wrong, it was unacceptable. He was in her bed and she'd known him—how long exactly? Not quite forty-eight hours.

But it was hard to maintain the self-loathing when he was *so* gorgeous. She had behaved horribly selfishly last night. She really had! She knew it but somehow she couldn't quite feel it, she couldn't quite regret it. She was too happy. She forced herself to think back over the events of the previous evening. Stephanie had arrived and landed all that terrible news on her doorstep. Then she'd disappeared in a flash! Pip had felt awful, just *awful*, then she'd felt frustrated and infuriated as she'd repeatedly called Steph, over and over again, only to be sent straight through to voicemail. How could Steph turn her phone off at a time like that? Pip would have chased after her but she couldn't very well wake up Chloe and bundle her into the car, could she?

She probably would never have answered the phone to Robbie at all but she assumed it was Steph finally returning one of hers and so she'd picked up in a hurry, not even pausing to check the caller ID. She probably wouldn't have allowed him to come round either if she hadn't been so agitated. She hadn't been thinking straight. She'd never had a guy back to her flat, there was Chloe to consider and, truthfully, no one had ever really intrigued or interested her enough for her to risk exposing them to her home. Not that she was afraid that they'd catch E. coli or salmonella crossing her doorway (yes, she was slovenly but not that slovenly!), it was more the risk of what *she* would be exposed to if she allowed a man into her home, into her life.

But, after an hour chatting on the phone (finishing off the bottle of champagne on her own was probably a mistake but Pip couldn't be blamed, it really did seem crazy to let Bollinger go to waste), she'd agreed to Robbie's suggestion that he pop round with another bottle. That was the thing with champagne, it wasn't the sort of drink that encouraged temperance. It was much more of an indulgence drink, a let-your-hair-down type of drink. Maybe she should have said no. She certainly hadn't played the evening out according to the rules of the various dating books she'd read. She probably should not have told him that he was perfect. Just because a man arrives at her house with a bottle of champers and a box of Cadbury's Roses was not a reason to think he was perfect, let alone tell him. Alcohol and chocs were probably standard issue for a booty call and she was in no doubt that she was indeed a booty call, what else could she be at that time of night? Of course Robbie said he just wanted to chat for longer, he wasn't going to come out and simply say he was horny.

When she opened the door to him, he struck her as being leaner and taller than she'd remembered but then, what did she know? She hadn't seen him standing up until that moment. She must have been a bit tipsy because she made some joke about theirs certainly not being a longstanding relationship. He'd smiled politely but clearly didn't really understand what she was going on about. Truthfully it wasn't her funniest comment ever, some way off it. She was never any good at being funny in front of men she fancied. She was always too nervous to be her best self. When she was with just Chloe or Steph she could catch balls, even juggle, she was witty and funny, but as she opened the door to Robbie, she'd tripped and banged her head and then said, 'Well, that trip wasn't as good as a trip to Margate.' This was something her grandfather used to say to her as a child, every time she went splat. Sometimes she wished she'd been born without a tongue.

Robbie was wearing combat trousers, they were slipping around his hips in a provocative, somewhat dangerously sexy way. A thick belt stopped an act of indecency and its weight seemed not only to hold up the trousers but also to anchor him to the ground. He stole her breath.

At least she'd managed to temper the way she'd told him he was perfect. She'd managed to be a little bit droll, as she'd served the compliment as a backhander. There must be points in the dating rule books for backhanded compliments rather than out-and-out straightforward ones lobbed over the net. It was just after he'd patiently listened to her offload Steph's dramatic story (maybe in retrospect she shouldn't have shared that particular tale of woe quite so quickly and willingly, the problem was Steph's upset was playing on her mind). He'd listened carefully and when she'd finished dishing up the gory details, instead of weighing in with some half-cooked solution to the problem or inadequate, ill-considered advice, he'd simply offered to massage her feet. Which at the time had seemed pretty damn perfect and she couldn't help telling him so.

'You are too good to be true. Champers, not cava, chocolates and now a foot massage. And do you know Cadbury's Roses are my absolute favourite, especially the purple ones with the hazelnut in caramel. It's official, you are the perfect man,' she'd declared, as she swung her feet on to his lap. Up until then they'd been sitting at a formal distance, each at one end of the sofa, careful not to actually touch each other.

'So I've been told,' he'd replied with a cocky but not altogether unattractive, grin.

'Hmmm.' Pip had paused and taken a moment to enjoy the foot rub. He circled his thumb on her instep in a way that provided so much pleasure it was probably illegal but she wasn't so keen on Robbie's reaction to her declaration that he was perfect. He accepted the compliment as though he was used to receiving it. She could only surmise that other women had benefited from this foot rub

250

too. Perhaps the alcohol, calorific goodies and rub were just standard practice on a Tuesday evening, she just happened to be this week's lucky recipient. She hadn't wanted to appear as soft as putty so, rallying, she'd managed to mutter, 'I've always been fascinated when meeting perfect people.'

'Why?'

'I like spotting the flaws that they are so desperately hiding.'

Robbie had gasped, pretending to be shocked or offended.

'Come on, no one is perfect,' she'd insisted.

'Seriously,' he said with a grin that suggested he was about to be anything other than serious, 'I've given it a lot of thought and I am.' His self-confidence should have been off-putting but Pip had been stunned to find that she liked it even more than the foot rub.

'No, you're not. You probably have a mad wife in the attic, or a gay lover in the closet or at the very least a stack of festering washing-up in your sink.'

Pip wished that all her metaphors had not been quite so domestic—attic, closet, sink. Marvellous. She *really* needed to get out more. If she'd had broader experiences then maybe she might have been able to accuse him of more glorious and adventurous crimes than neglected washing-up. Robbie had stared at her as though she was certifiable. She did sound a bit bonkers but then she wasn't the one claiming to be perfect. That was sheer madness. And vanity!

'OK, well, how about I stay until we've finished this bottle and we can chat about anything you like and I promise to be totally honest and you can see if you can discover my flaws, as you call them. Then we can decide if they are deal-breakers for you,' said Robbie.

'How will I know you are being honest with me? I don't know you well enough to recognise any tell-tale tics that expose you when you're fibbing.'

'Well, I won't be fibbing. I promise.'

'Just like that. No lies.'

'It's sort of a rule of mine.'

Pip had eyed Robbie sceptically but thought she had nothing to lose by quizzing him.

'Are you in a relationship?' she'd asked, going straight for the jugular. It wouldn't be the first time she'd fallen for someone hook, line and sinker only to discover that someone else already held the ownership deeds.

'No, I split up with my girlfriend of four years about eight months ago.'

'Why?'

'Long story.'

'I have time.'

'We weren't compatible. Not ultimately. Isn't that always why people split up?'

'It took you four years to work out that you weren't compatible?' Pip had asked suspiciously.

'No. It took three years to work it out and another for us both to accept it,' he'd replied plainly.

Pip laughed. Fair enough, it might have been the champagne, but this answer struck her as pretty perfect. It was truthful, straightforward and hinted at a man with insight.

'Were you faithful when you were with her?'

'Yes.'

'Have you ever been unfaithful?'

'Yes.'

'Ha,' said Pip triumphantly.

'When I was eighteen. I was deeply sorry and since then I've always sacked or been sacked before I jump into some new sack.'

'That sounds a bit like a practised line.'

'No, actually, as a matter of fact, it just came to me now. I'm a poet and I don't know it.'

'Maybe your flaw is your use of silly rhymes.'

'Maybe but is that a deal-breaker?'

'No, suppose not.' Pip had grinned.

She'd been impressed. No matter what she asked him, she found that his answers, while not predictable, were always believable and, seemingly, honest. He did have flaws but they weren't insurmountable. After grilling him for two hours while they finished off the bottle of champers and started in on the whisky she kept on the bookshelf, the worst things she'd managed to discover about him were that he nearly always drank directly from the milk carton, during washing crises he had been known to wear his underwear for two days in a row and that he occasionally masturbated in the shower. They weren't deal-breakers.

He'd discovered that she was a fragile, wounded, single mum, with little grasp on popular culture, an overactive imagination and an inability to talk for longer than twenty minutes without referring to her ex. On the plus side, she was refreshingly straightforward, the only game she was interested in playing was Monopoly (and then only if she could be the Top Hat), she was creative, independent, intelligent and drop-dead stunning to look at.

'So what now?' she'd asked after they'd drained

their whiskies.

'Well, now it's up to you, Pippa. It's all up to you. I could stay for another hour or so, or the night or longer. It's all up to you.' He'd stared at her with such sincerity when he said this that for a moment she felt incredibly powerful. He was putting her in charge, saying they could take this—this relationship or fling or whatever it was—at exactly the speed she wanted.

'Right,' she'd nodded.

'So what do you say?'

Pip had opened and closed her mouth. *No* was the word she was planning on finding, *no*. Perhaps *no, thank you* because she liked his Scottish charm and cheek and she had invited him over in the first place.

'Well . . .' She'd hesitated.

'It's all up to you. But you probably should know that I'm enormously well-endowed and a fabulous kisser,' he'd said with a grin.

Pip had laughed. 'Are you now?'

'Well, there's only one way to find out for sure.'

This was true enough.

Now, Pip checked the clock on her bedside table. It was 6 a.m. Did she dare wake him? Ought she ask him to leave before Chloe woke up? Probably. That was certainly the most sensible thing to do but somehow Pip couldn't bring herself to place her hand on his arm and gently shake him awake. It wasn't shyness about reaching out to him (after last night, when she'd had her hands all over his body, why would she worry about touching his arm?). The truth was she didn't want to wake him because she liked him in her bed. It had been a long, long, long, long time since she'd shared her bed in such a wonderful way. The problem was, despite Robbie talking about staying as long as she wanted him to, Pip couldn't help but fear that was unlikely. Once she woke him, he would go on his way and then that would probably be the last she'd ever see of him. Pip mentally stuck out her chin. Of course she hadn't ever really believed him when he'd said it was all up to her as to how long he stayed. She could spot a line when she was fed one, she wasn't a fool. But she'd wanted to nibble the line, what was the harm in that?

It had been nice, though. Last night had been very nice. Not just the sex, which she had to admit, was—well—very, *very* nice but she meant the rest of the night too. Watching him breathe, in out, in out, was lovely. Feeling him roll over in his sleep had been so pleasant. On some level, even hearing the gentle little putt of his snoring was reassuring.

Pip had suspected it to be the case. Obviously, she'd vigorously denied it, what self-respecting woman would admit to it? But last night, having his company, had categorically confirmed it. The fact was, she was lonely. Her loneliness was not debilitating, it was not all-consuming. She had Chloe—darling Chloe, the centre of her world— she had Steph and Steph's boys and her other friends and now she even had a contract with Selfridges and an emerging career but still, the loneliness had stained the air around her. It seemed to hang about like a bad smell.

She knew she couldn't keep him locked in her room.

Could she?

No, she really couldn't, no matter how much they'd laughed the night before, no matter that they'd talked into the early hours and had sex twice. Twice! She couldn't keep him a moment longer than he wanted to stay but she did wish he would stay.

Not for ever, obviously.

Well, not unless he wanted to stay for ever. Might he?

No, she was being silly, just joking. Of course not for ever but for the morning at least. She wondered whether she was capable of managing to get Chloe off to school without making her aware of Robbie's presence. Then she would be able to sneak back into bed and they could do it again. God, she'd missed sex. Not the energetic throes of orgasm (she hadn't actually had an orgasm last night, she'd had far too much to drink to hope for that) but she missed the closeness, the kissing, the holding one another. One more time wouldn't hurt, would it? She might as well. When did an opportunity like this come along? Not once since Dylan, she'd be mad to pass it up. Then they could have breakfast together. Maybe even go for a walk as the sun was seeping through the curtains, the weather looked promising.

She was close enough to smell last night's alcohol on his breath. Would she still be able to taste it on his lips if she kissed him? He was almost too long for her bed, his feet stuck out of the duvet. They were big, bony feet. The manliness of him was quite breathtaking. Pip and Chloe's world was so entirely feminine. They lived in a mass of floral scents, glitter, pretty stationery and mail order catalogues. They had a basket of small hand soaps in the bathroom, it didn't get more girly than that. Robbie was so different and unexpected. So exciting.

What was the best course of action? Should she wake him and ask him to be silent and beg him to stay but risk the fact that once he woke he might leave? Or should she just lock him in the bedroom, make Chloe breakfast with maximum noise (to drown out the sound of him hammering on the bedroom door and begging for his freedom) and hope against hope that he didn't shimmy down the drainpipe in a desperate attempt to escape from her clutches?

Imagine what the neighbours would say.

No, she couldn't risk it. On balance it made more sense to wake him and deal with him leaving before Chloe was any the wiser about her mother's loose morals and wild antics.

Pip placed the palm of her right hand firmly over Robbie's mouth and then gently shook him awake. The instant he opened his eyes she put her finger from her left hand to her lips and muttered, 'Don't say a word.' He nodded, like the hostage he no doubt felt himself to be, so she explained. 'My daughter mustn't know you are here. OK?' He nodded again. 'If you want to stay until after I've taken her to school, we could have sex again when I get back.' He nodded for a third time. 'But in the meantime, you must be a ninja, OK?' This time he licked her hand, which tickled and surprised her enough to loosen her grip.

'I like your agenda,' he whispered. 'But, Pippa, do we have time to move directly to the sex bit if I promise not to yell out when I come?'

This time it was Pip who nodded.

CHAPTER TWENTY-FIVE

Stephanie glanced at the clock. It was 6 a.m. which meant she'd had another night with hardly any sleep. She might have drifted off for ten minutes at a time but she didn't feel at all rested or ready to face the new day, she wasn't sure how she'd ever sleep soundly again. Her head was beginning to hurt so much she thought it might crack. She yawned and rubbed hard at her bleary eyes. She was still dressed in yesterday's clothes because when she'd finally come home and relieved Mrs Evans last night, she hadn't thought to have a bath or shower. She was too traumatised, too devastated to imagine managing something so mundane. Turning the taps, pouring in bubble bath and undressing would require a Herculean effort that Steph simply wasn't capable of. Instead she'd poured herself a glass of whisky—the drink her father recommended for shock—and then she'd dug out the large cream leather photo album that stored their wedding photos.

The photographer had worked with film and not a digital camera, which was unimaginable now. But Steph rather approved of film. A photographer had limited chances with film, he couldn't keep endlessly snapping, hoping that some of the shots would pass muster, comforting himself that if they didn't then there was always Photoshop. No, photographers who used film knew that they had limited chances and so they worked harder at capturing those fleeting, glittering moments, they captured life with more skill and conviction.

Stephanie loved her wedding photos as the photographer had managed to grab the instant of smug delight and splendid unfettered excitement. At least those moments were preserved between the acid-free sheets of paper. Safe from harm.

She was putting herself on the rack by looking at the photos, she knew that, but she wanted to put herself through that particular brand of pain. It was at least a pain she could control. Besides, on some drunken, disorientated, self-disgusted, subconscious level she deserved it. Her actions had been so extreme. So impulsive. It was pitiful that all she was capable of now was a pathetic longing to turn back time. Steph sat on a vicious and jagged knife edge and waited for more trouble to find her. She knew it would. There would be consequences for what she'd done last night. How could there not be?

Steph and Julian had married in the church where Steph had been christened and where they went on to have the three boys christened too. It was the prettiest, most soulful church imaginable, especially when it was floodlit at Christmas or decked with fruit and flowers for harvest festival. As the guests had arrived at their wedding that sunny Saturday afternoon fifteen years ago, they'd all gasped at the church's beauty and simplicity. Some of Steph's girlfriends considered moving house or even changing religion to secure such a perfect backdrop for their photos. It was a picture-postcard, small and charming Victorian church, built on the site of an ancient Saxon one. Steph always thought it was clever when someone built a church on a site that showcased God's handiwork and St Mary's-on-the-Hill definitely fell into that

259

category. Coming or going to a service, the congregation could pause at the church doors and enjoy views of rolling fields and dramatic woodland; on a clear day it was possible to see right across the county. Stephanie loved that vista. When she took in the scenes below her she always felt especially vital, connected and alive. She liked to stand on the top of a hill and imagine the endless possibilities that were stretched out below, possibilities parcelled up as other people's lives.

They'd held their reception in a warm and welcoming local hotel. They had been one of the first amongst their friends to get married and so no standard had been set as to what was expected from a wedding in terms of style or hospitality. Stephanie smiled when she remembered how impressed her aunts had been that the chairs in the reception room matched. Back then, weddings didn't include all-night champagne or even a paid-for bar, or personalised favours or engraved bronzed leaves as nameplates, they did not have fireworks at midnight and nor did their reception culminate in bacon rolls at dawn. Steph and Julian served one glass of champagne on arrival and red and white wine until the meal was finished. There was a misspelling or two on the nameplates, but no one minded. The party finished about an hour after the happy couple had changed into their specifically bought 'going away' clothes, they had been waved off to the sound of tin cans chasing the shaving foam-covered car. The decoration of the car wasn't even ironic or retro, it was for real.

It had been perfect.

Oh dear God.

Steph wore a wide dress with mutton-leg sleeves

and a heavily laced bodice. It looked very dated now, of course, but at the time it had been the envy of every girl in the church. Few women could pull off pure white (either because of their skin colouring or their colourful past) but the chaste gown suited Steph who had always been quite shy with the opposite sex and had a light golden skin tone. The dress was now carefully preserved, wrapped in tissue and stored in a box in their attic. It was a shame that you couldn't wrap up your actual marriage with the same care, thought Steph, a marriage seemed so much harder to preserve. She used to think that one day she might have a daughter who would want to wear her dress but that was never going to happen. Besides the fact that she had three sons, she couldn't imagine any modern bride making do with hand-me-downs, not even particularly cherished hand-me-downs.

Certainly, no one would want a gown from such an ill-fated marriage. The best thing she could do with it now was take it to a charity shop.

Julian, the best man and the groom's men had worn top hats and morning coats. Pip (her only bridesmaid) had worn emerald. It had been a pleasantly warm day. Not so hot that her make-up ran or people had to squint at the photographer but warm enough so that it was comfortable and favourable to spill out on to the patio to drink the champagne and to make the light choice of salmon and boiled potatoes appear wise, not just economical.

Stephanie's parents had paid for the entire event, they wouldn't hear of anything else. They'd been saving up for twenty-two years to seat one hundred and twenty guests. It was a matter of great pride to them. The thought of Steph's parents—so well-intentioned—caused Steph's heart to quicken. This mess would devastate them. What had she done? Something so, so terrible. Something unforgivable. What was she going to do next?

Stephanie's aunt had made the cake, which had been four tiers high and show-stopping. Not because it was exquisite but because the icing was rock-hard and Julian and Stephanie's combined strength hadn't been enough to enable them to slice into it. There'd been a lot of jokes about how to hold the knife more effectively. Their friends had playfully urged that Julian 'put the point in first', which had caused Steph a moment of embarrassment and discomfort because the old rellies had got the joke.

Steph was thinking about plunging the knife deep into the cake when the doorbell rang. She knew at once what it was. Trouble. It couldn't be anything other. Not at this time of the morning. Definitely, the only thing that called at this time was Trouble. At the very best, it might be Pip. She'd be hysterical that her best friend hadn't returned her calls all of last night. She'd probably done something impulsive and irresponsible (but ultimately well-meaning) like bundling Chloe into her banger of a car and dashing over here to see if she could help in any way. A wasted journey. No one could help. She was beyond help.

When the bell rang, Harry called out from his room.

'No, it's not time to get up yet, go back to sleep, darling. Don't worry,' she tried to reassure him, she needed to protect him for as long as possible, that was her job as a mother. But then, she hadn't behaved like a mother last night, which was why her voice was high and thin.

As she walked down the stairs she became aware of her grubbiness and worried that her breath smelt of whisky. Last night she should have bathed, put on pyjamas and fallen into bed, the familiar and simple ritual would have offered some sort of comfort, minuscule perhaps but something.

It wasn't Pip.

There was a policeman and a policewoman. Stephanie opened the door and stared at their uniforms. Their walkie-talkies, their torches, bulky belts and heavy boots all seemed so out of place on her pretty front step.

'Mrs Blake, wife of Julian Blake?' asked the policewoman. Stephanie must have nodded. 'There's been an accident. Can we come in?'

The policewoman glanced at Steph's cream carpet and then conscientiously wiped her feet on the mat before she crossed into Steph's world. Her vigorous stomping made Steph think the policewoman was trying to leave as much of the distress and grime belonging to her criminal world at the doorway. Too late, thought Steph. Too late. Filth and crime have already found their way into my home.

The policewoman was probably in her early thirties but her brief yet genuine smile suggested a calm confidence well beyond her years. Steph could smell cigarette smoke on her breath. She thought, she shouldn't smoke, this young policewoman, it's a horrible death, and then she thought, who could blame this woman for smoking? I'd smoke too if this was my job. Steph's thoughts were disconnected and non-sequential, it was to be expected considering the trauma and lack of sleep. She felt as though she was dragging her body through someone else's life. It wasn't a dreamlike state, not even nightmarish; the comfort of dreams and nightmares was that no matter how weird or upsetting, you knew you'd eventually wake up. Steph felt like she was two minutes behind reality, she couldn't catch up. She couldn't react quickly enough to save anything.

The policewoman wore heavy make-up, which seemed strange to Steph. Had she just started her shift? Who put make-up on at six in the morning? What type of woman stopped to apply midnight-blue eyeliner as she responded to a 999 call? A heartless, vain one? Or a woman who still had standards, someone who thought a level of formality was required at times like this? Steph didn't know. Didn't know anything. She let the woman lead her through to her own kitchen, where the policeman put on the kettle.

He was even younger than the woman. He was in his early twenties but he was one of those people who was happy with his youth, there was no sign of self-consciousness. He deftly moved around Steph's kitchen opening and closing cupboards until he found mugs and tea bags. He added milk and sugar to hers, even though she'd said she preferred it black.

'You need the sweetness,' he asserted. What a funny arrangement of words, thought Steph. She'd have expected him to say, 'It's good for shock.' Yet his words were apt. She did need sweetness. Stephanie was surprised to notice that the policeman wore a wedding ring on his finger, it didn't sit comfortably with the arrogance on his face. Steph wondered whether he was faithful to his wife. She doubted it. Or even if he was now, he probably wouldn't be as the years rolled by. He was strikingly handsome and knew it. His mother had probably taught him to believe he was doing the world a favour by simply existing.

These were the sort of ungracious thoughts that swirled around Steph's sleep-deprived, slightly hung-over mind. Until Monday lunchtime such mean-spirited, ugly thoughts had always been strangers to Steph but now she embraced them. She thought she ought to make friends with her inner bitch, she figured they might be keeping each other company for quite some time.

Then, finally, the policewoman began to talk and she said what Steph knew would be said.

'Your husband has been in an accident.' The policewoman held Steph's hands. She had warm hands despite coming in from outside. Her fingers felt like rice paper. Steph sat absolutely still and tried to manage these words.

'A hit-and-run, actually,' said the man. He didn't hold Steph's hand, he slurped his tea.

'He was discovered at four a.m. this morning.'

Steph gasped. She felt her blood slow, it seemed to freeze in her veins. Four a.m.

'When was the last time you saw your husband, Mrs Blake?' asked the policeman with a gruffness that was habitual to him.

Steph tried to think. 'Breakfast, yesterday.'

They'd hardly spoken a word. She'd made him toast as usual but he hadn't eaten it. He'd said he didn't have time because he was running late. She'd been disproportionately furious that he'd refused her breakfast, she'd felt that he was

265

rejecting her all over again, in yet another way. A tiny pathetic way. But still, another way. Why it mattered to her so much she wasn't sure. He was sleeping with someone else, he'd chosen someone else. He didn't want to be her husband anymore, not properly, so did it matter if he didn't want her wholewheat either? The toast went into the bin. She hadn't had an appetite either.

'Did you speak on the phone yesterday? Or text one another?' The policeman held his pencil over his notebook. 'Any contact at all?' He was poised, ready to write down whatever she said.

Contact. The word made Steph shudder. 'I sent him a text yesterday at teatime. About six.'

She'd sent out one final, frantic plea. She'd desperately hoped (although not really expected) that by sending him a text at the precise time she'd calculated he'd be greeting his mistress, he might have had a late-in-the-day flash of conscience and would suddenly turn round and travel home to her and the boys. Unsurprisingly her text, 'We're having shepherd's pie for tea,' had not done the job. She wished she could have thought of something more compelling.

'Were you expecting your husband home last night?'

'No. He often stays in town on a Tuesday,' replied Steph carefully. 'He said he might have to work late and stay in the company flat.'

She had no choice other than to continue to pretend that she thought this was the case. This was not the moment to say that she knew her husband was an adulterer and had been staying in a beautiful hotel with his bitch of a mistress. What good would come of that? As she uttered the lie, she comforted herself with the fact that until Monday, she would have thought she was telling the truth.

'In town? You thought your husband was in London?'

'Wasn't he?'

'No, Mrs Blake. He was staying at Highview Hotel, just a few miles down the road,' said the policeman. 'He was found in the car park. A guest was checking out early, to catch a plane, and they found him lying on the ground.'

The policewoman threw a look of censor at her colleague and then shared one of knowing sympathy with Stephanie.

CHAPTER TWENTY-SIX

Even now, Kirsten couldn't stop shaking, she folded her hands across her body, warming her fingers in her armpits but still she was cold and trembling.

Last night was officially the worst night of her life. No fucking doubt about it. Off the scale. Un-fucking-believable.

Much worse than the night when Daddy discovered that she smoked pot and made her go to that dorky support group full of skanky crackheads, she wasn't anything like any one of them, Mummy and Daddy had *so* overreacted. That was a very bad time. Smelly and so *humiliating*.

Worse than her graduation prom when, despite having spent literally hundreds of hours and hundreds of pounds finding the perfect dress, she'd turned up at the ball only to discover that Rachel Abbot was wearing the exact same one!

From the moment Kirsten had spotted the dress she'd loved it ferociously. It was a Jenny Packham. Admittedly, it was from her ready-to-wear collection but when Kirsten did get married she was going to have a Jenny Packham haute couture bridal gown. But as most of the other girls were opting for Top Shop maxis and stuff, because they were worried about their student debt, Kirsten was certain she'd create a stir—even in ready-to-wear. She wanted to give everyone something to remember her by, *for ever*. Something so magnificent that when she became famous (or at the very least was in the *Tatler* society pages) they'd say to themselves, 'Oh yes, Kirsten Elton, she always was gorgeous, she always was going to be *somebody*.' Secretly, Kirsten regretted the fact that her university didn't have a yearbook, like they did in America, she was sure she'd be voted the most likely to succeed, or maybe the most beautiful, if they had that category. It would have been nice to see it written down.

The dress was a buttercup yellow, which worked just beautifully with her bronzed skin. It was fitted, with delicate straps and had stunning diamanté detail around the bust. But the most magnificent thing about the dress was that it split to the thigh, flashing her toned and tanned legs whenever she strode forward; it was sold with matching hot pants. In summary, it was just too, too cool. From the moment she spotted it, Kirsten knew she'd do anything to get the dress, even give a blow job to one of Daddy's old cronies if necessary. As it happened it wasn't necessary, Mummy had persuaded Daddy that a dress like that was an investment. What had she called it? Quite the show-stopper.

Goes without saying, there was no question that Kirsten looked best in the dress. If she and Rachel Abbot were photographed side by side and put in one of those magazines where readers were asked to text in to vote for who wore it well, Kirsten would get one hundred per cent of the votes, it was a dead cert. Rachel Abbot was a size sixteen, she had acne and knees that were so cushioned they were practically entire sofas! What made a girl who looked like that think she should wear a Jenny Packham dress? In yellow! Rachel would have been much better in a black, slack dress, ideally with long sleeves. No offence but the fact was, Rachel Abbot was a hound. That was why it was so bad! If one of the other pretty girls had been wearing the same dress, Kirsten might have been able to laugh at the situation, perhaps she and the other pretty girl could have flirted with the guys, jokingly telling them that they were twins—boys never tired of that fantasy. But Rachel was so ugly that her choosing the same dress as Kirsten was humiliating! Kirsten's taste and style were called into question.

Obviously, Kirsten had had no alternative but to go home because the shame was too overwhelming. It was a pity really, because Jake Mason had hinted that they might have got together later on. He'd kept saying he'd been practising his foxtrot, which was a joke, clearly, there was never any question that they'd really have to foxtrot, more likely they'd get sweaty to

Lady Gaga and Pixie Lott but it did go to show that he wanted to dance with her. She'd been at home in bed, *alone*, by nine thirty, while all the other students had partied until five in the morning and only gone to bed after they'd cruised down the Thames to Richmond.

Such were the level of disasters and disappointments in Kirsten's life until now. The thought made Kirsten splutter, tears poured down her face again, mingling with snot and sweat. She seemed to be leaking everywhere. Oh Jesus, oh God, oh fuck, fuck, fuck. What was going to happen now? This was such a big, fucking, serious disaster. She hated the word serious; teachers, parents, mates, even boyfriends were forever hurling it at her and whenever she'd heard them use it she'd had to disagree. It was such an overused word. Learning stuff wasn't serious, which grade some stuck-up examiner awarded her wasn't serious, nicking stuff from Boots wasn't serious, not even if you were stupid enough to get caught like Holly Shaw (a ticking-off by the spinster store manager hardly amounted to a criminal record, did it?), having sex without a condom wasn't serious, that's why you could get the morning-after pill over the counter now. But this, this was serious.

Julian was dead.

Through the rain she'd watched him go down. He just folded like one of those old-fashioned deckchairs you still saw on beaches. Fuck, it was shocking. The yelling, his body falling on to the bonnet of the car and then slumping on to the ground. It made her sick just thinking of it. She hadn't gone to him and checked on him. She

270

hadn't even reported it. How could she? Why would she? At the moment no one knew of her existence. She certainly didn't want his wife finding out about her *now*. She'd just panicked and left. Left him alone.

The moment she'd got back to her flat Kirsten had run a hot, deep bath and climbed into it without pausing to check if the temperature was even bearable. The water was scalding and scorched her flesh but she hardly noticed. One of her flatmates had woken up and angrily complained about the lights going on and all the noise at such a late hour but Kirsten didn't give a toss. One small part of her brain was already calculating that it was important to form a tight alibi as to her whereabouts and so her flatmate knowing she was at home was a good thing. She'd yelled through the bathroom door that she'd been in bed for ages unable to sleep and that she was having a late-night bath in the hope that it might send her off. She was fairly sure her flatmate had bought it. Kirsten was used to finding herself in trouble and usually she managed to get out of it. Not always though. Oh fuck. Not always and she had to get out of this mess. She *had* to. Kirsten had cried, causing rivers of mascara to cascade down her pretty face. She'd hugged her knees tightly to her body and silently sobbed until the bathwater turned cold.

How was she going to get out of this mess? How? It was impossible to fix. He was dead.

CHAPTER TWENTY-SEVEN

'An ambulance has taken him to the Royal Surrey. I'm sure you want to get there as quickly as possible,' said the policewoman.

'He's not dead?' Steph felt a tidal wave of relief surge through her body.

'You thought he was dead?' the policeman asked suspiciously.

'You seemed so serious, so deathly,' stuttered Steph. She couldn't think, couldn't imagine, couldn't breathe. He was alive. Oh thank God, the bastard was alive. She took deep gasps of air but there wasn't enough oxygen in the room. She rushed to the kitchen window and flung it open. The sweet smell of dewy grass and the chill of the early spring morning cradled her. The officers watched her carefully.

'It *is* serious. A hit-and-run has severe legal consequences,' said the policeman grimly.

'And your husband isn't yet conscious,' added the policewoman. 'Where were you last night, Mrs Blake?'

The policewoman slipped the question into the room as stealthily as a small mouse creeping around looking for crumbs, yet Steph knew the danger.

'Me?' she asked stupidly, stalling for time. Her mind started to whizz and whirl, she was certain that the police would hear her forming excuses and considering explanations.

'Just routine to ask.' The policewoman smiled reassuringly.

'Yes. Of course.' Steph pulled the window closed and took a moment to lock it. 'I was at my friend's home. I was at Pip's. Philippa Foxton. We were having a celebratory drink, actually. She'd had some good news.'

'What time were you there?'

'I got there about seven and I left at about eleven, maybe eleven thirty.'

'She can verify that, can she?' asked the policeman bluntly.

'Yes, of course,' replied Steph firmly. She reached for her handbag, 'Now, should we get going?'

The neighbourhood watch scheme in Hilledge Grove was tested and passed with flying colours. Just as the officers were asking whether there was someone Stephanie could call to watch the boys while she rushed to the hospital to be at Julian's bedside, Mrs Hodgson from next door 'popped by'. She'd seen the police car and she wondered whether everything was all right. Steph was, for once, grateful for the fact that her neighbour was a nosy empty-nester with too much time on her hands. The thoughtful Christmas and birthday cards, occasional jars of homemade jam and donations of rhubarb from Stephanie's garden were all paid back, with dividends, when Mrs Hodgson ushered Steph to the police car insisting that there was no need to worry about the boys, she'd take care of everything.

Stephanie had never sat in a police car before. A thoroughly law-abiding citizen, she'd never so much as received a speeding ticket. She felt conspicuous and panicked as she ducked into the back seat. The policeman actually said, 'Mind your

273

head,' the way they did in films. Stephanie felt tears prick her eyes. How could this be her life? Her husband was in hospital, he was an adulterer, she was in a police car, a crime had been committed.

The car smelt of sweat, produced through adrenalin and dread. She wondered who else had sat in the back of this car. What sort of person? Pimps, drug dealers? Murderers? The world's lowlife. Now she was in the same seat. Stephanie's backside itched and her mind whirled.

They silently zipped through the streets. There was no traffic on the roads as yet, it was too early for Surrey to mooch into action. By contrast the hospital was heaving. There was a scattering of dazed and bloodied people waiting in A&E, a fair number of confused and restless patients aimlessly wandering the corridors, and seemingly endless grief-stricken, terrified souls hanging around the vending machines waiting for news about their loved ones. The angels of life and death didn't give a toss what time it was.

Steph was led through the endless corridors of beige lino, ushered through heavy swing doors and finally into an area which bore the signpost Intensive Care Unit. Steph thought it was a brutal notice. Sadly, it was entirely Ronseal, it did what it said on the tin. The people behind these doors required intensive care, ordinary care was inadequate, it wasn't enough to keep them safe and functioning.

The officers introduced Stephanie to a receptionist and then the policeman gave Steph his card. PC Terry Weybridge. He did it in such a way that suggested they were colleagues who'd met at a networking conference, he said they'd be in touch but his promise seemed more threatening than comforting. The policewoman also gave Steph her card. Her name was Sergeant Mary Jean Brown. The name was somehow reassuring. It was a solid, promising name. Steph thought that she might like to have had a cup of coffee with Mary Jean Brown under different circumstances. Say, for example, if they'd met at a book group, rather than over her comatose husband's body, Sergeant Mary Jean Brown was the sort of woman Steph would want to become friends with: calm, experienced, sympathetic. Steph felt confused and strangely bereft as she watched the policeman and woman walk back along the corridor, away from her. Shouldn't they have to stay with her, at least until she saw Julian? Who would prop her up now?

Stephanie was given a form, she was asked to sit down, offered some tea (which she refused), asked to sit down again (when had she stood up?), she couldn't answer the questions on the form, it was too confusing although usually she was efficient and accurate when completing questionnaires of any sort. Again she was asked if there was anyone she wanted to call.

Pip. The solution came to Steph straight like an arrow.

Pip would help. She'd fill out the forms and hold her hand. She'd bring tissues and maybe toothpaste and a deodorant. Steph could smell her own stale body. She recognised the smell, it was exactly the smell that was emitted when you unzipped a sleeping bag after a poor and restless night's sleep on a camping trip, sweet not sour.

Stephanie was not a natural camper. She liked

her home comforts far too much to think it was a good idea to use up Julian's precious leave battling with inclement weather on the Northumberland coast. Julian didn't subscribe to trips to Cornwall like the rest of Surrey, he preferred the brooding landscapes of the north. Steph would have liked to stick to five-star hotels which laid chocolates on the pillows when they turned down the beds. Yet she had never said as much and they camped at least twice a year over bank holiday weekends because Julian was firm in his belief that the boys would benefit from camping trips. He was staunch in his insistence that their boys ought to be the sort of boys who were comfortable with pegs, torches, compasses, portable gas stoves, light aluminium pan sets and groundsheets. It had been easy to be seduced. Cath Kidston had a lot to answer for. Steph had bought beautifully patterned cagoules, a floral parasol and brightly coloured melamine beakers, she'd donned spotty Wellington boots and gamely joined in. Despite the wet and the sweat and the mould and the cold, Stephanie admitted that she enjoyed herself in a slightly masochistic way, it was fun to see what she and her boys were physically capable of. Besides the bracing walks and daring boat trips, they played cards in the tent, Alfie kept hiding the aces, Harry smiled for three solid days. They fried sausages and heated tins of beans. The experience was like something out of an Enid Blyton book.

She'd give anything to be freezing on a beach right now.

Steph's eyes stung with lack of sleep. She worried that it wasn't nice to smell so stale when you had to meet a doctor. But if Pip came to her, who would look after Chloe? Maybe Steph should call her parents. She glanced at the clock. No, it was too early. They'd be so terrified to receive a call at this time in the morning. She'd have to wait an hour at least. Steph's mother had been the sort who dragged her daughter out of bed, bathed her and dressed her in her Sunday best before she'd take her to the doctors. Would she be cross with Steph for being so slovenly? Or would she understand? Steph didn't know the rules. It was Armageddon.

Steph waited and waited and waited, for what seemed to be hours, and then she checked the clock—four minutes had gone by. That couldn't be right, could it? Another age past, a nurse informed her that her husband was having tests. The nurse couldn't explain what the tests were for or how much longer they would take. Finally, a doctor came and stood in front of Steph. For a moment Steph lost confidence in whether he was actually a doctor. He was wearing a white coat and he looked worn out but then he said his name was *Mr* Khan. Mr Khan started to use words like, 'profound state of unconsciousness' and 'acute neurologic injuries'. The words whirled around Steph's head but would not settle in any sort of order.

'I want to see a doctor,' she insisted, she felt exposed and made susceptible by her confusion.

Mr Khan guided her to a chair in the corridor (no matter how often someone sat her down she seemed to jump back up again, a veritable Jack-in-the-Box). Seeing her confusion he gently explained he was a doctor, a consultant, a specialist if you like. That was a good thing, Steph told herself. He was a specialist. He'd know what he was talking

277

about, he'd have answers. Yet, needing a specialist was a bad thing. Very bad. Mr Khan had a gentle and practical face. He was born to do this job, a job where he had to win people's respect and trust within a heartbeat. Steph tried to concentrate on the tricky words that he was using. He was saying that the head trauma was caused by a blow. He didn't want to speculate on how that blow could have happened. All he'd say was that the police were investigating. He added that the good news was her husband had not sustained any other serious injuries, besides the blow to his head; he was badly bruised and had two cracked ribs but the specialist didn't seem to rate those. There was no internal bleeding or broken limbs that they were aware of but it was too early to fully comprehend the extent or exact nature of the trauma. They'd been running investigative tests and would continue to do so, as necessary.

'We'll know more presently. These cases are unpredictable. The underlying cause of coma is bilateral damage to the reticular formation of the midbrain, which is important in regulating sleep.'

Stephanie heard coma and nothing else.

Was she ready to see her husband now?

At the door to the hospital room, the doctor turned to Stephanie. He pushed his glasses further up the bridge of his nose, he had tiny beads of sweat nestled all the way along the top of his eyebrows. 'We find patients often respond well to a familiar voice at this early time. I do urge you to talk to your husband.'

If only I had, thought Steph. If only.

CHAPTER TWENTY-EIGHT

Pip practically sprinted Chloe to school. Initially her speed was because not only had she successfully managed to hide Robbie's presence from Chloe but she'd also successfully persuaded Robbie to stay put (it hadn't been that tricky, actually) and so she was motivated by the thought of dashing home for yet more sex. Who could blame her for enjoying the feast after such a long famine?

As she dashed to school her thoughts fled to Stephanie and Julian. Pip still couldn't believe it. Not really and truly. Julian an adulterer? No, it couldn't be true. However, about halfway to school, all thoughts of Stephanie and Julian were ousted as she was suddenly struck by the thought that Robbie might be some sort of professional thief. She hardly knew him! Well, other than in the Biblical sense. OK, last night, when they'd talked and talked, she had *felt* as though she'd known him for ages and she *felt* as though she could trust him but that was idiotic. The facts were a) she was a poor judge of character as far as men were concerned, b) she was unable to remember with any clarity a single thing they'd talked about last night anyway (other than she had an awful feeling she had perhaps dwelt a little too long on her break-up with Dylan), and c) she'd only met Robbie less than forty-eight hours ago, *even she* could not pass that off as a meaningful relationship. There was a chance that Robbie Donaldson had sweet-talked his way into her house and her knickers with the sole purpose of clearing out her home of all valuables. How had she ever bought into that male fertility nurse line? Who had heard of male fertility nurses? By the time she got back she might discover that her flat had been stripped of electrical equipment, and her sheets (if still there) would be cold.

However, as Pip risked life and limb (both hers and her daughter's) darting across the A road between the speeding cars (yet again she wished that she had the energy to start a sustained campaign for a zebra crossing), she consoled herself with the thought that even if Robbie was some sort of professional thief—who had gone to extreme lengths to lull her into a false sense of security—she had very little (actually nothing) of value for him to steal. Her TV was rented and insured through the rental company for the few quid it was worth, her DVD player had been purchased a couple of Christmases ago from Boots of all places (with points from her loyalty card) and she couldn't think that Robbie would be that interested in her hair dryer, her hair straighteners or her vibrator. Although her straighteners were GHD and invaluable to her, he just wouldn't get it.

Still, she ran home with her fingers crossed. She crossed the fingers on one hand in the hope that on her return she'd find all her possessions exactly where she'd left them and she crossed the fingers on the other hand in the hope that *he'd* be exactly where she'd left him; there was a danger that he'd have hot-footed it out of there the moment she and Chloe had closed the door behind them. She couldn't kid herself she was what was classically known as a great catch. She was thirty-something (best to stay a little vague as to the exact numerical value of that something) and a single mum, who while saved from the indignity of droopy boobs was suffering from a severe case of sagging self-confidence. Besides, it crossed her mind that running through the streets with her fingers crossed might lead some to believe that she was more than a little bit weird.

She put the key in the lock and gently pushed open the door to her flat. Instead of being greeted with tumbleweed or any signs of a robbery, Pip was greeted with the delicious smell of bacon grilling and the sight of Robbie in one of her aprons. It was a floral number, it took quite a body and an attitude to carry it off. But he did.

'I didn't know I had bacon in the fridge,' she commented, as she edged through the door and slipped out of her jacket.

'You didn't. In fact you didn't have much in, other than some really fancy crisps.'

'I used the last of the milk up on Chloe's Weetabix,' said Pip defensively. She was used to her homemaking skills not coming up to par but she wasn't used to anyone, other than Chloe, being aware that they didn't.

Robbie shrugged good-naturedly. 'I guessed that you probably do your big shop on a Wednesday. I never have anything in the house the day I'm due to go to the supermarket either.' Pip nodded. She was keen to accept his explanation, even though it was untrue. She didn't do a big shop on Wednesdays, or indeed any other day of the week, with any sort of regularity. She was far more likely to pick up a microwave meal and a few essentials like milk, tea bags and a copy of *Heat* magazine at the overpriced One Stop on the walk home from school. Robbie continued, 'I popped out and got some bacon, sausages, eggs and stuff. I found your spare key in the jam jar marked "spare key".'

'Right.' Not able to resist, Pip glanced towards the jar to check the key had been returned. It had. She couldn't decide if she was disappointed or relieved. It was too early to entirely rule out the possibility that the man was psycho and if that was the case she definitely didn't want him to have her key, on the other hand he might just be Prince Charming, in which case . . .

'I thought you might appreciate a big breakfast,' added Robbie.

'You mean to mop up my hangover?' said Pip with a weary grin.

'Erm, no, I was thinking of storing up some calories, considering all the energy you are going to use this morning,' replied Robbie with a much more confident, cheeky grin that, happily, left Pip in no doubt that he wasn't suggesting a jog around the park. 'Your timing is perfect. We're good to go,' he added, placing two plates stacked with attractive-looking cholesterol on to the table.

Pip, prone to inane chatter, particularly when nervous or embarrassed, surprised herself by relaxing into if not a comfortable silence then at least a definite silence while she ate. She found that instead of worrying about the fact that she hadn't had time to apply any make-up (not even the briefest wave of a mascara wand) she focused on the fact that this was the very first time she'd shared breakfast with anyone (other than Chloe) in this flat, it was also the first time anyone (other than Steph) had cooked for her in many years.

Again Pip's thoughts flew to Steph. What must she be going through? Pip resolved to call her the moment Robbie left.

Pip considered that she ought to feel awkward, especially when the yolk of the fried egg found its way down her chin and Robbie wiped it away with a mucky tea towel. She ought to be more self-conscious about the fact that the mugs that Robbie had brewed the tea in were both chipped and mismatched and that her washing (clean but revealing) lay in mountainous stacks around the kitchen (would he think it was a nice homely touch that her bras and tights were hung across the radiator?). But she found that no amount of chaos or muddle could chisel through her feelings of contentment and—good Lord—was the word security overstating the case? It felt pleasant having Robbie here in her messy kitchen. More than pleasant, it felt appropriate. It felt right.

Robbie was quite unlike any man she had ever dated in the past or, to put it more bluntly, he was quite unlike any man she had ever slept with in the past. He was entertaining, with funny stories aplenty (something Pip always admired in people) but he did not seem to consider himself a one-man show and expect her to be a silent and adoring audience. He often stopped mid-flow and asked things about her life. He listened to her answers. Really listened. He didn't listen in that way which made it obvious that he was simply queuing up his next amusing tale (a tale selected so it might place the speaker in a more flattering and impressive light), which was usually the case. On the rare occasions Pip did force herself out and about in a contrived attempt to meet new people (usually to a dinner party at Steph's house) Pip had noticed that people didn't really listen to one another anymore. Not sincerely. Often, she could practically see the cogs of people's minds whirling as they were supposed to be listening to her but in reality were impatiently waiting for the opportunity to start up again on another one of their own fascinating stories. The impatience and sense of one-upmanship always put her off her stride and invariably she'd throw away her punchline or lose the thread of her story, making her look pretty imbecilic, rather than witty and experienced. Robbie seemed to be genuinely interested in everything she had to say and therefore everything she had to say became increasingly interesting. Last night she'd always managed to make it to the punchline.

Some of the details of their conversations were coming back to her. She'd regaled him with tales of her time in Paris, she talked about the catfights between supermodels who, always hungry, were short-tempered and likely to argue over something as small and petty as a hairgrip or the right to the last carrot stick, and she'd recalled tales of glamorous parties, where champagne and caviar were considered basic necessities. Giggling, she'd admitted that she'd rarely enjoyed the lavish hospitality as, more often than not, she'd spent the evening behind the scenes hunting for a fresh bottle of purified water for an important client. The water was needed to fill and constantly refill his finger bowl which another (even more junior) assistant had to carry so that he could dunk his fingers after each canapé; his chubby but manicured digits were insured for hundreds of

284

thousands. He'd seemed really interested in her friendship with Steph and not in a juvenile, pervie 'any chance of a threesome?' way (which she often encountered whenever she talked to men about her special closeness to Steph) and he'd listened to her when she tried to explain how hard she found her parents' emigration to New Zealand which coincided horribly with becoming a single mum. He'd listened to her plans to visit them one year and suggested that maybe that would be next year, now she had the Selfridges contract.

His stories had centred round his amazing experiences at work, his antics with his mates and his chocolate Labrador's terrible behaviour.

Yes, last night, full of champagne and bonhomie, she'd been certain that she was fascinated and fascinating, that's why it hadn't been too tricky for her to hop into bed with him. This morning she was suffering from post-bed-hop regrets and misgivings. She'd rushed things. Again. No good ever came out of rushing things or, put less delicately, no good ever came of shagging a man on the first date because what was his incentive to come back? Everyone knew that. It was written on the stone slabs that Moses brought down from the mountain and while those self-help slash dating guidebooks didn't agree on much, they emphatically agreed on that. The problem was Pip wasn't a hold-back sort of girl, she was more of a heart-on-her-sleeve sort of girl. She knew that her grasp on reality was tremulous. Her family and Steph often accused her of being permanently suspended in fairy-tale land, which she thought was probably a just appraisal. Steph was always telling her the problem with fairy tales was that

285

they were full of doomed princesses. Poor Steph, she must believe that now, more than ever. Pip's mind briefly ran to Steph's calamity. She must call her friend soon. But not now. By refusing to answer Pip's calls last night Steph had made it clear that she wanted to be alone and sort through her mess by herself. She was formidable in her independent ways.

Pip knew she should probably try to be a bit more like Steph. She had to be a bit more realistic this time. There wasn't just her to consider, there was Chloe too. She shouldn't expect too much. She shouldn't charge ahead and risk confusing Chloe or terrifying Robbie. She ought to be a bit more sensible and measured about how things were likely to turn out between them. She'd been carried away on countless occasions. It was time for her to grow up. It was time to be more responsible. To look before she leapt. To pause before she plunged.

He was lovely, though. Look at the way the hairs on his forearms caught the light.

Was it just because he flattered her with his interest that she found him so compelling? she wondered. Or could it be his accent? She was a sucker for a Scottish accent, she always had been, ever since she watched *Braveheart* as a teenager (she also liked kilts). The thought of kilts ruined Pip's resolution to sensibly manage her expectations. She took a moment out from chewing sausage to project forward to her wedding to Robbie, she imagined him wearing a kilt and Chloe wearing a sweet little cream dress with a tartan sash. However, once she acknowledged that she didn't know what any of the guests would look

286

like on his side, she forced herself to settle back down to the present conversation and tried to focus on the here and now. Getting carried away was her worst failing and she had a few to pick from.

'That was delicious.' Pip smiled as she mopped up the last smudge of fried egg with a slice of white toast. 'I can't think when I last had a cooked breakfast. I think you must be trying to impress me,' she asserted with a flirty grin.

She was pleased with the tone she'd hit. She thought she sounded quite cool and in control, it was probably a good thing that she was unaware that she had a glob of ketchup on her white vest top which had happened to fall, like a target, on her proud and pointy nipple.

Robbie grinned back (he was aware of the ketchup blob and the erect nipple). Besides, he was pleased that the cooked breakfast had so obviously impressed her.

'And we've already had sex. Normally guys don't hang around for breakfast, let alone make it after they've got lucky,' Pip added. Robbie couldn't help but look a little shocked and a little concerned. Noticing his reaction, Pip reran, in her head, what she'd just said aloud. Ah, she'd just said she was a slut. 'Oh. I don't mean *my* men rarely stay for breakfast. I meant men *generally*,' she rushed to explain. 'I mean, there haven't been *my men* for, oh, *ages*. Well, since before Chloe was born. Just the one.' Oh God, now she sounded desperate. 'Dylan. I told you about him,' she added helplessly.

'Yes, you told me all about him,' said Robbie. He'd stopped smiling.

Pip paused. Had she gone on and on and on and

287

on about Dylan last night? She couldn't remember exactly. She did have a tendency to reminisce about him when she'd had a few. In fact, Steph said that it wasn't so much reminiscing as obsessing. Truthfully, although Pip would never admit as much to anyone, one of the reasons she liked to get drunk was it practically gave her permission to talk about Dylan. When she was sober, it was acknowledged that a couple of years after the split she shouldn't really still be mentioning her ex, let alone obsessing about him. But when she was drunk, people tended to cut more slack, they'd assume she was being irrational and emotional. This would be true. They'd assume that it was '*just* the drink talking'. This would not be true. She couldn't help herself. She really couldn't.

He'd locked her out. Simply told her that that was it, game over. He'd tossed her away and he'd thrown his baby away. He never even called or wrote to see how Chloe was getting on. Occasionally, he bunged a few hundred quid into their old bank account but not with any sort of regularity, Pip couldn't count on it. He usually remembered to send a birthday or Christmas card to Chloe, but not always. No one really believed her but her fury, her heartache, her mammoth disappointment wasn't for herself alone or even for herself *primarily*—it was for Chloe. It hurt. It hurt so much to know that she'd created a baby, actually brought a little being into the world, with the wrong man. With a man that was incapable (or unwilling) to take his responsibilities seriously. How could she have been so stupid? How could she have made such a gigantic mistake? Could she ever forgive herself? Pip knew that it was possible,

288

not feasible, not probable, but *possible* that one day she might fall in love again, she might even remarry. She'd have another husband, but how many shots did Chloe get at having another father? That was a once in a lifetime thing, wasn't it?

Shyly, Pip looked up at Robbie and wondered. Last night there had been a couple of moments when it seemed as though he knew exactly what she was thinking. She'd lunge for the bread knife and hack off her head if she thought he knew what she was thinking right now. It appeared so pathetic, so misguided and desperate to be weighing up her lay in terms of whether he was father material. That said, would Robbie make a good dad? *Could* Robbie be Chloe's second father? Her first father?

Was she rushing things?

Yes, yes she was. And she knew it. Such thoughts *were* pathetic, misguided and desperate—there was no *appear* about it.

They were also understandable.

As it happened, Robbie was squeezing out a tea bag, concentrating on making a fresh brew, he didn't seem too interested in what was going on in Pip's head that moment. She did find that other people seemed to switch from the sublime to the mundane with much more ease than she could manage. As Robbie handed her a refilled mug, she tried to decipher his slightly dazed expression. Was it the result of discovering the pile of used tea bags in the sink (similar size to most people's pile of grass cuttings), or the effects of the fabulous sex last night (a comforting thought but unlikely). No doubt he was thinking she was a total slut and he was probably regretting the effort he'd put into

289

making the breakfast now that she'd practically told him breakfast wasn't expected (therefore required) and that he could have slunk away at dawn. Or was he thinking she was as desperate as a woman shipwrecked on a desert island where the only sign of life was a well-run convent? Which was worse? Domestic disaster, local slut or totally desperate? None of these was the impression she wanted to give. What a pity.

She had a decision to make. She could say nothing more, allow him to shower and slip away, out of her life for ever, or she could try and explain herself. Properly explain herself and her life.

Pip thought about the night before, how it had been full of laughter and warm, deep kisses. And she thought about many, many nights before that one. Lonely ones, heartbreaking, humiliating and tedious ones. Last night had been neither lonely nor tedious. It had, in fact, been lovely.

'I think I'm a bad mother,' she blurted.

'Why's that?'

'It's not the ordinary stuff I worry about. Not the question of money, or using iron-on name tags rather than taking the time to sew them on or even the matter of tidiness and cleanliness.' She took a brief glance around the messy kitchen and casually shrugged off the disarray. 'That stuff I can handle. I might not be perfect but seriously, none of us are.' She paused and considered. 'Well, perhaps none other than my friend Stephanie. You know she organises her kids' wardrobes not only by season but by colour and they're boys!' Pip glanced at Robbie and thought she was in danger of confusing him or losing him, so she made an effort to stay on track. She took a deep breath and told him her deepest fear, the one thing she'd never said to anyone, even Steph. 'I think I created Chloe with the wrong man. With a disappointing man. And I'm worried that from day one all I've ever taught my little girl is that men stink.'

Pip was a crier. She cried at school Nativity plays (even when her child wasn't performing), she sometimes cried when she listened to beautiful pieces of music, whether it was a full orchestra performing on the radio or a busker pumping out a simple tune on his fiddle in the town centre. She cried at happy endings and sad ones in books and films. She cried when she watched the Queen place a wreath at the Cenotaph on Remembrance Sunday. She cried when she read poetry, when her hands got too cold, when the radiator leaked, when she got a bill, and she cried if she was late or lost.

Suddenly Pip realised she was not crying; usually, talking about Dylan or her daughter guaranteed tears. The combination of the two caused the sort of weeping that was not just a pretty, dainty tear meandering down her cheek but great big, ugly gulps, as though she was fighting for breath. But today, talking to Robbie, Pip was struck by an unfamiliar and delightful sense of calm.

'I love her so much and I'm terrified, utterly terrified, that I've made such a great big rotten mess,' she stated.

Was she benefiting from the famed comfort of strangers? Was it easier to admit this, her deepest, most vicious secret to him because he wasn't her best friend or her mother or even a school-gate mum? Robbie was a stranger, OK a stranger who was more than acquainted with her bikini line, but not someone who was likely to judge her (he had not even noticed that her legs were as hairy as a Highland cow's, let alone judged). As a stranger he was unlikely to offer inadequate words of comfort or worse still a cheery optimistic plan for her future. He probably didn't care enough to do either. That was probably why Pip felt able to share with him her most intimate thoughts. It was probably nothing to do with the fact he had a soothing, patient manner, the most generous smile and such exceptionally merry eyes. Pip had never really understood what it meant to have twinkling eyes until she met Robbie Donaldson but now she got it.

She must not get carried away.

She blamed the lack of sleep. That might at least explain her behaviour. She was tired and not thinking clearly. Yet, she had to admit that saying the words out loud was a distinct relief. She felt notably better. Her worst fear was less threatening once articulated. Some of the menace and shame had dissolved as though she'd broken the spell by simply finding her voice. What was the worst that could happen now? Well, besides Robbie agreeing with her, confirming that she was a dismal excuse for a mother and walking out of their lives before he'd helped with the washing-up. Pip stared at him and waited to hear what he had to say.

'I don't want to pick a fight on such a short acquaintance,' he said, in his oh-so-sexy Scottish accent, 'but I can't help but think that you're wrong.'

'What?'

'You're doing your best and no one can do more than that. It's not like you conceived Chloe with

Hitler, is it? So Dylan's a crap dad. Crap dads are ten a penny. It's not your fault.'

'It's not?'

'No, it's not. It's your problem, but not your fault. It's a problem you have to deal with and I think you're dealing very well.'

'You do?'

'Oh yes. And you can trust me, I'm a doctor.' Robbie smiled encouragingly.

'You said you were a nurse,' Pip pointed out.

'Well, near enough.'

'I guess.' She almost allowed herself to smile.

'Do I need to remind you about my fantastic bedside manner?' he asked.

Pip paused for a moment. Just long enough to notice the spring sunshine flooding through the kitchen window. The bright, warm rays landed like fairy dust on her cutlery, her sewing machine and Robbie's watch, causing everything to twinkle and glisten. Pip watched, mesmerised, as these normal household objects were suddenly and undoubtedly transformed into something much more beautiful and spectacular. Pip knew that all her friends and family despaired of her romantic nature, her willingness to interpret the most everyday occurrence as some sort of sign with a deeper meaning. They warned against her gullible nature, her overactive imagination, her sustained belief that she would be rescued, metaphorically kissed and brought back to life. She knew that if Stephanie were here now, she'd warn her to proceed with caution. Her mother would sigh with impatience and tell her that longevity in a relationship was rarely achieved if the lady was too easy with her favours. The mums at the school gates might tell her to hold out for a genuine doctor, who would earn considerably more than a nurse.

Pip thought they were all wrong.

'Yes, I think you may have to remind me of your fantastic bedside manner,' she said with a shy but inviting smile. She held out her hand and allowed him to lead her back to her bedroom.

CHAPTER TWENTY-NINE

Stephanie lost all sense of time. She was too shaken and stunned to feel tired or hungry so she had no idea that she'd skipped lunch and she'd forgotten that she'd hardly slept for two days straight. Operating on automatic pilot, she'd managed to briefly speak to her parents and Julian's father and she'd left three messages on Pip's answering machine this morning. She was depending on Mrs Hodgson's indiscretion to spread the news around her other friends and neighbours. The course of a tragedy would play out as it always did. Steph knew the ritual. Friends and neighbours would rally, they'd bake casseroles, draw up a schedule for childcare and offer to help in any way they could. Family would dash to their cars, pulling front doors closed behind them but not taking the time to double lock or set alarms, they'd be speeding along motorways now, hurrying to her side, praying to God they weren't too late, unsure what too late might be.

Stephanie knew this was the script because she'd helped out others in their times of need. There was that once, last October half-term break, when a school-mum pal, suffering from pre-eclampsia, went into early labour and Steph had taken in her two older children for nearly a week. Last winter she'd made fish pie every Friday for three months for an elderly neighbour who had lost his wife and his appetite. But, until today, Steph had only been a bit-part of the tragedies or she'd sat in the rafters watching the show, now she was centre stage. Steph had never craved limelight.

Steph's parents arrived at Julian's bedside by about mid-morning, she supposed. She guessed this because her father kept offering her coffee and he drank coffee in the morning and tea in the afternoon. She didn't want a bitter coffee from the vending machine and he probably knew as much but by agreeing to his offer she gave him a small chore. Everyone seemed keen to be of use and to be kept busy. She'd accepted her mum and dad's hugs and clung to their optimistic words of comfort. They were her *parents*, they must know something. She could trust them when they promised her everything would be OK. Right? Except when she looked into their eyes, there was no indication that they could match the reassurances with levels of confidence and so their words of comfort were rendered vacant, they looked just as terrified as she felt. And they didn't know the half.

CHAPTER THIRTY

Pip finally arrived at the hospital at two fifteen in the afternoon. Robbie had stayed at hers until quarter to eleven but then had had to dash off to work.

'Won't you be late?' she'd asked. She was sitting up in bed with the sheets pulled up to her chin. She was OK about being naked in front of him when she was horizontal and gravity worked with her and when he was naked too but now Robbie was fully clothed except for socks, he was running around the room trying to hunt those down.

'I'm already late,' he said, glancing at his watch with a mix of concern and amusement. 'I'll pretend I had an emergency dentist appointment or something.'

'That's not very responsible of you,' she'd teased, secretly pleased that she'd been able to distract him.

'No, it's not,' he said, shaking his head at his own recklessness. 'But in my defence I've never pulled such a stunt before.' He sat down on the bed then and treated her to another long lingering kiss. 'These are very exceptional circumstances,' he'd added.

She'd wanted to ask how exceptional and she'd wanted to carry on kissing him but she knew where it would lead.

'Come on, women need their eggs fertilising and you're the man for the job,' she'd said, gently pushing him away.

'I really have to explain to you exactly what my

job entails sometime,' he'd said with an amused smile. 'I'm not sure you've got it. But not right now. Right now, I have to go. Sadly.'

Despite her intention of calling Steph to see how she was managing, Pip had fallen into a deep and contented slumber the moment he'd pulled the door closed behind him. She couldn't remember sleeping as deeply for an age. She'd slept right through her phone ringing and her mobile beeping with text messages. She'd woken up refreshed and exhilarated; at least she had been until she'd heard Steph's messages.

She was a hurly-burly mass of contradictory and unhelpful emotions. First and foremost she was desperately concerned for Julian's health, naturally. He was in a coma. By God, that sounded serious. That was serious! Pip couldn't get her head around it at all. The problem with living a life packed full of soap operas and contrived reality TV was that when something genuinely authentic happened, it was impossible to understand its enormity. She'd had so much to take in over the last two days and frankly her mind was struggling to compute most of it. First she'd been told Julian was an adulterer, then (if she'd understood Steph's hysterically whispered messages) that Julian was a victim of a hit-and-run crime and therefore now in a coma. That was insane. Too shocking for words. And why was Steph whispering? Perhaps she didn't want to wake the other patients as she was ever so considerate, but then if Julian was on a coma ward, wouldn't it be a good thing to wake the patients? Pip didn't know. It was all too much. She'd called Steph immediately and had been frantic when she'd discovered Steph's phone line was dead.

297

Could it be that her phone was switched off? You did have to switch off phones in hospitals. Or maybe she was out of power. Pip imagined how many desperate and lonely calls Steph must have made to run out of power and she was deeply ashamed of herself. Too agitated to drive, she'd hopped into a taxi and headed off to the hospital.

From the back of the cab Pip called Mrs Amstell, Steph's mum, who would for all eternity be Mrs Amstell or Steph's mum to Pip but never Joan) and was relieved to find that Mr and Mrs Amstell were currently at the hospital with Steph. Mrs Amstell explained the situation as best she could and they'd discussed a series of complicated arrangements for the children's care. Pip was told that the boys had been packed off to school without any knowledge of the situation because Mrs Hodgson hadn't known what to tell them and so had decided to tell them nothing at all (although, as Steph had predicted, Mrs Hodgson had spent the entire morning on the phone speculating and gossiping with friends, neighbours and acquaintances). Now the school and the children needed to be told of the situation. The seriousness had to be stressed without instilling any sort of panic or fear. Pip offered to do the job but was somewhat relieved when it was suggested that she'd be more use sitting with Steph at the hospital and that, with the knowledge that she was on her way, the grandparents could leave and go directly to the school to deliver the news and try to offer some comfort to the children.

'Will they come and visit Julian after school?' Pip had asked Mrs Amstell.

'No, dear. I don't think so. Not yet at least. I

don't think it's a good idea that the boys see their dad like this.' Pip had felt her stomach lurch as she tried to envisage what to expect.

He didn't look like Julian. He looked like a sick person. Any sick person. All sick people. He was as pale as the sheet he lay on. Pip had last seen him on Monday morning, when he'd looked tanned, handsome and muscular. It was unbelievable to think that was just forty-eight hours ago. Now he looked puffy, pallid and disturbingly placid. The room was airless.

Pip put her hand on Julian's. 'Hey,' her voice came out quieter than she'd planned. She coughed and then spoke up with a forced jovial intonation that she doubted was appropriate. 'You are in a mess, aren't you, mate? What's been going on? Does it hurt?'

The nurse on the reception desk had said it was important to talk to Julian but the questions seemed ridiculous and Pip momentarily lost her confidence in her ability to carry on. Just then Steph pushed open the door to the room. Pip fell on her and drew her into the most enormous hug.

'Jesus, Steph, I am so, so sorry.'

Steph abruptly pulled away from Pip's arms and walked straight to Julian's bedside without so much as looking her friend in the face. She'd only been out of the room for a few moments, just long enough to pee, but she was swamped with a sickening feeling of dread. What if something had happened to him while she'd been out of the room? What if nothing had?

Pip felt rejected and hopeless. Her arms fell to her sides and swung there uselessly. 'I'm sorry I didn't get your calls this morning.' Guilt that she hadn't been available for her friend affected her tone of voice and she sounded shrill, rather than concerned or contrite.

'Oh, I realise you had Chloe to get to school, Mrs Hodgson managed the boys,' muttered Stephanie. 'I did try you a couple of times but when I didn't get a response I guessed you were probably working with your earphones on. I know you do that sometimes when you're really busy.'

Pip thought of her morning—hot and sweaty, enjoying Robbie's naked body, finally reaching a very satisfying orgasm and then falling into a profound sleep. She felt miserable.

'Yes, I was working,' she muttered. She felt uncomfortable lying to Steph at a time like this but since it was a time like this, she could hardly introduce the topic of Robbie.

Steph still hadn't so much as glanced at Pip. She hated taking her eyes off Julian, she was terrified that if she didn't watch him all the time something awful might happen. The thought made her grimace with a sad irony. Something *more* awful, she corrected herself. 'There was nothing you could do anyway,' she added.

'I suppose not. But I am sorry.'

'I guess you've already made quite some progress on the Selfridges order, have you?' Steph was not trying to sound censorial, she was hardly thinking about the words coming out of her mouth, she'd slipped into routine mode of appearing to take a polite interest in other people, and it had taken all her strength to do as much, but Pip was alert to criticism and felt wrong-footed. She knew it was impossible but it was as though Steph knew she'd been neglecting her friend and her work in order to have hot sex. Pip blushed.

'What sort of friend must I be? A terrible one, hey?' she groaned.

If she hoped for a response she was disappointed as Steph was too distracted by Julian's condition to really give any time to Pip's self-loathing. In this moment it was beyond Steph to dredge up her customary cheering pep talk. Shouldn't Pip be comforting her, even if it was accepted that in every other awkward social situation it did generally fall to Steph to come up with the correct ice-breaker or call up some pleasant small talk which was interesting and inclusive and yet not intimidating? It was clear that Pip was incredibly uncomfortable, she was never any good around sickness, Steph knew that, but Pip couldn't really expect to be put at ease in this situation, could she? This was horrifying and immense. It was draining all of Steph's energy and willpower to just stay upright in her chair. Truthfully, she wanted to collapse in a heap on Julian's bed, on Pip's shoulder or even on to the cold, tiled floor. It didn't really matter to her where she did her collapsing, she just longed to give in to the scale of this nightmare.

After a moment Pip coughed and then asked, 'So how is he?'

'He's in a coma,' stated Steph flatly.

Pip knew this and wanted to kick herself for her clumsiness but what was the right thing to say? 'He'll be OK, though, won't he?' she added.

'I don't know. They don't know,' Steph replied, nodding her head towards the open door that led to the hospital corridor and towards the army of doctors and nurses who, disappointingly, couldn't tell her anything concrete. Steph felt powerless and cheated. Weren't doctors supposed to know everything, fix everything? Isn't that why they went to college for years and years? Steph sighed, she knew her frustration was unreasonable but she couldn't help feeling resentment.

The bleak truth floored them both and they sat in silence with just the sound of medical machines whirring and nurses talking to one another outside the room.

After a while Pip asked, 'So what happened? What do the police say?'

The word police seemed to slap Steph, she flinched. 'They haven't said much, other than it being a hit-and-run. He was found at the hotel.'

'The Highview?'

'Yes.'

Pip shifted uncomfortably. 'That's awkward. How are you going to explain that to everyone?'

Steph shot Pip a quick look of frustration. 'He was working.'

'But—'

'Working, Pip,' Steph insisted with a grim determination.

'Right,' muttered Pip. Of course, what else could Steph say? What else *would* Steph say? She was wedded to keeping up appearances and this was not the moment for dramatic revelations. Julian's father was on the M25 right now, hurrying towards his son, and the three boys were to hear the terrible news about Julian's condition this afternoon, no one would want the matter made any more complicated. Anyway, it didn't matter one jot why Julian was at the hotel, did it? Pip didn't want to say anything that would further distress her friend, she certainly had no intention of telling anyone about the saucy texts on the phone, she was still clinging to the hope that the phone wasn't Julian's after all and that he wasn't having an affair—although the fact that he was found at Highview did seem to be quite damning evidence against him.

Stephanie was thinking about all the things she'd said about her husband to Pip yesterday. She'd said he was an idiot, he was cruel, a two-timing, double-dealing, faithless bastard. She'd howled that she hated him. And that she loved him. At least now she knew which it was.

'Would you mind not mentioning that we knew any differently when you talk to the police?' Steph said quietly.

'Why would I talk to them?' asked Pip.

'The police might want to talk to you. You know, just routine. They wanted to know where I was last night.'

'Oh. I see.'

'Nothing to worry about, Pip.'

'No, of course not.'

Neither of the women had taken their eyes off Julian throughout the exchange but despite their combined wishful thinking his eyelids did not flutter, nor did he tentatively attempt to mutter any words.

'I said I thought he was in London, because that's what he'd told me. I don't want him waking up to a scandal,' added Steph. 'That sort of nonsense isn't going to help his recovery, is it?'

'No. I understand,' agreed Pip. It was a good thing that Steph was having such a positive attitude and talking about when Julian would wake up.

'Do you have a newspaper?' Steph asked suddenly.

'I can go and get you one. Why?'

'I'd like to read to Julian. The nurses said he might recognise my voice. It might help.' Steph still didn't take her eyes off him, her anxiety stained the air.

'But papers are only full of bad news. Why don't you just chat to him?'

'About what, Pip? What do you suggest I talk to him about?'

'Your news,' replied Pip without thought.

'I haven't any good news either.'

'Oh. Yes. Right. Erm, I'll go and get a paper from the shop in the foyer.'

CHAPTER THIRTY-ONE

Steph had a pleasant melodic voice but Pip wasn't sure it was going to stimulate Julian. After she'd listened to Steph read headlines, bylines and copy on the financial and sports pages in *The Times*, she was left feeling stupefied. The room was a little too warm to be comfortable and if it hadn't been for the constant flow of nurses and doctors coming in and out of the room—checking charts, tweaking dials and prodding Julian—there would have been a serious danger that she might have dropped off to sleep. Pip did have a tendency to close down in times of stress. She'd spend most of her days, from door-slamming to decree absolute, under the duvet. Psychologists said that everyone had a fight or flight trigger, Pip had a snooze button.

Besides, what was the point of her being here? She felt helpless and in the way. Steph was acting strangely. Well, who was to say what was normal under these hideous circumstances? But Pip would have felt more comfortable if Steph had been prepared to talk about the thing that was so obviously sitting between them—the huge neon elephant in the room. What was Steph thinking and feeling? She wouldn't say. Pip wondered whether on some level Steph was punishing her because she hadn't responded as Steph hoped she would last night or because she hadn't been available this morning. Pip was unreasonably hurt that her friend was being so closed. Pip had always shared with Steph every single thought that passed through her head and every single feeling that had passed through her heart (even the less worthy feelings that passed somewhere quite a bit lower on her anatomy were divulged, discussed and dissected). Why wouldn't Steph tell her how she was feeling?

All that said, Pip didn't think this was the moment to trade her news. Hey, guess what, Steph? I think perhaps I might be falling in love! No, it definitely was not the moment.

Eventually the oppressive atmosphere became too much for Pip. She never liked hospitals; no matter how many people told her they were where people went to get better, that hadn't always been her experience. All she could smell, taste, see and hear was sickness. She glanced at her watch and wondered whether one hour and forty-five minutes was an acceptable amount of time to visit someone who didn't know you were there.

'Is there anything I can do, Steph?' she asked, as

305

she discreetly reached for her handbag.

'No, I don't think so. Just, you know . . .'

Steph didn't want to actually have to ask her friend to pray, or touch wood, or hope for the best or for any of the other usual crutches although she was frantically grasping at every option. Pip understood and squeezed Steph's hand, it was unusually clammy, which was probably not a surprise under the circumstances but normally Stephanie had such cool fingers, sometimes chilly.

'In that case I think I'll get back and see how Chloe and the boys are getting along. Maybe I could relieve your mum and she could come back here.'

'That's good of you.'

'Will you still be here?'

'Where else would I be?'

'Right, yes. Silly of me. Sorry,' muttered Pip, as she wished that she could spontaneously combust. Where had their usual comfortable familiarity gone? Never before had Pip felt she'd said the wrong thing to Steph, yet this afternoon when she most needed to say the absolutely right thing, she'd felt she'd been about as delicate as a medieval torturer keen to hurry through a couple of disembowelments and a ducking before sunset. 'Well, if you think of anything—anything at all— just say, won't you?'

'Yes, of course.' Pip leant in to hug her friend but Stephanie didn't melt into the embrace as usual, instead she remained brittle and distant. Pip felt a fresh wave of guilt. Perhaps she ought to stay, even if she didn't want to. 'Oh Pip, just one thing. Something and nothing really,' said Steph. She finally turned her gaze to meet her friend's.

'What? Anything.'

'I told the police that I stayed at your house until about eleven, maybe even half past, last night.'

'Oh. Why did you say that?'

'Because I'd mentioned that I went to yours at seven and that we had a drink. I shouldn't really have driven home when I did.'

No, she shouldn't have. She should have stayed and they could have talked about Steph's fears that Julian was having an affair. The opportunity to do so had obviously vanished for ever because clearly Steph had no intention of discussing it while he lay comatose. Which was understandable, Pip supposed. Imagine if he could hear them! Imagine if he couldn't. Pip just wanted to make Steph feel better, even in the smallest way she could.

'Well, it was just a glass of champagne. Not a binge session. I think it would have been OK to say you drove home at seven thirty.'

'Oh, probably, yes,' said Steph quickly. 'Even so, I was worried that they'd be funny about it. We drank the champagne out of a wine glass and those glasses are really a unit and a half. I couldn't remember all the rules about how much you're supposed to have drunk before you can drive. I thought if I added a couple of hours on then it would be OK, as my body would then have had time to digest the alcohol.'

'I see.' Pip mentally shrugged. God, Steph was such a worrier. Getting ticked off for drinking and driving was the last thing that would have been on Pip's mind if she'd ever had to face the same set of circumstances. Her best friend was astonishing.

'You understand,' said Steph.

'Yes, I do.' Pip zipped up her jacket, squeezed Julian's lifeless hand and then headed to the door. At the door she turned to her friend. Something was nagging her like an out-of-reach itch in the middle of her back or a damned fruit fly hanging around the grapes. The idea, only half formed, still fuzzy, would not be ignored. Pip knew she was being crazy but she had to ask. 'But you went straight home, right, Steph?'

'Yes, of course,' replied Stephanie without taking her eyes off her husband. 'Straight home.'

CHAPTER THIRTY-TWO

Steph breathed an enormous sigh of relief when Pip left the room. She hated lying to Pip and asking Pip to lie on her behalf. But what else could she do? Oh dear God, what could she do?

It was very unfortunate for Steph that she'd been born into the sort of family who firmly believed in God as a scary being, someone or something to be very, very afraid of. A being that might generously give with one hand but could just as swiftly take away with the other. A being that punished a woman for being tempted by a man who was not her husband. Her God was not interested in extenuating circumstances such as her husband nailing another woman. Her God demanded an eye for an eye. A tooth for a tooth.

An accident. It was an accident.

For the first time in her life, Steph envied Pip her lack of faith. Pip didn't believe in God at all but if she did, she'd probably believe in a hippy, female God who was known for bestowing beatific smiles and having endless reserves of forgiveness which she not only flung around like confetti but which she stored in designer handbags.

Oh, the guilt. The guilt and the fear. Stephanie was practically paralysed with both emotions. Her mind kept returning to last night and the guilt and fear were overwhelming. All-consuming. She could not think about it. No, she could not. She must not. If she did she might vomit. Best to keep busy. Best to nurse her husband. Best to be a good wife.

Steph leant close into her husband and then whispered in his ear, 'Get better, get better, please.' She sat back on her chair and then, unbidden, the thought of one of the rude texts she'd read on his phone leapt into her mind. She leaned forward again and added, 'You bastard.'

CHAPTER THIRTY-THREE

Pip practically ran down the corridor, away from the sickroom; she was keen to exit the hospital as quickly as possible. She was wearing high-heeled boots and the sound of her scurrying away reverberated through the wards. It wasn't noble of her, she knew as much. Yet, irrationally, knowing that she was behaving poorly made her keener still to put distance between herself and Steph's tragedy.

Pip was viciously disappointed with herself. She'd occasionally fantasised about being just the sort of person who would be good in a crisis, empathetic, patient and practical. She knew this was slightly twisted but she'd even, once or twice, thought she'd actually like something to go wrong for Steph so that she could step up to the plate and show Steph just how useful she could be. Horrible thing to admit, really, but Steph had been a rock to her throughout her terrible break-up and last night, after the initial shock and disbelief regarding Julian's affair, a teeny tiny part of Pip thought that maybe some good could come out of Steph's awful situation. Perhaps she could talk Steph off the ledge, stay calm and convince her that there had been a hideous mix-up, or at least she could buy the tissues to mop up the tears when they both accepted the painful truth. Yes, Pip had always been certain that she'd be empathetic, patient and practical if ever Stephanie needed her. But a coma? A coma was too big.

Pip was terrified and overwhelmed and as such she was incapable of thinking straight, never her forte. She was being totally illogical. It was not logical to think her best friend was behaving weirdly just because she had lied to the police about the small matter of when she left Pip's house. So what? Pip had lied to the police on a quite a few occasions. She always claimed not to have been aware that she was speeding or that she was parked in a residents-only bay (not that it did her any good, her driver's licence had more points than her supermarket loyalty card). The odd lie to a person in authority was not a big deal. Pip had lied to teachers when, on a bright day, she fancied a trip to the seaside and wanted to take Chloe out of school (although whether Miss Fletcher really thought Chloe was susceptible to throat infections or not was debatable). She lied on her CV about the glaring gaps between employment (again, not especially effectively, as most potential employees were alert to the failings of a candidate who had more breaks in their career than the four-finger Kit-Kat bar).

It was just that Stephanie didn't lie. Not to ticket officers, or teachers or anyone. Why would she lie to the police?

Pip shook her head and took deep gulps of the spring air in order to clear her foggy mind. She was being stupid, probably because her conscience was inflamed. She should have sat all evening and all night with Steph, she should have held her hand and whispered in a soft voice that everything was going to be all right but she simply could not make herself do it. Julian's inert state frightened her. The smell of disinfectant and sickness that oozed throughout the hospital was too much for her. *Was* everything going to be all right?

Pip was desperate to feel life, to touch life. She needed to be out in the open, to allow the freshness of the spring breeze to wash over her body and run through her hair. This situation was unprecedented and far, far too big for her to cope with in any other way than bite-size pieces. Her selfishness appalled her but it was unavoidable. Pip ran out of the hospital and towards the bus stop in too much of a hurry to notice anyone else. She slapped bang into him.

'Sorry, sorry,' she muttered without looking up to see who she was apologising to.

'Not at all, my fault,' he replied automatically and then he recognised the thick, blonde hair and long thin limbs that were flailing around hazardously. 'Hey.' He threw out a big grin.

'Pippa.'

'Robbie? Bloody hell, what are the chances?'

'Well, quite high. I work here and you so obviously *are* stalking me. Couldn't keep away from me, hey? God, I must be good.' He delivered his line with a huge beam, but Pip was embarrassed, guilty and worried so she wasn't in the mood for his jovial cracks.

'I'm visiting a friend, actually. He's in a coma,' she said starkly.

'Shit. Sorry, Pippa.' Robbie looked instantly stricken, it was a difficult statement to recover from. He fingered his stubble and looked mortified. 'Oh, Pippa. Wow. I am so sorry.'

The coma stunt was low. It was an effective conversation-stopper but did she really want to stop the conversation? No, she wanted his attention. Besides, it was wrong to elicit sympathy when she hadn't even managed to sit with Julian and keep Steph company for so much as an entire afternoon. Pip regretted being so brutal and tried to make up by giving a bit more detail.

'Yeah, I'm sorry too. It's Julian, Steph's husband.'

'Steph's husband? The adulterer?'

Maybe she had given too much detail already. Last night she had been unable to resist telling Robbie all about Steph's predicament, but now it seemed extremely grubby to hear Julian branded as something so low, especially when he was in such a desperate position. 'We don't know he's an adulterer for sure,' said Pip weakly.

'Come on, Pippa. Were you born yesterday? The phone message from the hotel, the cheeky texts. It's an open and shut case.'

312

'He was found at the hotel,' admitted Pip.

'Was it a heart attack?'

Clearly Robbie's mind was now full of images of Julian in full bondage gear tied to the bed with a buxom woman astride him, shagging him to death. Pip felt protective and snapped, 'It was a hit-and-run, actually. He was found in the car park.'

'Shit.' Robbie looked stunned. He blurted the first thought in his head. 'Did your friend Steph do it?'

'For God's sake!' Pip glared at him. 'Why would you say a thing like that?'

'Sorry, sorry. Stupid thing to say. Bloody stupid of me.' Robbie held up his hands as though he was surrendering under fire. 'It's just that it usually is the spouse who's culpable if there's any sort of out-of-the-ordinary violence. Statistics show that. And what with her just discovering that he had a mistress.'

'Shut up, Robbie.'

'Right.' He clamped his mouth shut.

The thought was too ridiculous. Too shocking. She had to put the idea right out of her head. No one who knew Stephanie could ever have articulated such a wild fantasy. Was he joking? Well, it was a stupid, sick joke. Ridiculous.

Robbie and Pip silently stared at their feet. He was wearing scruffy Converse trainers which made his feet look very long indeed. Pip suddenly had a flashback to their night together. Once again colour rushed to her cheeks. That was so inappropriate of her! But it wasn't her fault, it was a subconscious connection. It wasn't even a scientific rule—big feet did not necessarily mean that a man was well-endowed, although it did in

313

this case. Even so, being well-endowed did not guarantee a good performance in the sack, although—again—it did in this case. If only his brain was as big as his dick, thought Pip very crossly and somewhat unfairly, as she dragged her eyes up from the ground in order to glare at him. How could he have said something so awful about Steph? He met her gaze.

'I'm really sorry, Pippa. That was an unbelievably stupid thing for me to say. Of course I'm not suggesting that your friend is capable of anything like attempted murder. Hell, things are bad enough without that sort of idea being mooted.'

'Yes, yes they are,' snarled Pip.

'The problem is I say stupid things when I'm nervous,' he confessed.

'You're nervous?'

'Massively.'

'Because you think my friend is a killer?'

'No, because you're so great and I don't want to mess this up.' He dragged his fingers through his longish hair and looked around the hospital car park.

'Really?' Pip felt a warm glow in the pit of her belly.

'Yeah, really. I know you can't tell. Saying your best mate is the prime suspect in her husband's hit-and-run is probably not a great way to show you that I don't want to mess this up.'

'No, I mean the other bit. You really think I'm great?'

'Yes, I do,' he stated plainly.

'That's nice to know.' Pip breathed out, calmly accepting the compliment. The words settled in

314

her head and she felt a rare rush of confidence. She looked at her watch. 'Look, I'm sorry, I'm not ducking out on you. It's just that—'

'This is a bad time,' he suggested.

'Very bad,' she confirmed.

'Can I help you? Can I drive you somewhere?'

Pip hesitated, it would be much quicker to accept a lift than to travel by bus and there was a huge queue snaking from the taxi rank, she'd have to wait an age for a cab. 'I do need to get to Steph's as soon as possible but I won't be much company,' she warned.

'We don't have to talk. Hell, it might be a way forwards.'

'Yes, it might,' she said and she allowed herself a brief grin.

'Let me help you,' he urged. The request was made with such rare sincerity that Pip felt temporarily at a loss. She understood that she was being presented with a singular opportunity. It was as though he was tempting her to collapse into a big fluffy cloud, a cloud that would carry her along and protect her. 'I want to help and I can,' he added.

She believed him and she thought that maybe he was talking about offering more help than just a lift. It wasn't rational. It wasn't considered. It was a belief, or maybe not even that, maybe just a hope. Whatever it was, Pip knew Robbie Donaldson was a big deal. It was undeniable that he'd come along at a uniquely inconvenient time, it was hideously confusing to feel so excited and optimistic about one thing while feeling utterly gutted about another. The contradiction was exhausting.

Yet . . .

315

She nodded. She thought that perhaps she did need help. Oddly, knowing she was going to get it made her feel considerably stronger.

CHAPTER THIRTY-FOUR

Kirsten had once watched a TV programme about people being hypnotised so that they'd give up fags or stop pigging out. It was nothing to do with dangling fob watches; it was just a case of replacing negative thoughts with positive suggestions. It didn't sound too difficult, it had to be worth a shot. All day Kirsten had repeated the same mantra, 'This is not my fault. Not my fault. Not my fault. None of this is my fault.' The hypno guy on the TV had said it could take a few days for your negative subconscious to accept the positive suggestions that you were repeating but that it always worked. If that was right then she reckoned that by Friday night she might really believe that none of this was her fault.

At first, she hadn't thought she had it in her to get out of bed and go into work this morning, not after what she'd been through—what she'd seen— it was a big ask. But some sort of survival instinct told her she had to, if she was absent she'd have explaining to do. A doctor's note or something might have to be dredged up and while she was certain she could convince a doctor to give her a sick note (she looked like shit after spending half the night in the bath and she'd probably caught her death of cold) all in all it was probably not a good idea to draw attention to herself right now. She could have justifiably had the day off, it wouldn't be pulling a sickie because she had actually felt very sick on the journey into work but all the same it was probably best to carry on as normal. Not my fault. Not my fault. The thing that was bothering her was that she'd known that there would be an announcement about Jules's death and she wasn't sure how she ought to react.

She thought of herself as a pretty good actress. She'd wanted to be an actress at one point, when she was a kid. She'd gone to drama classes on Saturday mornings for a few months. She'd been quite into it until she'd overheard some bitch of a teacher talking to one of the other kid's mums. The teacher had said that while Kirsten's acting was OK, she was really heavy on her feet and she couldn't sing a note. The teacher said she wasn't 'drama school material'. Kirsten thought that the bitch of a teacher was probably just jealous because she was far prettier than the teacher had ever been and the teacher was an old hag now. It was all over for her and she was doing nothing more fabulous with her life than teaching a bunch of bratty schoolkids how to project to the back of the town hall. Still, Kirsten had packed in the drama lessons after that as she hadn't wanted to line the old bag's pockets. There was nothing they could teach her anyhow, she was a natural. She could make herself cry if she needed to (which came in handy as a teenager when guilt-tripping Daddy over how much he worked and how little she saw of him, just a couple of tears and he'd always bung her twenty quid) and hadn't she always managed to convince *really* boring blokes they were way more interesting than they could

317

possibly hope to be? Plus, she'd never in her life had an orgasm but every man she'd ever been with thought they were super studs and that she came every time because she'd watched enough porn to know what was expected. If that wasn't natural talent, she didn't know what was. Kirsten hadn't gone in for acting in the end. She still secretly thought that maybe, one day, she'd be walking down the street and some talent agent might spot her, which would be cool. But she wasn't stupid, she knew that it could take years and years and years before you made it big time if you went to drama school and auditioned for poxy parts at poxy local theatres and all that, and Kirsten was in too much of a hurry to be rich to take years and years building a career.

So how should she react to news of Jules's death? She'd practised her surprised look in the bathroom mirror before she set off to work. Plus, her horrified one. Which would be the most appropriate? Would people expect her to be more surprised or horrified? She'd have to see how the other PAs acted and just do whatever they did. No one knew she had been Jules's lover and therefore they wouldn't expect her to act any differently from anyone else, looking heartbroken would be an unnecessary shade to her performance. She was genuinely interested to see how everyone would react. Jules was really popular in the office. Had been, she corrected herself, it was odd getting used to the fact he'd gone. Not my fault. Not my fault. None of this is my fault. His fault. His wife's fault. Not my fault. She was sure everyone would be very sad. Thinking about it now, it was a bit of a shame she'd never confided her affair to anyone. From time to time she had considered telling Ellie, who sat at the desk next to hers, and if she had told Ellie, then Ellie would certainly have made a special fuss of her at a time like this. She'd have made the tea all day, instead of them having to take turns like usual, and she'd have answered Kirsten's phones too probably—that sort of thing—because she'd have known Kirsten was gutted.

Anyway, when the announcement did come, Kirsten hadn't had to act. She *was* genuinely surprised, you could have knocked her over with a feather. And she was relieved. My God, so relieved. He wasn't dead. Just in a coma. She'd actually cried for real. People had mistaken her relief for shock and Ellie did make the tea all day. He wasn't dead. That was brilliant.

Halfway through the day the excitement and relief began to drain away as Kirsten heard rumours that the police were going to be coming into the office to ask a few people questions. Why? No one here knew what had happened to him, except her of course, and she sure as hell wasn't going to be saying a word. There were loads of other rumours going around too. Some people said he was still going to die, while others said he was going to live but wouldn't be able to walk again. Since Kirsten had heard he was in hospital, in a stable but critical condition, she'd thought that he'd wake up by about teatime. Whenever they said 'stable but critical' on *Grey's Anatomy*, the person always woke up by the end of the episode (suffering from nothing more than a really bad headache). She'd thought that if Jules woke up with nothing worse than a bad headache then everything would be OK. He was unlikely to want to tell anyone what they were doing at the hotel and how his accident came about. He wouldn't mention her being with him. No one else knew about her. He'd never mentioned her to anyone. That was the point of mistresses, they were invisible, a fact that used to piss her off but it was something she was now grateful for.

Kirsten kept her head down all day. She finally got round to all that electronic filing which she'd avoided doing since she started her job. She left the office at five on the dot, as usual. Other than the filing and the muttering (not my fault, not my fault), Kirsten behaved as she normally did.

CHAPTER THIRTY-FIVE

Mr and Mrs Amstell, Harry, Alfie and Chloe rushed to the door as soon as they heard Pip ring the bell.

'Any news?' they demanded in a chorus.

Pip shook her head. 'Same, no change.'

'That's good, isn't it?' asked Alfie desperately. 'He's not worse.'

'Come into the kitchen and finish your tea, Alfie darling. Where's Freddie? Go and call him. I think you'll find him glued to the box,' said Mrs Amstell to her grandson, saving Pip the difficulty of responding to his question. Pip noticed Mrs Amstell was trembling like a leaf in the wind, even though the house was warm. She glanced at Mr Amstell, he appeared grey and reduced. He put Pip in mind of a rabbit boxed in a cage, anxious and twitching.

Harry lingered in the hallway, keen to eavesdrop on the adult conversation that was no doubt about to take place between Pip and his grandparents. Alfie was such an idiot, he thought. A total baby. Of course the news 'no change' was not good news. Dad was in a coma. They *wanted* a change.

Pip noticed Harry skulking and pulled him into a hug; over the top of his head she threw out a half shrug, half grimace at the grandparents. When she released Harry, Pip said, 'Harry, there are two casserole dishes on the doorstep, will you go and bring them inside?' She had an idea that it was best to keep the oldest boys occupied.

'More food?' gasped Mrs Amstell. 'People are so kind. And so *efficient.*' She was unable to hide her surprise. 'There was a dish on the step when we returned from school. I wasn't quite sure what it was at first. A bean, lentil and tofu stew, I think.'

'I suppose news has got round fast,' added Mr Amstell. 'Shocking things such as this do bring out the best in people.'

'The tofu stew came in a very smart dish and it was boxed in some sort of heat-retaining container, the like of which I've never come across,' added his wife. 'There was no note. I don't know who to return it to.'

'Don't worry. These things have a way of sorting themselves out. The right lady will make herself known when she needs to,' reassured Pip.

Mrs Amstell looked relieved and then confessed, 'We didn't actually eat the stew.'

'Oh?'

'No. I'd already promised the children chicken nuggets and chips.' The grandma looked sheepish.

321

Pip was flattered that someone might think she was the sort of mother who demanded anything more sophisticated from her child's food than it filled up the belly of said child.

'Things are bad enough without health food,' muttered Mr Amstell.

Pip smiled. 'I'll take over with the children if you want to get back to the hospital. I think Steph would appreciate seeing you. Julian's dad might be there by now too.'

'Yes. Good idea. I'd like to talk to the doctors,' said Mr Amstell. Mrs Amstell ran around the house gathering up bits that might offer some comfort to Steph or be of use to Julian, a bar of chocolate, clean clothes, the book that Steph had by her bed, his iPod and the portable speakers. She put everything into large canvas shopping bags and she tucked a huge cream box under her arm.

'What's in the box?' asked Pip.

'It's their wedding album. I found it on the breakfast bar. They must have been looking at their photos quite recently. Isn't that touching? They're such a close couple.' Mrs Amstell looked momentarily stricken at the thought of how close she believed them to be but Pip was pretty certain that destroying the fantasy wasn't going to offer much reassurance. 'I thought Steph might like to have them by her side. I thought it might be comforting.'

'Oh,' said Pip. So that was how Steph had spent her evening, nothing suspicious, only heartbreaking. Pip clearly imagined exactly why Steph might have been looking at the photos last night. She'd have been looking at them in rage, feeling rejection and regret. What would she feel when her mother presented them to her now? Pip had no idea. What was Steph thinking? There was a chance that Steph might find the photos a comfort or she might hurl them out of the hospital window. Who knew?

Pip closed the door on Steph's parents and turned back to the four children. The boys all stared at her with expressions that clearly communicated that they thought she was in charge and could solve things. She was, after all, the adult. Notably, Chloe's expression was less expecting, more pleading.

OK. Get with the programme, she instructed herself. She *was* the adult. She was in charge. Robbie thought she was great. The knowledge somehow helped her to be a bit less pathetic than she was naturally inclined. She *could* step up to the plate as she'd always imagined. She could be empathetic, patient and practical, it was *not* too late. But where to start? She should clear away the evidence of chicken nuggets and chips (the debris in the sink and ketchup around the kids' faces). They had enjoyed arctic roll too, the cardboard wrapping hadn't been put in the recycling box and vivid yellow drops of vanilla ice cream had dripped on the table and floor. Steph's parents must have bought that especially because Pip couldn't imagine such a thing in Steph's freezer. Steph firmly believed you are what you eat and she didn't see any of her boys as arctic roll or minced, mechanically separated meat held together with phosphate salts, some chicken skin and antioxidants derived from petroleum. Wednesday night was normally toad-in-the-hole night, with roasted onion gravy and two accompanying

323

vegetables. All ingredients were organic and most were bought at the local farmers' market. Usually Pip and Chloe loved coming round on a Wednesday even if it meant that they had to abide by the house rule, anyone who didn't eat all their veg had a choice—no pudding or no TV.

What would Steph do right now?

Pip started to stack the dishwasher, and then she wiped down all the surfaces and cleaned the kitchen floor. After that she supervised homework, bathed Freddie and Chloe and sat outside the bathroom while Harry and Alfie took it in turns to bath themselves. She did respect their right to privacy but she was far too nervous to remain downstairs in front of the TV while they managed themselves; what if one of them slipped in the bath? This home already had enough tragedy to deal with. She read stories to the children and tucked them into their beds, or rather the beds they'd opted for tonight—they all piled into Steph and Julian's bed, except for Chloe, she settled into the top bunk in Alfie's room. Surprisingly, all the children fell asleep almost the moment their heads had hit their pillows. Pip had expected resistance but found resilience.

It was about 9 p.m. and Pip was just putting a load of washing in the machine when Mr and Mrs Amstell arrived home. Unfortunately, they had not been able to persuade Steph to come home too.

'She's going to sleep on a camp bed by his side,' said Mr Amstell.

'Devoted,' noted Mrs Amstell with a sad smile.

'Demented,' contradicted her husband. 'She needs a decent night's sleep. She won't be any help to anyone if she gets sick too. She looks bloody awful.'

It was decided that Pip should stay. There was no point in disturbing Chloe and catching a bus across town at that time of night.

Pip was grateful to slip between the clean sheets on Alfie's bottom bunk (they smelt of alpine mountains) and, like the children, despite the turbulence in her mind, she was asleep within moments. She didn't know what time it was when her mobile started to ring and woke her. She had sent Robbie a text just before she'd nodded off (nothing heavy, just a quick thank you for the lift) so her mobile was right by her bed. She scrabbled around in the dark and swiftly picked it up as she didn't want the ringtone to wake Chloe.

'Hello,' she whispered.

'I suppose the truth is he might die,' said Stephanie. The statement was so shockingly bleak and accurate that Pip didn't know how to respond. She could hear the tears in Steph's voice. Glancing at her watch she saw it was three in the morning, the loneliest and most terrifying time. Pip wished she could put her arms around Steph. 'He might . . .' Steph paused and searched for the exact word. 'He might stop. You know? Cease to be.'

'You can't think like that,' said Pip as she slipped out of bed and, pulling the duvet around her shoulders, climbed inside Alfie's toy cupboard. She sat on something plastic and painful but managed not to yell out but instead silently pulled the door behind her, she didn't want to wake anyone.

'I can't think any other way. He's been so busy these past few years. We both have. I've focused on the boys. I don't regret that but I haven't had much of him recently.'

Both women were thinking about the other woman, whoever she might be. How much of him had she had? Stephanie had thought she'd been sharing Julian with his work, which wasn't at all unusual; they even had a name for women with husbands who appeared to be married to their work—corporate widows. 'Better that than a golf widow,' Steph had been known to joke with her girlfriends. 'At least corporate widows get their mortgages paid!' But truthfully she'd never been happy with the situation, just reconciled. She'd married an ambitious, bright man so a few nights alone with the remote control were to be expected. But since Monday—when she'd discovered that she had not been sharing him with the financial markets, spreadsheets and budgets, that she'd been sharing him with someone else, with flesh and blood—it hurt. It hurt so much. It tore at her from inside.

'I'd thought sharing him was the worst thing in the world but to have none of him, or there to be none of him, it's inconceivable,' Steph whispered. 'I can't imagine how I'd cope with that.'

Pip shook her head desolately, lost for words. It struck her as odd that they were here, in the twenty-first century, in the western world, to all intents and purposes at the top of the food chain and yet they were both rendered dumb with shock at the thought of death. Life they had come to understand. Pip had sat in the very same hospital where Julian now lay comatose while Stephanie had pushed out two of her three boys and Stephanie had been at Pip's bedside throughout Chloe's birth. Life she understood. That raw and wonderful miracle was explicable, but this thunderous horror—death. They didn't have a clue.

'It will be OK,' muttered Pip but she knew her words were pathetic and fallible. What did she know? He might not be. Last year, there had been a mum who Pip used to nod to at the school gate, a smiley woman whom Pip always meant to strike up a conversation with. She never had, the school gate was always so frantic and then Pip noticed the smiley woman's absence. She asked around and was told she'd died suddenly, on her way to Blockbusters. Here one minute, not the next. Left a husband and two kids. Left a gap. A void. It was an aneurism.

It was an anathema. Death was an anathema.

Julian was so full of life. So full of shit, thought Pip not unpleasantly but instead with a weary, matey smile.

'I haven't had a rehearsal,' muttered Steph. Her thoughts were non-sequential, her voice was cracked and she was whispering too, so Pip struggled to understand her friend. Pip wondered where she was making the call from. Not a toy cupboard. Maybe the visitors' room. Pip had been in hospital visitors' rooms in the past, she hated them. The TV was always blaring no matter what time of day or night it was and invariably it was stuck on a news channel which poured out nothing other than doom and gloom. The furniture was universally drab, brown and shabby, the sort of furniture that had been popular in the 1980s, particularly in former Soviet Union countries. And the occupants? The people who took refuge in these rooms? They were desperate and fearful and they wore their fear and desperation openly. Pip wished Steph was sharing closet space with remote control cars and Lego pieces, no matter how uncomfortable.

'What do you mean, you haven't had a rehearsal?'

'My mum and dad are still with me.'

'Thank God.'

'Of course. But what I mean is I've only ever lost my mother-in-law and my dog. When Hilary died, the pain I felt was mostly for Julian. After seeing her suffer, I was almost relieved to let her slip away. And other than that, a bloody poodle.' Stephanie had been devastated by the loss of Sugar. There was still a picture of her on the fireplace and the mutt's red lead still hung in the garage. 'I've experienced nothing to prepare me,' she explained.

'Nothing could,' pointed out Pip.

Pip had lost grandparents, uncles, cousins, friends, her godmother and, in a different way, her husband. Pip was not a stranger to loss. She'd secretly always envied Stephanie her untainted innocence. Until this week, it had always seemed as though Steph dwelt in a childish, cloud nine paradise, she slipped through life untarnished, not stained and spoilt like Pip felt herself to be. It was as though Stephanie had been treated with a special chemical like her carpets, a stain-resistant spray.

Suddenly Steph started to sob. She sounded as though she was struggling for breath.

'It will be all right,' said Pip helplessly. She couldn't think of anything more pertinent or original.

'No, no, it won't because you see there's something else. Something terrible I need to tell you. It's all my fault.' Steph was spitting out her words between gasps for air. She mumbled something more but Pip couldn't make out exactly what she was saying between the howling, sniffing and the gulping.

'Say that again, Steph. I can't understand you. Count to ten. Take a deep breath. You're not making sense. It sounds as though you are saying this is all your fault.'

But Pip realised she was talking to a dead line. Steph had hung up. Pip called her back but her phone was switched off. Steph didn't want to be reached. Pip was left with nothing other than the austere tones of a disconnected line.

What did she mean, it was all her fault?

Thursday

CHAPTER THIRTY-SIX

Steph looked closely at her husband's features as she sometimes liked to do when he was sleeping at home. It was easier to deal with the coma if she thought of it as a deep sleep, rather than what it really was—obliteration. To do this she had to use all her powers of determination to ignore the tube in his windpipe that connected him to a machine that helped him breathe. She would not look at the needle plugged into the vein in his hand, which was joined to the tube which enabled an intravenous drip of medication and food. She ignored the catheter that led to the bag of yellow urine, hanging slackly next to her husband's bed.

Over the years Steph had watched as Julian lost some of his sharpness, some of the indescribable quality that had made him so attractive to her way back when. The sharp, elusive quality had been replaced by a familiar softness which she'd been comfortable with. This morning, she frantically searched his face for the familiarity and the softness but it wasn't there. It had melted away. She didn't know this doughy, lifeless face. It didn't belong to her husband.

Julian had always been the better sleeper of the two, she was often restless. Night-time was her time to run through to-do lists and to mentally tick off what she'd achieved with her day, her week or month—what she'd achieved with her life. She used to enjoy studying her soundly sleeping husband, as she'd found his obvious contentment and confidence in whatever he had done that day heartening. She used to have absolute faith that her family were on the right track and that he'd keep them all there, somehow; his easy, deep sleeping proved it. Until last May, that was.

Since May, since Subhash, Steph's night-time vigils over Julian had become less about marvelling at his sharp bone structure, nor was he a backdrop to her domestic mental arithmetic (clean shoes plus numerous structured activities, plus healthy packed lunch, plus limited screen time equals good mum, tick). No, since May, she'd stare at her husband in an effort to try to anchor herself, to level and calm herself. She'd gaze at the fine lines around Julian's eyes, the slightly bluish tinge under his eyes, his hairline, his wayward eyebrows—all of which she knew intimately—and she would remind herself that he was a good man, a man who worked hard for her and for their boys, a decent man and her chosen life partner. As she'd stared at her husband, drinking him in, consuming him—in order to remind herself just how lucky she was— she had tried (so very, very hard) to block out Subhash. She'd tried to ignore the feeling that she was just waiting. Waiting until she forgot Subhash. Waiting until she became tired of thinking about him. This thought now doused Steph with an intense, overwhelming feeling of guilt and shame and regret, just as though someone had thrown a bucket of icy water over her.

How would she ever sleep again after Tuesday?

Julian hated hospitals. This thought had haunted Stephanie since she'd arrived here. How would he get better when he was in the one place on earth that he despised? They hadn't always bothered him. He'd attended all three of the boys' births and regarded hospitals as very useful places where his wife went to safely give birth to their bouncing baby boys. Julian was not the type to entertain the idea of a home birth. He rejected that suggestion when he heard that a new mattress would no doubt be required despite the plastic sheets that the midwife could readily supply. The fear and loathing began two years after Freddie was born.

She had asked her mother to bring in the teal cashmere throw that they kept on their bed, Steph wanted to cover up the utilitarian hospital blanket, and she'd also asked for some cushions to scatter on the visitors' chairs. At the very least they needed the children's pictures Blu-tacked to the wall covering those glum signs reminding people to wash their hands. Steph sighed as she hopelessly and helplessly glanced around the room. Would such tiny touches help? Probably not. The reason Julian had a hatred of hospitals was too big to be covered up with a cashmere throw.

They hadn't been actively trying to have another baby but they weren't always as careful as they could be. When Stephanie had skipped her period, her heart had skipped a beat too, she was so thrilled. Three healthy, lovely children were a joy, a blessing and a godsend. A fourth would be a marvel. Steph didn't mind that she became so huge so quickly. After three pregnancies it was reasonable to assume her stomach muscles had simply given up, she looked five months gone at the point when she calculated that she was just ten weeks down the line. As with the other pregnancies, she was forever nipping to the loo and her boobs were sore and lumpy, she even had a bit of extra hair growth (sadly not on her head!) but there was no sickness and she was generally much more lethargic than she had been during all her other pregnancies. The slight variations in the symptoms were enough to convince Stephanie that they were having a girl this time. She hadn't rushed to take a test, she hadn't believed it was necessary after three babies, she knew her body well enough. Instead, she'd dragged out the sacks of baby clothes that were bagged up and stored in the loft and begun to re-sort and re-wash anything in white or neutral greens and yellows, although even as she meticulously salvaged Babygros she knew she was kidding herself, there was no way she'd be able to resist a pink fest. She'd had none of the superstitious caution that she'd had before, the fourth time round she was all about practicality. The way she saw it was, the more she could get done in this first trimester, before she was too tired or bulky, the better. She'd begun to browse around baby shops, drawing up lists of equipment she might need to replace and equipment that might make do, just one more time. She had liked nothing more than lying in bed at night, next to Julian, reading through naming books.

'Rose?' she suggested.

'Beautiful.'

'Daisy?'

'Very pretty.'

'Lily?'

'Also gorgeous but I draw the line at Hyacinth,' Julian had said. This had made her giggle.

But then she'd started to get terrible pains in her stomach, agonising piercing cramps; her biggest fear was that she was miscarrying. She went to the doctor and he immediately redirected her to hospital. By the time Julian arrived at the hospital, just a few hours later, she'd already found out that she wasn't miscarrying because she wasn't growing a beautiful baby girl as she'd hoped, just some nasty, enormous ovarian cysts.

The vast majority of these cysts go away without treatment. Some are inconveniently persistent and positioned, and therefore have to be removed; most of these can be operated on without hurting the ovaries. In a very small percentage of cases the cysts are eradicated along with the chances of ever having any more babies. After a series of tests and scans, it was established that Steph had the latter type.

Oh, of course Steph knew she was very lucky, very lucky indeed. She already had three children, what possible need could there be for another one? A fourth would be an unnecessary luxury, at least that's what the few well-meaning friends and family who knew of her condition implied. Even Pip pointed out that things could have been a lot, lot worse. And yes, they could. She was so incredibly lucky that the cysts turned out to be benign and no further treatment was required. No chemo, no radiography. Pip's marriage was in tatters at this point, she was drowning in her own particular brand of agony, so it was hard for her to imagine Steph's pain. How could she possibly be grieving? There never was a baby. How could she grieve for their never-was baby?

When Julian had come to pick her up after her hospital stay, he'd ignored her instructions to bring along the children. Instead he had left Freddie with Mrs Evans and the eldest two had gone to school as normal. He'd correctly anticipated that Steph would be weak and pale and sore.

'A boisterous two year old inadvertently using you as a trampoline would not be the best idea,' he'd gently explained as she'd desperately searched behind him for any sign of her brood. 'Will my cuddles do?' he'd asked as he'd pulled her into a careful hug. She'd poured herself into his embrace, surprised to find that his big, firm arms offered absolute comfort. She'd been in hospital for two nights and he knew she'd missed her boys but he hadn't brought them in to visit as Steph had been too drugged up the first night and too delicate the second, they'd have been rowdy on both occasions. 'Come on, let's get out of here,' he'd said. They'd signed papers and then fled from the hospital as though they were jailbirds.

Julian had not brought her flowers or (God forbid) helium balloons the way other husbands might have. Steph remembered her mother had been quite irritated with him because she thought he was showing a lack of consideration. Steph knew the opposite was the case. Julian would not ruin her favourite flowers by bringing them to her at such a time, ever after forcing her to associate peonies with her loss. He had not tried to disguise or decorate the room; he had not shied away from what it was. Horrible. And for that she'd been extremely grateful.

He hadn't taken her directly home. It was a bright, warm day and Julian had driven straight through the town centre and towards the country. They parked below St Mary's-on-the-Hill, the church where they'd married, and there he revealed that he'd packed a picnic. He'd fussed

338

around Steph, insisting that she remained sitting in the car until he'd set everything up. He'd told her it was all to be a surprise and she wasn't to watch him as he staggered up and down the hill a few times, lugging deckchairs (normally they sat on the rug but he'd brought along deckchairs to make her more comfortable), the picnic rug and hamper. He'd then momentarily lost confidence in his plan; would she be able to manage the walk to the spot just beyond the church that offered the most glorious view?

'Actually, I fancy a walk,' she'd insisted.

'That's what I first thought. Fresh air in your lungs,' he'd replied. She'd noticed that he was sweating. She wasn't sure if it was the exertion of setting up the picnic or worry, as he tentatively took her arm and led the way.

It was the most beautiful picnic spread Stephanie had ever seen. No wonder Julian was out of puff. There were slices of prosciutto and cantaloupe melon, crayfish tails served with delicious lime and coriander, a dressed crab, an enormous selection of cheeses, including Steph's favourite Cornish brie, a pot of olives, bread rolls and a mixed summer salad with basil and cherry tomatoes.

'Find a good website?' she'd asked with a knowing beam.

'Yup,' he'd admitted with a grin. 'But I picked the champagne.' It was Krug.

Steph had gasped. 'That's madness, Julian. We won't be able to manage more than a glass each. I'm on medication and you're driving. We'll have to throw most of it away. How much did it cost?'

'Don't worry about it. Not today. I brought your

crystal glasses.' She'd gasped again, this time at the thought of her crystal being hauled around in a picnic hamper. 'It tastes better and they make a great sound when clinked together,' he'd pointed out as he eased the cork out of the bottle.

'What's the toast?' she'd asked, giving in to his determination.

'Us,' he'd replied firmly.

And there were flowers. Somehow (and Steph had subsequently given a great deal of thought as to how exactly there were flowers but never quite fathomed it) Julian had managed to cart a bunch and a plastic vase of water up the hill while she was looking the other way. Plonked in the middle of the rug was a vase of pale pink roses, just opening lilies and big, fat, wild daisies. Roses, lilies and daisies. Steph had stared at the flowers and furiously blinked away tears.

'I thought we needed to have some kind of formal way of saying, I don't know, maybe goodbye,' said Julian quietly.

'There never was a baby,' Steph sensibly pointed out, as doctors and nurses and family and friends had sensibly pointed out to her. Not to be cruel but in a misguided attempt to comfort her.

'I know. I think we need to say goodbye to our never-was baby.'

Steph nodded, unable to speak because of all the love that was choking her. He understood. He'd understood that she hated her body, she felt it had let her down, she felt unfeminine and useless. He'd understood that she was grieving and angry and extremely sad. He'd understood that these emotions did not mean that she was ungrateful or unaware of all she already had. He'd understood her.

How had that man put his dick into another woman?

Steph's head spun. She didn't know what to feel or think. This situation was beyond difficult. Now as she stared at her husband's face, tracing the lines that ran like rivers from his eyes, she felt bemused and displaced. Who was this man? She'd thought she'd known and trusted him. She thought she'd known herself.

She'd known nothing. Now she had nothing. She'd been better off before.

Stephanie glanced across at her father-in-law. He was holding a copy of *The Times*, folded at the crossword page, but Steph knew that he was just pretending to be interested in the quiz. Usually he could rattle off all the answers to clues, up and down, within twenty minutes. He'd been holding the paper for three hours now and Steph hadn't seen him write a single letter. He looked pallid and drawn. She could only imagine the fear and despair that was surrounding the widower as he watched his eldest son lie still. He'd contacted Julian's brother who lived in Canada; he'd had to make one of those dreaded calls where you have nothing but bad news. James had asked whether he ought to get on a plane right away. Her father-in-law had been forced to admit it might be best.

She'd been here for over twenty-four hours now, here by his bedside staring at the same things. She simply sat. Still. Like Julian. She was not finding sitting at the hospital as difficult as everyone imagined. She was naturally a patient woman, used to waiting, biding or filling in time. The truth was that there were a lot of dead hours in Stephanie's day. Hours when she sat in the car between one child's school finishing time and the next, hours when she sat in dusty, draughty, smelly school halls while the boys fenced or played music in a recital. She stood on the side of games pitches and cheered modest and robust attempts to chase some ball or other. She did not mind, she'd never counted up the hours and worked out the days—perhaps weeks—of her life that were washed away in this manner. Because standing on sidelines, sitting in the audience, waiting in line, was her life. And it was valid, she thought indignantly. She was continuing, preserving, nurturing the next generation. What could be finer? What could be more important? But she did wonder if it was the fact that Freddie was now in full-time school, her last baby bird flown the nest, which had led to her thing with Subhash. Had there suddenly been simply too many hours to fill? Could all this destruction and mess and confusion simply be a product of boredom?

Steph could list every encounter she'd ever had with Subhash, because there were so few. Had their rarity inflated their worth? It hadn't felt like that on Tuesday but on Tuesday she was desperate and hurt. So hurt. She'd shared endless days with Julian. Birthdays blurred in her memory, was it last year she'd bought him tickets for Twickenham to see England or the year before? Christmases were all fun but they became interchangeable, the only thing that distinguished one from the other was the pyjamas the boys wore when opening their gifts. They had twenty years' worth of days, weekends that bled into bank holidays that melted into weekdays. They had sunny days, wet days. Happy days, sad days. Months, seasons. A lifetime. Was it going to end?

Stephanie carefully tried to process exactly what Mr Khan had said when he last popped in to check on Julian. The doctor had explained that a comatose person is defined as such when the person in question cannot be awakened, fails to respond normally to pain or light, does not have sleep-wake cycles, and does not take voluntary actions. They are still.

Julian was still.

He was still Julian.

Steph played with the words until they stopped making sense. She should really go home and have a shower, check on the kids as the doctors and nurses, her parents and father-in-law had begged her to, maybe try and get some sleep herself. She couldn't imagine sleeping. It was funny but since Julian lost consciousness she had only managed to snatch the briefest of catnaps. Was it possible that on some sort of spiritual level they were still behaving as a ying to the yang? Maybe she should try to get a proper night's sleep; if she did, then maybe he'd wake. This theory seemed quite reasonable, just as convincing as any scientific theory the doctors might come up with. They hadn't—as it happened—come up with any definitive theory which would mean he'd wake up. All they could tell her was that apparently it was unlikely that there would be a sudden eureka moment when Julian woke up, and said, 'Stephanie, my—'

My what? What would Julian say if he could? My darling? My deserted? My detested?

But Mr Khan had taken great pains to explain to

343

her that those moments were unlikely anyway, they were the sole preserve of Hollywood. Julian's recovery (pray God there was one) would be flagged by a twitching toe, a moment or two of consciousness.

Slowly, gently, with as much courtesy as possible, it had been explained that the outcomes of a coma ranged considerably. Steph had pushed for details.

'What range are we talking about here, Mr Khan?'

'Well, there may be a full recovery, Mrs Blake,' he'd assured her.

'Or?'

'Or not,' he'd admitted.

'Worst-case scenario?'

'It never does any good to dwell on the worst-case scenario,' the consultant had replied. He was too used to this type of conversation to be uncomfortable with it. He wasn't embarrassed, he was just aware it was an unhelpful avenue to pursue, more of a cul-de-sac, in fact. As a doctor, as a human being, he preferred to dwell on the positive until it was scientifically ridiculous to do so.

'Comas generally last a few days to a few weeks,' he'd explained. 'They rarely last more than about five weeks.'

'But they can?' asked Steph.

'Some have lasted as long as several years,' he admitted. Mr Khan saw a realist in this patient's wife and wanted to treat her questions with a dignity and honesty that her no-nonsense demeanour deserved but as he'd replied, he'd noticed she swayed as though she was about to

344

collapse, and he'd put a steadying arm on her elbow. 'There is no point in speculating,' he said firmly. 'The outcome for coma depends on the cause, location, severity and extent of neurological damage. A deeper coma alone does not necessarily mean a slimmer chance of recovery, because some people in a deep coma recover well while others in a so-called milder coma sometimes fail to improve.'

Stephanie hated this information because it informed her of precisely nothing at all, it told her less than she thought she already knew. There were no guarantees, no certainties.

CHAPTER THIRTY-SEVEN

Mr and Mrs Amstell took all four children to school while Pip slept. They didn't know about the late-night phone call from Steph but they wanted to be occupied and being in charge of four children ensured that. When Pip woke up and found she was alone in the house, she saw her opportunity. She hardly dared acknowledge the thought in her head. Did she really think Steph might have done something so terrible and desperate? It was too, too awful to imagine and yet she had imagined it. Pip didn't want to entertain the possibility of something so heartbreaking and dire but it was becoming harder and harder to draw any other conclusion. Steph had lied to the police and asked her for an alibi and Robbie said that it was usually the spouse who was responsible for this sort of thing. A crime of passion, was it? And then there was the fact that last night Steph had said it was all her fault. What else could she have possibly meant? Nothing else. The thought made Pip tremble.

Pip felt extremely underhand as she flicked through Stephanie's telephone book and found Mrs Evans' number. She tried to tell herself that she wasn't really checking up on Stephanie, not as such. No. Rather, she was just confirming her friend's story, so that when the moment came for Pip to talk to the police, she could be certain that she said exactly what Stephanie wanted her to say and that she had understood everything correctly. Of *course* Steph had gone straight home, just as she'd said. She'd probably spent the night sadly pawing over her wedding photos. How could she consider for even a moment that Steph might have mowed down her husband? And yet Pip knew she would not rest until she made the call.

'Hello, Mrs Evans, it's Philippa Foxton here. Steph's friend. Do you remember?'

'Oh yes, of course I remember you, Pip, dear. Yes. How is Mrs Blake?' asked Mrs Evans, keenly. A slither of irrational irritation shimmied through Pip's body. How come Steph's cleaner slash babysitter called Steph Mrs Blake and yet she was comfortable calling Pip, Pip? Why not Ms Foxton? Pip wondered what she was lacking that would guarantee the gravitas that Steph seemed to acquire so easily. A cleaner of her own? A detached house? A husband, she thought bleakly.

'Well, she's bearing up. Considering the circumstances,' replied Pip.

'I imagine she's being very brave. Such a dignified woman.'

'Yes.'

'Is she at his bedside?'

'Constantly.'

'Of course.' This seemed to be the answer Mrs Evans was hoping for.

'It's very difficult, as you can imagine,' replied Pip, as she wondered how she could pull the conversation around to the thing that she most needed to ask.

'The poor woman. I've thought of nothing else. A hit-and-run! Fancy. Such a terrible thing. Such a lovely family. What a thing to have happened.' Mrs Evans struggled to keep the animation out of her voice. Certainly, she wished this dreadful thing had never happened but since it had, she couldn't help being rather excited to be involved. This was by far the most thrilling thing that had happened to Mrs Evans *ever*. This was a significantly better drama than the fight with her insurance company about her claim.

'Absolutely,' murmured Pip.

'So, he's still in a coma, is he?'

'Yes, I'm afraid so. I'll make sure you are among the first to know if there's any improvement. I know you must be very worried as you're so close to the family,' added Pip. She nervously fiddled with the pencil that Stephanie always kept next to the phone.

'Oh yes. I am, very. I was there babysitting the very night it happened, you know.'

'Yes, Steph mentioned it.' Pip's heart pounded as she realised they were edging towards the thing she needed to talk about.

'That's right because she was at yours, wasn't she?' Mrs Evans had no doubt mulled over these details countless times for the entertainment of her friends, neighbours and any general passers-by that she'd managed to collar. An update from Pip (even if that update amounted to there being no news other than there was no change in Mr Blake's condition) would give her more fodder for the gossips.

'Yes, she was with me.' Pip knew that she needed to get used to saying this.

'Celebrating some good news, she said.'

'Yes.'

Mrs Evans tried to recall the details. 'Haven't you got some job altering clothes or something? Do you do hems? I've a pair of my hubby's trousers that need taking up, if you are looking for work. I haven't got round to them and they've been lying in a heap on the bedroom floor for weeks now.'

'Actually, I was awarded a rather large contract with Selfridges, designing and making my own products,' said Pip stiffly.

'Oh, I see,' said Mrs Evans. Clearly she didn't and Pip felt somewhat disappointed that the announcement of her important news had failed to impress. In fact, truthfully, it was rather frustrating that her important news had been completely overshadowed by Julian's dramas. His affair and his coma had out-trumped her successful bid for financial independence. Pip knew she was being a bit petty and possibly a bit sick but she couldn't help herself. This was her moment, by rights she should be shining but instead she was fretting over her friend's troubles. She didn't resent it as such; she just wished it wasn't the case. Why wasn't life tidier? 'You must have had a good night,' said Mrs Evans, with a hint of censor and charmless finger-

348

pointing. 'The hour Mrs Blake finally rolled in! After midnight.' The tut-tutting was implicit. 'And it's not often you see her tipsy. Still, at least she had the sense to leave her car at yours and get a cab.'

Pip froze. She felt the blood in her body slow to a grinding halt. Stephanie came home after midnight and she was *drunk*. She didn't bring her car home. Why not? Where was the car now? Oh my God. Oh my God. Oh my God. The words tumbled around Pip's head, she wasn't sure if she was blaspheming or praying. Steph had said she'd gone straight home. Why would she lie? Oh God, Pip didn't want to think about the answer to that question.

'After midnight? You're certain?'

'Absolutely,' replied Mrs Evans firmly. 'I remember it clearly because I'd just been watching *The Krypton Factor* on ITV. I do love that show. Well, frankly, I'm not interested in the show but I do like to see that Ben Shephard. Now, there's a handsome man! I told the police as much. Not that I think Ben Shephard is handsome, no. No. I told them that I'd been watching *The Krypton Factor*. It had just finished. I think they were impressed. I know because I was just looking for something else to watch.'

'Got to go,' said Pip, and she hung up on Mrs Evans without even bothering to say goodbye.

Pip ran to the drawer where Steph kept her keys. Their house was so grand that they had a detached garage. Pip grabbed the garage keys and dashed outside. She had to see the car's absence for herself, if only to discern who Steph was telling the most lies to. Pip hit a brick wall when she

349

found the Audi was snugly parked up in the garage, right next to the kids' bikes, scooters, Rollerblades and wellingtons. Steph *had* driven it home. Yet she'd made a point of telling Mrs Evans that she'd caught a cab. Why? And she'd only got home after midnight. And where had she been? She'd made a point of telling Pip she'd gone straight home after leaving hers. What had she been doing?

There was only one answer. Pip was struggling to breathe. It was unbelievable. Yet she believed it. It was such a mess. Yet it was clear-cut. Stephanie had put Julian in a coma. Stephanie had tried to kill Julian.

Pip darted back into the house and rushed to Steph's downstairs loo, she splashed cold water on her clammy face. How could this be? Stephanie, kind, thoughtful, careful Stephanie—a killer? Admittedly, she'd always said she'd rather be widowed than divorced but she'd been kidding, right? Every wife makes jokes like that. Steph wouldn't try to kill her husband just to guarantee her social standing and avoid the embarrassment and hassle of divorce, would she? No amount of sympathetically donated casserole dishes were worth that, surely. She'd been kidding when she said she'd have killed Julian if he'd done what Dylan had done, hadn't she?

Apparently not.

Pip leant her head against the mirror. The cool, smooth surface did nothing to clear her hot head. The small room swirled around her and her world fell apart.

CHAPTER THIRTY-EIGHT

Pip forced herself to go back out to the garage. She frantically circled the car to see if she could find any further evidence of the hit-and-run. She didn't know what exactly to expect, not part of Julian's brain on the windscreen necessarily but perhaps a dent in the car. There would be some signs of impact, wouldn't there? A cold chill crawled over Pip's skin, she felt as though she was being slowly lowered into a bath of ice when she spotted a dent and a long scratch on the front of the car on the left-hand side. Pip's legs buckled under her.

She was torn. She had to get to Stephanie as quickly as possible but she didn't want to drive this car, this weapon. Was it tampering with evidence? The thought was crushing.

'Fuck!' she said aloud. She glanced around, wondering if she'd attracted the attention of the neighbours. 'Fuck, Steph. How could you?' Pip's car was still at her house. What choice did she have? She jumped in and started up the engine. She had been itching to drive this car, ever since Julian brought it home, how could she have imagined—even in her wildest dreams—that the scenario would be so gross and tragic?

Pip drove at a dangerous speed and in a careless fashion all the way to the hospital. She was certain she'd been caught by a traffic camera as she scooted through the amber lights in the town centre but she couldn't worry about that now.

Pip parked across two spaces. As she jumped out of the car another driver, looking for a spot, started to yell at her. He was a bald guy with a tattooed head and he had two young children in the back of his car. Pip thought that he shouldn't use that sort of language in front of little kids but she didn't waste time telling him so, nor did she bother to straighten up the car. She was pretty sure that when she came out of the hospital he'd have added another dent to the Audi. She didn't care.

Pip charged along the corridors, nearly colliding with two separate wheelchairs. No one yelled, 'Where's the fire?' because it was a place full of emergencies and desperate people, although the old guy who was wheeling himself and his catheter towards the foyer shop did point out that if, in her haste, she'd dislodged his bag, she'd have come off worse than him.

Pip flew into Julian's room and without stopping to check whether they were alone she demanded, 'So where were you, Steph?'

Stephanie glanced over at her father-in-law. He appeared startled. Steph surmised he must have finally nodded off in the armchair, hiding behind his crossword, and she'd simply failed to notice. Pip's hasty entrance had jolted him awake.

'Harold, would you mind going to the cafeteria and getting me a hot chocolate, please?' asked Steph, with apparent calm. Pip was horrified by her friend's composure. Pip felt hysterical and she hadn't tried to kill her husband! How could Steph be so poised? Her husband was in a coma, for fuck's sake.

Harold said he was pleased to stretch his legs if Pip was prepared to keep Steph company for a few moments. In a low voice, but one Steph could hear perfectly well, he added that he didn't like her to be alone. Pip felt a surge of anger shoot through her body. Would old Mr Blake be quite so considerate of his daughter-in-law's feelings if he'd known she was the one that had put his son in hospital? No, he bloody wouldn't. Steph did not deserve all this attention and consideration, it was disgusting. He asked if he could bring Pip a hot chocolate too but she abruptly refused. He said he'd bring back crisps or sandwiches if there was anything appetising. She nodded although the thought of eating anything made her feel sick. The moment he left the room, Pip turned back to Steph and demanded again, 'So where were you?'

'I told you. At home,' replied Steph, knowing at once what Pip was talking about, just as though they'd had the conversation about alibis only a moment before.

'But you weren't. That's a lie.' The word 'lie' sat swollen and raw between them. 'I checked with Mrs Evans. She said you got back after midnight! You left mine at seven thirty and yet you didn't get home until midnight. That's four and a half hours lost. Where were you?' demanded Pip.

'Who are you? Nancy Drew?' replied Steph crossly.

Pip gasped. She wasn't used to sarcasm from Steph. She'd expected a flustered denial or a tearful, heart-wrenching confession but not cold sarcasm. Pip felt she didn't know Steph at all. 'You used to say you'd rather see Julian dead than be divorced.'

'Have I said that?' Steph glanced at her husband punctured with tubes and couldn't believe she might have said that, even as a joke.

'Yes, you have. A number of times,' insisted Pip

firmly.

'Maybe, before we married.'

'After.'

'As a joke.'

'I thought so but maybe you were serious.'

'Oh, Pip. That's just the sort of thing people say before they have any idea what death means. Or what marriage means either, come to that. Besides, stop talking about Julian as though he's dying, he might be able to hear us,' she added in a whisper.

Pip dropped to her knees and took hold of Steph's hand. Steph needed to face what she'd done and confess. It would be much better all round. It was only a matter of time before the police worked it out and then—oh God, Pip couldn't think about what might happen then. An arrest, a court case, jail—the children! She had to get her friend to admit to what had happened. She tried another tack. She would elicit a confession. 'It was a wet night, Stephanie, and you'd had a drink at mine,' she said tentatively. She hoped her tone seemed understanding.

'Yes, a drink, I wasn't drunk, you make me sound like a drunk,' said Steph wearily.

'But you *were* drunk when you got back to yours, Mrs Evans told me.' Steph would not look at her friend, she continued to stare at the wall behind Julian's bed, it was painted a peach colour, Steph had never been fond of peach, now she hated the shade. 'When and where did you get drunk?' insisted Pip.

'This is absurd,' said Steph quietly. Her passivity unnerved Pip, it seemed sinister. Too calm and collected. Shouldn't Steph be ranting or tearful, outraged or indignant? Her silence pretty much

354

amounted to a confession.

'It's a new car. You aren't used to it. It's big. Under the circumstances . . .' Pip broke off.

'What? What are you saying?' Steph finally snapped her head in Pip's direction but Pip wished she hadn't. She looked furious. Pip thought of Medusa and wondered whether she might actually turn to stone.

'Perhaps you went to the hotel just to talk to him,' reasoned Pip quietly.

As she'd dashed over to the hospital she'd thought about how the events must have panned out on Tuesday night at Highview. She'd imagined Stephanie driving up the gravel path, heading towards the car park. She'd probably planned on shaming Julian or maybe just getting a look at the other woman. Pip imagined Steph walking in on her husband and the other woman. They would have yelled at one another. Steph might have threatened him with losing everything he had, including the boys. That was the usual way these things went. Then Steph would have marched off, Julian might have followed her, perhaps the row had escalated in the car park. Pip could see it all so clearly. Steph might have tried to drive away and Julian had got in front of the car somehow. Nothing premeditated, just a terrible, terrible accident.

Pip continued. 'I don't imagine you went there expecting to cause this sort of trouble. Not to cause any trouble at all. Even though Robbie thinks it's usually the spouse that's the culprit in a case like this,' she added thoughtlessly.

'Who's Robbie?' asked Steph, puzzled.

'He's—well, my boyfriend.' Pip wondered if she

355

was being accurate in calling Robbie her boyfriend, she wasn't sure, it was difficult to know. Steph was the person she'd normally discuss exactly this sort of matter with but it was awkward, bordering on the impossible, to chat about the matter with Steph right now. 'Kind of my boyfriend. I think. You know, he's the man I met on the train going into London on Monday. I told you about him.'

Steph couldn't remember ever hearing his name mentioned. She stared at Pip in bewilderment.

'We're sort of an item now,' added Pip.

'An item?'

'I haven't had a chance to tell you all about it,' muttered Pip defensively.

'I'm so sorry my husband's critical condition has curbed your updates on your sex life,' snapped Steph, with uncharacteristic aggression. 'So, this Robbie thinks I'm responsible and you believe him.'

'I just—'

'A man you met on Monday?'

'No, no, I'm not saying that,' said Pip helplessly. She was saying that, in fact, but it just didn't sound that great when Steph played it back to her. 'He's a really nice guy.'

'Oh I don't doubt, another one of your lust-haves that you were always so famed for.'

'That's not fair, Steph.'

'Isn't it?' They fell into an embarrassed and angry silence until Steph asked, 'How long have we known each other, Pip?'

'Over thirty years,' said Pip with a tired sigh. She understood Steph's point but just didn't think it proved her innocence. 'I imagine you probably just went to the hotel to really see if Julian was there.

356

But you were upset and it was raining.'

Steph stared at Pip stonily.

'I'm just saying that under the circumstances it would be likely that you had an accident.' Stephanie gasped but Pip was determined to carry on. 'And, you know, that might mean you panicked. And since then you've been—I don't know— confused and you've felt that you didn't dare tell anyone what really happened. Even me.'

'This really isn't the time to start getting fanciful, Pip,' warned Steph.

'I'm not.'

A silence dropped between them. It was like a sudden storm cloud, dark, all-engulfing and promising nothing but a downpour.

'You think I could have done this?' Steph spoke in a whisper as she pointed to her husband. Pip didn't answer and all they both heard was the hum of the hospital machines.

Pip didn't want to think it but yes, yes she did. 'Where were you, Steph?' she asked. Tears were stinging her eyes like small scratches.

Steph considered. Should she simply tell Pip about Subhash? It wasn't something she wanted to confess to and certainly not now, not over Julian's still body. There had been many, many occasions when Steph had been tempted to tell Pip about Subhash but she never had. Not because she thought Pip might judge her—Steph accepted that she deserved to be judged and, besides, no one could judge her quite as severely as she judged herself—Steph's reticence was down to the fact that Subhash was married. Her friendship with him (for want of a more accurate label) was not just her secret, it was his too. And, more than that, any

357

potential fallout from revealing the secret threatened to damage not just her marriage but to shatter his too, to hurt not just *her* spouse but *his* too. One thing Stephanie was surer of now, more than ever, was that she would *never ever* want another woman to feel the way she'd felt when she found Julian's phone. It was sickening. No good would come of her confessing to her relationship with Subhash now. Only harm.

'I can't tell you,' whispered Steph. She squeezed her friend's hand. 'But I'm begging you to trust me.' Pip shook her head ever so slightly and Steph thought hard about how she could get her on side. 'Who knows that my father is a gambling addict?' she asked.

'What?'

'At school, who did I tell that my father was a gambling addict? That we nearly lost our house because of it.'

'Well, me.'

'Just you.' The shame and fear of scandal had almost crippled Steph and her mother at the time. Mrs Amstell was torn between standing by her man, who was desperate and out of control, or losing him and losing face. Those had been difficult times that even now Steph hated to revisit.

'But he's hasn't been near a casino in twenty-two years, Steph.'

Stephanie scowled briefly. Didn't Pip get the point she was making? 'And who knows that when I gave birth to Freddie that I cried for ten days because I couldn't bond with him and I wanted a girl?'

'Me.'

'Just you. Not even Julian knows how badly I

358

wanted my third son to be a girl. Who knows that when I cough I leak wee?'

'OK, Stephanie, I get it. But it's not on the same scale, is it?'

Stephanie, eternally proper and gracious, thought that confessing to piddling was pretty major actually, but she didn't say so.

'I'm just trying to demonstrate to you that I would tell you if I could,' whispered Steph.

Pip sighed. She'd encountered her friend's steely reserve before, she wasn't hopeful that Steph would suddenly be worn down, relent and detail exactly where she was in those missing hours. What sort of trouble could she be in? Well, besides the obvious shedloads of trouble.

'He's going to be OK,' said Steph as though it was as simple as her wanting it to be the case.

'What if he's not?' asked Pip. 'Last night you didn't seem to think he would be and you said it was all your fault.' Pip was really battling with her tears now. She felt like a child who had just discovered Father Christmas didn't exist, he was just some fat shop employee who had no choice but to dress up in an itchy scarlet suit or else he'd be out of a job.

'I was extremely tired and I wasn't thinking straight. Besides, on some level, I think this is my fault,' admitted Steph.

'How?' cried Pip in frustration. 'What do you mean by that? What did you do? What do you know?' Pip realised she had lost her battle not to blub. There was a fat tear rolling down her cheek, she carefully wiped it away but it was almost instantly replaced with another one, again forcing Pip's hand to fly into action. It put Steph in mind of frantic windscreen wipers, dashing from left to right to clear the window so a driver could see properly.

'It's complicated.' Steph locked her gaze on her friend's and said, 'Pip, I'm asking you to trust me. Do you trust me, Pip?'

Pip wanted to. Stephanie was her oldest and best friend, but Steph wasn't helping her here. Pip carefully stood up and backed away.

'I need you to say that I was with you,' added Steph.

Pip looked out of the window at the hospital car park. Despite it being a bright spring day, everything looked dingy and bleak. She watched as visitors locked their car doors and then hurried to the reception, head down, dispirited. Litter was being buffeted across the concrete and Pip thought of the times she'd felt like a little scrap of litter, not much better than pummelled rubbish, and at moments like those it was always Steph who had buoyed her up and seen her through. Friendship was a form of mutual selflessness, an intricate and delicate exercise in give and take and trust-building, through which people who are not related become honorary family. Thirty years of their shared experiences, secrets and even expenses had led to an unconditional acceptance, allegiance and dependence. Pip knew that Steph, an only child, happily thought of her as the sibling she'd never had and while she herself did have a younger brother, she often said Steph was like a sister to her. And she meant it. Stephanie was her best friend, undoubtedly. She was her oldest friend. Thirty years meant something. It meant such a lot. How much? How much did she owe

Steph?

But then Pip had been Julian's friend for twenty years. OK, so their friendship wasn't as intense, a collection of jocular chats rather than a plethora of soul-sharing moments, but he'd always been patient and inclusive with her. God, she was so disappointed that he'd had an affair, sickened, disgusted. Devastated. But no matter what, he didn't deserve to end up like this. In a coma. Lifeless. Finished?

'Just tell me, Stephanie, that you didn't do it. Just answer me straight out and I'll believe you. No more will be said on the matter. Tell me it wasn't you who ran Julian over.'

Stephanie gazed at Pip and slowly and sadly said, 'I'm your best friend, Pip, so I'm going to pretend you never said that. It's idiotic that you're asking me if I tried to kill my husband.'

Pip sighed. Steph had avoided answering the question. Certain as she had always been that her friend wouldn't lie to her she was now sure that Steph had driven the car that had ploughed into Julian.

CHAPTER THIRTY-NINE

'Mrs Foxton? Mrs Philippa Foxton?'

'Ms, actually,' said Pip.

'I'm Sergeant Mary Jean Brown and this is my colleague Police Constable Terry Weybridge. I wonder if you'd mind answering a few questions.'

'I've been expecting you,' said Pip as she held her flat door wide open. As soon as she'd uttered the words she deeply regretted them. They sounded ominous and weighty. 'Can I make you a cup of tea?' she added more breezily.

Yes, a cup of tea, brilliant idea, that would give her a few more minutes to order her thoughts; besides, she always made a cuppa for anyone who had to come into her home to do any sort of work, plumbers and decorators, etc. She found that the willingness of these guys to do a really good job could be influenced depending on whether or not she offered them a chocolate Hobnob. Such a small price compared to the call-out charge on a second plumber if the initial plumber felt disgruntled and chose to bodge it and leg it. Not that she'd had a decorator at this flat, she hadn't had any spare cash and so she'd had to manage by herself, well, not really by herself. She'd had to manage with Steph's help. Steph had arrived one Tuesday morning, armed with huge pots of buttercup-yellow paint, and she'd dragged Pip out of bed, insisting that they redecorate the sitting room. Pip had appreciated the gesture but she hated the colour. It had taken her until they were halfway through painting the biggest wall before she found the courage to admit as much. Stephanie had called her a 'daft bat' for not saying so earlier, if she wanted to say 'pathetic bitch' she resisted. They'd driven to Homebase and Pip chose a more sophisticated mauve. They ate their way through about a dozen packets of Hobnobs before they finished all the rooms.

Pip might not have had any decorators in her flat but she had been visited by the guy who fixed her boiler, the guy who fixed her leaky shower and the guy she'd called when she thought all her

362

sockets had blown up and they were left without electricity (although it turned out that they were without electricity because she'd forgotten to pay her bill and she'd been cut off).

Pip wondered whether to offer the police chocolate Hobnobs or plain old Rich Tea. How good did she want them to be at their job?

She could actually see her hand shaking as she handed over the mugs, so could the police; the policewoman hadn't taken her eyes off Pip's quivering hand (although the policeman was checking out far less worthy parts of her anatomy—it was a fact that her bum did look good in these jeans). Pip put the plate of biscuits on the table and told everyone to help themselves.

'Thanks a lot,' said Sergeant Mary Jean Brown, with a brief but genuine smile of appreciation. 'We probably won't take up more than a couple of minutes of your time but I'm parched. We'll be out of your way in a jiffy.'

Pip hoped so.

'She's got a mouth made of asbestos, she drinks her tea scalding hot,' added the policeman. Pip thought it was rather nice that they knew one another so well, in a job as tough as theirs it must be comforting to work in pairs. Steph liked her tea black although she still missed sugar (which she'd given up six years ago). There wasn't another living soul that Pip knew as well as she knew Steph. Or, at least, that's what she'd believed. 'Are you some sort of dressmaker?' asked the PC, nodding towards her sewing machine and the pile of fabric.

'I make aprons, party bags and bunting, that sort of thing,' replied Pip.

The policeman shot her a questioning glance.

He was questioning what the hell use was bunting in the twenty-first century; Pip thought he was concerned about whether she was ever paid cash in hand.

'If I sell anything I keep all the receipts. I declare everything. I pay tax and I'm VAT registered.' It was all true, Stephanie had insisted that Pip ran her business properly, even when the business was tiny. She'd said it was important that Pip took her own work seriously. Pip had been a bit fed up with Steph at the time, she'd been very aware of the immediate benefit of cash in hand, but she was glad she had followed Steph's advice now. For all Pip knew, these cops might be snooping for their cousins at Her Majesty's Revenue and Customs.

The policeman smirked and nodded, practically reading Pip's mind. 'OK, let's get down to it,' he said, flipping open his notebook. The sergeant said nothing, she was hovering above the biscuit plate deciding between the Hobnob and the Rich Tea. 'Can you tell me where you were on Tuesday evening?'

'This Tuesday?' asked Pip, which was a bit daft as he was unlikely to be talking about next Tuesday.

'Yes, Tuesday the twenty-third of March.'

'Here at home, with my daughter and Steph.'

'Stephanie Blake?'

'Yes.'

'What time was Mrs Blake with you?'

'She came over at about six thirty, maybe seven. We had a glass of champers. We were celebrating my new job.'

Pip could imagine exactly how the conversation

might continue:

'She stayed for a chat and then headed home at about eleven thirty, or no, thinking about it, it was probably closer to quarter to twelve. My boyfriend called round about then, I remember I was just seeing Steph out the door,' Pip might add. She liked the idea of that extra little flourish—the bit about her boyfriend. She liked it for two reasons. One, she liked saying the word boyfriend (it had been a while!), and two, her story sounded more authentic by adding a little detail like that.

'So your boyfriend saw Mrs Blake here at your place, at eleven thirty, he can confirm that?' the policeman would ask.

She was an idiot! What made her think adding that little flourish was a good idea? She could hardly ask Robbie to lie for Steph too. 'Erm, no.' She'd have to think quickly. 'Steph had just driven off. They were a few minutes apart. Only five or ten minutes between them, at the most,' she might garble. 'And she only had one glass of champagne, I drank the rest of the bottle alone,' Pip could add.

The policeman and woman would exchange a glance. Pip would momentarily panic that perhaps they doubted her story or maybe they thought it was too rehearsed. She'd been continually running through the fake times in her head so that she didn't slip up and drop Stephanie in it.

'What time did Mrs Blake leave your house?' asked the policeman. Pip jumped as she was brought back to the reality of here and now.

'She didn't stay long. Maybe half an hour. She left about seven thirty while I was putting my daughter to bed.'

Sergeant Mary Jean Brown stopped thinking

about dippy biscuits. She snapped her head round to face Pip. 'You are quite certain of that?'

'Absolutely,' said Pip with a deep, regretful sigh. She wished it wasn't the case. She wished she was unsure or at least that she had the cheek or guts to lie to the police but she hadn't. The sergeant and the PC exchanged a glance. 'And I know she's told you she was with me. But she wasn't. I was on the phone to my boyfriend from about nine thirty and he came over at eleven. You can check with him if you like. Or I suppose you could check my phone records, whatever it is that you do.'

She wasn't sure what they did but she was pretty certain it would be thorough and revealing, that's why she'd had no choice. Funnily enough, saying the word boyfriend didn't cause even the tiniest shard of excitement for her.

'Did Mrs Blake tell you where she was going after she left you?'

'No, she just rushed out,' sighed Pip. She felt she was tying a noose, fastening it tightly around Steph's neck. 'But I can make a guess,' she sighed.

'What would you guess?' asked the PC.

'I imagine she went to see her husband at Highview Hotel.' Pip thought she might choke on her own words.

'She knew he was there?'

'Yes.' Pip knew she was leading Stephanie to the position over the trap door.

'Can you tell me what sort of frame of mind she was in when she left your flat?' asked Sergeant Brown.

'She was upset,' admitted Pip, reaching for the lever that opened the trap door.

'Why was she upset?' probed the policewoman.

366

'Because she'd just discovered her husband was having an affair,' said Pip, pulling the lever. She'd left Steph dangling.

'Bingo!' said the PC excitedly, as he leapt from his chair and started to walk purposefully out of the kitchen and into the hall.

Sergeant Mary Jean Brown rose from the table with no outward sign of excitement. Her eager PC had been insisting that there was something shifty about Mrs Blake since they first called on her yesterday morning to tell her the news about her husband being involved in a hit-and-run. 'She's hiding something!' he'd crowed, time after time. Mary Jean had thought that Mrs Blake wasn't so much hiding something as hiding *from* something. She was probably hiding from the fact that her husband had been regularly visiting a very smart hotel, with a very young girl, for months— according to the hotel staff. She wished PC Weybridge had been wrong (not least because he'd now be insufferable) because if Mrs Blake knew about her husband's affair, there was motive for the crime and, as she'd lied about her alibi, it now appeared she had opportunity. Sergeant Brown felt for the kids.

'Thank you for your time, Ms Foxton. We'll see ourselves out.'

Pip nodded and then her head sank to the dining-room table. She wondered how she'd ever lift it again.

CHAPTER FORTY

Not my fault. Not my fault. Not my fault. None of this is my fault.

This morning Kirsten had woken up expecting to feel much better. She thought that by now her brain would be quite some way to accepting the positive suggestions of the mantra and she'd be free to think about the entire incident in an altogether different light. The hypno guy on the TV programme had said that success was guaranteed but he'd admitted that the timing was variable. A lot depended on how determined you were and how often you reinforced the suggestive message. Kirsten had thought she'd be fine by now because she was very strong-willed but she still felt awful on Thursday morning when she heard there had been no change.

People in the office kept saying that his chances of ever coming round were reduced significantly the longer he stayed in a coma, these first few days were vitally important. That pissed Kirsten off a bit, actually, the way people spread that sort of stuff (always in hushed whispers, always with a fake look of concern). Were they doctors? No. They were bankers and they didn't know anything much. It just made them feel important repeating that doom and gloom stuff. Well, it might make them feel important but it made her feel awful. It *wasn't* her fault but she did have a heart and it wasn't nice thinking about Jules lying in hospital and being in pain. Although did people in comas feel pain? She wasn't sure. Probably not and even if they did, the doctors would give him loads of great drugs to help with that. Lucky sod, she could do with some drugs to take her out of her head right now!

As she'd been especially efficient yesterday, she found she didn't have anything to keep her busy. Well, except for that self-assessment PowerPoint presentation course that HR kept asking her to complete but she couldn't be arsed to do that. She called HR and explained that everyone in her department was really traumatised, her included. 'I wouldn't get a representative score today.'

Kirsten tried to tune out from all the gossip about Jules. She logged on to Asos.com with the idea of buying some new shoes but no matter how awesome the courts, flats or heels were, for the first time in her life, internet shopping couldn't hold her attention.

'I was sorry to hear about Julian Blake. Any news?' The question startled her and she jumped about a foot in the air. Kirsten looked up and was surprised to see Jake Mason leaning over her desk. She quickly clicked back to her work emails. They may have gone to uni together but he was management and she was a PA, there was a divide, a them and us, and while she didn't expect him to dob her in for internet shopping, she didn't completely rule out the idea either.

'How would I know? I just know what everyone else knows,' she snapped abruptly.

It wasn't that she wanted to be especially narky with Jake (although she was never especially nice to him because she did hate hot guys thinking she liked them, they were arrogant enough without her fanning their egos, plus she was still a bit pissed off that he'd never again suggested they grab a sandwich) but, besides all that, the thing was, she was feeling really edgy today and probably couldn't have rustled up her usual flirtatious manner even if she'd wanted to. 'He's not my boss. I'm not his PA, Rosie O'Grady is,' she added.

Jake raised an eyebrow a fraction and then leant over her computer screen and said quietly, 'Really? I thought you were a family friend or something. I thought maybe your dad knew him.'

'Why would you say that?'

'Well, just,' Jake paused, 'something and nothing.' He stared right at her. He had big blue eyes that were framed by the longest lashes, lashes that actually curled up at the end. They were beautiful.

Kirsten was startled. She'd always thought Jake was hot and sexy, quite a laugh and funny and all that but she hadn't noticed, until this moment, how beautiful he was. And he looked *bothered*. Kirsten, a girl who spent a lot of effort trying not to look bothered about anything at all, noticed his intensity straightaway. She was someone who had managed to not look bothered even as she stood in front of the Taj Mahal, the Grand Canyon and the Sydney Opera House, all of which her parents had shown her and her brother in a relentless—and doomed—attempt to get her to react passionately to something other than the performance of the *X Factor* contestants. Somehow, a lifetime of studied indifference had alerted her to genuine— what would her mother call it?—genuine concern.

'What are you insinuating?' she asked suspiciously. She didn't trust him, no matter how beautiful or concerned he looked. In fact, she made it a rule to trust beautiful boys less than the ugly ones.

'Nothing,' replied Jake. He shrugged. 'I just thought if he was a particular family friend, then you'd be more upset than most and I wanted you to know . . .' Jake broke his gaze away from hers now, he rubbed the back of his neck and then glanced at his watch and garbled, 'I wanted you to know that you can trust me to be your friend too. Got it?'

Before she could reply, he rushed off, leaving Kirsten to wonder what exactly he meant and what *exactly* he knew.

Was he saying that he thought she got the job because Daddy had put in a good word for her with Jules? Why would Daddy know Jules? Daddy was ancient! He was forty-eight. Forty-eight, which might as well be fifty! At fifty, didn't they start measuring you up for your coffin suit! Jules was only thirty-nine. Thirty-nine was still young-ish. Or at least it was a distinguished age. How could Jake think Jules might be mates with an oldie like her father? Although, Ellie had once commented that Kirsten's father was very distinguished-looking, yes, those were the exact words she'd used. Whenever Daddy was in town and had time to take Kirsten for lunch, Ellie always made a thing about coming down into reception to say hi to him. She was always ridiculously flirty but it had never crossed Kirsten's mind that Ellie might seriously find her father attractive in the same way she found Jules attractive. She'd thought Ellie had been humouring an old man!

The way she'd humoured Alan Edwardson up until last month? The thought came out of nowhere and Kirsten wished it had stayed there. It was an uncomfortable, embarrassing thought. How old was Alan exactly? She wasn't certain. She knew his kids were still teenagers so she'd always assumed he was a bit younger than her own father but then her parents had married when they were really young. They'd had her and her brother quite quickly. How old was Alan Edwardson? Kirsten turned to her screen and quickly pulled down his details from the company info-net. OMG, Alan Edwardson was *fifty-one*. A geriatric. He was older than her father! She'd had sex with someone older than her father! Kirsten felt ill. That was gross! Why hadn't she thought of that before? Just because his kids were younger than she was didn't necessarily mean he was younger than her father. He'd probably had kids late in life because he couldn't persuade anyone to marry him! It was such a gross-out, disgusting thought that Kirsten pushed it to the back of her mind. Instead, she concentrated on what Jake had said about him thinking Jules was a family friend.

Maybe he did believe that.

And yet . . .

Kirsten thought back to the way Jake had held her gaze and then the way he hadn't been able to hold her gaze. He'd seemed really *real* and then really shifty! What was it he'd said? He'd thought Jules was a family friend *or something*. Kirsten shuddered as though a hairy spider had just scuttled over her back.

Jake knew!

He knew that she was Jules's *friend*, by which, of course, he meant lover. He knew that much, she was sure of it. How did he know? Had he spotted her with Jules? He'd spotted her in the lift with

Mark that time but, as far as she knew, he hadn't ever seen her with Jules. As far as she knew. But it was possible. Maybe at Jeroboam? She hadn't always been as discreet as she might have been.

And what did he mean when he said that she could trust him to be her friend too? Did he mean he wanted to shag her? He must mean that. What else did any man ever mean when they were being nice to her? They might say something like, 'You'll go far in this company,' or 'You're not just a pretty face, are you?' or even, 'Can I get you a glass of water from the cooler?' but they meant they wanted to shag her. They always meant that.

If, last week, anyone had asked Kirsten whether she'd mind shagging Jake Mason, she'd have admitted that no, she wouldn't mind, not at all. Obviously. He was hot and young and fun. Besides the great eyelashes and huge blue eyes, he had broad shoulders and a slim waist and flat stomach which suggested a six-pack that the guy on the Diet Coke ads might be proud of. She probably would have questioned whether he had the resources to cough up all the stuff she expected a boyfriend to deliver but she might have waived her usual material demands, just for a bit of fun.

Kirsten had always thought that having sex with someone was the goal. Or, to be more accurate, to get them to want to have sex with her was the goal. She found it difficult to explain but she believed that to be linked with a man in that way gave her some sort of power or status or security. It marked her out, it made her different. Her brother said she was wrong. He said all blokes wanted sex all the time, with pretty much anyone, and being the someone who happened to agree to sex was 'no big shakes'. Kirsten disagreed. Getting married men to have sex with you (aka risk all for you), wasn't as easy as everyone believed. Some blokes were quite resistant, at least in the beginning, it took a certain skill and charm to convince them to take the plunge. Ones like Jules, for example, had to be convinced that she was worth the effort. She'd really had to work at him in the early days. Some might say that she'd thrown herself at him at every opportunity (they might even say that as though it was a bad thing). What was wrong with turning up the charm to full throttle? She'd put a lot of effort in with Jules, she really had wanted to be connected to him. She'd wanted that shimmering kudos.

That's what she had thought.

But then, when she started having sex with lots of men, she'd become a little less sure. Just recently, she'd started to have a nagging feeling that maybe *they* had the power—the men she slept with—and, besides, her mother was always going on that sex should not have anything to do with power and status anyway, she said it was supposed to be about love. Ha, easy for her to say when she was married to Daddy, he was loaded and, anyway, Mummy probably didn't even have to have sex anymore because they were so old and used to each other.

But, in the last few days, when the men she was sleeping with had started to dump her, she'd been faced with the fact that having sex with someone didn't provide any security at all. Quite the opposite. That's why that last night with Jules she'd felt futile, hopeless, weak and bloody idiotic. Even if she couldn't carefully separate out each of those emotions, she knew she felt humiliated. Horribly, totally, irretrievably humiliated.

So now the idea of shagging Jake was a damn sight less appealing. How could it possibly be fun? Especially since his overture was motivated by the fact that he thought she was the office bike and as one of the cyclists was unavoidably detained in hospital, he was offering himself up as stand-in. It wasn't flattering.

Her thoughts were interrupted by her phone ringing.

'Yes?'

'Jake here.'

'What?' she asked irritably.

He coughed and then said, 'I wondered whether you wanted to go for a drink after work.'

'With you?'

'Well, I'm guessing you'd also be interested in having a drink with Robert Pattinson if he asked, but he's not asking so yes, with me.' Kirsten looked up and glanced across the open-plan office to where Jake sat. He stared back at her. And smiled.

It was, undeniably, a lovely smile. Kirsten could see that. It was sexy and broad but it was also . . . Kirsten looked carefully, it was also something else. His smile caused a slight twinge in her stomach. A sort of happy, contented feeling, a bit like the feeling she got on the rare occasions she allowed herself to drink hot chocolate, but even better than that. A drink with Jake wasn't the worst idea in the world. Let's face it, she had nothing better to do. She definitely didn't want to go home and sit in her gloomy flat all night. Alone. No, no way. She wasn't good at being on her own at the best of times and this wasn't the best of times. She needed to get back into the swing of things. Flirting with men—having dinner, having sex, having a laugh (sometimes)—was her thing. The way she saw it was that if she was now known as the office bike there was probably a string of men hoping they might be the next one to take her for a ride and none of them would be as fit as Jake. She'd need to start looking for another job soon anyway. No matter what happened to Jules, she'd need a clean start away from this office. With that in mind, it wouldn't do her any harm to kill some time with Jake, he'd probably be able to help her write up a decent CV.

'Where?' she asked, not yet decided as to whether she'd accept. 'Jeroboam?'

'I was thinking the Hare and Hound.'

'A pub?' she squawked in disbelief.

The Hare and Hound was an ancient, grungy pub near the tube station, about five minutes' walk from the office. Kirsten was horrified. They didn't sell champagne or cocktails of any sort. No one she knew ever went there! When she walked past it, it was always full of scruffy students and, sometimes, even tourists.

'Jeroboam is really pricey,' pointed out Jake.

'You tight-arse! You're on that graduate scheme thing, aren't you? You earn a fortune,' replied Kirsten, not considering whether or not saying the first thing that came into her head was a good idea.

'Yes, I do. Well, a good amount,' said Jake. 'But you don't and I didn't want to embarrass you when it came to your round.'

'My round!'

'Besides, it's quieter in there. It will be easier to talk. See you at the Hare and Hound at six.'

Then he rang off. Kirsten was so miffed that he thought she might be buying a round that for a few moments she considered not turning up but the thought of her empty flat spooked her so she downgraded her punishment to not redoing her make-up before the date. Then she reasoned what would she do between five (when she knocked off) and six (when he did)? She certainly wouldn't want to stay at her desk, so she might as well nip to the loos and reapply, although it was definitely *not* because he was worth making an effort for. The Hare and Hound! Paying for a round! Who did Jake Mason think he was?

CHAPTER FORTY-ONE

Stephanie was finding it harder and harder to stay awake, let alone stay focused. She longed to go home, have a bath, put on a clean pair of pyjamas and then go to bed. She wanted to fall asleep and then wake up and discover this had all been a terrible dream. She wanted for none of this to have happened or, at least, if it had to have happened then not to her. Stephanie knew this was an unreasonable thought. She deserved this as much as the next person. Possibly more. But she didn't want it to be true, not at all.

The smell of the hospital was beginning to bother her. Disinfectant and industrially laundered sheets offered no comfort. She longed for the smells of her home. Fresh ginger candles, flowers from the garden, food cooking in the oven, the children's bubble bath on the landing in the evenings. She even missed the awful smells. The boys' rooms usually smelt of muddy, moist trainers, illegal snacks and not totally clean clothes—despite the fact that Steph was always tackling a laundry pile the size of Mount Everest. She often thought that home life was a series of smells—the boys' kitbags, clean shirts, ground coffee, burnt toast. She wondered if other people's family lives could be distilled into a series of sights or sounds or textures.

In the morning, the first thing she always noticed was the smell of Julian's warm skin. He never smelt badly, not sweaty or anything, he simply smelt of the smell that Stephanie had come to know as Julian. It was familiar and comforting. Steph leant forward and sniffed her husband's hand. He smelt of the antiseptic they'd swabbed him with before they pushed the needle into him. It was distressing. Harrowing. Some mornings Stephanie would throw back the duvet and she'd smell her own body and occasionally sex too. When? When had that last happened, that the sheets smelt of sex? Weeks ago? Maybe a month? Maybe two? Steph had once loved Julian in a way that meant going just a few days without sex was unthinkable, let alone a few weeks, their lust had been so utterly and completely consuming. She'd loved him as much as her young heart was capable and in the only way it was capable. But after they married and had the children, she lost the habit of loving him that way. Lost the rhythm. Their love, quite naturally, was sometimes tinged with nit-picking and petty essential marital logistics. Steph was forever telling herself that this new manifestation had solidity and a constancy which compensated. But she'd been lying to herself.

So many lies.

Sitting in the hospital had given Stephanie plenty of time to think, she could do little else. She thought about the times—long, long ago—when she and Julian had been little more than children themselves but blithely unaware that was the case. They'd thought they were incredibly sophisticated and mature when, following graduation, they'd taken their first holiday away together, a road trip from San Francisco to Vegas. Steph recalled the trip, for the first time in a long time, and was surprised by how clearly she remembered the cheap motels they stayed in, the duvets they slipped under, the rib meals they ate. She recalled the fat, sleek bodies of the seals that splashed around the pier in San Francisco and she remembered giggling as they'd been thrown around a tram as it hopped over the hills. They'd played pool in shabby, off-the-beaten-track bars, she could almost hear the music playing and the thwack of the balls hitting against one another, before rolling into their designated pockets. She'd cleared the table, surprised everyone. She could smell the dust of the desert, see the glare of Vegas and feel the heat on their young bodies. Feel the heat *in* their young bodies.

There had been so much loving. They'd fused into one another. They fitted and belonged. Sex, yes, lots of it but besides that—as well as that— there had been hand-holding, caressing and kissing. In those days Julian couldn't sit next to her without resting his hand on her knee and when he spoke to her he always used to tuck her long hair behind her ear because he said he liked to look at her entire face. Her hair was much shorter now, short hair was so much more practical and the only hand she ever held was Freddie's sticky one.

Stephanie brought her memories more up to date. She wallowed in warm thoughts of weddings, christenings, birthdays and dinner parties and more simple, everyday occasions. She thought of Julian playing Lego with the boys, the Mother's Day when they set off the fire alarm while making her pancakes and their bickering about where the Christmas tree should go (Julian preferred the hall, Steph the living room). There had been good times, lots of them. They had enjoyed many fabulous holidays since the road trip and they visited highly acclaimed restaurants to eat sensational meals and drink fine wines, they watched entertaining movies and they'd had deep, thoughtful conversations and shallow, hilarious ones as well.

Steph's thoughts ebbed and flowed to the rhythm of nurses' shoes click-clacking up and down the corridors and a murmuring chorus of concerned voices as visitors stopped by and then went on their way. Sometimes, when she was alone with Julian, she talked to him and shared her memories, other times visitors would inhibit her flow.

'I'm sorry,' she whispered. 'I'm sorry about Subhash.' She paused, hoping against hope for some sort of miracle. She half expected him to suddenly sit up, reach for her hand and say, 'That's all right, my love. It's me who should be apologising.' But he didn't move. Not a flicker.

Once again fury jumped up from her stomach and sat, tasting like bile, in her mouth. She leant her head into her hands. God, this was hard. So bloody hard. She didn't even know if the fury and bile was due to the fact that he owed her a mammoth, off-the-scale, hard-to-accept apology or the fact that he couldn't give it.

'Haven't I been a good wife?' she asked him, angrily. It was the question she'd wanted to ask ever since she found the incriminating phone. She meant, 'Do I deserve this in some way? Is this my fault?' She was scrambling about for an explanation. 'I'm pretty sure I have been a good wife,' she added, indignantly answering her own question. 'Even when I didn't want to be and surely that's when it counts the most. Isn't it?' No response. 'OK, so maybe I've never ever considered wearing suspenders and a peek-a-boo bra and greeting you in the bedroom with handcuffs and a riding crop but seriously, do those wives really exist?' She paused, but this question also slapped against silence. She sighed and then clarified. 'And I said *wives*. Of course there's always going to be some daft little tart who will provide this service, but I bet you every pound we have that if you ever married the daft little tart she would fling away the peek-a-boo bra before she walked down the aisle.'

Steph gasped at the thought. He mustn't ever marry this daft little tart, this other woman. He mustn't even think about it! Nor must she. He was *her* husband. She was *his* wife. Panicked, Steph's thoughts went into free fall. 'I've washed and cleaned and cooked and ironed and given you three wonderful children,' she pointed out crossly. Then she considered that she sounded a lot like some dowdy Victorian wife and for a fraction of a moment she was relieved Julian was in a coma and hadn't heard her desperation.

The truth was it hadn't all been about housework and childcare. There came a point in their marriage where they had enough cash for someone else to do a lot of the domestic dross and so she'd spent her time finding other ways to make Julian's life as pleasant as possible. She'd booked mini breaks to interesting cities and she'd reserved tickets to important cultural exhibitions and concerts.

'And I spent ages on eBay tracking down the original nineteen seventies *Star Wars* figurines because you once told me that as a child you'd adored your set and since then you'd lost them. They're just plastic dolls! And I spent literally hours!' she pointed out with indignation.

Hadn't he appreciated anything? Steph sighed. Even she realised that a plastic Princess Leia was unlikely to turn him on as much as the possibility of having sex with another woman. The thought was overwhelming. Sickening. Even now, having lived for three days with the knowledge that her husband was an adulterer (the longest three days of her life) she still did not know what to do with the nasty, icy, solid fact. How exactly ought she to react to it? She'd tried to get revenge by meeting up with Subhash—that had been disastrous. She'd considered walking away from Julian, but how could she when he lay in a coma and there was absolutely no chance whatsoever that he could run after her? And she'd tried to ignore the fact altogether—at least outwardly that had been the most successful route. She had not divulged his secret to anyone other than Pip. She had not confided in her parents, or confessed the true state of affairs to the police and she certainly had not coughed it up in anger to the children. She had been restrained and careful. She'd tried to be dignified.

Of course, she'd spent hours sitting here by Julian's bedside, imagining this woman. This Other Woman. She'd clawed and scratched at the thought of her. Steph felt like a rat gnawing at its own foot that was lodged in a trap, she'd tried to free herself so that she could limp away from the very thought of this woman but it was impossible.

Even though Steph had just called the woman a daft little tart, she feared this was unlikely to be the case. She thought that the other woman must be a high flyer, super intellectual type because Julian wouldn't waste himself on a bimbo. Surely. And no doubt, besides being a brainiac, she'd be glamorous too, Stephanie supposed. The Other Woman would have manicured finger and toenails, they would probably be painted an edgy but sophisticated, on-trend midnight-blue colour—or similar. Steph never dared to paint hers anything more exciting than nude or a pretty pink for holidays. She'd have an eternally tidy bikini line. Oh God, let's face it, she'd probably had the area in question lasered into a permanent Brazilian or a Hollywood. There would be no stray stubborn hairs crawling around her inner thighs when she went to the swimming baths. Not that Steph could imagine Julian's mistress ever having to endure the local public swimming pool, which was made up of fifty per cent eye-stinging disinfectant and fifty per cent eye-stinging kids' urine. She'd have amazing legs that stretched to her armpits. She'd be so incredibly beautiful, terrifyingly cerebral and witty that every other female would vanish in her presence. Steph clearly had, at least as far as Julian was concerned, which was all that mattered to Steph. The imaginings of this woman's tight waist, cellulite-free bottom, interesting laugh and orgasmic groan haunted Steph.

The thought of the affair made her boil.

It made her weak.

Steph glared at her lifeless husband. 'And I've *always* supported you through stressful times at work. And you know there've been enough of them.' Still, he did not reply. The only sound was her livid, shallow breathing. She wished to God she could rile him. She'd like to hear him form his defence. Maybe he'd point out he'd done his share of supporting too. He'd been fantastic with her throughout the pregnancies and when the boys were tiny, people had commented upon how much of a family man he was. So many men bailed at that point, either through panic or maybe there was an affliction that affected men more severely than women which created a genuine repugnance to dirty nappies (odd that so many men would become squeamish when they were undoubtedly the smellier of the two sexes). Steph didn't necessarily mean that they all bailed in such a dramatic way as Dylan had, they didn't all actually leave the country. Most were happy enough to linger in the office five nights a week or nip to the pub until the really grotty part of childhood was safely dealt with and passed through and then they'd pick up the reins and carry on. But Julian had not lingered in the office or hidden behind the dartboard at their local, he had been a hands-on

384

dad.

She'd like to hear him point out that he hadn't minded when she'd slept with chilled cabbage leaves in her bra (in an effort to ease her throbbing nipples when she breastfed), and that he'd wiped his share of runny noses and bums and that he was even known to make tea for the children on Saturdays (fish fingers, chips and beans being his modest but adequate and welcome specialty). He played football with them, he took them swimming. He always booked her car in for servicing because she didn't like dealing with mechanics and he sometimes picked up a box of Ferrero Rocher chocolates for her, without there being any sort of occasion. Steph could hear him, in her head, robustly defending his abilities as a husband and father.

'I've always been generous with money and I've never had debts,' he would say. Something he knew she was terrified of since she'd lived through a childhood which, while generally happy and always loving, was blighted with financial insecurity because of her father's gambling addiction. 'I'm polite and inclusive with your friends and family,' he might add. 'And even when I stopped pouring on the passion or even tenderness, I continued to treat you appropriately. Maybe I haven't nourished you with the same intense kindness and thoughtfulness as I did in years past, my affections might have dulled down to respect and consideration. But isn't that enough?' Would he be shouting by this point in their exchange? Or contrite? Steph didn't know.

Steph thought about it and was certain. She had been a good wife, he had been a good husband, theirs was a good marriage. Until the affair.

Steph sighed again. The problem was, even in her head she couldn't make him say, 'I love *you*.'

CHAPTER FORTY-TWO

Pip had never felt more alone. Her stomach turned to liquid, mercury probably, she felt poisonous. She sat in the kitchen, stomach sloshing, heart melting and considered her actions. The problem was, while she knew she had done the proper and truthful thing, it somehow felt a lot like the wrong thing. It felt a lot like betrayal. Usually, whenever she had any sort of panic about anything (from the colour her hair had turned out after using a home dye kit, to being drastically overdrawn and not able to afford Chloe's school trip) Pip would call Steph. Stephanie would always soothe and suggest, calm and correct. But Pip could hardly call Steph now, could she? What would she say? 'Sorry, I think you drove into your husband, probably not in cold blood, more likely in a hot rage, so I've just told that lovely policewoman as much.' No, that wouldn't do.

Pip glanced at the clock. It was time to pick up Chloe from school. Had she sat here, frozen, for all those hours? Following pick-up, Pip had to take Chloe to her swimming lesson. After swimming Chloe might have some homework to do and then she'd need bathing and putting to bed. That was what Pip would concentrate on. Thank God she had Chloe to keep her sane.

Much later, after Pip had watched Chloe receive

her 200 metres swimming certificate, after they had read two chapters of *Charlotte's Web* and Chloe had fallen asleep, Pip found herself once again at her kitchen table, her mind full of Steph, and Julian and Steph, and the police and Steph. Pip picked up her mobile and began to flick through the contact list to see who she might turn to for a bit of solace. Not her parents, they were in New Zealand and it was goodness knows what time for them right now—the middle of the afternoon probably, or the middle of the night? Most likely they'd be having a barbie with the neighbours and they wouldn't be free to talk. Not that she'd ever called her parents when they were having a barbie with neighbours, let alone any other social occasion that prevented them from talking, she was in fact conjuring this scenario from hours of watching *Neighbours*, the Australian soap, and while she knew New Zealand was a totally different country and the scenario may or may not be at all accurate, the truth was she didn't feel comfortable calling her parents with this drama. Her brother would be at work and would be stunned to hear from her. They had a habit of calling one another on birthdays and holidays but they rarely bothered in-between; if she called he'd assume someone had died.

She had girlfriends other than Steph, of course. When she and Dylan had been a couple they went to dinner parties every weekend and met friends in bars and restaurants at least twice during the week. They'd had a great social life. But Pip knew they had not had great friends. When Dylan left, no one brought tureens to her door. Well, she hadn't had a door for them to do so. She'd moved in with Steph

387

almost straightaway. Steph hadn't brought tureens to her door, she'd done more than that, she'd brought a tray to her bedside and, on the odd occasion, she'd actually spoon-fed her. Back to Steph. Pip's stomach churned again. There were about a dozen telephone numbers of mothers of children in Chloe's class. But Pip didn't feel she was able to call those women for anything more urgent than a discussion on lift-sharing to a netball game. Those women had never known the perky, spiky, fun-loving Pip and while that Pip hadn't been in evidence much these past few years, Steph at least knew she had once existed and for that reason Pip always felt her true self around Steph. Back to Steph. The truth was they hadn't needed other friends, not really. Not while they had each other. Practically all of Pip's memories were intricately woven into the fabric of Steph's life. They were meshed and indistinguishable. Now it felt as though she had taken her shiny, sharp needlework scissors and severed them. Without Steph she wasn't even sure she existed.

The other names in her contact list were the names of the guys she'd fleetingly dated since Dylan and she had divorced and even some of those she'd dated before him. Why on earth was she still storing those numbers? Pip demanded of herself. The pre-Dylan boyfriends were likely to be married and have Von Trapp size families by now, she would never ever speak to any of them again, and the post-Dylan contacts couldn't really even be described as boyfriends. Most of those relationships hadn't managed to last quite as long as a mayfly's life cycle. Of course when she'd been crushed by the brevity of these affairs, Steph had always been on hand to console her.

Time slipped away as Pip's thoughts continually flew back to Steph. It was after half past ten before Pip came across Robbie's number. She hesitated. This was a lot to land at the door of a new relationship. But who else could she talk to? There was a serious chance that she was some sort of needy, overly dependent type and no doubt she'd have to see a counsellor about that at some stage but not right now. This wasn't her moment to make a bid for independent living. She called Robbie.

'Hi, I was just going to call you.' He sounded genuinely happy to hear her voice.

'Beat you to it.'

'I wanted to know if there had been any change in your friend's condition.'

'No, no change, except that I might have put his wife in jail.'

Pip filled Robbie in with the details of the conversation she'd had with Steph this morning and the one she'd had with the police this afternoon.

'Shit,' he gasped.

'Yup, that about covers it.'

'But you had to tell the truth, Pippa. And the truth is she wasn't with you.'

'I know.'

'Do you think she's really capable of such a thing?'

'Do you?'

'I don't know her, she's your friend.'

'I think it's safe to say it's out of character,' said Pip, not able to keep sarcasm out of her voice. 'But she was desperate. Besides, why would she lie to me and say she went straight home when Mrs Evans said she didn't? Where can she have been in those lost hours?'

'Shagging someone?' suggested Robbie.

'What?'

'Is that possible?'

'No, no, it's ludicrous, it's—'

'More or less ludicrous than her trying to kill her husband?' probed Robbie calmly.

'Fuck.' Pip took a deep breath and considered the possibility. It wasn't a great explanation but it was at least an explanation. Why the hell hadn't she thought of that? If Steph was having an affair, she would see that as about as big a crime as a hit-and-run, she would not want to share the details. Oh the stupid, stupid woman. Pip wasn't sure if she meant Steph or herself. 'Damn! Can you come over here and look after Chloe? I need to see Steph.'

'On my way.'

CHAPTER FORTY-THREE

Kirsten arrived at the pub at ten past six, she wasn't going to sit and wait for him, no matter how long his eyelashes were! Thinking about her day, it was a case of so far, so good. The police had arrived this afternoon, as rumoured, but she had not been one of the people called by HR for an interview. The police, it seemed, only wanted to talk to Jules's line manager and they'd checked his schedule with his PA. They had not linked her to him. Not my fault. Not my fault. And a drink with

Jake Mason, well, that was unexpected and not all bad. As she pushed open the heavy wooden door she was hit by an unfamiliar, yet not completely unpleasant, smell of beer-soaked carpets and the noise of animated chatter which, almost but not quite, drowned out the pop song that was playing on the jukebox. Kirsten had become used to posh wine bars that smelt of expensive aftershave and where competitive braying drowned out the sound of indistinguishable (but very trendy) lounge tunes. This place struck her as altogether different in ways she couldn't yet assess.

The light of the spring evening rushed through the original nineteenth-century stained-glass windows, throwing slashes of colour that played on the optics behind the bar. The dark oak floorboards were splattered and made sticky from slopped drinks and scuffed by thousands of feet scraping out a good time. The chairs were a hotchpotch, none of them matched and most of them were threadbare. Kirsten had grown up in a home which had expensive leather three-piece suites in the reception room and the conservatory, and pristine nests of tables liberally scattered throughout the house so she was surprised to find that she appreciated the casual, quirky muddle of functional, tatty furniture. It was nothing like the ugly, cheap, modern crap that her flat was full of. These chairs seemed to hold on to the good times that they'd witnessed; the furniture in her flat had never witnessed any good times, she was pretty sure of that and if it had, all evidence had slipped off the mean veneers. Strangely, and Kirsten really didn't give it too much thought, the pub had a soothing effect on her; for the first time in longer than she cared to admit, she felt almost relaxed. Maybe the hypnosis was working. Not my fault. She took a deep breath in and out, to the count of three.

Kirsten spotted Jake immediately. He was sitting in the snug in the corner, reading a magazine. Not the sort of magazine she enjoyed, the cover had a picture of President Obama rather than Gerard Butler, but Kirsten was glad that at least he wasn't reading that big pink paper that Jules liked. When Jules had read that big pink paper across the breakfast table at Highview, she'd found that there were absolutely no pictures to look at at all! Not that she imagined that scenario was going to be a problem to her in the future. Kirsten couldn't decide if Jake was genuinely oblivious to the admiring looks he was attracting from the various gangs of girls scattered around the pub or whether he was just pretending to be so. It was quite a laugh watching their faces drop as she flounced over to him and dropped a big smacker on his cheek. It was quite a different sort of reaction to the reaction she got when she was with Alan or Brian or Mark or even Jules. When she was with those guys, women might have flung envious looks her way but they were always tempered with knowing ones. The barmaids and waitresses knew the deal Kirsten had struck with those men.

Jake looked quite surprised by the smacker too. Surprised but chuffed. He looked like a man who knew his luck was in. He pointed to the vodka and cranberry on the table and said, 'I seem to remember vodka was your poison at uni.'

'Thanks.' Kirsten had always tried to avoid

drinking beer or cheap white wine at uni, the way all the other girls did, she liked to stand out from the crowd whenever she could.

'And I couldn't decide between cranberry and orange. Both have loads of vitamin C but I went for the cranberry in the end. Nice colour.' Kirsten wasn't sure whether he was laughing at her but she didn't really care because it was a double. She swallowed a glug. 'I bought some crisps too.'

'I don't eat carbs in the week,' said Kirsten.

'That figures. You always have a hungry look about you. Go on, knock yourself out. I promise you won't balloon up to Beth Ditto size during the course of the evening.' Kirsten was starving, she hadn't been able to face food since Tuesday night, she figured one crisp couldn't hurt her. As she munched her first crisp she thought, actually, an entire bag was unlikely to hurt her either, nor would washing it down with another vodka.

'Easy, tiger,' said Jake with some concern, as he watched her knock back the vodka. 'That was a double.'

'Yeah, yeah, I get it. It's my round. What you having?'

'I didn't mean that. I just meant that's a lot to—'

'I'm a big girl. I can look after myself,' interrupted Kirsten impatiently. Now she was here in the pub she'd decided that she just wanted to get out of her head as quickly as possible. Not at all surprising when you considered what she'd been through recently. She was under tons of stress since the *incident*, it was all seriously horrible and, since the police hadn't called her in for questioning this afternoon, she now had something to celebrate. Getting pissed was the order of the day.

Besides, she found that she was always quite nervous around Jake. She had no idea why. It wasn't like he earned as much as her boyfriends nor was he in a position to promote her. It *really* didn't matter what she said to him or what he thought of her. Not really. She tossed her head back so that her hair bounced on her shoulders. 'I'm good. I can handle my drink. What do you want?'

Jake looked at her doubtfully but didn't say anything other than, 'I'm still OK with this Becks, thanks.'

Kirsten bought herself another double vodka, this time with Red Bull. Jake was probably right about her needing vitamin C but she needed to be flying more. As she threaded through the happy crowd, making her way back to Jake, she ignored the fact that the room was swaying ever so slightly. She sat down with a thud, temporarily forgetting the importance of floating elegantly, as if to suggest she was weightless, which was what she usually did around men. That seemed such an effort right now.

'So, to what do I owe the pleasure of this invite?' she asked. She didn't see the point in beating around the bush.

'We're old uni buddies. What could be more natural than us meeting up for a drink and a catch-up?'

'We weren't really buddies,' said Kirsten. She didn't want to sound petulant, exactly, but she found she couldn't stop herself, it was her default setting.

'True. You didn't talk to me that much when we were at uni,' agreed Jake. 'Which means this drink is overdue. Besides, I think you hang out with old dudes too much. They say a change is as good as a rest.' Kirsten thought she probably ought to be offended but she had to admit, he might have a point. It was fun being in this bar populated by people with full heads of hair. 'And, as I said earlier, I thought you could do with a friend,' Jake added, carefully.

Here we go, thought Kirsten. Let's get down to it. This is when he asks me if I want to go for dinner at a nearby hotel or (if he's cutting corners) maybe straight back to his. Either way, it's clear what's on the menu—me.

'I wondered whether you'd like someone to go with you to the hospital. I thought perhaps you were worrying about him but didn't know how you could respectably visit,' added Jake.

Kirsten's mouth fell open. She'd realised that he had connected her to Jules, office bike and so on, that's why they were here, but for one awful moment Kirsten thought he must have connected her to Tuesday evening too. Oh fuck. What would it take to shut him up? More than sex? Money? She didn't have any money.

'What do you want?' she asked, terrified.

'Nothing.' He looked at her from under his fringe and then added, 'To help. I think you're an idiot to be seeing a married man. But as you are, I thought maybe, I mean, it can't be easy, hearing everything second-hand. Not having a clue what's going on or what happened to him.'

Oh thank God, he didn't know! Not everything, at least. Kirsten allowed herself to breathe again. Not my fault, not my fault. She was so focused on repeating the mantra that she almost missed what

Jake was saying next.

'Being into someone you can't have is very difficult.' Jake—normally a confident, almost cocksure type—was mortified about having to make this speech but he couldn't stop himself.

'I'm not into him.'

'Really?' Jake looked delighted to hear it. Kirsten sighed, less thrilled with the confession.

'Not in the way you mean.' No, the fact was, she wasn't in love with him. She never had been. She'd wanted him to leave his wife and kids, she'd wanted him to herself, she'd even wanted to marry him and to be the sole benefactor of his substantial income and considerable status but she was not in love with him. She'd needed him, or at least she needed someone, to pick up where her parents had left off. She didn't want to be on her own, doubted she could be. What sort of person did that make her?

'You're not in love with Mark Dealy, are you?' Jake looked horrified.

'No!' Fuck, she hoped he wasn't going to humiliate her and ask her if she was in love with Brian Ford or Alan Edwardson as well. She didn't think she could stand the idea of beautiful Jake bringing those names into their evening. She knew he was probably here to get for himself a bit of what she so obviously spread around so easily but couldn't they at least place a semblance of decorum on the proceedings? Would he insist on calling her on all her mistakes? Kirsten felt uncomfortably grubby. Suddenly she was feeling so many things she hadn't felt before and none of them were very nice. She felt dirty and scared and sad and sorry. Really sorry. Oh God, was she about

396

to cry? She could feel tears pricking the back of her eyes. She furiously blinked them back. The stupid, poxy hypno stuff clearly wasn't working.

Despite her efforts, Jake noticed the tears welling. 'I think you would feel better if you saw him. We can go to the hospital together, if you like. You're less likely to draw attention to yourself if I'm there. People will just think we're concerned colleagues. Probably take us for a couple, which will keep the heat away. I'll call and find out about visiting hours.'

Maybe she should go and see Jules. Jake might be right, it might help her feel better if she saw him. It might put her mind at rest, a bit. In her mind Julian was really ill and once she saw him he might not be *that* bad. Besides, when he woke up, he might like to hear that she'd visited. It might help him feel decent towards her when he got better if he heard that she'd made the effort. She nodded.

Jake made a couple of calls on his mobile and then turned back to Kirsten who had at least managed to see off the threat of tears. 'I think we'll be too late if we set off now. Visiting hours finish at eight. Maybe we should go tomorrow.'

Kirsten smiled, relieved. Tomorrow was good. It wasn't *now*, which was a huge advantage because it would be a schlep to the hospital and not what you'd call a pleasant trip. Besides, tomorrow meant they could finish their drinks, maybe go for a bite, even on to a club, she'd have to see how the night panned out. Anyway, she'd see Jake two nights in a row. Like a relationship. Not that she was saying she wanted a relationship with Jake but she could think of worse things. 'OK.'

'Yeah, you'll look and feel better after a night's sleep.'

'Look better?' asked Kirsten indignantly.

'You know, stronger.'

'A good night's sleep?'

'I'll call you a cab.'

'But—'

'Don't worry about the cost. I'll put it on one of my job numbers. And maybe you should think of taking a day's holiday tomorrow. I will too. We can go to the hospital in the afternoon. I'll meet you at three, say, at Waterloo?'

Jake called for a company cab and before Kirsten could say Kurt Geiger she found herself bundled into a car without so much as a chaste kiss on the cheek. It was really, really frustrating that he was taking over everything and bossing her about and not even making a move! Really frustrating.

And a little bit lovely.

CHAPTER FORTY-FOUR

As Jake watched the cab disappear round the corner he thought that he was pretty sure that Kirsten was the sort of girl his grandmother would describe as 'no better than she ought to be' and the sort of girl his mother had had nightmares about him bringing home since he was about five years old and came home with a stray puppy that turned out to be not only flea-ridden but ferocious too and had snarled at his baby brothers. On the other hand, his father would be delighted as she was a particular pleasure to look at.

Jake set off towards the tube station, enjoying the warm evening stroll. He could not believe Kirsten was as bad as she tried to appear, as bad as she clearly considered herself to be. Not deep down. No, she had to be better than that, or at least, she might be *able* to be better than that, given a chance. Jake wanted to give her a chance. Another chance.

Like most men at Thames Valley University, Jake had noticed Kirsten during fresher week; she was hard to miss. He'd tried to strike up a conversation with her on a number of occasions but, frankly, she'd never seemed interested. He'd asked around, and it was generally agreed that she was more than a bit spoilt. The other girls on Kirsten's course, who appeared to live to gossip about Kirsten, insinuated that she had a daddy complex and was, unfortunately, drawn to older, wealthier guys. They seemed to think it was a result of her father's behaviour; apparently he bounced between obscenely indulging her and practically ignoring her and never quite hit the note that would prove he simply valued her. Jake was lucky enough to have doting, firm but fair parents. He'd been brought up to value himself and look for the value in others.

It was stupid of Kirsten to get mixed up with Julian Blake—fact. But you don't choose who you fall for. He knew that much. It was true that she had a tendency towards the caustic but that was possibly because she hadn't found anyone she could be sweet about, yet. Maybe he could help with that. Jake was bursting with a particular brand of idealism and heroism that tended to be the preserve of the young, a little like a desire and an ability to stay up all night to watch back-to-back episodes of *The Wire*. Older people may have the desire but lacked the staying power. Jake liked a challenge and there was no doubt that she'd be that.

He really was sort of into her.

CHAPTER FORTY-FIVE

Once again, all three boys snuggled up in Steph and Julian's bed, despite Harry's cross grumbles that, last night, Alfie had been unable to stay put in his designated part of the bed.

'He kept flinging his arms and legs over my side,' moaned the eldest boy, indignantly. 'It's like sleeping with an elephant-sized, zombie mud wrestler. He woke me up at least twice.'

'You can always sleep in your own bed, if you want to,' pointed out Steph gently.

'No, better not. I think they like me in there,' whispered Harry confidentially, as he quickly scampered after his younger brothers who were already in their parents' room. He leapt into bed without any more discussion. The fact was they all needed to feel the weight of their siblings' arms and legs, breath and cuddles, even if that meant disturbed sleep. Steph lay down next to them, waiting for them to drop off.

Freddie, who was simply happy to have his mum home again, popped his thumb in his mouth and fell asleep quickly. He was the only thumb-sucker of the three. The other two had sucked dummies for a short spell but had easily been persuaded to give them up. Steph knew that she had to convince Freddie to break the habit, he was five years old, but she never could bring herself to scold him because he looked so adorable with his thumb in his mouth. Adorable and endearing and a little bit vulnerable, he put her in mind of one of Peter Pan's lost boys and no one could scold a lost boy.

Harry and Alfie didn't find it as easy to settle to sleep. They repeatedly asked when Julian would be home. Steph walked a fine line of optimism and realism. She told her boys that their daddy would probably take a long time to get well. She did not allow the fearful thought, that he might not get well, bubble out of her mouth.

'Shall I read to you?'

'Yes.'

She read three chapters of a rather scary child-spy book which encouraged the boys to liveliness, rather than helped them drift into sleep. So they then played long rounds of the memory game, 'I went to the shop and bought . . .' A game that Harry usually dismissed as childish and beneath his dignity, tonight he fell in with the suggestion. Anything rather than face his nightmares or, worse, stare at the ceiling for hours. Alfie fell asleep as he was 'buying' risotto, strawberries and tapioca, at about 9 p.m.

'I think I win,' yawned Harry.

'Yes, darling, you do,' said Steph, stealing the opportunity to plant a rare kiss on the forehead of her eleven year old.

'I always do,' he added proudly.

'Yes, darling, you do,' agreed Steph, astounded that even at a time like this her sons were competitive. 'But you are the oldest,' she reminded him.

'I don't think you should have allowed fruit for f. Alfie should have had to come up with something different,' he mumbled sleepily.

'I felt like being lenient,' murmured Steph. Harry allowed her to curl her body around his as he lay on his side, wrapped around Alfie, who in turn held fast on to Freddie. 'Besides, I couldn't think of anything that began with an f.'

'Fromage frais, foie gras, fondue, frogs legs,' Harry suggested with another yawn and a hint of superiority. Steph wondered whether her son's food choices (or his hint of superiority) reflected well on her. She remembered back to their last holiday in France where she had been quite insistent that the children tried the local cuisine. As the boys had struggled with raw meats and smelly cheeses, Pip had allowed Chloe to exist on a diet of French fries and crêpes, which she argued were also local cuisine. Of course the boys had hated Steph for her rule. Every mealtime had been like a cold war. Steph now wondered why she'd ever cared, was it worth the struggle? She was unsure. High standards were so uncomfortable and alienating.

'Fish fingers, fudge, Frosties,' she added trying for a bit of late-in-the-day balance.

'Imagine if you had a day where you could only eat food beginning with one letter,' mused Harry, as he fought sleep.

'Which letter would you pick?'

He thought about it for a while. 'C. Chocolate, cherries, croissants, cake, crisps. Cashew nuts. Do cashew nuts count?'

'Definitely,' said Steph as she knew her eldest loved cashew nuts, especially the honey-roasted variety. She often threw them into salads to make carrots and celery more palatable. Steph wondered whether, when this was all over and Julian was home (please, please), they might have such a day. A day when they ate nothing but food beginning with the letter C. It seemed so impossibly careless. So unlike anything they ever did as a family.

Harry finally fell asleep after mumbling, 'Coco Pops.' They lay nested like Russian matryoshka dolls, except, thought Steph, generally matryoshka dolls came in sets of five.

The warmth and comfort of her sons' bodies and her sheer exhaustion, after days of scarcely any sleep, finally won through and Steph fell asleep almost the moment Harry did. When she woke up it was pitch black outside. The sound of her father coughing in his sleep had woken her. She wished it hadn't because the moment she was awake she knew she would not fall back to sleep again. Her first thought was that she wanted to go back to the hospital to be near Julian. She'd only been persuaded to leave his side because her mother had insisted the boys needed her too and Julian's father had taken a room in a nearby hotel and his brother, James, had arrived from Canada and was now sitting vigil. He'd promised to call Steph if there was the slightest change. Bleary-eyed, Steph felt around the bedside table for her phone. There were three text messages. They were all from Subhash, two words: 'You OK?' She deleted the records and checked the time, it was only almost midnight, witching hour, she'd thought it was later. Carefully, she edged out of the bed and then slipped downstairs to make a cup of chamomile tea.

Having longed to be home she was now surprised to find that her home seemed alien. After two days and a night at the hospital she had become accustomed to the constant muffled hustle and bustle of the ward staff and the whirr of the machines that were keeping her husband alive. Her house seemed so deathly silent by comparison, and distant. Distant from Julian, who was distant from everyone. Who had been distant from her even before this. Steph sighed. The house was alien because her husband had another woman.

Steph put the kettle on and while the water boiled she retrieved Julian's mobile phone. Her fingers were so icy that it was difficult for her to open the menu and find the messages icon and open the inbox. The words, so vile and wild and erotic, tore at her heart once again. She had to develop the self-control to stop looking at the messages, it wasn't helping matters. She snapped the phone closed, she needed some chamomile tea.

What was this woman thinking now? Was she wondering where Julian was? What had happened to her last Tuesday? Had she turned up at the hotel and gone to the room? Had she lain, scantily clad, waiting for him? At what time had his mistress given up expecting him? Stephanie assumed that waiting around was part of the deal for a mistress. No dirty socks to wash but no expectation that you could depend on appointments.

Steph's phone vibrated and caused her to leap. She checked the caller ID, hoping and dreading that it was the hospital, imagining it might be

Subhash and finding it was Pip.

'Hi.'

'I'm outside. I didn't want to ring the bell, in case I disturbed the kids. I didn't imagine you'd be sleeping. Can you let me in?'

Steph hurried to the front door and opened it to her friend. Cool night air flew through the house. Steph shivered and pulled her dressing gown tightly around her. Pip must be freezing too as she was shaking like a leaf. Steph barely recognised her; she looked thinner than she'd looked this morning, certainly more gaunt and withered.

'Robbie said to me that you might not have knocked down Julian but you might be having an affair,' garbled Pip. Steph heard the sentence clearly enough but it seemed to punch her in the head, leaving her dazed. 'I told him that was stupid. You are the last person in the world who would have an affair but then I began to wonder.' Steph could hear panic and confusion in Pip's voice and see turmoil in her face. 'Are you, Steph? I began to think that might make sense. That might be something you wouldn't want to tell me.'

Steph took a deep breath. She wouldn't lie to Pip. Her relationship with Subhash was not anything she'd ever wanted to have to confess to, let alone discuss and dissect, but she would not lie to Pip. Maybe offering up the explanation might be a help—to them both.

'Yes, your Robbie has got it this time,' said Steph, with an irritated emphasis on the man's name. Who the hell was this Robbie anyway? She'd never even met him and yet he knew more about her than her own mother did. Steph didn't like it. 'Quite the detective, isn't he? Come into the kitchen. I'll pour you a cup of chamomile. I don't know if it does any good but I'm drinking it by the gallon.'

Pip followed Steph into the kitchen. She took one look at the herb tea and shook her head. It looked horribly like urine and that put her in mind of Julian's catheter.

'Anything stronger?' she asked.

'Coffee,' deadpanned Steph. She didn't want what she had to say tonight to be further confused by alcohol consumption.

'OK,' agreed Pip, reluctantly.

They didn't speak while the coffee brewed. Small talk would have been an insult and the necessary big talk was so massive that attention couldn't be split between that and spooning heaps of coffee into the cafetière. It was clear to both of them that they could only start to talk once they were ensconced in the sun room, which was in fact anything other than sunny at that moment; it was dark and cold and draughty, but Steph chose to sit there because it was the room furthest away from the sleeping boys and she didn't want to risk them overhearing what she had to say.

'I met him last May. He's called Subhash Sharma. He runs his own solar power business.'

Pip thought that it was so like Steph to reel out the credentials first, as though she was throwing some sort of drinks party and introducing two strangers. 'This is John Smith, he's an architect and this is Jane Jones, she's a dentist.' Pip always hated it when people did that, it was assuming a person's job was their identity. Since Pip had followed a very sketchy career path, she'd always feared an introduction along the lines of, 'This is

Pip Foxton, she's a fiasco.'

'He asked me to go to dinner.' Stephanie smiled at the memory. Even now, in amongst all this mess and confusion, she found that thinking of Subhash—standing in the doorway of the coffee shop, cheerfully grinning at her—lit her up from the inside. She thought it probably always would. Always. A terribly long time.

'Oh my God,' replied Pip, catching Steph's expression and understanding it entirely. She was struggling with the thought that Steph was having an affair almost as much as she'd struggled with the thought that she might have attempted to kill her husband. 'But you said no. You said you were married, right?' Pip sounded anxious and irritated at once.

'Yes, that's exactly what I said,' Stephanie replied, with another sigh. 'But he said, I think even married women have to eat, don't they?' Stephanie recalled his carefully enunciated lilting tone. She could hear his words as clear as a bell.

'And you said no again,' Pip suggested, quite firmly.

'But married women *do* eat, Pip.' Stephanie looked Pip in the eye; she searched for some understanding, hoped for a little bit of tolerance.

'So you went for dinner,' groaned Pip, exhibiting nothing other than despair. 'Is he married as well?' she demanded angrily.

Steph nodded.

Pip glared.

It was a shootout at the OK Corral.

Steph was married. This impertinent stranger was married. This was a clearcut situation. This was unforgivable. Pip could *never* condone affairs.

407

She'd lived through the consequences of Dylan's treachery. This sort of situation was black and white for her. From time to time over the past couple of years, married or partnered men had hit on Pip. She'd realised that in some vague, inadequate way they might have offered a short-term answer to her perpetual loneliness but she'd never ever been tempted to take them up on their offers of drinks or dinners. Pip knew that there was always a wife to consider and even a wife who didn't understand, that no longer liked sex or who hated his mother, was still due respect. She would never ever put another woman through what she'd been through. The matter was non-negotiable.

Stephanie knew this and it took all her courage to continue. 'Not dinner, no. Never dinner. The children.' She nodded her head in the direction of the stairs and Pip was unsure if Steph meant that she hadn't accepted a dinner invite because she had babysitting issues or because she knew it was wrong to have an affair and the children were the physical embodiment of her fifteen-year marriage. Had they served as mini Jiminy Crickets? She hoped it was the latter and imagined it was the former. 'We had lunch,' admitted Steph. 'And then—then it was as you'd predict,' she added sheepishly.

Pip saw it vividly. Yes, she knew how such things went. The urgent glances, the breathless sighs, the dashing to find a hotel, the impatience to unlock the door, the handbag cast to one side and then the duvet tossed to the floor. She saw it clearly because she'd lived the scene a hundred times, a thousand times, in her head. Usually, different protagonists featured in her imaginings, Dylan and *that slut* had always starred in her show, but now she saw Steph and some stranger shredding pantyhose. Pip rubbed her eyes with the palms of her hands. No, no, it was too ghastly. Steph? Stephanie Amstell? She unconsciously fell back on her friend's maiden name, the name she'd used for Steph for fifteen years before the fifteen years she'd called her Stephanie Blake. How terrible it was that after thirty years of knowing someone, you found out you don't know them at all. Pip felt her world shake as though she was some sort of victim of time travel. The years vanished. Nothing was certain, Pip had no knowledge. She had no past. Stephanie Amstell was an adulterer.

Steph read her friend's mind as she always had. 'Pip, I know this must upset you. And I've disappointed you but I really need you to hear me out.' Steph moved towards Pip and laid her hand on her friend's. Pip pulled back as though she'd been stung and grabbed her coffee mug.

'Spare me, Steph. Spare me the pathetic, predictable details about how you've never felt this way about anyone before or you didn't mean it to happen or you didn't want to hurt anyone.'

'But no one was hurt,' insisted Stephanie, except perhaps herself and Subhash but she didn't think this was the moment for that level of detail. 'At least, not by me. I'm not Dylan.'

'I can't see a difference between you,' snapped Pip.

Stephanie considered this. Perhaps there wasn't a difference after all but she'd always hoped and thought there was. She'd tried to be better. Didn't that count? Looking at Pip's stony expression right now, Steph thought perhaps it didn't. She decided to try to tackle the problem from another angle. 'You have to think it's better that I was with Subhash than I attempted to kill my husband,' she pointed out reasonably.

Pip hung her head and then admitted, 'I could never have condoned you mowing down Julian, but in a strange way I almost understood it.'

Steph gasped. 'You're kidding.'

'No, I'm not. I thought you'd just lost it. You know. After years of keeping your cool and being so, oh, I don't know, so flawless, I thought you'd just gone mad and behaved like we all do. Badly.'

'And you'd have been OK with that?' asked Steph in amazement.

'Not OK, no. But I'd have understood a rare moment of madness.' Pip shrugged.

'But you can't understand my relationship with Subhash?' Steph pleaded.

'You know my thoughts on adultery,' mumbled Pip as she sipped her coffee.

Steph knew Pip well enough to guess that she was probably struggling to swallow her drink; she was simply using the coffee as a way of avoiding eye contact. Yes, yes, Steph knew Pip's views on adultery. Actually they coincided with her own, although Pip was unlikely to believe it right now. Pip's position of no excuses, no explanation, and no extenuating circumstances had meant Steph had never been able to confide in her in all these long, lonely and confusing months. That's why she was in such a mess because she couldn't bear the idea of Pip loathing her, the way she loathed other people who casually broke vows and hearts.

From the moment Pip had linked their names in the school playground, all those years ago, Steph had loved Philippa Foxton with an absolute sincerity and intensity. There was nothing she wouldn't do for her friend. She'd worked hard, perhaps too hard, to hold on to Pip's favour. When they were teenagers she'd broken curfews and drunk bitter-tasting alcohol if Pip wanted her to. When they were in their twenties she'd watched Pip's flourishing career with as much pride as if it had been her own and she'd felt Pip's heartbreaks almost as acutely as if they had been her own. During their thirties, on paper at least, it seemed that Steph was the one that was constantly giving to Pip, her time, her home, her nutritious meals, lifts and holidays, but Steph had never seen their friendship that way.

Pip had saved Steph's life.

Stephanie Amstell would have shrivelled up and disappeared if Pip hadn't noticed her as she skulked near the hopscotch, she was sure of it. If Pip, with all her confidence, allure and glamour had not singled her out, she would have stayed as tiny as Mrs Pepper Pot for her entire life. She doubted she would have been the sort of woman to have gone on to marry a man like Julian or to have the boys she had, she might not have even managed to hold coffee mornings for charity or even mastered the art of making meringue go stiff. Indeed, part of Steph's motivation to become an exemplary mother and homemaker was to complement Pip's skill set; on some level Steph enticed Pip into her life with freshly baked scones and tips on the exam system. Pip's approval mattered to Stephanie.

But now there were bigger things at stake. Part of Steph's motivation to become an exemplary

411

mother and homemaker was Pip but the bigger part was Julian, Harry, Alfie and Freddie.

The silence between them was tense and bloated like a balloon, Steph had to pop it.

'But now at least you understand why I need you to tell the police I was with you on Tuesday,' she mumbled. Pip blanched but Steph was too concerned with insisting on her own point to notice. 'Because if—when—Julian pulls through this, do you think it will help his recovery if he finds out where I was that night?'

Still angry and confused and guilty, Pip spat, 'Surely you could just explain that you were having an eye-for-an-eye shag after discovering that he was screwing some floozy.' Steph glanced warily at the ceiling, would Pip's voice carry?

'Shush. The boys, my mum and dad.'

'I mean, two wrongs make a right, don't they, Steph? That was what you were thinking.'

'I don't know what I was thinking but I didn't sleep with Subhash,' stated Steph calmly, despite her belief that revealing this level of detail was undignified.

'What, and you think it makes a difference that you didn't happen to shag him on that particular Tuesday?'

'I didn't ever *shag him*, as you so delicately put it.'

'What? But you said you were having an affair. You said Robbie was right,' Pip faltered.

'I thought, maybe, I was in love. That's an affair, isn't it.' Steph wasn't asking a question, she was stating the situation as she saw it.

'No sex?'

'No, no sex.' Steph fidgeted uncomfortably.

'No handjobs or blow jobs or fingering?' Pip was looking for clarification.

'Pip!'

'Sorry, I'm just trying to understand. Snogging?'

'I really hate that word.'

'Everyone does, but no one has come up with anything better.'

'Once. We kissed once. On Tuesday,' admitted Steph. 'We kissed and I drank the mini bar dry. He drove me home.'

'Ah.' Now Pip understood everything. Of course she understood why Steph might have flung herself into the arms of a longstanding flirtation—because really that's all it was. How could Steph accuse her of being the fanciful one when she described a couple of lunches as an affair? It was Steph who didn't have a grasp. Pip didn't blame Steph for the flirtation or the fling—she got it. Betrayal was a great motivator for stupid acts. And Pip understood that the Steph she knew wouldn't have been able to go though with sex, even if she'd wanted to, even if her husband was shagging another woman. That was not Steph's way. And finally, Pip understood the guilt and the dread of exposure that Steph would so keenly feel if people knew where she'd been on Tuesday. Now, if ever, Steph needed to cling to her respectability. Yes, Pip understood everything.

'He's a really lovely man, kind, decent, attentive, you know.'

Pip nodded, indeed perhaps for the first time she was gaining some understanding of what it was like to know a man of that sort. Robbie.

'Julian and I, well, we were victims of the age-old story. A little too used to one another, I think.

413

We'd started to take one another for granted. We'd become wallpaper in each other's lives. For a while there I thought I was in love with Subhash. Maybe I was. It was flattering. Exciting. Who knows.' Stephanie paused and looked out into the garden. The night wasn't so black now, there was the first breathy hint of light. Soon the garden would be steeped in a gash of golden light dividing the shadowy garden shrubs and the shimmering dark blue sky. An hour ago it was yesterday, in another few hours tomorrow would be today, right now was a peculiar limbo.

'Love is so much more complicated than I thought it was. I was so dim.' Steph clamped her hands to the sides of her head and squeezed. Pip wondered if she was trying to stop her head exploding or was she hoping to implode? 'I was so smug. I thought I had it all worked out. Then Subhash came along. And then I found out about Julian's affair and now, now I find that I hate and love my husband with such ferocity that I feel I'm being ripped apart. Pip, it's all so sickeningly confusing. I had no idea being an adult was so hard.'

'Oh, Steph, I'm sorry.' Pip jumped off her chair and knelt down beside Steph. 'Why didn't you tell me any of this?'

'How could I? I know I have exactly what you want. You'd have thought me ungrateful and greedy if I'd told you it wasn't enough.'

'No, I—' Pip stopped herself. Yeah, she would have.

'I have the perfect set-up. Admitting it's anything less than perfect ruins things for everyone.'

Pip realised that she had never given her friend any room to be less than perfect. Pip often declared that Steph was the ideal mother, that she was a wonderful cook, a flawless hostess and most importantly that she had a watertight marriage. She hadn't even listened when Steph had told her Julian was having an affair. She hadn't wanted to believe it, so she hadn't believed it. She'd insisted there must be some mistake. She'd forced Steph to look for someone else to confide in. Since Dylan had deserted her, Pip's designated role was heartbroken single mum in need of saving, and Steph's designated role was happily married mother of three, joined at the hip to her first love. Pip thought perhaps *she'd* been the one who had designated these roles and now she wondered if they were truly helpful. The roles hadn't left much room for her own growth or Steph's mistakes.

'Subhash says he wants to leave his wife for me. But I know for certain I don't want that. I worked it out on Tuesday night, after he kissed me. When it became real, I suppose. I don't want him but he's a good man and I definitely don't want him embroiled in this mess. I don't want things getting any more complicated. That's why I need you to lie for me, Pip. I'm so sorry to ask you but everything I have has to be focused on Julian and helping Julian get better. Do you understand?'

Oh shit, thought Pip. What she said was, 'What if Julian gets better and leaves you for this other woman?'

'Oh, I've thought of that. I realise that's quite likely, actually,' said Steph with a shrug that was designed to hide her dread but didn't. 'I believe a near-death experience often results in more daring

415

behaviour. People suddenly grasp at what they really want, rather than lazily putting up with what they have, but I'll have to cross that bridge when I come to it. All I know is I can't be the one to leave. Not now. Not even before. I want to stay. It's not fashionable. I know some people will think I'm a fool but I want to stand by him. It's what I believe.'

'What if he doesn't recover, Steph?' asked Pip quietly.

Stephanie glared at her friend, shocked that she'd said the unsayable but aware that someone had to say it and Pip, as her oldest friend, probably had that right.

'If he doesn't get better then I'll be on my own. What I do know is I can't make things worse right now. There's already shedloads to deal with.' Pip froze as she thought perhaps she had already made things worse. 'Subhash has a wife and I don't want to hurt her the way I've been hurt. The way you were. I don't want him being dragged into this and forced to offer up an alibi for me. That's a lot to pay for just one kiss. I don't want any more hurt.'

'Right,' said Pip carefully.

'Do you understand?'

'Yes, Steph. I understand now. I just wish you'd told me all of this before.'

'I was . . . It was . . . difficult.' Pip knew all about having to say something that was difficult. 'So will you lie for me, to the police? I know it's asking a lot but I haven't done anything illegal. You believe me now, don't you?'

'Yes, I believe you.'

'So, will you provide an alibi?'

Pip realised that if she was any sort of a friend she'd now explain to Steph exactly what she'd said

416

to the police. And if Steph was half the person Pip thought she was, she'd understand. Surely, Steph would understand that she couldn't lie to the police, not without any sort of explanation as to where Steph had been. Surely, she'd understand why she had told the police about Steph discovering Julian's affair and the fact that Stephanie had dashed out of the house upset on the night in question. Or maybe she would consider that an unnecessary detail.

Pip was ashamed to discover that if coming clean at this point defined her as any sort of a decent friend then she was *not* any sort of a decent friend.

'Look at the time,' she exclaimed suddenly, and not especially convincingly. 'It's great that we've cleared so much up. Obviously still a lot to talk about but I have to get back. I've left Chloe with Robbie.'

Steph was horrified. 'The man you met on Monday?'

'She's asleep.' Pip suddenly felt once again flung back into her position of inadequate mother defending her decisions to a more superior breed.

'What if she wakes up? She'll be frightened to see a stranger in the house. I take it there hasn't been any formal introduction.'

'No, there hasn't. I've had things on my mind.' Pip had stood up and was backing towards the door. 'He's a nurse. He's trustworthy. I was stuck.' Pip had never left Chloe with anyone other than Steph and she felt irritated with Steph for drawing attention to this possible but rare lapse of judgement. 'Sometimes, Steph, you expect too much of people. Do you know that?' she snapped

417

irritably.

'Yes, I expect a lot but I give a lot too.'

Pip knew this was true but felt too desperate to be fair.

Friday

CHAPTER FORTY-SIX

For the second time Sergeant Brown and PC Weybridge arrived at Stephanie's house early in the morning. They were perfectly polite and possibly all the more terrifying for that. They kept their faces impressively impassive as they asked Steph if she'd like to accompany them back to the police station to answer a few questions. It was only when Steph said, 'No, I'm sorry, I can't come right now, I have to go to the hospital and see my husband,' that she detected a flicker of expression. The policeman looked smug and then seemed to realise that was not the suitable response so altered his face so that he looked stern. The policewoman looked surprised.

'I don't think you understand, Mrs Blake. If you are not prepared to accompany us to the police station, then we'd be forced to insist you do so,' said the young policeman gruffly.

Were they arresting her? Steph shook her head, uncertain as to how this could have come about. Going to the police station was such a waste of time. It was one thing absenting herself from Julian's bedside because she was putting their children to bed and reading night-time stories, altogether another to waste time at a police station.

'But surely there's no need for that. You can ask me anything you want right now. Come through to the sitting room,' said Steph, as she fingered the collar of her shirt. She'd chosen a pretty purple shirt this morning, it was one that Julian had once commented 'suited her' and so she'd decided to wear it today, to make an effort, although she was very well aware that she was making an effort for a man who couldn't react to light or sound and breathed through a tube and a machine.

'We just want to run through some of the details on your statement, Mrs Blake,' said Sergeant Brown. Steph noticed that the policewoman didn't seem to emit the same sympathetic vibe as she had the first time she'd visited Steph, in fact she seemed irritated. Her tone of voice had a hint of impatience and exasperation to it, it was similar to the tone of voice Steph used on the boys when she found out that one or other of them had broken or lost something and wouldn't own up.

'You said you were with your friend, Ms Foxton,' chipped in the PC.

'That's right.'

'You arrived at seven.'

'Thereabouts.'

'And you left at about eleven, maybe eleven thirty.' The policeman was reading from his notebook.

Stephanie noticed that all three of her boys and both her parents had now congregated in the hall. Her mother was still wearing her dressing gown as she'd spent the morning concentrating on helping the boys find their school uniforms and ensuring they all ate an adequate enough breakfast, she looked wizened and wary. Steph's father was at least dressed in his day clothes. He never came downstairs without showering and dressing first, not even on Christmas morning. Steph had never seen him in his pyjamas, except once when he was bed-bound with a particularly vicious bout of flu.

His rule was that once up, you should get dressed, open the curtains and, ideally, go for a walk, he believed each day should be greeted with some enthusiasm. Yet this morning he did not look at all enthusiastic, he looked alarmed.

Steph glanced at her sons. She needed to be getting them in the car. They would be late for school otherwise. Freddie had the least idea as to what was going on in their household at the moment and so did not look as bemused and afraid as the other two. He had the courage and curiosity to creep forward and stand close to the policeman, eyeing the PC's walkie-talkie with delighted interest. Alfie slipped his hand into his mother's, he was pale and passive. Harry looked at the police with outrage and resentment. He couldn't comprehend why they had ever come to *his* door to deliver such terrible news as they had this week. Why not next door? Or the door of some other kid in his class? Any door other than this one in Hilledge Grove. It wasn't fair.

'Yes, I was with Pip from seven to eleven thirty,' Steph lied again. 'You can talk to her and she will confirm those times. I really don't see any need for me to come to the station. My husband is critically ill. I need to be with him.' Steph could hear her own hysteria. She wasn't helping her case and she wasn't helping her boys. Alfie threw her a frightened glance.

'We have talked to Ms Foxton and I'm afraid there seems to be some discrepancy in the timings. We could discuss this here or you could come down to the station, Mrs Blake.' Sergeant Brown threw out a fleeting look that caught all the boys and her parents like helpless, hopeless fish in a net.

'I'll get my coat,' replied Steph with a sigh.

CHAPTER FORTY-SEVEN

It had been an unexpectedly warm day, unseasonably so. The spring sun sat squarely on the shoulders of young men and mercilessly on the bat wings of older women in strappy tops who really would have been better advised to keep their jackets on. It was a peculiarly English thing, Pip decided, this unwise and rather too enthusiastic basking. Nowhere else on the planet would similar temperatures lead to an injudicious display of flesh. Pip had found the surprise heat infuriating, what was going on with the weather this week? Why was everything so unsettled and changeable? One moment it was pouring down, the next it was the sort of weather where people chose to go to riverside pubs after work, to drink beer and flick nuts at the ducks. She felt the unpredictability of the weather was somehow contributing to the week's uncertainty, at the very least it was highlighting her tremulous time.

Pip would have preferred it to be dull today, gloomy cloud or even electric storms might have suited her mood better; besides, she was certainly too busy and stressed to enjoy the warmth. She'd spent the entire morning in an internet café, desperately trying to do something to right her wrong. Normally, she liked spending time in the internet café near the library. Dave, the guy who ran the place, was cheerful and non-condescending. He always offered free technical advice and sometimes he threw in a free coffee too, if business was going well. Today the café had been empty, presumably everyone else had clear consciences and they were out sunning themselves in the town park. After all, how many people in Riverford had betrayed their best friends through a lack of trust in the last twenty-four hours? Pip thought it was probably just her. She'd never felt so isolated and forlorn before, not even when Dylan left her. At least then she knew the travesty wasn't her fault.

Dave clearly resented the fact he had to stay open for Pip, rather than join the sun worshippers. So much was obvious from the way he said the coffee machine was broken and then didn't even give her a straw—let alone a glass—to go with her Diet Coke. He'd probably been planning on shutting shop and sneaking out until Pip arrived with her pen and paper and good intentions. As a result Dave hadn't taken any interest whatsoever in her project, which was unusual but useful. She really wasn't up to lying about what she was doing but nor did she want to explain herself.

Pip had little to go on, other than three facts. She knew his name, she knew that he ran a business that had something to do with a solar power, and she knew that he was married. The third fact, although the most pertinent to Steph, was the least helpful when it came to her amateur sleuthing. However, Googling had proven fruitful. She'd come across a couple of articles about Subhash being awarded various regional awards for business and she also discovered he had an OBE. She wondered whether Steph knew this. Maybe she did, but it just wasn't the sort of thing you mentioned to your best friend about your sort of lover while your husband was in a coma. After some further investigating, Pip had found a telephone number for Subhash's company and called to make contact but a fiercely efficient PA had refused to interrupt his meeting to bring him to the phone. Pip had been forced to leave a message that Steph's friend had called and could he call back immediately. It was a matter of some importance. 'Steph's friend,' the PA had repeated with some scepticism. Pip felt as if she was twelve and back in the playground, announcing to some boy that her friend fancied his friend. It all seemed very desperate.

Subhash had rung back at three thirty. He apologised profusely for being so tardy.

'I've just this minute got out of my meeting. I wish I'd been called to the phone when you rang. Is she OK? Is everything OK? I haven't been able to reach her,' he garbled. The love and concern in his voice was unmistakable.

Pip felt sorry for him. She explained who she was and said that yes, Steph was OK but things were complicated. 'I think it might be easier to explain if we met up.'

'I can meet you now.'

Half an hour later Pip and Chloe sat in the lobby of the local theatre, waiting for Subhash. Pip glanced out of the window and across the river to the groups of revellers that were desperately soaking up the afternoon rays. The sun's warmth oozed in people's smiles and their loud, overexcited voices. It was much cooler inside the theatre lobby, where the air con was a little too robust. Pip often felt the cold, but she'd learnt not to ever make much of the fact because people always replied that her problem was that her bones needed considerably more padding. Of course, they didn't mean it, her angular, jutting joints—cheekbones, wrists, hips, knees—were envied. If it was true that a woman could never be too rich or too thin then Pip thought she'd got half of it right, although she couldn't help wishing it was the other half.

The lobby was quiet. Occasionally a woman might pop in off the street to talk to someone in the box office or pick up a programme. Three such ladies stopped by as Pip waited for Subhash. Pip thought that the women were the sort of women who expected their pleasures to be tasteful and their fun to be safe and restrained, women who operated on a muted level and were no longer ever exuberant and wholeheartedly joyful. Was Stephanie like those women? Pip wondered. Was Steph happy or resentful of her life of tasteful pleasures? Pip thought she should know that much about her best friend but it was hard to make the call when she was sitting in a theatre lobby, waiting for Steph's bit of fun which she had not been able to restrain and which had consequently bled all over her life. Pip remembered making love to Robbie on Tuesday night and a slow smile spread across her face and a warm feeling ran through her body. She was not like those women, she'd tasted abandoned pleasure, just this week. Who would have imagined that, after two years of hibernation and many years of humiliation? In all of this tragic confusion she'd barely had time to think about what a miracle Robbie was. But he was a miracle of sorts. He was a start. A possibility.

Pip had had no choice but to bring Chloe along to this peculiar rendezvous. She now realised how much she relied on Steph for babysitting. Usually, whenever she had a half-hour appointment after school, she was able to drop off Chloe with Steph. Although, until recently, Pip hadn't had much call to rush around the streets of Riverford; if she'd ever had a reason, it used to be something more mundane like a parents' night at Chloe's school rather than a desperate dash to dredge up an alibi for her friend, to clear her of any possible involvement in said friend's husband's hit-and-run! When had life become so complicated? Pip had considered calling Robbie and asking him to help out with babysitting again but she'd decided against it. It was one thing to ask him to babysit when Chloe was tucked up in bed and not likely to cause any aggro, it was altogether another to expect him to make her tea and oversee homework. Besides, Pip didn't want Chloe's first introduction to Robbie to be a hurried, scrambled-together event. She wanted the three of them to take their time over that initial meeting, to give it some gravitas and lots of good intention. Because she did hope . . . She couldn't help but imagine . . . Pip did not dare complete the sentences, not even in her head. She thought it was enough to tempt fate by suggesting (even to herself!) that perhaps, once all this mess was sorted out, the three of them could spend a day together in London, maybe visit the zoo or the Science Museum. Would Chloe like that?

Pip glanced at her daughter who was unenthusiastically eating a skinny banana and raisin loaf cake. Clearly the cake was as tasteless as it was worthy. Cakes oughtn't to be worthy, they ought to be gooey and yummy but the selection available in the theatre's café was limited. Pip secretly believed that arts venues, such as this theatre, were often unnecessarily austere. It was almost as though the theatre manager was concerned that anyone might have too much *fun* here and therefore instructed the caterers to only sell cakes stuffed with bran and dried fruit. Pip had no idea why Subhash had suggested they meet here at the theatre in the first place, it was a slightly odd place to hook up but he'd seemed determined.

She spotted him straightaway, he walked directly towards her. Pip wondered whether (and how) Steph had described her.

'Philippa Foxton?'

'For my sins,' said Pip, meaning it.

Right now she would have very much liked to be someone else, someone with a smaller mouth, perhaps, or a bigger capacity to trust. Pip wondered how they ought to greet one another. She considered wrapping Subhash in an enormous bear hug, after all she had really quite terrible news to dish up, but then she thought hugging might be a bit weird. She didn't want him thinking she was coming on to him or that she was some sort of drippy hippy, so instead she pumped his hand up and down with unnecessary vigour.

'And this is my daughter, Chloe.'

Chloe and Subhash shook hands too and then Pip dispatched Chloe (and her Nintendo DS) to a nearby table. Pip would have liked her daughter to sit and draw or maybe learn her times tables but realistically she needed thirty minutes of uninterrupted time and the truth was only the DS would enable that.

Pip carefully and concisely brought Subhash up to date with the events of the week. On cue, his so obviously intelligent face flooded with concern and shock. Pip faltered when it came to explaining her part in the drama.

'So the hit-and-run happened when she was with me?' he asked.

'Yes, so it seems.'

'And she asked you for an alibi?'

'Yes.'

'But you didn't give her it.'

'No.' Pip felt shame flood her body again but instead of blushing she felt as though all her blood had run to her feet. This was perhaps fitting as her world was upside down.

'Why not?' He seemed bemused.

'I thought—I thought that, maybe, she *had* done it.'

'You thought that of Stephanie?'

'For a time.'

'Strange.'

Pip glared at Subhash. In that one word it seemed to her that he'd understood everything. He'd understood how she had failed Steph. How she had doubted and betrayed her. He didn't have to say so but Pip knew that he thought Steph would have given her the alibi, even if it had meant lying to the police and even if she hadn't been able to account for the missing hours. Maybe that was wrong. Maybe it was right. Pip didn't know anymore. All she knew was that Steph would have done as much for her because there was nothing Steph would not do for her. Pip, it seemed, had limits.

430

'Of course I'll step forward and explain that she was with me. Let's go to the police station right this moment,' said Subhash firmly. He stood up, his chair scraped along the wooden floor and inside Pip's head, his impressive height was shown to its full advantage. Pip could understand why Steph had fallen for this man. He oozed integrity and simplicity, but he was no fool, he was clearly quite unafraid. He was a lot like Steph. Pip tugged at the sleeve of his jacket, indicating that he had to sit down again.

'She doesn't want you to do that.'

'Sorry?'

'She doesn't want you or your wife to get embroiled in this.'

Subhash saw at once what that must mean. 'She's staying with him. Isn't she? She's standing by her man.' He collapsed back into the chair, folding in on himself. He put Pip in mind of a crumpled sheet of paper, upon which the beginnings of an idea had once been sketched but now the idea wasn't going to be developed. The paper was screwed into a ball and tossed aside into a rubbish bin.

'I think so,' and then more firmly Pip admitted, 'Yes, she is.'

'If he gets well, she'll choose him.'

'And even if he does not,' said Pip carefully. She knew Subhash must be hurting but she believed Steph had made the right decision. She thought Steph ought to be with Julian—not the Julian who sent mucky and heartbreaking texts to another woman and then screwed her in a fancy hotel, but the other Julian. Steph ought to stay with the trustworthy, ambitious, honourable and steadfast

431

Julian. He was the one that deserved Steph. Oh God, it was complicated.

'I thought this would be her choice almost the moment she kissed me. I hoped I was wrong when she stayed with me and got drunk on miniatures but Steph is not the sort of woman who could ever manage to—' He broke off.

'Have an affair?' suggested Pip.

'To hurt,' clarified Subhash. 'I had no right hoping for it. How is he? The husband.'

'Not good.'

'And Steph?'

Pip shrugged. 'I haven't spoken to her today. I've been trying to find you and I've had to pick up Chloe and . . .' Pip stopped talking. It appeared that no matter how much she did for Steph, it never seemed quite enough. There was too much debt. Steph had thoroughly looked after her when she'd most needed it, yet when Steph had turned to her for help, she had let her down. Would she ever be able to fix this? Suddenly Pip felt unsure that she could. She had thought about Steph pretty much all day. She'd tracked down Subhash but she'd also had to whip up that sample apron for Selfridges, she couldn't keep putting it off. After she'd popped that in the post she'd quickly dashed to the supermarket because there was absolutely nothing in the fridge or cupboards, they were even out of the basics like washing powder, cornflakes and ketchup. Pip couldn't really afford to keep buying that sort of thing at the local corner store when they were half the price at the supermarket. Then she'd had to collect Chloe from school so she hadn't called Steph or Mr and Mrs Amstell today for an update. She had managed to find the time to call the hospital earlier that morning but had only been told the usual 'no change in his condition', which told her precisely nothing, actually. From the way Subhash was staring at her right now, Pip thought she was a failure as a friend. Thinking about Steph all day was not enough. Action was needed.

'I'll call her now,' she mumbled. Pip tried Steph's mobile but there was no answer, the phone was dead or off again. 'She's probably at the hospital. They don't allow mobile phones to be switched on there. I'll try her home number, her mother or father will be there.'

Subhash didn't know Pip very well at all, despite Stephanie's numerous colourful and complimentary personality sketches, but he didn't need to know her well to understand that when she managed to talk to Stephanie's family, she was burdened with more bad news. The colour drained from her face, her fingers drummed up and down on the table and she sat in a blatant pool of anxiety. He listened to a series of 'uh huhs', 'ohs', and 'OK, OK', before Pip hung up.

'Well?'

'They've taken Steph into the police station for questioning. She's been there all day. Her father is looking for a good lawyer.'

CHAPTER FORTY-EIGHT

Steph was put in a small room which had a tiny Formica table and three plastic chairs in the centre of it and very little else. Notably, there was no window and so the air felt stale, it had been breathed in and out too many times. The chairs were arranged so that one chair was on one side of the tatty table and two on the other. The set-up was stark and intimidating. Sergeant Brown said she was to wait until someone came to talk to her. Steph tried not to show her frustration or fear.

'And how long might that be?' She'd wanted to sound polite but her voice came out strident and shrill.

'There's been a big security alert in the shopping precinct. We're quite tied up,' the sergeant explained. 'It won't be a bomb. It'll just be some bored kids. Setting off alarms and making crank calls.'

'Let's hope,' observed Steph.

'Well, yes.' The policewoman looked uncomfortable and Steph wished she'd kept her mouth shut. She didn't know much about police procedure but she knew enough about human nature to realise that this process would not be speeded up if she came across as an unlikable smart-arse.

So, as an afterthought, Steph commented, 'It's marvellous that you are taking it so seriously.' Then she wanted to kick herself. What else would the police do with a bomb alert? Or a dubious alibi to a hit-and-run case, for that matter. Serious was their thing.

'It creates a lot of paperwork,' added the policewoman with a sigh.

'I can imagine. What a nuisance,' Stephanie tut-tutted.

What was wrong with her? Nerves, she supposed. She couldn't seem to find the right tone.

A bomb scare was more than a nuisance. Forgetting your sturdy, re-usable shopping bags when you went to the supermarket was a nuisance. A bomb scare was a tragedy. The problem was Steph had been up close and personal with tragedy this week and had been forced to keep her chin up and carry on as normal, no matter how unnatural normal felt. Now, she no longer knew what normal was. She sounded like an idiot. A clueless idiot.

The sergeant asked if she wanted a cup of tea. Steph said no thank you but someone brought her a cup anyway. A young policeman, he looked as though he was about a year older than Harry. At first, Steph ignored the tea in the chipped mug but after what seemed like a lifetime of being left alone in the room she eventually took a sip, simply because it was something to do. The tea was milky and sugary which suggested they'd recognised she was in shock.

Steph looked around the room. It was even less interesting than a dentist's waiting room, at least there she might expect to find some dog-eared, three-year-old magazines about antiques or horse riding. In the police interview room there was nothing to read except the posters on the walls which cautioned drivers to hide their valuables and lock their doors. Steph thought perhaps she ought to have locked Julian up more carefully so he was safe from stray drivers and perhaps she should have hidden him away so he was protected from loose, enticing women. There was a clock on the wall that slowly counted out time. Steph had been left on her own for twenty-two minutes now. She wondered whether all the police staff were really very busy or whether this was part of the process.

Maybe they wanted to make her sweat or give her time to think. Was she on an enormous naughty step and her 'time out' was supposed to bring her to her senses?

Steph knew she was unlikely to be deprived of food or water, she didn't expect that she would be beaten or even threatened. She was a middle-class woman of a certain age, who lived in Riverford. There would be a lawyer and a series of uncomfortable questions.

And yet.

And yet it was torture. Stephanie Blake was a woman who had always lived her life well. She'd tried to be a good person, a good neighbour, friend, daughter, mother and wife. It hadn't always been easy. Sometimes, it had been tricky but she rarely gossiped, she found no pleasure in insulting, slighting or hurting and she felt uncomfortable lying. She wasn't a saint. Sometimes, she did fall into gossip and she could be a little snobby or impatient but she was aware of these faults and tried hard to keep them in check. She had tried to be good. So what had gone wrong? How could she possibly be here, in a stale room breathing in the air criminals had expunged?

Julian's affair? Her thing with Subhash? What came first? The chicken or the egg?

Carefully she bent forward and rested her cheek on the scratched Formica table. The cool plastic took some of the heat out of her cheeks. She wasn't sure if she was hot with fury or with shame but she burned.

Steph stayed still with her head resting on the table for a long time. Exhaustion might have overwhelmed her and she might have even

436

dropped off to sleep for a few moments, it was hard to know because asleep or awake she fought nightmares.

Why weren't the police coming to talk to her?

What would she say if they did?

It was now obvious that Pip had decided not to offer an alibi. Stephanie was hurt. It wasn't a searing, gaping hole of a pain, like the pain of knowing her husband had screwed someone else, it wasn't even like the pain she'd felt for months when she'd imagined that she wanted to be with Subhash and knew that she couldn't be. It was a throbbing, insistent pain. Betrayal and heartache, it seemed, came in many, many guises.

Stupid, scatty, spineless Pip. The anger bubbled in Steph's chest and head. It rushed about like hot lava but there was nowhere for it to flow. She should be with Julian right now. Or the children. She shouldn't be here. Pip could have saved her from this indignity, at least. What would it have cost her to tell this lie? It was not as though Pip was above lying, she did it all the time if it suited her needs. *Her* needs! That was the point. Steph hadn't asked anything of Pip for years now. Probably the last time she'd asked for a favour was almost twenty years ago when she had first introduced Pip and Julian. She'd asked Pip not to be too charming around him.

Steph remembered the conversation so clearly. Pip had travelled to Birmingham for Steph's nineteenth birthday celebration. Steph and many of her friends, including Julian, were meeting in the student bar and then, if the night had the right vibe and the students had enough cash, their plan was to go a local pizzeria and finally on to a

437

nightclub. Steph and Julian were just good friends at that stage. Ostensibly. Even so, she'd had the foresight to warn Pip off. Julian and Steph could never become an item if he'd had a dalliance with Pip first.

'What do you mean *too* charming?' Pip had giggled as she linked her arm through Steph's. It was a chilly late February evening and they were briskly walking to the pub to save a couple of quid on bus fares.

'Don't seduce him,' Steph had clarified.

'Me?' Pip looked startled, as though she thought the idea was absurd. Steph never knew for certain whether Pip honestly didn't know how attractive she was to the opposite sex or whether she was just good at playing disingenuous.

'You seduce everyone you meet, Pip, whether it's consciously or not,' Steph had found herself having to explain. 'So I'm asking you to take care *not* to seduce Julian. OK?'

'I thought you said there was nothing going on between the two of you.'

'There isn't. But who knows—'

'One day there might be,' Pip had finished Steph's sentence as she so often did. The girls had collapsed into giggles, their hot breath causing plumes in the cold night air. They looked like a couple of happy baby dragons.

Pip had been as good as her word and had never tried to be particularly charming in *that* way with Julian. Whatever signals she sent out to the rest of the male population that first night, in the shabby pub, the tacky pizzeria and the sweaty nightclub (it had been a great birthday), Pip had managed to direct all her compelling allure away from Julian.

She'd been friendly and interesting but not too friendly and not too interesting. Steph had been extremely grateful for Pip's sensitivity and had never asked anything of Pip since. Now, Steph was beginning to wonder whether she'd been far too grateful to Pip. Perhaps she should have continued to demand various favours over the years, big and small, to keep Pip in the habit of granting them. Perhaps she could have requested the odd cup of sugar and maybe she could have worked up to asking for a kidney. OK, Steph didn't need a kidney but then Pip might have been more rehearsed in the art of granting favours when it came to providing an alibi.

Suddenly, a terrible thought occurred to Steph. Maybe Pip hadn't actually even granted her that favour. Maybe, she simply hadn't fancied Julian anyway, he certainly wasn't her type, and that was the reason she hadn't tried to charm him. Or maybe (and this theory was even harder to believe in light of Pip's legendary beauty and Julian's recent infidelity but Steph ran the idea around her head anyway), maybe Julian simply wasn't interested in Pip and had been impervious to any charms she might have displayed. Was that possible? Steph didn't know. She was too wound up to think properly. One thing she did know was that she had found herself doing endless favours for Pip. She was always helping out with Chloe's childcare. Pip asked for advice about everything, from which brand of flour she should bake with to whether or not she should employ an accountant. Steph had helped decorate Pip's flat and she was always lending her clothes and bags and even their spare bedroom. She was continually giving Pip lifts from A to B and back again.

Pip owed her!

But it was impossible for Steph to be unjust. A lifetime of being reasonable and seeing things from everyone's point of view (which was a great help when adjudicating tussles between the children) meant that she had no choice but to understand Pip's side of this. Had Pip *asked* for all of the stuff she had done for her over the years? No, she had not. Steph knew that she had helped with these things and Pip had always been delighted to receive help but Pip had not specifically asked for all these favours. Not all. And even if she had asked, at no point had she held a gun to Steph's head. Steph had given her support, her time and even her resources freely because she loved Pip. Pip was like a sister to her. There was nothing she wouldn't do for Pip.

That's what hurt.

Steph considered lying on the floor of the small interview room, rolling around on the scuffed lino and howling until she was hoarse. She had been betrayed by her husband in the worst way and now by her friend in an equally damning manner; her husband was in a coma and therefore unable to defend or explain himself but also not a fit receptacle for her anger. Her parents and children were no doubt traumatised, there would probably be permanent psychological damage. She imagined a strange reversal of type, her parents seeking psychiatric help, lying on a leather couch while a bespectacled doctor listened as they blamed all their woes and insecurities on her—their criminal daughter. Couldn't Pip at least have mentioned last night that she wasn't prepared to offer an alibi? Then Stephanie would have had time to think of something else or she might have behaved differently this morning. At the very least she could have protected the children and her parents from the excruciating scene in the hallway. How much had the boys understood? Did they know that their mother had lied to the police and that she was in deep trouble? Deep, deep trouble. How worried they must be.

Lying on the floor and howling until she was hoarse was indeed an option but Steph knew it wasn't acceptable behaviour. The truth was she had to take some responsibility for this mess she was in. She had been with Subhash that night and she hadn't wanted to say so. Steph took a deep breath and then let the air back out through her nose. She clawed through her fuggy mind for some reasonableness and a sense of proportion. Perhaps she shouldn't blame Pip for not lying to the police. It was a big ask—she realised that. When it came to the crunch, it had probably been too nerve-racking. Lying about a parking ticket was quite a different thing to lying about someone's whereabouts during an investigation into a hit-and-run (and anyway Steph had never approved of Pip lying about parking tickets).

Steph's stomach rumbled. She hadn't eaten properly for days and she'd had nothing for breakfast this morning, other than a cup of tea. How long had she been in this room now? A glance at the clock confirmed that she'd been here for just over an hour. If she had been surer of the system (was she wishing she was a more hardened criminal?) she might have had the confidence to bang on the door and yell out that she knew her rights and someone had to talk to her soon but, as it was, she didn't know her rights. Not at all. The sergeant and the PC had been keen to point out that she wasn't under arrest and that she didn't need a lawyer, although she could have one if she preferred. She had said it was unnecessary. Now she thought perhaps she could do with some legal advice. She'd lied to the police and they knew it. That wasn't good. She didn't even know if the door was locked or watched, maybe she could simply stand up and walk right out of here. For all that she didn't know, the questions remained the same. When would they come and talk to her? What would she say when they did?

As she wasn't under arrest she had not had to hand over any of her possessions. Steph picked up her handbag from the floor and began to root through it for some sort of entertainment. It wasn't that she was bored, far from it, but she was becoming irrational, going round in circles, and she needed something to keep her mind and her hands busy.

Steph's bag stored her life, or at least everything that was important to her in her life. There were house and car keys and her purse naturally, but those articles didn't offer any sort of diversion. This wasn't the moment to empty her bulging purse of receipts (she had a tendency to hang on to receipts, sometimes for longer that the item purchased even lasted). Nor was this the moment to do her make-up although she did have mascara and a lip salve tucked inside one of the bag's pockets. There were two phones, hers and Julian's adultery phone. Hers was out of power and she definitely didn't want to reread Julian's sex texts

442

again. Then, tucked inside the zip pocket, Steph spotted what she was hoping to find, a tiny photo album in which she stored the school photographs of her boys. School photographs were never the most complimentary or unique photographs, more often than not the moments captured were ones of distraction or embarrassment, yet Steph had a fondness for these photos. She was attracted to the regularity they represented. She liked to flick through the album and look at how her children had grown. There were only three photos of Freddie, one taken at nursery, one from his reception class and the latest. There were three more of Alfie and a total of nine photos of Harry. She took a moment to pull the pictures from the album and then she lined them up on the Formica table. Harry's photos first, beneath those Alfie's and then little Freddie's. She cast her eyes over the inverted pyramid of snaps.

How quickly they grew. In a blink of an eye Harry had transformed from a chubby-cheeked cherub to a brooding tweenager. He'd once had dimpled knees and now all his joints jutted out at awkward angles, he put Steph in mind of one of those collapsible clothes horses that her mother used to use to air clothes—a series of sharp slants and tilts. His body was at the stage that suggested (threatened) that muscles might suddenly flourish. He was so often anxious or irritated these days. Steph glanced at his photos and tried to pinpoint a year when the easy smiles and giggles were no longer offered up. He was her oldest and yet in some ways she felt most protective of him. She'd never quite shaken the feeling that he was their experiment. They'd been so clueless when he was first born, sometimes she thought it was a miracle he'd made it this far, trapped as he was between her inexperience and her paranoia. She had managed, though, she had mothered him as best she could and now here he was, at an age when a boy needed his father.

Stephanie carefully examined Alfie's photos. His beauty always surprised her. His piercing eyes and wide, frank beam seemed so out of place in this dingy police room, Steph was ashamed that she'd brought him here, even his 2D form deserved better. Then there was her baby. Freddie still had a rosebud mouth that was nearly always prepared to pucker up and bestow a kiss. That would probably end this year if he was anything like his brothers. Soon he would place conditions upon his kisses, only exchanging them for gifts or as greetings and *never* at the school gate. The school photos did not prove that Freddie had skin that felt as soft as butter, although that was the case, and they did not reveal his trademark flexibility, which came with soft, young bones. He was so bendy that the rest of the family marvelled when they caught him watching TV, a foot hooked up behind his ear as though this position was the most natural and comfortable on earth. The foot-hook always raised a laugh, even from Harry. The photos didn't smell like her boys, or sound like them; when she stroked the glossy paper the photos did not feel warm and soft and yet they captivated her, held her, shook her. Steph felt weak with longing.

Suddenly, it struck her. Through the fuzziness that sat like wire wool in her head—a product of lack of sleep and food—and through her sturdy ideals and her ancient loyalties. What was she thinking of? Her husband might die. The thought had crept up on her over the past few days and she'd always tried to slap it away, she'd been absolutely unprepared to think about anything so catastrophic. So final. But now she really couldn't push the thought out of her head. It spread like ink, staining every thought. The boys would have no father! And here she was, in a police interview room, which was just a sneeze away from a courtroom and becoming someone's little bitch while she rested at Her Majesty's pleasure!

Of course she must tell the police the truth and she must get Subhash to tell the truth too and she was very, very sorry that his wife might be embroiled in this whole messy business but better that than her children being brought up by strangers! She'd tried to protect Subhash because she cared for him, deeply. But he was not hers to worry about. Not really, not in the final analysis. He was a grown man. A grown man who had tried to enter into an illicit relationship with a grown woman. He was better able to cope with the consequences of her telling the truth than her little boys were able to cope with the consequences if she didn't tell the truth.

Hell, she had to get out of here. Now, as quickly as possible. Pip had been right to be honest with the police. They were the police, for Christ's sake. As messy and ugly as the truth was, it had to be heard. In fact, it usually was—even when people tried to bury it. Didn't Julian's stupid phone prove that much? The thing she had with Subhash, it was just an affair. Not even an affair! Would it be so dreadful facing a bit of gossip? No, after everything she'd been through, she thought the only dreadful thing would be not getting through to the other end.

Not getting out.

CHAPTER FORTY-NINE

'Oh no. No.' Pip's voice was squeaky and her breath seemed squeezed. 'Imagine if, imagine if he dies and she's not even with him because she's being questioned. She'd never forgive me.' Tears sprang into Pip's eyes.

Subhash wasn't often moved to anger, let alone rage. It simply wasn't part of his personality. He was firm, yes (bordering on the obstinate), strong and determined but he rarely found the need, either in his private or business life, to raise his voice. He found lowering it and forcing people to lean closer to him in order to glean his pearls of wisdom was so much more effective (and admittedly so much more sinister, if sinister was required). Yet this Pip, this woman whom Steph had always described as her best and most wonderful friend, *Pip* made him want to blow a fuse. He wanted to rip off her juvenile, pretty head or at least shake her vigorously on the off chance the messages in her brain might jiggle around a bit and reconnect in a more helpful way. She was meddlesome and ineffectual and self-indulgent! He could feel his blood pressure rising. Then a thought struck him—Steph wouldn't like him like this. He'd often had this thought over the last ten months, if ever he was being impatient or dismissive or even just lacklustre. He'd consider that Steph wouldn't appreciate him being less than his best. Steph helped him be a better man. He had to get a grip.

'One thing at a time. We need to go to the police station *immediately* and tell them that Steph was with me on Tuesday night. At least we can get Steph out of there.'

'I told you, she doesn't want you involved,' said Pip. She wondered what the police station was like. Would it be cold? It was bound to be intimidating. Poor Steph.

'I understand but I don't think I can do what she wants. I *am* involved.' Subhash considered for a moment. 'We need someone else to confirm the story that she was with me.'

'Brilliant. Yes. Where did you go?' demanded Pip.

'Actually, we went to Highview.'

'Highview! No.'

'Yes, you know that lovely hotel—'

'That's where he was found!' Pip had turned white. Chloe came across to the table to find out why this man was upsetting her mother.

'Why are you shouting, Mummy?' asked Chloe, throwing a suspicious look at Subhash. Pip stared at her daughter and was at a loss as to how she should answer. Had she been shouting?

'Darling, don't worry. Mummy is just rehearsing a play.' Chloe looked unconvinced. 'Yes, a play. We're in a theatre, aren't we? This man is auditioning me.' Pip had no idea why this idiotic explanation had sprung to her mind but was it any more stupid than the idea that the Easter bunny existed? No, it was not and in fact it might be a damn sight more useful as Chloe was defiantly loitering at the table and refusing to be ushered away even though Pip tried to bribe her with the offer of lemonade. Pip turned her attention back to Subhash and she started to exchange information with him, while pretending that she was following a script. The irony wasn't lost on Pip, she longed for there to be a script for her to follow. The truth was she felt as though she was freefalling through a Greek tragedy.

'That's where the incident happened. That's where he was found!'

'You didn't mention that.'

'I didn't think it was important.' Pip could only imagine what sort of revenge Stephanie had been trying to extract when she'd taken her would-be lover to the exact same hotel where she knew her husband was cocooned with his mistress. But it hadn't worked for her. She couldn't do the eye-for-an-eye thing and now the mess was more profound. Steph had been at the scene of the crime. Pip searched her heart and considered what this new information meant to her. Did she again believe the possibility that Steph was guilty of this crime? No, no, she did not. Pip had thought about Steph all day. She'd remembered her hundreds of kindnesses, her strict moral codes and her legendary calm in a crisis. She believed in Steph's innocence. She turned to Subhash.

'Did you do it?'

Subhash looked surprised and then furious. 'For goodness' sake, woman, will you stop flinging around ridiculous allegations and concentrate on how we can help Stephanie!'

'But did you? You haven't answered the question.'

448

'No, I did not do it.' Subhash bit down on his lip in a huge effort to remain composed. 'But it looks bad,' he admitted.

'Were you seen?' Pip demanded. Only a minute ago their being seen promised to solve everything, now Pip feared it was going to make a bigger mess.

'Of course we were seen, we booked a room.'

'Shit. Shit.' Pip turned to Chloe. 'Sorry, darling.'

'That's OK. You're only acting.'

'We should still go to the police,' said Subhash. 'I'll explain she was with me that night. We didn't leave the room.'

Pip threw him a despairing and dismayed glance. 'The police might not believe you.'

'Why wouldn't they believe me?'

'Because you are so clearly in love with her,' said Pip with a weary sigh. It was obvious to Pip that Subhash would say anything to help or protect Steph, he would lie to the police. The thought made her feel even more inadequate. OK, he didn't actually have to lie but Pip was pretty sure he would have done so if he'd been asked to. If she could see that much, the police might think so too. Would they know he was telling the truth when the truth was so unexpected—they were there and they had motive but they had nothing to do with the crime? Plus, if Steph was at this moment being questioned and she was continuing to say she was with Pip, his coming forward would have no positive effect on the situation at all. In fact, it would only confuse things further. The police would, at best, start to think that Steph was a bit unhinged and at worst that she'd tried to murder her husband with the help of her lover. Perhaps Subhash was also seeing the difficulties of his proposed knight in shining armour thing, he said nothing for a while. Pip could almost hear his mind whirl.

'Has anyone talked to the mistress?'

'Sorry?'

'Julian's mistress. Well, isn't she a likely culprit?'

'I hadn't thought of that,' gasped Pip.

'No disrespect intended, Philippa Foxton, but I don't think you are cut out for the job of detective,' snapped Subhash.

'Didn't you get the part, Mummy?' piped up Chloe. Normally, she found following the conversations of grown-ups was pretty simple, if a little bit dull. They usually talked about the same things, which were how expensive everything was and what they should do or had done at the weekend. But Chloe was finding this conversation very tricky to follow. She hadn't got a clue. She hadn't even known that her mummy wanted to be an actress. Had she got the part? Pip didn't answer her daughter.

'This other woman, what's her name?'

'I don't know.'

'When did he see her last?'

'I'm not sure. They were planning on meeting that night but I'd assumed she'd stood him up or he got knocked down before he made it into the hotel.' Subhash stared at Pip with incomprehension. How could she not have seen this? Were her eyes so misty with jealousy of Stephanie or her mind so fogged with a need for drama and complexities that she'd missed this obvious avenue and instead pursued the ludicrous thought that Steph might be to blame for this terrible incident?

'I'm going to go to the police station, right now, to tell them everything I know. You should too.' Subhash pushed his chair back and stood up in such a hurry that the chair would have toppled over if Chloe hadn't rushed to steady it.

'Yes, OK,' mumbled Pip. But even as she agreed she knew she had to do one more thing first. She had to find this mistress. She would go to Julian's office and talk to his colleagues and friends. The chances were this woman worked with Julian, when else would he have had time to meet anyone? Someone would know something. These things were never as secret as the adulterers hoped they were. She was sure she could persuade somebody to give her a name. She used to have a way of eliciting information out of men, they always wanted to please her, it just required a bit of flirtation. She was rusty but she was certain she could dredge up the necessary skill so that they'd be falling over themselves to blab on Julian. And if that didn't work, then she would go to the hospital. She'd check with the nurses to see if anyone else had called to ask about Julian's health or had visited unbeknown to her or Steph. If this woman had a heart or even a conscience she'd have done that much, surely. She would find this woman. She would clear Steph's name.

Pip held out her hand for Subhash to shake but he was already halfway out of the door.

'Mummy?' Chloe was now aimlessly flicking through leaflets advertising up-and-coming shows. To all intents and purposes it looked as though she was totally uninterested in the conversation she'd just been privy to.

'Yes, darling?'

'Isn't it funny that your play has a character called Julian? Like Uncle Julian, hey?'

'Erm, yes. But it's not a very unusual name,' said Pip. She started to gather up her bag. She found Chloe's DS under a chair and put it in her pocket.

'Isn't it? I thought it was. There isn't a Julian in my class at school.'

'Isn't there?' Pip took hold of her daughter's hand and made to leave the theatre.

'No, there isn't. How many other Julians do you know?'

'Well, there's Julian Lennon and—' Pip's mind went blank. She really didn't have time for this now. Were there any other famous Julians? She wished she'd never come up with this stupid story about auditions. That was the problem with telling a lie, it inevitably led to other lies.

'Who's Julian Lennon?'

'He's a musician. John Lennon's son.'

'Who's John Lennon?'

Oh God, Pip could do with a babysitter. She needed to think. They stood in the street and Pip looked left and right. She could carry on up this road and walk ten minutes to the police station. To her left was the train station where she could catch a train to London but there was no point in going to Julian's office now, by the time she got there everyone would be leaving for the evening, no one would want to chat. To her right was the bus stop, she could catch a bus to the hospital. It was a longer shot that she'd find answers at the hospital but at least she'd feel as though she was doing something. She couldn't just go home. She needed to try to help Steph. To make it up to Steph. She marched Chloe to the bus stop.

'Mummy?'

'Yes, darling?' Pip swallowed her exasperated sigh.

'Does your play have a happy ending?'

'I don't know, darling. I really don't know.'

CHAPTER FIFTY

'I'm sorry, Mrs Blake. But we aren't ready to let you leave the station yet,' said the PC bluntly.

'Why? Why not? You have my statement.' Steph glanced at her lawyer. He had grey hair and glasses, he looked more like a bus conductor than a lawyer. Steph had imagined someone a little more dynamic. A little more powerful. Oh God, she had a lawyer. What a bloody mess. How had she let it get this far?

This morning she'd banged on the door and asked to speak to Sergeant Mary Jean Brown, Steph had explained that she'd like to change her statement. She'd hoped to revive that deep level of humanity in the sergeant that she'd sensed at the outset but she'd been advised that she ought to wait until her lawyer arrived.

'I don't need a lawyer,' she insisted.

'You want to change your statement.'

'Well, yes.'

'I strongly recommend a lawyer. We can arrange one for you or you can instruct someone independently.'

'Well, how long will that take?'

'Someone will be with you in a couple of hours.'

During her interview, they pointed out that Mrs

453

Evans had said in her statement that Steph had arrived home near midnight and that she was, in fact, tipsy that night.

'Yes, yes, it's all true,' said Steph impatiently. All she wanted was to get back to the hospital. Why was this taking so long? Her lawyer glanced at her and there was something in his expression that seemed to want to hush her. 'What?' Steph demanded. 'There's no problem. I'm just telling the truth. I should have done so in the first place. I didn't hurt Julian. I would never hurt him. I was with Mr Subhash Sharma.'

'Your lover?' asked the PC.

'My friend,' clarified Steph.

'So, you're not in a sexual relationship with Mr Sharma?'

'No, I'm not.' Steph thought the room was uncomfortably hot.

'Yet the hotel staff testified that you took a room together that night at Highview, where your husband was injured.'

'Yes.' Steph knew it looked bad.

'Your housekeeper says that you were in an unusually violent mood that day.'

'She said what?'

'That you threw your chopping board and knife at the kitchen wall.'

'I don't think I threw the knife.' Steph tried to remember. She didn't want to be dishonest but Mrs Evans was being misleading.

'Your housekeeper said you went out to buy paint to cover up the damage.'

'I didn't buy any paint. The woman likes a drama. She cheats her insurance claims, do you know that? She's an unreliable witness.' Steph

454

knew she sounded shrewish and panicked. It was because she was shrewish and panicked.

'But you were angry, Mrs Blake,' added Sergeant Brown in a sympathetic tone.

'Well, yes, naturally,' admitted Steph. There was no point in denying that. Any fool would know as much.

'And hurt and despairing.'

'Well, yes.'

'Vengeful?' probed the PC keenly.

'I was upset.' Steph glanced at the tape recorder.

'Did you smash or break anything else other than the chopping board?'

'No. I— The chopping board didn't break.'

'Did you want to?'

The violence had been such a release. To see the wall stained and chipped had felt wonderful, exhilarating. Yes, she'd wanted to smash something else.

'Well, maybe,' she admitted.

'The glassware perhaps? Or the crockery?'

Steph thought back. 'Both. I wanted to smash glasses and plates and cups and saucers. I wanted to fling, crush, crash and demolish until everything we owned was destroyed. I wanted to plunge the chopping knife into the cushions and gouge out their innards. I wanted to gash and shred our bed sheets.' When she finished she realised she must have been yelling when she couldn't catch her breath.

Her lawyer had a grey face now, as well as grey hair.

CHAPTER FIFTY-ONE

Kirsten had enjoyed her train ride to Riverford with Jake. They hadn't talked about Jules. They talked about other people that they worked with and people they'd been to uni with. Not in a bitchy way. Jake didn't really go in for that, he was keener to tell her how well everyone was doing and that, when he met up with any of his old gang, they always asked after her.

'I can imagine,' she'd muttered.

They'd talked about V Festival and Party in the Park. It was a laugh being with someone who actually knew the bands you were on about and even had their own thoughts on them. Mark Deally reckoned he was hip because he had Cheryl Cole on his iPod. How sad was that? Jake had talked about his family. He was clearly from one of those families that were into each other, they probably played charades at Christmas and had roast dinners every Sunday. She doubted he'd ever had to put a lock on his bedroom door to keep out snooping parents when he'd lived at home. Then again he probably didn't have a pot habit that he was trying to hide. To her astonishment, he claimed he'd *never* nicked anything off his younger brothers.

'What? Not even a shirt?' Kirsten asked in disbelief.

'I'd just ask to borrow it if I needed something of theirs,' said Jake with a slightly confused grin.

'Right.' Kirsten wondered whether Jake was, like, uber-square or were his brothers terrified of him and therefore happy to hand over their goods if he asked? She'd nicked things off her brother all the time when she'd lived at home, money, fags, T-shirts, his iPod. She thought it was probably best not to mention to Jake that until she was fourteen years old, it had been practically a tradition for her to open all her brother's Christmas presents on Christmas Eve and swap tags if she thought he was getting cooler stuff than she was. The tradition was only abandoned because once she was fourteen her parents stopped buying Christmas presents and just wrote large cheques instead.

The train and taxi journey flew by and before Kirsten knew it they were at the hospital. She had often visited people in hospital before. When she was about sixteen there was a whole spate of occasions when her mates found their way on to a ward with some sort of attention-seeking affliction. One of her friends had her stomach pumped after a half-hearted, melodramatic attempt to end it all, another had an abortion, a third had twins (poor cow!) and a couple of others were treated for bulimia, anorexia, depression or a combination of the above. It wasn't because all of Kirsten's friends were drama queens that she'd ended up visiting the hospital on so many occasions at such desperate times. It was more a case of her liking to make friends with girls who were in crisis, and this was not because she was the milk of human kindness and believed her mother's saying that 'a friend in need is a friend indeed', it was just she liked to be up close and personal with the gossip. When she'd visited Sicky Vicky, the bulimic, Vicky had actually asked if they'd ever met before and Mad Mel had cried for a nurse and asked to have her removed, calling her an evil cow and no sort of friend. Kirsten thought it was probably the medication that made her go so mental, that or she'd heard that Kirsten was the one who had coined the name Mad Mel in the first place. Anyway, Kirsten had thought that these experiences would all stand her in good stead when she visited Jules. She did not expect to be shocked or frightened. Or moved.

'Are you OK? You're as white as a ghost,' said Jake. Kirsten was aware that he'd slipped his arm around her shoulders but she couldn't feel any pleasure in the intimacy at all.

'He looks like a ghost,' she whispered, staring at the shadow of a man lying still on the bed.

Jake coughed uncomfortably. He couldn't deny it. Julian looked as though he was at death's door. The truth was Julian *was* at death's door. He was shrivelled, grey and frail. It was a lot to take in. Knowing something and seeing it were two very different things. It was like watching the ten o' clock news, everyone knew there were wars and famines and torture and murders in the world but it wasn't very real unless you stood where the victim stood, or at least where the cameraman stood.

'He looks so completely different from when I last saw him,' gasped Kirsten.

Then she started to make strange sounds. She was gulping at the air as though she couldn't get enough. Had she forgotten how to breathe? She was shaking so much she looked as though she was body-popping. Jake realised she was in shock and questioned his own judgement in bringing her here. He'd never imagined Kirsten would take it this badly. She'd said she wasn't that into Julian. He'd thought she'd meant that what they had going on was just a bit of ill-considered, mindless fun. But that clearly wasn't the case. Kirsten was devastated to see Julian in such a mess.

'Come on now,' he mumbled but he wasn't certain what he meant by that or what good it was. He just needed her to hold it together. Julian's brother, who'd said a brief hello to them and then gone to chat to the doctor, might be back any moment. What would he think if he came into the room and Kirsten was lying prone across the bed practically passing out? The last thing Jake wanted was for the family to guess Julian had a mistress. His poor wife must be going through enough right now without that sort of complication.

'He looks so weak and frail,' muttered Kirsten through her gasps. 'He might actually die.' This comment was pushed out as a squeak. She couldn't believe it. She couldn't imagine it. Of course the thought had skittered across her mind, loads, since Tuesday, she wasn't an animal. Tuesday had been terrifying and part of her had lived in constant fear that at any minute she might hear the news that he'd died but she hadn't thought much about what that would actually *mean*. She'd mostly been worried about her involvement in the incident.

'This is not my fault,' whispered Kirsten. Jake had to lean close to her to hear properly.

'No, of course not. No one is saying that,' he said soothingly.

'In many ways, it's his *own* fault. He practically asked for it,' she added as she moved closer to the bed. Jake didn't follow her. He let his arm slip to his side.

459

'What do you mean?' he asked carefully.

What had she ever done to him? Well, before Tuesday? Nothing. Nothing at all. She'd kept her side of the unwritten deal, she'd been a perfect mistress! She'd always been available, she'd always made an effort to look super cute, she'd tried to be funny and interesting (she'd taken such care to stockpile interesting facts about Paris Hilton and *Celebrity Big Brother* so that she'd always have something to talk to him about), and she'd *swallowed*! She did not deserve to be treated the way he'd treated her! How dare he think he could just brush her off like a piece of fluff, toss her away like a used tissue!

This was not her fault. It was just a reaction. You know, a consequence. An accident.

Kirsten tried to be indignant but she was simply terrified. The resulting adrenalin surged through her body causing her to quake even more, she felt a lot like she'd felt last Tuesday. My God, she didn't know whether she was coming or going. It *was not* her fault. It really wasn't. She hadn't asked him to start the affair and she certainly hadn't asked him to finish it! Because he'd started and then finished the affair, she was bound to be upset and accidents do tend to happen when people are upset! And because *he* was married, *he* was the one that insisted on going to an out-of-the-way place, which was why she had been driving in the first place. Daddy was right, it was a huge car for her to handle (Daddy should have stuck to his guns and not allowed her to drive it, no matter how much Mummy had begged him to—he was a tiny bit to blame for this whole disaster too). Not as much as Jules, though. It was really Jules's own fault. She

460

hadn't asked him to chase after her, had she? He'd leapt out in front of the car, she couldn't have stopped, no one could have.

It was not her fault.

She panicked. It was understandable. To be honest, it was a miracle that she hadn't killed *herself* on her drive back up the A3 that night. She couldn't even remember much about how she'd managed to get back to her flat, she just drove. The lack of recall might be to do with the champagne she'd drunk earlier on or it might have been shock. Because, fuck, it was shocking. The yelling, the thud, his body falling on to the bonnet of her car and then slumping heavily on to the ground. It made her sick just thinking of it. Through the rainy car window she'd watched him slump in front of her and she'd just driven away.

'What did you say?' asked Jake.

'The yelling, the thud, I just drove away,' whispered Kirsten. Oh fuck, how much of that had she just said aloud? How much had stayed in her head and how much had escaped into this room?

CHAPTER FIFTY-TWO

Her lips, her hips, her tits punched out at Pip, almost embarrassing Pip by being so blatantly sensual in a hospital room. The woman, or rather girl, was mesmerising, it was no wonder Julian had fallen so utterly and completely in . . . In what? In love with her? In lust for certain. Poor, poor Stephanie, how could she compete with this vision of gorgeousness? Pip gazed at the girl's long, long,

461

sexy, gently muscular legs, her high bum and pert tits. It was a fact that this girl-woman's ribs had never been pushed aside to accommodate a growing baby, her skin hadn't stretched, sagged, wrinkled or simply slipped to her ankles, the way it seemed to do once you'd reached Pip and Steph's age. The girl-woman was blonde and tanned and toned and honed. She had flawless skin and make-up, she wore tight-fitting, up-to-the-minute clothes and shoes. She was perfect.

Except for the sewage that was spurting out of her mouth. The dirt that she'd held in her head. The mess that had squeezed her heart.

Pip listened as the mistress poured out vile words over Julian's bed. Pip was aware that the young man in the room was swaying with confusion, he looked as though he'd just been thumped as he listened to all the gory details about that night.

'Chloe, go and find a nurse, now,' said Pip. She couldn't let her daughter listen to this but she couldn't miss a word herself. Chloe heard the urgency and determination in her mother's voice and sped off without argument.

The girl-woman was unstoppable. She was hysterical, crying and yelling. Sometimes addressing the comatose Julian, sometimes the handsome guy who was with her, sometimes it seemed as though she didn't know anyone else was in the room, she just needed to talk.

'I couldn't get a massage, not even that. I deserved that much, didn't I? But that silly bitch in the spa embarrassed me beyond limits so I stomped back to the room and shook Jules awake, insisting he dress for dinner. He did, eventually, but we didn't sit down until nearly ten. I was starving! And then we ate in one of those hideous painful, sulky silences. You know? You know what I mean?' She turned angrily to Jake. 'Like married people! I mean it was humiliating. But I certainly wasn't going to be the one that made the effort to keep the conversation going, no way! After all, it was his fault that we were having such a shit time. I ate three courses. I didn't even care if the hotel staff kept looking at their watches and yawning, really obviously. I ordered coffee too. He owed me!'

Jake slumped down into a visitor's chair. He held his head in his hands. 'Jesus, Kirsten.'

'Back in the room I thought again. Tried to calm down.' There was no evidence of calm now, Kirsten paced around Julian's small room like a cheetah in a zoo cage. 'What I figured was that if I fell out with Jules that would leave me with just Mark because it was the day after Brian Ford had dumped me. But I *know* Mark's a bastard. He's sexy, true, but cold. A little too hooked on power games and sometimes even I just want to be cuddled, you know? Don't you men *ever* realise that?'

Kirsten stared at Jake accusingly. He shook his young head sadly, not sure what to say to this lost girl. She didn't care. She carried on. She was finding it a strange relief to get her story out in the open at last. It had been a hard secret to carry around this week. No fun at all. Not like having an affair, that sort of secret was thrilling and exciting and— Kirsten's gaze drifted over to the comatose Julian. Well, no. Maybe not thrilling and exciting. Not anymore. There was no fun left in any of it.

463

'I just like pretty things, expensive things. It's just what I'm used to. I *always* thought I'd marry a wealthy guy. I'm not the first woman to think that, am I? And Jules was my best shot,' Kirsten explained desperately. She wanted Jake to understand. She needed him to. People had to listen to her. They had to understand her. 'So I performed, erm, this really salacious striptease to try to cheer him up. It didn't work. He just looked a bit awkward. So I was, you know—desperate.' This bit was difficult to explain but if she didn't tell it how it was, it might stay trapped in her head for ever. She had to get it out. She'd go insane if it stayed there. 'So I'm standing, in nothing but Agent Provocateur, and I lean in to kiss him and guess what he did? He backed away from me! I asked him if he was sickening from something. And you know what he replied?'

'What?' asked Jake, although he felt squeamish and uncomfortable and was pretty sure he didn't want to know.

'He said, "A bit. I'm a bit sick of this. Of you."'

The memory of Julian's words assaulted Kirsten all over again. She felt the fury and disappointment, the humiliation and the desperation, resurface. But this time, it was worse, this time she also felt a hideous sense of bleakness and sorrow. What had she done? Tears streamed down her face now, her make-up was no longer perfect, there were rivers of mascara cascading down the neck of her white T-shirt. Her chest ached, it was hard to breathe, to speak, to simply stand up.

'Oh God, I wanted to punch him in his stupid, bored-looking face and in his stomach. I wanted to punch him over and over again. Punch the life out of him. I wanted to kill him in that moment. *He* was sick? *He* was sick? Well, he wasn't alone! *I* was sick too. I was sick of people using me and then ditching me.' She glowered at Julian as though she might punch him right that moment but instead she took another breath and continued. 'I was sick of going down on men, sick of faking orgasms, I was sick of their stupid unfunny jokes and their middle-aged fucking crises. It's degrading.' Kirsten turned her glare on Jake again. 'But I didn't punch him. Instead, I just got dressed. I was silently seething as he went on and on. He mistook my silence to be, I don't know, some sort of calm acceptance of his viewpoint. He probably thought I was a good little well-behaved mistress who would slink away, now he'd had enough of me. He probably thought that I'd disappear without causing him any trouble or inconvenience. But with each word Julian uttered, I became eaten up with rage. You know? I've never known anything like it. He kept saying stuff that I didn't agree with and he kept assuming I did agree. It was annoying. Really, really annoying. It was so, so fucking patronising.'

Why was Jake looking at her like that? Like she was some sort of animal? And who was that woman in the room, who looked so shocked and worried? Not Julian's wife. Too thin for his wife. Kirsten couldn't work it out. It was all rushing around her head. Julian's machine was beeping and loads of people were staring at her. Pointing at her. The woman. And now a kid. They were sort of lunging at her as though they wanted to trap her. Jake was telling everyone to calm down. Now there

465

was a nurse, with a grim mouth and really ugly shoes, she was demanding to know who Kirsten was. The room was so full. The nurse was yelling that everyone had to get out. Get out of the room. Two more nurses did the opposite, they ran in but they weren't interested in Kirsten, they ran straight to Julian. Then a doctor charged into the room as well. Kirsten saw her chance. She dashed for the door, not so much because the nurse had told them to, more because she needed to make a break for it. In a flash and despite her killer heels, she was off. She sprinted along the corridor, straight into the waiting arms of Sergeant Mary Jean Brown.

Kirsten kicked and fought, flashing her knickers because her designer skirt was so short. PC Weybridge watched as the dishevelled beauty struggled with his superior officer and he just wished he could have filmed it on his phone.

CHAPTER FIFTY-THREE

'OK, Mrs Blake, thank you for your time, you can go now,' said a middle-aged policeman that Stephanie hadn't seen up until now.

'Sorry?' Was he joking?

'You're free to go. We have your statement. We'll be in touch.'

Steph was confused, they'd had her statement for hours, how come she could suddenly leave now? She glanced at her lawyer but the lawyer was already packing up papers, it was clear this wasn't the moment to question the logic of the powers that be. Steph thanked the officer, nodded at her lawyer, grabbed her bag and bolted for the door. She didn't really take in what the lawyer was calling after her. She'd get the details later, right now all she needed was to get to the hospital to see Julian. In the reception she briefly glanced around, hoping to spot her parents but they weren't there. Presumably they were at the hospital or taking care of the boys. She couldn't expect them to be waiting on her. She asked the policeman at the reception desk if she could borrow a phone to call a cab.

'Mine's out of power,' she explained.

'Take my cab. It will be here any moment now. I called it ten minutes ago.'

Steph recognised the voice before she turned to face him. 'Subhash.' Ah, now she understood why she'd suddenly been released. He smiled and together they walked the two or three steps out of the police station on to the street. After being in the windowless room all day, Steph was surprised to find it was a beautiful day. The sun slapped down on the pavements, throwing off a glare that caused her to squint. 'You came forward. That's why they let me go.'

'I think so, yes.'

'I'm sorry you had to get involved.'

'My call.'

Steph nodded. 'Thank you.'

Subhash nodded stiffly. 'I think they are pursuing a different line of inquiry now,' he explained. 'They are looking for Julian's mistress. Some of the hotel staff have confirmed we were there but someone saw us leave the hotel grounds. Do you remember, you wanted to drive but I wouldn't let you because you'd had too much to drink, then the moment I was behind the wheel I clipped the car against their garden wall, despite being stone-cold sober? The night porter came out to check I hadn't damaged his damn wall or shrub. Apparently he watched us drive all the way along the drive and on to the A road. I guess he was really worried about his shrubs.'

'Yes, I think I remember that.' Steph had forgotten but now he mentioned it, the hazy memory was stirred.

'She was there too, that night, the mistress, but no one saw her leave,' added Subhash, carefully.

'I see.' Steph didn't know what to say. The thought had never occurred to her. 'Why would his mistress knock him over?' she mused aloud.

'Maybe he was leaving her,' suggested Subhash. 'Maybe Julian chose you.'

Steph looked up at Subhash with total gratitude. He saw her tear-stained, careworn face break into the biggest, broadest, most definite smile he'd ever witnessed.

'Do you think?' she asked, almost breathless.

Subhash nodded. 'How could he not?' he replied quietly. He looked away and concentrated on the spot a few inches above her head. He would choose this woman too, if he could, if she'd have him. But she would not, he knew that and now he would have to accept it. Once and for all. He took deep breaths and let the warm spring air fill his body. 'I can see the cab, you better get going. I imagine you are desperate to get to the hospital.'

Subhash waved to the driver and the cab pulled up next to them, he held open the back door for Stephanie. Before she bent to get in the car, she turned to him and placed a gentle kiss on his cheek. 'You've been an amazing friend, Subhash.

Throughout this. Before this. Thank you.'

'My pleasure,' he said, swallowing down the grief at hearing his love relegated to mere friendship. 'Take care of yourself, Stephanie Blake.'

'You too. Goodbye.'

Subhash stayed on the pavement until the cab was out of sight. The sun caught the wing mirror, causing a brief sparkle. He reached into his pocket and pulled out his phone. He called another cab. It was time to go home.

CHAPTER FIFTY-FOUR

Kirsten told the police all about that night. They seemed more than happy to listen to every one of the details. They didn't look shocked or deflated like Jake, or furious like that skinny woman. She just got to have her say.

Kirsten had been so *sick*. There was no other word for it. Her anger had started deep in the pit of her stomach and from there it had rushed through her bloodstream, into her mind, causing everything to go fuzzy and then blank. She'd tried to listen to Jules. Tried to concentrate on what he had to say but she didn't agree with him.

No, she did not agree that they both had 'always known it was just a bit of fun'. No, she did not think that 'all good things had to come to an end'. No, she did not have 'lots of great guys her own age queuing up to date her'. And no, no, bloody no, she did not agree that they had to 'think about his wife and kids now'. Why the sudden attack of

469

conscience? Wasn't it a bit late in the day for that?

It hurt. Rejection was a nasty thing. She felt grubby and ugly. Used. He made her feel bad. Very, very bad about herself. Kirsten had somehow managed to fake a sense of serenity, that she was a million miles away from him as she'd pulled on her clothes and reached for her bag and car keys. Surely, once he realised she was going to leave him, he'd try to stop her, she'd reasoned to herself. Once he understood what he was losing, he'd regret all the things he'd just said, wouldn't he? But then, she'd caught his reflection in the mirror hung on the hotel bedroom wall and he'd looked *relieved*, almost happy! It had been the final insult.

'Maybe you're right,' she'd said stiffly. 'It is time you started doing the right thing by your family.'

'I'm so glad you understand,' Julian had replied. 'No hard feelings, hey? We had fun, didn't we?'

My God, it was as though he was about to offer his hand for her to shake! She'd smiled coldly and said, 'I think the best thing to do is tell your wife exactly what's been going on. Let's make a fresh start and all that.'

The colour had flooded from Julian's face. It was quite comical really, if you thought about it. 'Oh no. No. I don't think there's any need for that.' He'd laughed nervously and inappropriately.

'Oh, I do,' Kirsten had replied firmly, as she made for the door.

She'd quickly put some distance between them. She was younger and fitter than he was and he'd had to pause to find the room key. Jules probably hadn't wanted to risk making a fool of himself in front of the night porter because he'd slowed down his run to a fast walk as he passed through reception. He needn't have bothered, the night porter was nowhere to be seen, he'd been in the bathroom, otherwise the whole thing would have been witnessed.

Jules had followed her outside. She'd parked in the furthest extremity of the car park because she'd been nervous about reversing into any of the tighter but more convenient spots. She'd heard him charge along the gravel path, he was in such a state that he hadn't even noticed his own wife's car, neatly parked close to the reception. He'd run on and on, towards the headlamps of Kirsten's car. Kirsten realised that all he cared about was stopping her. He had to! Of course he didn't want his wife to know about any of this. It was clear that he thought it would be the worst thing in the world if she found out. He didn't want to hurt his wife. He'd never planned to hurt her. Kirsten understood; Jules loved his wife.

That was clearly his only thought.

That was his last thought.

CHAPTER FIFTY-FIVE

It was after 7 p.m. by the time Stephanie arrived at the hospital, visitors were swarming out of the wards and private rooms, rushing through the corridors. Some were dashing, secretly keen to leave the sickness and sorrow behind and get on with their weekend, others were reluctant to step away from their loved ones' beds and walked while looking back over their shoulders. Steph felt like a trout swimming upstream.

'Excuse me, excuse me, can I get past?' she mumbled repeatedly. A few sensed her urgency and desperation and stepped aside for her, many were too wrapped up in their own dramas to make allowances.

All day in the police station, in the cab and as she wound her way through the labyrinth of corridors, hundreds of thoughts had tumbled around her mind. First and foremost she thought of Julian. Julian had chosen her? That's what Subhash believed had happened that night. Was it true? Was it possible? Please, God, oh please, God. Steph was now certain that all that mattered was that she and Julian had the chance to patch this up, pick up the pieces and mend their marriage. If he loved her, if he'd chosen her then she could forgive him.

After he'd done a lot of grovelling of course.

A *lot* of grovelling.

But she knew she could. Fifteen years of marriage, three sons, weekends that bled into bank holidays that melted into weekdays. All those sunny days, wet days, happy days, sad days that she'd been remembering. The months and seasons, and their never-was baby meant more than Subhash's sincere friendship and shimmering flirtation and so it certainly meant a damn sight more than a phone full of grubby texts and a bit of thoughtless sex in a hotel room.

She loved him. Right now she wasn't proud of him or even pleased with him. But she still loved her husband and she was so desperately worried about him.

Stephanie also thought about her boys. Harry had Julian's sporting ability and competitive spirit.

Alfie's beautiful eyes were his father's gift, and darling Freddie already showed signs of inheriting Julian's sense of humour. They were terrific boys. Wonderful. They were *their* boys. Julian's and hers. They'd made them. Given them life.

Steph thought about Pip. Bloody Pip. Poor Pip. Sometimes selfish, sometimes perfect Pip. God, she'd tear a strip off her if she hadn't managed to send that bloody sample to Selfridges yet. Pip must not muck up this chance at her new career. Pip was at the starting line again. She'd been around the block but now there were new chances, new possibilities. Please God this Robbie wasn't a total waster like Dylan. Or Philippe or Jacob or any of the others. What had Pip said he did for a living? A fertility nurse? Well, it was different and somehow promising. Less flashy than the musicians and photographers and male models and such that Pip had dated in the past.

Even though her husband was in a coma, Steph felt hopeful. Although she'd only been detained by the police for the best part of a day, she suddenly valued her freedom so much more than she ever had. She wanted to celebrate or at least appreciate every single minute. She wanted time to count. She'd been bored and frustrated when she'd let Subhash into her life. She'd allowed time to become stale and sloppy. Once the boys were all at school, she'd lost her verve and focus. Never again. Finally, Steph could see her future quite clearly once more. Julian would get better. They'd go home. They'd have a day where they'd eat nothing other than cherries and chocolate and crisps and cashew nuts. Everything would be just fine.

Steph sped through the doors that said Intensive

Care Unit. She heard someone call out her name.

'Mrs Blake, Mrs Blake.'

But she didn't pause. She just had to be with Julian. She pushed open the door to his room and ran in.

The bed was empty.

It had been stripped.

The room was bleak and blank. No sign of Harold or James or her parents. No sign of *Julian*.

'Mrs Blake, Mrs Blake.' The nurse repeating her name was now at her side.

'Where is he?' asked Steph. But she knew.

The nurse put her hand on Steph's arm. 'You don't know? You haven't been told? I'm sorry, someone should have spoken to you. He's gone.' The nurse spoke with great tenderness and care but this news could not be anything other than annihilating.

Stephanie threw both her hands over her mouth to stop herself screaming. She understood. She was too late. Tears were in her eyes and nose in a moment. She felt the room wobble around her. She couldn't take her eyes off his empty bed. There were no good luck cards, no throw, and no cushions. It had all been cleared out already. She'd been at the police station when she should have been here. She could have been here but Pip hadn't given her an alibi. Or maybe she wasn't here because she hadn't told the truth—she'd been so ashamed about where she'd been on that night. It didn't matter which way you looked at it. It was all over. Julian was dead. He was dead. He'd gone.

CHAPTER FIFTY-SIX

'Somebody should have told you, Mrs Blake,' said the nurse. She was a compact woman, with short brown hair that could only just be scraped back into a ponytail. She seemed kind, sensible and practical, all the things Steph normally loved in a person but Steph hated the woman for delivering this destroying news. The nurse was unaware that Steph loathed her and she gently guided Steph to a chair. 'You poor woman. You've been through such a lot,' she mumbled. She poured Steph some water from the jug on the bedside table and watched while she drank it.

'I'm sorry, it must be such a shock. But it is good news. Finally.'

'Sorry?'

'He's out of intensive care. He's gone to a ward because he's spoken a few words. First, he moved his foot, that was this morning, at about eleven. We've been trying to get in touch with you but we couldn't reach you. Then, this afternoon, there was a rumpus with his colleagues, and he started to say a few words. All your family are with him now. Including your sons.'

'What? Where?' Steph couldn't take it in. She'd thought he was dead. Gone. She'd said gone. 'He's not dead?'

'No.' Now the nurse looked confused. 'He's gone to a ward. Ward number thirty-two, I think. I'll check for you. He's spoken, Mrs Blake. There's every sign that there'll be a full recovery.'

'What were his words? What did he say first?'

Steph asked excitedly.

'I think he said shut up,' said the nurse with a beam. 'Then he said Stephanie.'

CHAPTER FIFTY-SEVEN

Stephanie thought there was a very good chance that she'd drop dead herself before she found ward thirty-two, her heart was beating so furiously. He was alive! His first word (after shut up) had been Stephanie. He was alive and coming out of his coma. Thankyouthankyouthankyou, God. Now, she'd have a chance to tell him what a total bastard he was and what hell he'd put her through.

And how much she loved him and what she was prepared to go through.

The ward was quite a small one, there were only four beds in it. Julian was in the one in the far right-hand corner. Even though it was against visiting rules (each patient was officially limited to two visitors at a time) he was surrounded by the people who loved him; the nurses had obviously decided to turn a blind eye. Steph paused in the doorway to gather her breath and her thoughts. She'd done the same thing just before she walked down the aisle to marry him all those years ago. In many ways she felt like she was making that decision all over again. She was committing to him. She was giving herself to him.

She had time to notice that there was no longer a tube in his neck, he was breathing through an oxygen mask. He was still lying down but he was smiling at something her mother had said. The colour had crept back into her mother's cheeks, she was laughing unstintingly, the joke registered in her eyes. Freddie was sitting on his granny's knee, he was walking a small Pokémon model up and down her arm, Alfie was on the end of his dad's bed and Harry was standing so close that he was practically in the bed with Julian. All three boys were beaming and chatting and pretty soon they would be squabbling, the relief was palpable and overwhelming. They had been granted a reprieve too. They'd been allowed to re-enter their own lives.

Her father and Julian's brother were chatting to one another. Their voices were ebullient and a little too loud for a hospital ward. Excitedly they cut across one another, simply too cheerful to be polite or proper. Harold, Julian's father, was by contrast silent. He'd been strong and steadfast throughout the last few days but now he looked sapped. Now he knew his son was out of danger he no longer felt the need to sit upright and tense on the edge of the chair as though he was urging his son on, hoping against hope that he'd slice through the ribbon and make it to the end of the race to have a tickertape moment. Julian had won. Harold was now so relaxed he looked boneless. He was flopped in amongst the cushions on the visitor's chair, not bothering to contribute to any of the conversations going on around him, simply happy to stare at his son—in gratitude and with love.

Pip and Chloe were at the foot of the bed, they were talking to a nurse, a male nurse. Well, not so much talking, more giggling, sort of flirting—even Chloe! Oh, a thought occurred to Steph, might he be *the* male nurse? Was that Robbie? Very possibly

477

because he had gorgeous sparkling eyes and high cheekbones and while Pip didn't usually fall for nurses, she often fell for sparkling eyes and sharp cheekbones.

Julian's eyes flicked towards the doorway almost as though he sensed his wife, at least as though he was waiting for her. He saw that Steph was standing in a pool of grief and relief, regret and happiness. All the visitors followed his gaze and then the ward erupted into spontaneous shouts of glee and demands as to where she'd been and why wasn't her phone charged up! What had taken her so long? They'd been so worried about her. Her family and friends swarmed, demanding and delivering hugs, beaming at her, congratulating her and then, as though they'd passed some telepathic signal, they melted away.

'We'll give you some peace and privacy.'

'He's been asking for you.'

'We'll take the boys home, get them put to bed.'

Steph stood next to her husband's bed and they locked eyes. The silence spoke volumes and stretched for miles. Eventually she retreated into the obvious ice-breaker. 'How are you feeling?'

'Good, good,' muttered Julian. His voice was scratchy but then he had a hole in his throat so that was understandable. She raised her eyebrows, questioningly. 'No really. I'm good, I'm so bloody grateful,' he gasped.

'Right.' Steph nodded but found she couldn't really say as much as she wanted. Tears had erupted from nowhere, *again*. The first she realised was when she noted the neck of her shirt was wet.

'I'm grateful to be alive.' Steph had to lean very

478

close to her husband's mouth to hear him properly, the oxygen mask and the hole in his throat were making things tricky. 'Because I wanted to live—'

'Well, of course.'

Julian moved his oxygen mask away from his mouth. He wanted to be clear. Steph gasped. 'Put it back on.'

'I'm OK,' he assured her. 'I wanted to live with you and the boys.' He paused then scanned his wife's face in order to ascertain exactly what she knew. He read her like a book. She knew everything. He would have told her anyhow and then said what he had to say; now he knew he just had to get to the crux. 'I wanted to live so that I could say sorry, Steph. To say I'm really, completely and off the scale sorry.'

'It doesn't cover it,' said Steph.

'No, I know, absolutely. I'm just saying . . .' Julian caught his wife's grin. He'd seen that exact same grin many times in the past. She'd thrown him that particular grin over the student union bar, on the sidelines of rugby matches, when she accepted his proposal, when she handed him his newborns and on countless other occasions. But he couldn't remember when he'd last seen that particular grin, he thought she'd forgotten how to do it and so he was very glad to see it again. It was a grin that was full of promise and gladness and magnificent, unregulated excitement. It had a hint of the flirt too.

'I am sorry. I was stupid and—'

Steph shook her head. 'Don't try and explain it all now, Julian. Just get better. We can talk later. We have plenty of time.'

'Do we? Do we have plenty of time?' He hadn't

been certain. Even getting well didn't guarantee he'd still have plenty of time with Steph, not after what he'd done.

'Oh God, don't you start crying too. It's like a tsunami in here,' laughed Steph through her own tears.

'It's the drugs, not emotion,' said Julian. 'I'm a British man,' he joked.

'Yes, exactly.'

Julian stared at his wife with total gratitude and admiration. 'So what's next?' he asked.

In that one sentence Julian acknowledged something that all partners know but occasionally forget. The truth is, sometimes one of you has no idea. One of you makes a mistake. One of you screws it all up. But it's OK because there are two of you. That's the point. So the other can pick up the reins for a while. Keep the wagons rolling. Until the one who has no idea and has screwed it all up finds a way back on to the track.

'Like I said, first you have to get better. And then when you are, when there are no machines feeding you, or draining you, or monitoring your heart rate or your blood pressure or your oxygen levels, well, then we're going to throw a big party.'

'We will?' Julian smiled.

'Yes. A massive, alcohol-fuelled party with incredibly loud music and no seating plan, there might not be chairs at all, in fact. And we're going to drag the rug into the middle of the sitting room and that will be our makeshift dance floor.'

'A dance floor?'

'Upon which you are going to gyrate and whirl regardless of rhythm. You, Julian Blake are going to dance until you are clammy.'

Five Months Later

It had been decided that the day after the trial, Stephanie, Julian and the boys, Pip, Robbie and Chloe would go to the beach for a picnic. After the months of tension and a day in the stale courtroom Steph knew she would have a need to breathe sea air, for the wind to catch her hair and for her to feel sand beneath her toes. When she'd mooted as much to Julian, he'd at once agreed that it was a brilliant idea. His office had been very generous with regard to him taking days off work, possibly because both his manager and Julian knew it was only a matter of time before he had to resign from the company and find a new position elsewhere. Even without Kirsten's presence, the scandal simmered. Julian realised that while he probably deserved to be the object of ridicule and speculation, he didn't much enjoy it. He'd be better off starting with a clean slate in a new company. He didn't really mind too much if the new role meant less money, as long as it meant fewer hours.

Once Pip heard about the plan to picnic on the beach, she'd asked whether she, Chloe and Robbie might come along too. Stephanie gracefully accepted the addition to the party; some things never changed and Pip crashing her plans was probably one of them, for which Steph was secretly grateful and relieved. Steph wanted Pip to be at the picnic, it was an occasion. The party Steph had promised Julian at his hospital bedside was planned for next month, it wouldn't have been right to have a party straight after the trial. That party was a celebration of Julian's return to health and somehow that had to be kept separate from the trauma and drama of the trial. But, getting through the trial was a milestone and ought to be marked in some way.

They settled on the unspoilt sands, in front of the picture-perfect colourful beach huts, and they faced the sparkling sea. Julian and Robbie set to work erecting wind shields, because it was notoriously nippy at West Wittering beach, especially now in late summer. The men set up deckchairs and debated where the rug might best be positioned.

'They are like a couple of tom cats marking out their territory,' whispered Pip with a grin.

Steph just rolled her eyes and concentrated on rubbing suncream on the limbs of the fidgeting boys. Chloe was carefully applying her own cream. Once the men and children had scampered off to the sea edge to jump waves and even swim if they got the nerve, Steph and Pip started to unpack the food.

Pip had been planning her contribution to the picnic for a week now. She wanted to make an effort. She'd made three different types of sandwiches (cheese and pickle, ham and bacon and egg and cress). She was fully aware that there wasn't a single sane human being on the planet, let alone on the picnic, who actually enjoyed eating cress and no doubt she'd find herself picking out the green stuff from Chloe's sandwiches but she believed the cress necessary as it added a bit of colour and pizzazz, although that might be overstating the case. She'd baked too—a blue cheese and broccoli quiche and flapjacks. Plus (and this was possibly her triumph) Chloe and she had visited a local farm on Sunday and picked punnets full of organic strawberries. Pip pulled out the food from her rucksack and laid the Tupperware boxes on the picnic rug with the sort of reverence that is usually reserved for ancient religious artefacts.

Stephanie felt the waves of self-satisfaction and pride her friend was emitting and duly commented, 'Wow, those sandwiches look yummy.'

Pip beamed, for once she was satisfied that her efforts might not appear too pathetic in comparison to Stephanie's superior domestic goddess skills. But, almost instantly, her beam was replaced with an expression of stunned incomprehension—Stephanie was unpacking *shop-bought* sandwiches, a huge tub of *shop-bought* hummus and another of tzatziki from her wicker picnic basket.

Steph caught Pip's expression and laughed. 'What? I've bought a few convenience bits and pieces, I haven't sacrificed my firstborn on the picnic rug, get over it.' She laughed. 'Besides, I chopped my own carrots and I did bake these brownies.'

'Oh, thank God. I thought you'd been body-snatched,' giggled Pip.

'I've found it necessary to cut a few corners recently. I don't have the time I had before. Thank goodness. I can't tell you how boring it was that my biggest triumph of the day used to be that I'd baked a delicious fish pie. A pie that the boys and Julian would devour without comment or notice, I might add. Over these past few months I've had to think about different things. Julian's health for one but after that as well.'

'You're really enjoying your life coaching course, aren't you?' asked Pip.

'Love it,' nodded Steph as she reached for one of Pip's sandwiches, bit into it and made appreciative noises.

'We should have thought of it before. You're just the perfect person to become a life coach. You are a wonderful listener and you have a great ability to ask questions which get to the real heart of the issue.'

'Do I?'

'Yes! And you are a fantastic motivator. You even managed to motivate me.'

'How are things going with Selfridges?' Steph asked this question from time to time but tried not to ask too often. She wanted to show her interest and enthusiasm but she didn't want it to appear that she was continually checking up on Pip.

'Fab. Other than that very first order the buyer placed, I've hit all my deadlines. Perhaps this is because she's an experienced buyer and has ordered cautiously, aware that I'm a one-woman show,' added Pip.

'Or perhaps it's because you've found your confidence and niche at last,' replied Steph.

'Yeah, maybe. I'm beginning to grow into who I thought I might be. You know. I'm not quite ready for Philippa yet, but I'm halfway there, I'm certainly Pippa. Who knew growing up would take so long?' Pip flashed a wide grin.

Stephanie glanced up and took a moment to watch her husband and boys play in the waves. The children were all in swim gear but Julian and Robbie had only rolled up their shirtsleeves and trouser legs. Now great splodges of fabric had been made darker by the children's energetic splashing. Julian didn't seem to have noticed, or if he had, he didn't care. He chased Harry, Alfie and Chloe in circles, spraying and splattering anyone in his way until they were all doused. Stephanie watched as Julian noticed (the very moment she did) that Freddie looked a bit out of it and was probably moments away from frustrated tears, being the youngest he never had any hope of winning a game, sometimes he struggled just to keep up. Julian swooped down and hoisted Freddie on to his shoulders and then together they chased Robbie further into the sea than he wanted to go. 'We didn't think of my life coaching before because I wasn't ready before,' mused Steph. 'The time is right now.'

It was true that the course was perfect for her. A nurse had suggested she ought to think of possibly trying to gain a few formal qualifications as a life coach, after having observed Steph throughout Julian's recuperation.

At first Steph had protested. 'Oh no, I'm no Florence Nightingale,' she'd laughed.

'I'm not saying you are. It's just that people like talking to you. You get so many people to open up to you, patients and their visitors alike. I think you'd be a natural,' the nurse had insisted.

Stephanie had been surprised when over the following weeks she realised that she hadn't entirely dismissed the idea. She kept imagining what it would be like to go on a course, gain a qualification and re-enter the workforce. Not full-time. That wouldn't suit her at all. The boys needed her to be around now more than ever and frankly she needed to be around them now more than ever, but if she could find something to do during school hours, that would be ideal. Something other than have lunch with charming men who believed they were in love with her. Something she could chat about with Julian when he arrived home from the office. Something that rooted her and helped her feel more robust in her own right. Yes, it would be better all around.

Julian had loved the idea and had been very encouraging. In fact Julian seemed to love everything about Steph at the moment. He complimented her on her apple crumble (she hadn't ruined the moment by admitting that, too, was shop-bought), he complimented her on her appearance (he'd said her new haircut was 'very modern and suited her', and neither she nor the Visa bill had prompted him to notice). He took a greater interest in her day's activities and thanked her when she reported calling his father for updates and news. He carefully listened when she told him about her dalliance with Subhash and, while he struggled, he found it in him to admit that Subhash sounded like 'a decent bloke', although he had demanded reassurances that she would never see him again; that she didn't want to do so.

Yes, Julian seemed to love everything about Steph and Steph loved Julian. She loved him on days like this, days that were full of chatter and laughter, when the white wine would flow and the kids would collect pebbles and go home smelling of sunshine. But she also loved him on the occasional days when she fought great surges of anger that flowed through her body and seemed desperate to gush out all over him, maybe even drown him. She loved him when she yelled at him, 'How could you have done it?' and when he held her close, stroking her hair, telling her over and over again that he was sorry, so very sorry, and he would never make the same mistake again. She loved him enough to be sure she believed him.

Julian had helped find the life coaching course. Steph had been terrified the moment she entered the big town hall, which smelt of new paint, to join the seminar. But it hadn't taken her too long to realise that the place was full of people just like her. Not just full of women who were a certain age, a certain class and recovering from a certain heartache, no, not that. The delegates came in all shapes and sizes, there were stressed-out city execs looking for a new direction, there were middle-aged women teachers who realised they had a lot to give, there were recently retired men not at all ready to call it a day, there were survivors of crime or illness, optimists, dreamers, planners, good Samaritans, idealists and realists. Some were younger than Steph, others older. Some were fatter or thinner, more facial hair or less hair on their heads, one man was in a wheelchair and one woman was accompanied by a guide dog. Probably the only thing they all had in common was that they were all rather wary about coming through the door and committing to the course. They were all a little bit terrified but they wanted to give it a go. Give helping a go. Give life a go. By the morning tea break Steph realised that the fluttering in her stomach was not so much nerves as excitement.

'I'm glad you love the course so much,' smiled Pip.

'It's funny but training to be a life coach has

taught me such a lot.'

'Like what?' Pip was sitting in one of the two deckchairs the Blakes had brought along. She was nibbling a carrot and gazing at Robbie but her attention was on Steph, which Steph understood and appreciated.

Steph thought that the course was helping her to move on from the past and break through the self-imposed blocks that might have held her back, she was addressing confidence issues, partly, and also she was resisting pigeon-holing herself. She was a mother and a wife, a great mother and wife, but she was also Stephanie, an individual. It felt good remembering as much.

'Oh, you know, I'm getting better at solving my own problems.' Steph was sitting on the rug, she was barefoot and liked the feel of burrowing her toes into the sand.

'I think you've always been pretty good at that.'

'Do you?' Steph was pleased and surprised.

'Absolutely. To the point where it seemed you didn't have any.'

'But we all have problems,' pointed out Steph.

'I know.' Pip felt uncomfortable. She had never quite managed to get over the guilt of letting down her best friend when she was most needed. Her shame and remorse was sharp and persistent. She'd apologised numerous times and sincerely tried to explain how scared and confused she'd been, but neither her regret nor the fact that Steph always gracefully accepted her apologies and said that she understood seemed to have a soothing effect on her conscience.

Pip knew that now the trial was behind them she had to apologise again. Maybe this time would be the last time. Could things ever be completely forgiven and forgotten? Pip hoped so.

'You know I'm so very sorry, don't you, Steph? Sorry I didn't give you the alibi.'

'Yes, I know that. And you know I'm sorry I ever asked you to do so. It wasn't fair of me.'

Usually the two women stopped this conversation here but there was something else that Pip knew she needed to say. She took a deep breath and then said, 'But I think you'd have lied for me.'

Steph shrugged, uncertain. 'You know what, I don't know whether I would have, I've thought about it a lot since. I don't know what I would have done when it came to the wire. That's the point, isn't it? Sometimes we don't know ourselves as well as we think and that's when we start to make a mess of things. When we lose ourselves, or misjudge ourselves.'

'Or when we lose others, misjudge others,' added Pip shyly.

'Quite.'

Stephanie and Pip both stared out towards the sea. The waves rolled rhythmically on the shore. The sound was comforting and soothing; its peaceful hypnotic qualities couldn't be disturbed even by the noisy children on the beach or the screeching seagulls in the sky. Steph thought that perhaps people were attracted to the sea because the waves were so consistent and so persistent. Always there, rushing on to the shore. Always coming and going and coming again. Humans were the same. We try our best. Sometimes we run all the way up the shore and other times we fall short of target. So we have another go. Endlessly.

491

Hopefully.

'How do you feel about the sentence?' asked Pip, deciding to address the elephant on the beach.

'Suspension of her driving licence for two years and fifty hours' community service seems perfectly correct to me. We didn't want a custodial sentence for Kirsten. Not after her mother came and visited me.'

'That must have taken some courage.'

'Yes, but we'd all do it for our children, wouldn't we? Mrs Elton helped me see that Kirsten isn't much more than a child. She made a mistake. Mrs Elton thought they had too, as parents. She was distraught, couldn't stop talking about how much they'd indulged Kirsten. They'd given her everything she could have dreamt of materially and they'd encouraged her to think of little else other than her looks but, understandably I suppose, she'd become a brat and they'd lost control. They thought they were teaching her a lesson when they cut off her cash flow but it was too little too late, it led to more desperate behaviour. By then Kirsten had come to believe that older, rich men were her only career option.'

Pip glanced over to Chloe. She felt some sympathy for Mr and Mrs Elton; it was hard for a parent to deny their child goodies or to resist telling them they were adorable. At least being hard up meant that she'd never be able to ruin Chloe. 'I guess they did make mistakes, didn't they?'

'Which of us didn't, in this entire mess? I think Kirsten's learnt her lesson. Her mother said she's seeing a really nice boy of her own age now.'

'I think that's the bloke who was with her at the

hospital. He was in court too. Wow, he must be quite some amazing guy to stick around through all this. Hot too. Did you notice him?'

Steph shook her head.

'I hope she knows how lucky she is,' added Pip.

Steph couldn't comment. She found it hard thinking about Kirsten. She hadn't believed the girl ought to be punished any more severely for the hit-and-run than she had been; after all, the circumstances were extraordinary. The court had made attempts to understand the mental state of the hit-and-run driver and Julian had testified that Kirsten knocked him over by accident, that there was no ill intention. Steph would never know for certain whether this was true. No one other than Kirsten could know for sure. She might have panicked. She might have wanted him dead. It was the other crime that Kirsten had committed that Steph still found extremely hard to deal with. Admittedly, it was becoming easier, day by day, as Julian continued to reassure her and to show his love for her, but the fact was Kirsten would never be on Stephanie's Christmas card list.

At least Subhash had been kept out of the mess; that was something Steph was grateful for. Julian had supported her in that decision and, as the case had become much more straightforward following Julian's recovery and Kirsten's confession, there was no need for Subhash to testify. Steph was relieved that his wife would not be embarrassed or embroiled. She hoped that Subhash had found a way to reignite the passion between him and Paadini or if not that, then she hoped he'd found some other way to be happy. She'd never know about that either. She had not seen Subhash since the day at the police station and she didn't want to.

'She looked like a different girl in court from when I saw her in hospital that day,' pointed out Pip. 'No heels, hardly any make-up. Of course she might have been dressing for court, her lawyer might have advised her to appear more demure.'

'I don't think so.'

'No, nor do I. She looked subdued and repentant. I don't think she could have faked that.'

Pip decided to pretend that she hadn't noticed just how beautiful Kirsten's new vulnerability had made her. If there had been anything to criticise about Kirsten's looks, it was that she appeared too confident, almost brassy. Her new fragility and uncertainty was immensely more attractive. When the judge passed the sentence, it seemed that the entire court had sighed with relief, Kirsten more than anyone. She'd thanked the judge, her lawyer and then tightly hugged her parents and boyfriend, she looked weak with gratitude. Yes, she was someone who had learnt a lesson. Her first.

'So you're happy then?' asked Pip tentatively.

Steph stretched her legs out in front of her and eased herself back, propped up on her elbows. 'Never happier,' she replied honestly and confidently.

'Even after everything? I mean it can't be easy.'

'No, it's not. Not always. But I think we're a bit like a vase that's been knocked over and smashed into lots of pieces but a vase that's loved so much that instead of being chucked, we've been carefully glued back together. So now while we're no longer pristine and shiny, we are aware that we are loved and we've endured and that seems somehow more important than being pristine and shiny. So yes,

I'm very happy. How about you?'

'Not that Robbie and I are like a new vase yet, never mind a broken and fixed one,' said Pip. 'Robbie, Chloe and I are more like a brand new jigsaw just being fitted together, we're enjoying the relief and comfort of the pieces slipping into place.'

Steph turned to Pip and saw at once that she was misty-eyed. 'Pip! Are you crying because you are meant to be the creative one and your analogy is so much weaker than mine?'

Pip laughed and swallowed her tears. 'I know, I know. I'm just so happy. And you're happy and it's all really great.'

'Yes, it is, isn't it.' The women beamed at one another cloaked in the sort of love that had thickened and solidified over the years. 'Pip?'

'Yes?'

'You're not pregnant, are you?'

'What makes you ask that?'

'You prepared a picnic, that's basically nesting, now you're crying, and the fact that we've been sitting on this beach for more than half an hour and you haven't reached for the corkscrew yet.'

Pip grinned and said, 'Do you know what, I'm starving. Should I go and get the children and men so we can start in on this picnic properly?' Within a flash Pip was up and scampering to the shoreline.

Steph laughed and called after her, 'You haven't answered my question. That's not a proper answer! Do you mean you're starving because you're pregnant? Are you or aren't you?'

But Steph couldn't catch Pip's answer, it was caught on the roar of the waves coming and going. Persistent. Consistent. Endlessly hopeful.

495

ACKNOWLEDGMENTS

Thank you, Jane Morpeth, the most wonderful editor anyone could ask for and I say that as a girl with very high standards indeed! It is a joy to work with you and your amazing team. At the risk of sounding like I'm accepting an Oscar I'd like to thank Georgina Moore and Rosie Gailer for their persistence and creative brilliance. Aslan Byrne and the magnificent sales force—at home, abroad, key account and regional—you are all so talented, tremendous and tenacious. A special thank you to Kate Byrne and Harriet Bourton for wisdom and support. Thank you to the marketing and design team who are the most sparkly, scintillating and smiley crew imaginable, particularly Vicky Cowell and Sam Habib who understand the importance of soft focus.

Thank you, Jonny Geller, again!

A massive thank you is due to Police Officer Liz Chatfield and Youth Offending Link Officer Nellie Williams as well as nurses Carol Wordley, Katie Rawson, Tracey Corbett and Pamela Rourke. Thank you all for taking time out of your incredibly busy and vital schedules to answer my questions about police procedure and nursing coma victims. You are terrific women and briefly alluding to your heroic work in this novel has been a humbling experience for me. I ought to add any inaccuracies in procedure or practice are my poetic licence!

Thank you to the wonderful retailers and librarians that work so hard to engage readers and, erm, well, frankly, sell books.

Thank you to all my readers, without you there's no point in writing a word!

I'd like to warmly acknowledge Rob and Becky Booker, once again, for their wonderfully generous support of Sparks, the children's medical research charity. The remit of Sparks is to fund research across the entire spectrum of paediatric medicine. Their goal is for all babies to be born healthy and stay healthy. To learn more about Sparks visit www.sparks.org.uk.

Finally, I'd also like to warmly acknowledge Valerie Satterfield and her daughter, Mary Jean Brown, for their wonderfully generous support of Room to Read, a charity that seeks to transform the lives of millions of children in developing countries by focusing on literacy and gender equality in education. To learn more about Room to Read visit www.roomtoread.org.